Comme

Proceedings of the Commercial Convention, held in Detroit, July 11th, 12th, 13th, and 14th, 1865

SALZWASSER VERLAG

Commercial Convention

Proceedings of the Commercial Convention, held in Detroit, July 11th, 12th, 13th, and 14th, 1865

Reprint of the original, first published in 1865.

1st Edition 2022 | ISBN: 978-3-75258-942-9

Verlag (Publisher): Salzwasser Verlag GmbH, Zeilweg 44, 60439 Frankfurt, Deutschland
Vertretungsberechtigt (Authorized to represent): E. Roepke, Zeilweg 44, 60439 Frankfurt, Deutschland
Druck (Print): Books on Demand GmbH, In de Tarpen 42, 22848 Norderstedt, Deutschland

PROCEEDINGS

OF THE

COMMERCIAL CONVENTION,

HELD IN DETROIT,

JULY 11TH, 12TH, 13TH AND 14TH, 1865.

PUBLISHED BY ORDER OF THE CONVENTION.

DETROIT

1865.

ORIGIN OF THE CONVENTION.

THE project of a Convention of Boards of Trade, for the purpose of deliberating upon important subjects intimately connected with the great Business Interests of the Country, had its origin in resolutions (which will be found embodied in the circular letter below) introduced in the Board of Trade of the City of Detroit, by H. P. Bridge, Esq., on the 28th February, 1865. Their introduction was made the occasion of a few general remarks upon their merits, both by the mover and Duncan Stewart, Esq., pointing out the advantages and benefits that would naturally result from such an assemblage; but inasmuch as the project was one of great importance, Mr. Bridge, to afford opportunity for due deliberation, waived the question of its endorsement at the time, asking a postponement for one week, which was accordingly done. The resolutions came up in due course on the 6th March, when they were unanimously adopted, and the following Circular Letter was sent to the various Boards of Trade and Chambers of Commerce:

BOARD OF TRADE ROOMS, DETROIT, MICH., March, 1865.

At a meeting of this Association on the 6th inst., the following resolutions, after full discussion, were unanimously adopted:

Resolved, That the President be requested to address circular letters to the presiding officers of the several Boards of Trade in the loyal States and British Provinces, asking the appointment of delegates to attend a Convention to be held during the approaching summer, for the consideration of the following subjects, viz.:

Commerce, Finance, Communications of Transit from the West to the Seaboard, Reciprocal Trade between the United States and the British Provinces, and such other business as may come before the Convention not of a purely local or political character.

Resolved, That Detroit is a central and convenient place for the Convention to meet, and we hereby tender the Board of Trade Rooms for its accommodation.

In conformity with the foregoing resolutions, calling a Convention, the objects being therein stated, I shall simply ask for them your careful consideration, and, if approved of, that your Association will cordially co-operate by sending a suitable number of its members to the proposed Convention, to assist in discussing the various and important commercial questions which may properly come before it.

It is believed that this is eminently a proper time for the business men of this country, through their several Boards of Trade and Chambers of Commerce, to meet in council, to discuss matters of Finance and Commerce, and thus give to the people at large the life-long experience of men devoted to commercial affairs. Such discussion cannot produce evil, and may result in material good.

I would beg leave to name the second Tuesday in July, proximo, for the Convention to meet in Detroit. If any other time or place should be thought more desirable by a majority of the Boards, their views will be adopted. When we hear from the several Boards of Trade on the subject, this Association will communicate their action to you.

Hoping to hear from you at your earliest convenience,

Your obedient servant,

JOSEPH ASPINALL,

President.

The Circular Letter having met with a favorable response from every organization to which it had been addressed, the following call for the assembling of the Convention was then issued:

BOARD OF TRADE ROOMS, DETROIT, MICH., May 25, 1865.

The Circular Letter which this Board had the honor to issue to the Boards of Trade and Chambers of Commerce of the United States and British North American Provinces, proposing a Commercial Convention for the discussion of the subjects therein stated, has met a favorable response from the Associations addressed, promising to co-operate, by sending a suitable delegation to represent them; also, approving of the time and place of meeting.

In accordance with this unanimity of sentiment, this Board, therefore, calls the Convention to meet in the Detroit Board of Trade Building, in the forenoon of the 11th day of July next.

All Commercial Associations about to participate, are requested to report to this Board, at the earliest possible moment, the number of delegates they desire to send, in order that suitable accommodations may be provided for them in the Convention.

It is not advisable to limit the number of delegates representing each Board, some having already appointed ten, and others twelve members. It is proposed to leave it to the Convention to decide the mode of voting, and to establish rules for its organization.

Through the kind liberality of Railroad and Steamboat Companies, arrangements have been made by this Board for the free transmission of delegates to and from Detroit by the following lines, centering in Detroit:

Michigan Central Railroad.

Michigan Southern and Northern Indiana Railroad.

Great Western Railway of Canada.

Grand Trunk and Buffalo and Lake Huron Railways of Canada.

Detroit and Milwaukee Railroad.

Detroit and Cleveland Steamboat Line.

Passes will be sent over the above lines on receiving from the respective Boards the names of the delegates desiring them.

All arrangements for transmission of delegates over railroads or other lines connecting with the above named lines, must be made by the several Commercial Associations participating in the Convention.

I am, Dear Sir,

Yours very truly,

JOSEPH ASPINALL,

President.

COMMERCIAL CONVENTION.

FIRST DAY.

TUESDAY, July 11, 1865.

THE Convention assembled at 11 o'clock, and was called to order by Joseph Aspinall, Esq., President of the Board of Trade of the City of Detroit.

The Right Rev. Samuel A. McCoskry, Bishop of the Diocese of Michigan, was then introduced to the Convention, and implored the Divine blessing on its labors in the following words:

Most merciful God, our Heavenly Father, we would recognize Thee as the Author of all our comforts, the Director of all our ways. From Thee every good and perfect gift comes, and without Thee nothing is strong, nothing is holy. On this occasion we desire to acknowledge our dependence upon Thee. We wish Thy richest blessing to descend upon this assembly. May all their deliberations tend to bind every part of the nation in the closest bonds of peace and love. May there be one heart and one mind in all their efforts to place on a free and fair basis the commercial relations of this land and all the nations of the earth, so that reciprocal benefits may be enjoyed by all. May they exert the immense influence placed in their hands, not only to extend the blessings of civilization, but to send the gospel of our blessed Lord to the remotest nations of the earth. May they be happy instruments in hastening the day when commerce shall be the hand-maid of true religion, and all nations shall acknowledge one common Lord and Saviour. O, God, we bless Thee for the mercies bestowed upon the nation. Thou hast been exceedingly gracious unto this land; continue Thy favor and protection to us. Let truth and justice, brotherly kindness and charity, concord and unity, so exist among us that the stability of our laws shall make the nation a praise in the earth.

And so direct and dispose the hearts of our rulers, that they, knowing whose servants they are, may, above all things, seek the Lord and His glory; and that we, duly considering whose authority they have, may faithfully serve them and obey them in Thee and for Thee, according to Thy blessed Word, ordained through Jesus Christ our Lord. Amen.

Joseph Aspinall, Esq., delivered the following address:

In the name of the Board of Trade, and of the citizens of Detroit, I have great pleasure in welcoming you to our City. Although this Convention has met for purely commercial purposes, yet I trust our intercourse may be not only profitable, but pleasant and agreeable.

In opening the deliberative proceedings of this large and influential assemblage, permit me, gentlemen, in the outset, to remark, that Detroit, although having initiated the call for this Convention, has no object to serve or point to gain for herself, but is only desirous of sharing, in common with the great Northwest, in the advantages to be derived from the grave discussions of the many important subjects to come before the Convention.

The objects of calling together this Convention of Commercial Associations are set forth in the circular issued by the Detroit Board of Trade to the various Boards of Trade and Chambers of Commerce of the United States, and of the British North American Provinces.

The subjects named therein are as follows: Commerce, Finance, Communications of Transit from the West to the Seaboard, Reciprocal Trade between the United States and the British North American Provinces, and any other business which may come before the Convention not of purely local or political character.

These subjects should be openly discussed, and an interchange of views freely expressed. After four years of rebellion of appalling magnitude, which, at one time, struck fierce blows at the commercial life of the country, and threatened the very existence of the Republic, unsettling all commercial values, and completely changing the financial system of the country, entailing a large debt and burdensome taxation, which, as initiated, falls chiefly upon commercial men—the commercial men of the country feel that they have special claims on the Government. Their undivided efforts, great sacrifices, and patriotic support, with the blessing of God, have largely contributed in restoring the Union, and bringing about a happy and glorious peace.

We feel that it is only by a wise and judicious policy on the part of the Government, that we shall be enabled to justly and honorably meet the demands it may impose upon us. Commerce must bear the burden of taxation, and business men are the best judges of their own wants, and what will most conduce to their prosperity; therefore, it behooves them to take deeper interest in governmental affairs.

This is believed to be the most propitious time for business men to meet in council, and calmly discuss commercial matters, and recommend such measures as, in their judgment, will conduce to the general good and prosperity. This is the primary object of this Convention. If we do not fully succeed in accomplishing all we desire at this meeting, our efforts cannot but result in some good; and by inaugurating a system of periodical Conventions of Commercial Associations, where all matters pertaining to commerce may be discussed, it must have a weight and influence that will command respect.

Were the participations in these Conventions extended to the Commercial Associations of all nations with whom we have commercial dealings, we would have a power and influence for good to the commercial world which cannot now be estimated.

Finance, the basis of all commercial prosperity, is dependent upon a firm and stable financial system readily convertible at all times. It is, therefore, a subject of the greatest importance to this Convention, and commercial men, and, doubtless, will meet with appropriate consideration.

Communication of transit between the Great Lakes and the seaboard is of vital importance to the Northwest. The continued prosperity of the Great West demands additional outlets to the seaboard, and to the markets of the world, for its agricultural, mineral, and other products, which will crowd every outlet as fast as constructed.

In ordinary business seasons, property accumulates at transhipping points, causing ruinous detention and great fluctuations in cost of transportation, which increases the hazard and uncertainties of all legitimate business.

The West has long felt the exorbitant transfer charges and tax levied by the State of New York upon its products passing through the Erie Canal, which is assessed regardless of the demand or value of the property at the place of destination, which, together, oftentimes exceed the Canal and Hudson River freight to New York, or lake transportation of one thousand miles, sometimes equaling the latter and the Ocean freight from New York to Europe together, or even what the Western farmer realizes upon coarse grains at the place of production. The Buffalo combination of elevating and warehouse charges on Western produce passing through Buffalo has no parallel in commercial transportation, realizing to its founders, every one or two years, dividends and rents equal to the value of the elevating property.

Any measures which can be devised to ensure the West cheap and speedy transportation on its products to tide-water, will promote the immediate prosperity of the people East and West.

Reciprocal trade between the United States and the British North American Provinces, is a subject fraught with deep interest to both countries, especially as the present Treaty, which has produced so much good, is so soon to be terminated. The increased trade between the two countries during the ten years of the Treaty may be seen in Mr. Secretary Chase's Report of Trade and Commerce of the United States for the year 1864, which shows that the commerce of the United States with the British North American Provinces is equal to the trade with Austria, Russia, Prussia, Spain, and Portugal together.

The best commercial minds of the country have questioned the propriety of abrogating the Treaty, believing in such judicious amendments being made as would increase its usefulness and be mutually beneficial.

The navigation of the St. Lawrence River and Canals, in their present condition, has failed to be a sufficiently important equivalent. But as the natural outlet of the Great Lakes, the navigation is susceptible of being improved to give a safe and clear draft of fourteen feet to tide water, which, to the future welfare of the great and growing Northwest, is imperative.

A liberal Reciprocal Treaty, based upon just principles to the British American Provinces and the United States, is demanded by every consideration of good neighborhood and wise statesmanship, such as will guarantee to the West these improvements on the St. Lawrence River and Canals, as the commerce of the lakes is destined to fill every avenue to the ocean.

A Ship Canal around the Falls of Niagara on the American side, is a work of importance, of a purely national character, linking together two great lakes within our own territory. That it has not been accomplished long ago is a reflection upon the wisdom of our own Government.

A uniform decimal system of weights and measures of all merchandise is a subject worthy the consideration of the Government of the United States and the British American Provinces, whose business relations are so intermingled, that it would be a great convenience, as well as a saving of labor.

These and other important recommendatory subjects which will be introduced, should be discussed by the representative men of this country, assembled at this Convention, with harmony and unison becoming the dignity and circumspection of such a body, eschewing all sectional, local, or political subjects, for the general good.

Having in mind the great danger of overloading this, the first Commercial Convention, with too many demands, and thereby risking the good which might otherwise be obtained, less pressing or important subjects should be left over for the recommendation of a future Convention.

The call for this Convention it will be seen, in the circular issued by the Detroit Board of Trade, was confined entirely to Boards of Trade and Chambers of Commerce, and their members. These Commercial Associations being composed of the chief business or commercial men of the country, it was thought desirable that the business of this Convention should be confided to their hands. This is proven to have been a wise provision, as this Convention has attracted extraordinary attention. Some of the Boards have appointed unusually large delegations, and in some instances not altogether of their own members.

The applications from cities and organizations of all kinds to be represented have been most numerous, but the committee having the matter in charge has not felt authorized to go beyond the call issued to the Boards of Trade and Chambers of Commerce, of which we are happy to say every known organized commercial board in the United States and British American Provinces is believed to be represented, to the number of some forty-two Commercial Associations.

Some Commercial Boards South and on the frontier of the late rebellious States are at present disorganized, and are, of course, not represented in this Convention.

The following Boards have reported and are represented in the Convention:

Board of Trade, ...	Albany, N. Y.
Board of Trade, ...	Buffalo, N. Y.
Board of Trade, ...	Bay City, Mich.
Board of Trade, ...	Boston, Mass.
Mercantile Association, ...	Bangor, Me.
Corn Exchange, ...	Boston, Mass.
Board of Trade, ...	Chicago, Ill.
Mercantile Association, . . .	Chicago, Ill.
Chamber of Commerce, ...	Cairo, Ill.
Chamber of Commerce, . . .	Cincinnati, O.
Board of Trade, ...	Cleveland, O.
Board of Trade, ...	Coburg, C. W.
Chamber of Commerce, ...	Charlottetown, P. E. Island.
Board of Trade, ...	Detroit, Mich.
Board of Trade, ...	Erie, Pa.
Chamber of Commerce, . . .	Halifax, N. S.
Board of Trade, ...	Hamilton, C. W.
Board of Trade, ...	Kingston, C. W.
Michigan Central Board of Trade, .	Kalamazoo, Mich.
Board of Trade, ...	London, C. W.
Board of Trade, ...	Montreal, C. E.
Corn Exchange Association, . .	Montreal, C. E.
Chamber of Commerce, ...	Milwaukee, Wis.
Chamber of Commerce, . . .	New York.
Commercial Association, ...	New York.
Board of Trade, ...	Oswego, N. Y.
Board of Trade, ...	Ottawa, C. W.

Board of Trade, ...	Philadelphia, Pa.
Corn Exchange Association, ...	Philadelphia, Pa.
Board of Trade, ...	Portland, Me.
Board of Trade, ...	Pittsburgh, Pa.
Board of Trade, ...	Quebec, C. E.
Board of Trade, . . , . .	St. Paul, Minn.
Board of Trade, ...	St. Louis, Mo.
Chamber of Commerce, ...	St. John, N. B.
Board of Trade, ...	Springfield, Ohio.
Board of Trade, ...	Stratford, C. W.
Board of Trade, ...	East Saginaw, Mich.
Board of Trade, ...	St. Catharines, C. W.
Board of Trade, ...	Toledo, Ohio.
Board of Trade, ...	Toronto, C. W.
Board of Trade, ...	Troy, N. Y.
Board of Trade, ...	Windsor, C. W.

In order to facilitate the organization of the Convention, by permission, I would move that Mr. Barton Able, President of the St. Louis Board, be appointed President *pro tem.* of the Convention, and Ray Haddock, Secretary of the Detroit Board, be appointed as Secretary *pro tem.*

Mr. Fraley, of Philadelphia, stated that a delegation was present from the Coal Exchange, Philadelphia, which was not mentioned in the list read by the Chairman.

Mr. Aspinall said there were many Boards of similar character throughout the country representing special interests, such as coal, petroleum, lumber, etc., but it had been thought best in sending out invitations, not to go outside the Boards of Trade and Commerce. The admission of the Coal Board of Philadelphia would be a matter for consideration after the Convention was organized.

Mr. Fraley insisted on the immediate recognition of the delegates from the Board in question. He thought it would be a signal want of courtesy to Philadelphia if it was refused.

Another gentleman, from Philadelphia, submitted a motion to admit the Coal Board.

After some further discussion, this motion was withdrawn until the President *pro tem.* should be appointed.

The nomination of President and Secretary *pro tem.*, as proposed by Mr. Aspinall, were agreed to.

Gen. W. K. Strong, of New York, moved that a Committee of two be appointed to conduct the

President to the Chair, which was agreed to, and Messrs. Strong and Bridge were appointed.

Mr. Able, on taking the chair, addressed the Convention as follows:

GENTLEMEN OF THE CONVENTION,—I return you for this high honor, my sincere thanks on behalf of the city of St. Louis. I know well it is not conferred upon me as an individual, but that it is conferred upon the great city to which I belong and which I love so well. I hope that the deliberations of this great convention may be marked by that moderation and sagacity which usually marks the deliberations of all great mercantile assemblies. The country has just emerged from one of the most terrible rebellions which ever afflicted any nation on the face of the earth—it has triumphantly emerged from that rebellion—and it is meet and proper that the commercial men of the country should meet together, and consult on the great measures referred to in the programme which has just been read by the President of the Board of Trade of the City of Detroit. The sentiment which has been expressed on the part of that gentleman, I endorse on the part of St. Louis; she has no private or selfish interests to serve in this convention. Her delegates come here with no other object than to benefit—if it be in their power—the great commercial interests of the country, the whole country, and nothing but the country. (Cheers.) This being a convention of business men, it is not proper that I should detain you by making a speech. I will content myself by simply again thanking you for the honor you have done me.

Hon. Hiram Walbridge offered the following resolution:

Resolved, That a committee of one from each Board of Trade or Chamber of Commerce here represented be appointed by the several Boards, to report the names of permanent officers for the Convention.

A gentleman from Philadelphia insisted that now was the time to settle the question as to the admission of the delegation from the Coal Board of that city.

The President ruled the question out of order for the present.

Gen. Strong, of New York, moved the following:

Resolved, That the presence here of a large and influential delegation from the British North American Provinces, gives us great pleasure, and we respectfully request them to name a delegate from each Board of Trade to act on the Committee of Permanent Organization. He understood these gentlemen had some delicacy about taking part in the organization of the Convention, and he wished them to understand that the Convention received them with open arms.

Gen. Walbridge's motion was put and carried.

Hon. T. Ryan, of Montreal, wished to offer a word of explanation on the part of the delegation from the British North American Provinces. They felt that it was a very graceful compliment which was paid to the Provinces of British North America, when the invitation was extended to them to send delegates to the Convention, but in considering this morning the course they should take, having accepted the invitation, they arrived at the conclusion that it would be more becoming and delicate on their part to abstain from giving any vote in the organization of the Convention. There were various subjects embraced in the call in which the delegates from the Provinces could have no voice; there were only two subjects, those of the Reciprocal Trade and Internal Communication, in which they could be considered directly interested, and being strangers to the gentlemen who might probably be proposed to fill the chair and vice-chairs, they had thought it would be better to leave the organization of the Convention in the hands of the gentlemen from the United States, being perfectly satisfied to rely on the good sense, good feeling, justice, and fair play of those gentlemen. (Applause.) On any question that might divide them, the gentlemen from the British Provinces had no desire to throw their vote in the balance on one side or the other, because if they did so they would be voting with reference to gentlemen of whose merits they were ignorant. He hoped, therefore, the Convention would excuse them from voting on matters relating to organization.

Gen. Strong, while appreciating the diffidence and modesty of the gentleman who had just spoken, thought nevertheless it was a duty incumbent on the gentlemen here, representing the commercial associations of the United States, to put on record the resolution he had moved. One of the most important points to be considered by the Convention was one which affected both countries, and it was desirable that the gentlemen from the British Provinces should participate in all the deliberations of the Convention. Whether they would persist in the course indicated by the gentleman from Canada, he could not say; but he hoped his resolution would go on record, so that it might be seen that these gentlemen had been received in a spirit of the most entire friendship and cordiality.

Mr. Spaulding, of Cleveland, said there could be no objection to extend to their friends from the British Provinces the right hand of fellowship so far as there was any community of interest between them. At the same time, he admired the honor and delicacy shown by those gentlemen; and as they were only interested in one important subject that was to come before the Convention, it was well to consider whether they should not be excused, as they desired, from taking part in organizing the assembly. It was not to be supposed that they had come here to assist us, for instance, in suggesting a suitable tariff for the United States, or in planning a canal around the Falls of Niagara to compete with their Welland Canal.

Hon. Joseph Howe, of Halifax, expressed himself to a similar effect as Mr. Ryan had already done, with regard to its being more becoming in the gentlemen from the British Provinces to abstain from voting on the appointment of permanent officers, as they could not be supposed to be acquainted with the merits of the various gentlemen likely to be candidates.

Mr. Scammon, of Chicago, said the gentlemen from the British Provinces were as much members of this Convention as the gentlemen from the United States, and he could not, therefore, see any propriety in the resolution. It would be quite as proper for the Canadians to pass resolutions inviting the gentlemen from the Mississippi valley to participate in the deliberations of this Convention, as for them to pass resolutions inviting the Canadians. He moved that the resolution be laid on the table.

After further discussion, Gen. Strong withdrew his resolution.

Hon. J. V. L. Pruyn offered the following resolution:

Resolved, That a committee of two from each State, and from each of the British Provinces represented in the Convention, be appointed on Credentials, and that they report prior to the announcement of the Committee on Permanent Organization, in order that each body entitled to admission may be represented in said organization.

Mr. Taylor, of Minnesota, said he had just learned that a representation from a portion of the British territory on this continent, which could not be properly designated as a province, was on its way to this City, and he had to state that the delegation from Minnesota were anxious that these representatives should take seats with them, if they could be recognized otherwise as not coming from a province. He referred to the large interior portion of British America, extending between Lake Superior and the Rocky Mountains, and capable, if the colonizing enterprise of the English people should reach it, of forming four provinces, each as important as the State of Ohio. (Hear, hear). The Red River Settlement, which had been for fifty years an inland, remote, sequestered country, would probably send, a distance of more than two thousand miles, an intelligent citizen to represent them and their interests on this floor; and if he could not be received as a provincial delegate, the Minnesota delegation would invite the representative of Red River to take a seat with themselves.

Mr. Pruyn's resolution was agreed to.

On motion of Mr. Pruyn, the delegates accredited by the Coal Exchange of Philadelphia were admitted.

On motion of Mr. Randolph, of Chicago, the Convention took a recess of ten minutes.

After recess, the following Committees were announced:

COMMITTEE ON CREDENTIALS.

New York,	D. C. Littlejohn, J. V. L. Pruyn.
Illinois,	Robert McChesney, Wm. Barker.
Missouri,	Samuel Plant, E. B. Kirby.
Pennsylvania,	Samuel V. Merrick, C. B. Herron.
Wisconsin,	Daniel Wells, W. P. McLaren.
Minnesota,	D. D. Merrill, N. B. Harwood.
Maine,	A. K. Shurtleff, S. P. Strickland.
Ohio,	M. R. Waite, J. P. Robinson.
Massachusetts,	Hamilton A. Hill, Curtis Guild.
Michigan,	H. P. Bridge, B. J. Brown.
Iowa,	James Putnam.
Canada,	P. Redpath, J. G. Worts.
New Brunswick,	A. E. Botsford, W. H. Steeves.
Nova Scotia,	T. J. Archibald, Wm. J. Stairs.
Prince Edward's Island,	George Coles, Frederick Brecken.

COMMITTEE ON ORGANIZATION.

Albany,	C. T. Shepard.
Buffalo,	Lewis F. Allen.
Bay City,	H. M. Fitzhugh.
Boston,	Joseph F. Ropes.
Bangor,	Samuel F. Dane.
Chicago Board of Trade,	J. Young Scammon.
Chicago Mercantile Association,	W. F. Allen.
Cairo,	D. M. Munn.
Cincinnati,	S. Lester Taylor.
Cleveland,	Rufus P. Spaulding.
Cobourg, C. W.,	Declined to act.

Charlotteville, P. E. I.,	Declined.
Detroit,	James F. Joy.
Erie,	M. R. Barr.
Halifax,	Declined.
Hamilton,	Declined.
Kingston,	Declined.
Kalamazoo,	C. S. May.
London,	Declined.
Montreal,	Declined.
Milwaukee,	Thos. Whitney.
New York Chamber of Commerce,	Gen. W. K. Strong.
New York Commercial Association,	R. P. Getty.
Oswego,	A. P. Grant.
Ottawa,	Declined.
Philadelphia Board of Trade,	Frederick Fraley.
Philadelphia Coal Exchange,	G. S. Reppelier.
Philadelphia Corn Exchange,	Thos. Allman.
Portland,	T. C. Hersey.
Pittsburgh,	Geo. H. Thurston.
Quebec,	Declined.
St. Paul,	John Nichols.
St. Louis,	Thos. Richeson.
St. John,	Declined.
Springfield, Ohio,	W. Warner.
Stratford,	Declined.
East Saginaw,	W. L. P. Little.
St. Catharines,	Declined.
Toledo,	Dennison P. Smith.
Toronto,	Declined.
Troy,	G. C. Burdett.
Windsor,	Declined.
Lumber Dealers' Association, Albany,	R. H. Waterman.

On motion of Mr. Joy, of Detroit, the Committee on Organization were instructed to fix the vote of each delegation, and report rules for the government of the Convention.

The Convention took a recess until 3 o'clock P. M.

AFTERNOON SESSION.

The Convention was called to order by the temporary Chairman at 3 P. M.

Hon. J. V. L. Pruyn, of Albany, Chairman of the Committee on Credentials, submitted the following Report:

The Committee adopted as a basis of their action the following resolutions:

1st. That all delegates from Commercial Associations, properly appointed, and in attendance on the Convention, be credited as members thereof.

2d. That all organizations recognized by the Detroit Board of Trade, and reported to the Convention by the President of that Board, be received as entitled to representation in the Convention.

3d. That in the judgment of this Committee, whenever more than one organization from any one City or place be admitted to representation in this Convention, the admission of such organization should not be allowed to increase the vote of that locality.

4th. That, as a matter of courtesy, the representatives of the Trustees of Niagara Falls Village,. and the City of Burlington, Iowa, be admitted to seats upon the floor of the Convention, without votes.

The names of the gentlemen composing the several delegations were then reported by the Committee, as follows:

Albany Board of Trade.

Hon. John V. L. Pruyn,	C. W. Armstrong,	William P. Irwin,
Hon. Lyman Tremain,	Samuel Rankin,	B. H. Mills,
Sylvester Hale,	John Lane,	Lee Chamberlain,
Henry Lansing,	Wm. Lacy,	John W. Russell,
William H. Taylor,	Charles T. Shepard,	John Tracey.

Albany Lumber Association.

S. B. Towner,	W. Dickson,	R. H. Waterman.
William Birdsall,		

Bangor (Maine) Board of Trade.

Hon. Samuel Dale,	S. P. Strickland,	H. E. Prentiss,
Hon. Hannibal Hamlin,	Hon. A. D. Manson,	George W. Hammett,
Charles Hayward,	S. W. Thaxter,	Hon. Charles Stetson,
J. M. Sabine,	Hon. S. H. Blake,	Hon. John Appleton.

Bay City Board of Trade.

N. B. Bradley,	C. E. Jennison,	J. E. Lewis,
M. Fitzhugh,	J. McEwan,	C. C. Fitzhugh,
O. M. Fowler,	A. E. McLain,	C. H. Denison.
H. H. Hatch,		

Belleville Delegation.

Hon. B. Flint,	George Nelson,	J. C. Walbridge,
Thomas Kelso,	Hep. Corby,	George Vair.
A. Damond,	W. B. Roblin,	

Boston Board of Trade.

James C. Converse,	Curtis Guild,	Gerry W. Cochrane,
Joseph S. Ropes,	W. W. Greenough,	William Hilton.
Hamilton A. Hill,	Lorenzo Sabine,	

Buffalo Board of Trade.

Hon. Israel P. Hatch,	George P. Bently,	E. P. Dorr,
Wm. Thurstone,	J. D. Hayes,	D. P. Dobbins,
Hon. E. S. Prosser,	S. S. Guthrie,	Hon. George S. Hazard,
Hon. Lewis F. Allen,	John Allen, jr.,	Joseph Larned,
Hon. S. V. R. Watson,	Jason Parker,	J. N. Matthews.
P. S. Marsh,	Cyrus Clarke,	

Burlington, Iowa.

James Putnam.

Cairo Chamber of Commerce.

William Barker,	Charles Scudder,	G. D. Williamson,
Hon. Wm. H. Green,	J. W. Trover,	John M. Cyrus,
B. M. Munn,	J. B. Humphreys,	Dyas F. Parker.
S. S. Homans,		

Chicago Board of Trade.

Charles Randolph,	M. C. Sherman,	C. W. Magill,
William Nason,	T. J. Bronson,	R. McChesney,

W. D. Houteling,
John V. Farwell,
Col. J. H. Bowen,
W. F. Coolbaugh,
Col. J. L. Hancock,
Asa Dow,
R. P. Whitney,
R. S. Jennings,
B. F. Culver,
J. W. Finley,
P. L. Underwood,
Col. B. S. Shepard,
Harrold Sprague,
T. P. Lawrence,
J. C. Dore,
J. H. Dole,
Col. Luther Haven,
Murry Nelson,
Solon Cummings,
T. S. Phillips,
D. H. Denton,
B. F. Jacobs,
Ira Y. Munn,
E. F. Lawrence,
Hugh McLennan,
N. K. Fairbank,
E. Wood,
F. B. Brown,
Clinton Furbish,
R. S. King,
T. Inglis,
J. Young Scammon.

Chicago Mercantile Association.

Charles Walker,
H. W. Hinsdale,
W. T. Allen,
W. G. Hibbard,
Edwin Burnham.

Cincinnati Chamber of Commerce.

W. W. Scarborough,
Lewis Worthington,
Adolph Wood,
Robert Brown,
James McKeehan,
Thomas G. Mitchell,
S. Lester Taylor,
Thomas Sherlock,
Joseph C. Butler,
John W. Hartwell.

Cleveland Board of Trade.

R. T. Lyon,
I. H. Clark,
W. Murray,
A. I. Begges,
G. W. Gardner,
S. N. Goodale,
Hon. R. P. Spaulding,
Hon. J. P. Robinson,
N. Sachrider,
A. Burgess,
J. C. Sage,
M. C. Younglove,
J. M. Hughes,
George Sprague,
Alton Pope,
William Wellhouse,
G. F. Otis,
C. W. Coe,
O. C. Scovill,
J. F. Freeman.

Cobourg Board of Trade.

Alexander Frazer,
John Sutherland,
E. A. Macnachtan,
Thomas N. Gibbs,
Abram Farewell,
George Currie,
A. McNaughton.

Detroit Board of Trade.

Joseph Aspinall,
H. P. Bridge,
James F. Joy,
R. W. King,
Duncan Stewart,
Moses W. Field,
George W. Bissell,
John R. Jones,
Alex. Lewis,
John Hutchings,
Franklin Moore,
Richard Hawley,
Christian H. Buhl,
A. E. Bissell,
E. B. Ward.

East Saginaw Board of Trade.

W. L. P. Little,	B. J. Brown,	M. B. Hass,
S. W. Yawkey,	S. B. Bliss,	M. Jeffers,
J. T. Burnham.	William L. Webber.	J. S. Estabrook.

Erie Board of Trade.

John Clemens,	M. R. Barr,	John W. Shannon.

Halifax Chamber of Commerce.

Hon. Joseph Howe,	Thomas Killiam,	D. R. Eaton,
Hon. T. D. Archibald,	R. P. Grant,	B. N. Salter.
Wm. J. Stairs,		

Hamilton (C. W.) Board of Trade.

Hon. Isaac Buchanan,	D. MacInnes,	John Proctor,
Adam Brown,	Edward Browne,	William Osborne,
William Irvine,	J. M. Williams,	Henry Parker.

Kingston (C. W.) Board of Trade.

John P. Litchfield,	W. G. Kinghorn,	Hon. Walker Ross,
R. M. Rose,	G. S. Hobart,	Thomas Donnelly,
John Shaw,	E. Chenn,	G. Stricker,
John Fraser,	D. Barker,	J. F. McCuaig.

London (C. W.) Board of Trade.

C. P. Smith,	Hon. C. Leonard,	W. W. Wallace,
C. Hunt,	Dr. D. Farrar,	Thomas Churcher,
F. Smith,	E. Havaran,	Robert Reid.
F. Rowland,	J. Bissell,	

Michigan Central Board of Trade.

Charles S. May,	C. Sherman,	George W. Fish,
H. E. Haskell,	H. Carpenter,	A. Sherman,
F. H. Chase,	H. F. Colbech,	George Ingersoll.
J. B. Merrill,		

Milwaukee Chamber of Commerce.

William Young,	William P. McLaren,	D. Wells, jr.,
Thomas Whitney,	F. Layton,	C. L Sholes,
George I. Jones,	E. Roddis,	J. Johnston.
G. D. Norris,	C. W. Willard,	

Montreal Corn Exchange.

Hon. J. L. Beaudry,	E. H. King,	Henry Thomas,
Hon. L. Renaud,	John Grant,	James Law,
Hon. L. Holton,	John Greenshields,	Walter Shanly,
Hon. Thomas Ryan,	C. J. Brydges,	Thomas Cramp,
Hugh Allan,	Thomas Rimmer,	W. H. A. Davies,
Peter Redpath,	D. Masson,	Wm. J. Patterson.
John McLennan,	Alfred Brown,	

New York Chamber of Commerce.

Hon. Hiram Walbridge,	Gen. W. K. Strong,	L. J. N. Stark,
Hon. J. S. T. Stranahan,	Louis J. Belloni, jr.,	N. S. Bentley.
S. DeWitt Bloodgood,		

New York Commercial Association.

Edward Hincken,	Frederic Sherwood,	Edgar Hyatt,
W. H. Harris,	Edward Cromwell,	A. J. Wood,
E. W. Coleman,	Robert P. Getty,	A. D. VanWagenen.
Augustus E. Masters,	F. A. Fisher,	

Oswego Board of Trade.

Hon. DeW. C. Littlejohn,	R. F. Sage,	J. L. McWhorter,
A. P. Grant,	H. C. Wright,	L. B. Crocker,
Henry Fitzhugh,	A. G. Cook,	B. Hagaman,
Cheney Ames,	W. H. Herrick,	Oscar E. Shepard,
Luther Wright,	George Ames,	Charles Parker,
Elias Root,	D. DeWolf,	N. B. Wright,
J. C. Churchill,	O. H. Hastings,	L. B. Robe,
E. B. Talcott,	George B. Sloan,	D. W. Erwin,
A. C. Mattoon,	A. B. Randall,	B. B. Burt,
Willard Johnson,	W. A. Rundell,	S. B. Johnson.

Ottawa (C. W.) Board of Trade.

Hon. James Skead,	Edward McGilleray,	Thomas Hunton,
Edward Griffin,	Hon. J. M. Currier,	George H. Perry.

Perth County, C. W.

P. R. Jarvis.

Philadelphia Board of Trade.

Samuel V. Merrick, Frederick Fraley, John M. Kennedy, Edward Y. Townsend, George L. Buzby, Charles S. Ogden, John Welsh, A. G. Cattell, Charles Macalester, Edward C. Biddle, Samuel E. Stokes, John Sparhawk, George N. Tatham, John P. Crozer, Dr. William Elder.

Philadelphia Coal Exchange Association.

O. W. Davis, G. S. Reppelier, J. Rommel, J. Tucker, J. G. C. Morris.

Philadelphia Corn Exchange Association.

John Derbyshire, Thomas Allman, Samuel Hartrauft, Joseph W. Miller, Joseph S. Perot, Charles Knecht, C. J. Hoffman, Henry Budd.

Pittsburgh Board of Trade.

William M. Shum, James I. Bennett, George H. Thurston, C. B. Herron,

Port Hope Delegation.

Ralph Jones, James O'Neil, John Fowler, William Frasier, James Smith.

Portland Board of Trade.

T. C. Hersey, A. K. Shurtleff, T. E. Twitchell, M. N. Rich, J. S. Bedloe, R. M. Richardson.

Prince Edward's Island Board of Trade.

Hon. George Coles. Frederick Breeken, William Heard.

Quebec Board of Trade.

Hon. Malcolm Cameron, James G. Moss, Henry Fry, P. Garmean, T. H. Grant, James Dean, T. H. Dunn, Henry Dinning, L. Tetu.

Representatives of Niagara Village.

John T. Bush, Horace N. Day, John Fisk.

Springfield (Ohio) Board of Trade.

William Warner, Thomas S. McGraw, J. D. Sharon.

St. Catharines (C. W.) Board of Trade.

Hon. Wm. McGiverin,
Hon. James G. Currie,
James Douglas,
C. Yale,
H. H. Collyer,
Robert Laurie,
William Eccles.

St. John (N. B.) Board of Trade.

Hon. A. E. Botsford,
Hon. W. H. Steeves,
William Parks, Esq.,
John Boyd, Esq.,
C. H. Fairweather,
Hon. Charles Fisher,
John Pickard, Esq.,
John Boulton, Esq.,

St. Louis Board of Trade.

Thomas Richeson,
H. F. Driller,
Barton Able,
J. O. Broadhead,
Nathan Cole.
J. H. Alexander,
W. S. Mosely,
R. S. Elliott,
J. L. Butler,
C. E. Slayback,
G. A. Maguire,
Samuel Treat,
Samuel Plant,
S. M. Edgell,
E. B. Kirby,
G. W. Chadbourne,
J. G. Pratner,
P. L. Wilkinson,
A. B. Garrison,
P. G. Gerhart.

St. Paul Board of Trade.

Daniel W. Ingersoll,
Hon. J. W. Taylor,
John Nicols,
D. D. Merrill,
N. B. Harwood,
W. J. Smith.

Toledo Board of Trade.

Denison B. Smith,
M. D. Carrington,
Charles A. King,
W. W. Griffith,
F. Bissell,
C. Waggoner,
G. E. Pomeroy,
M. R. Waite,
D. E. Gardner,
A. Reid,
T. H. Hoag,
H. S. Walbridge.

Troy Board of Trade.

Hon. David L. Seymour,
George C. Burdett,
L. A. Battershall,
Martin J. Townsend,
Chauncey O. Grum,
Jason C. Osgood,
Lorenzo D. Collins,
T. M. Tibbetts,
A. B. Morgan,
T. A. Tellenhaust,
Elias Ross,
Oliver Bascom,
T. T. Vaughn,
George W. Goff.

Windsor (C. W.) Board of Trade.

James Dougall,
Henry Kennedy,
Louis Meveux,
H. C. Guillot,
D. Cameron,
John McDonald,
James Lambie.

Toronto Board of Trade.

James G. Worts,	Hon. John McMurrich,	William Elliott,
Robert Spratt,	Hon. A. M. Smith,	Dalrymple Crawford,
Hon. Wm. McMasters,	Charles Robertson,	John Boyd,
	Erastus Wyman.	

Mr. Mitchell, of Cincinnati, moved to accept the Report. Carried.

Mr. W. F. Coolbaugh, of Chicago, moved to strike out all that part of the fourth resolution reported by the Committee which related to the delegate from Burlington, Iowa—lost, ayes 75, noes 85.

After further debate, Mr. Stranahan, of New York, moved to strike out the third resolution, the Committee on Organization being prepared to report on that subject. The motion was agreed to.

The report, as amended, was adopted.

Gen. W. K. Strong, of New York, from the Committee on Permanent Organization, submitted the following report:

Your Committee appointed to report the names for permanent officers of this Convention, whose duty it should be to frame rules for its government, beg leave to report that they have unanimously selected as the presiding officer of this Convention, a distinguished citizen of New York. His name, and those of the other officers, are as follows:

PRESIDENT,

Hon. HIRAM WALBRIDGE, of New York.

VICE PRESIDENTS,

Hon. H. Hamlin, Maine, at large.	J. C. Converse, Massachusetts.
Hon. Chas. Walker, Illinois at large.	T. E. Twitchel, Maine.
D. L. Seymour, New York.	W. L. P. Little, Michigan.
Geo. F. Davis, Ohio.	Hon. Jos. Howe, Nova Scotia.
D. W. Ingersoll, Minnesota.	Hon. W. Park, New Brunswick.
S. M. Edsall, Missouri.	Hon. Thos. Ryan,
W. Young, Wisconsin.	Hon. Wm. McMasters, Canada.
Chas. Randolph, Illinois.	Hon. Geo. Coles, P. E. Island.

James I. Bennett, Pennsylvania.

SECRETARIES,

Wm. Lacy, New York.	Ray Haddock, Michigan.

Adam Brown, Canada.

The Committee also reported the following resolutions embracing rules for the government of the Convention:

Resolved, That the rules of the House of Representatives in the United States Congress govern the proceedings of this Convention, with the following exceptions, to-wit:

1. No person shall speak more than ten minutes upon the same question without first obtaining the leave of the Convention.
2. No person shall speak more than once upon the same subject, without express leave of the Convention.
3. Each commercial association represented in this Convention shall be entitled to one vote only upon the disposition of questions submitted for action.
4. The formal disposition of all questions submitted for action to this Convention shall be made by voting *vica voce,* in which each association represented shall cast one vote.

Mr. Bentley, of New York, moved to adopt so much of the Report as related to the permanent organization of the Convention—carried.

On motion, Messrs. Pruyn and Strong, of New York, were appointed a Committee to conduct the President to the Chair.

The Committee then introduced the Hon. Hiram Walbridge to the Convention, who spoke as follows:

Gentlemen of the Convention,—I return to you my most sincere thanks for this manifestation of your regard. I shall endeavor to bring to the discharge of the duties of the chair whatever is requisite to creditably perform those duties in a manner so as to advance the great objects which have brought us together. I do not forget the character of the constituencies which we represent. This is the first great commercial assemblage which has been brought together in this country since the termination of that great rebellion which shook the earth beneath our feet. I do not forget that this rebellion was brought to its triumphant close mostly by the energies and through the exertions of the men of business in this country. But I am gratified that that rebellion is over, and that now when we have to enter upon the discharge of the duties incident to our new position, the business men of the country have stepped in advance, so as to exercise, I trust, hereafter their legitimate influence in the administration of public affairs. (Hear, hear.) The commercial and business men of this country have suffered their interests too long to be confided to the hands of politicians, and it is now their duty to step forward and exert their own legitimate influence in behalf of peace and the great measures we hope to accomplish in the future. I am much gratified to see that this Convention has brought together such large and influential delegates from the British Provinces of North America. (Hear, hear.) I trust that the community of sentiment which has brought them here, may eventuate in causing still closer relations to exist between them and us. (Cheers and laughter.) I hope that the deliberations of this Convention will eventuate in a treaty, which shall be just to them, and not inconsistent with the dignity, the honor and the welfare of the people of the United States. (Cheers.) Justice and equity in the commercial business and political intercourse between the two countries is what each has a right to demand, and on that we most earnestly insist, if the action of the Convention is to secure the approbation of the powerful constituencies we represent. And if, gentlemen, from this Convention new sentiments shall spring up between us and them, which shall eventuate in still more fraternal relations, I can only say to them that such is the peculiar character of our institutions that while we leave to the States the administration of their local concerns, giving to the general government the requisite power and authority to supervise the whole, our system admits of indefinite expansion — (cheers and laughter) — and if hereafter, in the providence of God, they should seek association with us, and help to discharge the debt this rebellion has created, it will relieve us from the anguish we have felt at the course they have heretofore pursued in reference to our internicine war. (Cheers.)

The Detroit Board of Trade, in naming the objects to which the attention of this Convention will be directed, has most properly placed Commerce in the front rank. They doubtless realized that the Constitution of the United States itself resulted from the necessities of Commerce. While, therefore, we sustain the commercial men of the country, we uphold the Constitution of the country, and maintain the honor and glory of the republic. (Cheers.) The second subject to which our consideration is invited is that of finance. There may be other systems better than ours; but I can conceive of none better than that which pledges the entire resources of the country to the just payment of its debts. A universal sentiment of execration for all time to come must rest upon any man who would repudiate any portion of the debt of the country. (Prolonged cheers.) The next great question — the third in order — is the opening of the means of transit between the West and the Seaboard. Gentlemen, when I stand here and look to the resources of the illimitable West, capable not only of sustaining one hundred millions of men here, but also capable of feeding another hundred million of men on the European continent, I ask you to multiply the facilities for placing this grain in the European markets at a price below what it can be grown there. When you have done that you may dispense with ministers and diplomacy, for when you control the food of a people, you control their sentiments. Do your best, this mighty West will crowd these avenues to the seaboard to place this food in the Eastern markets. These are the three questions, together with that of reciprocity, which we are invited to consider, and to which I shall endeavor, as your presiding officer, to hold the Convention, to the exclusion of all extraneous matter. (Cheers.) I do not forget that we have sacrificed much in leaving our business. We have come to this common altar to extend a welcome to our friends from the British Provinces, at the same time trusting that the result of the deliberations of this meeting may tend to the honor, the prosperity, dignity, and interest of the people of these Provinces, and to the honor, the prosperity, dignity and renown of the people of the United States. (Loud cheers.)

The other officers were requested to take seats upon the platform, and all of them who were present did so. There were loud calls for Ex-Vice President Hamlin, but a delegate reported that he was not present. He shortly entered the room, however, when the calls were renewed. The Chair requested him to come forward and take a seat upon the platform.

Mr. Hamlin rose and returned thanks for the honor conferred, but declined and requested the election of another Vice President in his place.

The President said that he must object to that as he wished the benefit of the Vice President's experience and advice, but the latter persisted in declining the honor.

The question being on the adoption of the resolutions reported by the Committee,

Mr. Lewis F. Allen, of Buffalo, called for a division on each resolution. The first, second and third resolutions were adopted.

Mr. Bowen, of Chicago, moved to amend the fourth resolution so that the representation in Convention should be based on population of cities.

Mr. Joy stated that the Committee had considered this, and decided that it would be impracticable. It must be remembered that the different States and Cities are not the population of the whole country, and that parties who come from these Cities may represent the sentiments and interests of the people among whom they live, and the representation of the opinion of these cities may just as well come from these citizens as from a commercial body. Some States have large delegations, others have small, and considering the whole, and canvassing every mode of representation, the Committee came to the conclusion that one vote from an association would declare its sentiment as well as a dozen. Therefore, we have made this recommendation.

The motion of Mr. Bowen was lost, and the fourth resolution was then adopted.

Mr. Kennedy, of Philadelphia, moved that the Committee on Organization be also appointed a Committee on Resolutions.

Mr. Joy moved the appointment of a committee of five to report order of business, the questions of transit to the East, and Reciprocity to be first taken up, as the Canadian delegates are most interested in those questions.

Mr. Kennedy suggested that his resolution did not conflict with this, the only objection being that the Canadians would not be represented.

Mr. Joy expressed the opinion that the committee proposed by Mr. Kennedy, would be too large.

Mr. Littlejohn offered the following:

Resolved, That five Committees, to consist of five members each, be appointed by the President of the Convention to consider respectively the following subjects:

Commerce.

Finance.

Communications of Transit from the West to the Seaboard.

Reciprocal Trade between the United States and British Provinces.

River and Harbor Improvements.

To which shall be referred all resolutions pertaining to those questions, and the Committees respectively shall have power to report upon the subjects referred to them.

Mr. Kennedy withdrew his resolution.

Mr. Joy moved to increase the above Committees to seven each, which was agreed to, and Mr. Littlejohn's resolution, as amended, was adopted.

Mr. Elliott, of St. Louis, moved the appointment of a Committee of seven on Miscellaneous Business, which was carried.

The Chair suggested that some consideration was necessary before such important appointments, and accordingly, on motion of Barton Able, a recess was taken until 7 o'clock.

EVENING SESSION.

Mr. Littlejohn moved that the number on the six Committees to be appointed by the President, be increased to nine, which was carried.

The President then announced the following Committees:

ON TRANSIT.

Hon. D. C. Littlejohn,	Oswego.
E. S. Prosser,	Buffalo.
Duncan Stewart,	Detroit.
R. S. Elliott,	St. Louis.
J. C. Converse,	Boston.
T. C. Hersey,	Portland.
C. F. Randolph,	Chicago.
R. P. Spaulding,	Cleveland.
D. B. Smith,	Toledo.

The following gentlemen were appointed on the part

of the British Provinces, to lay before the Committee their views on the question of Transit:

Hon. Malcolm Cameron,	Quebec.
Mr. John McLellan,	Montreal.
William McGivern, M. P. P.	St. Catharines.
George H. Perry,	Ottawa.

ON RECIPROCITY.

Hon. J. F. Joy,	Detroit.
M. R. Waite,	Toledo.
Israel T. Hatch,	Buffalo.
J. W. Taylor,	St. Paul.
Frederick Fraley,	Philadelphia.
S. DeWitt Bloodgood,	New York.
Daniel Wells,	Milwaukee.
J. Lester Taylor,	Cincinnati.
Geo. C. Burdett,	Troy.

The Chair stated that the Provincial delegations had declined to name members of the Committee, but would like to name the following gentlemen as a Committee of conference on their part, on the question of Reciprocity, viz:

Hon. Joseph Howe,	Halifax, N. S.
Hon. Thomas Ryan,	Montreal.
J. G. Worts,	Toronto.
Henry Fry,	Quebec.
John Boulton,	St. John.

On motion, the request of the Provincial delegation was acceded to, and the above gentlemen were appointed.

The Chair stated that the Canadians and delegates from the Lower Provinces, desired that the gentlemen named from their delegations be regarded as not voting, but simply to afford information in Committee.

Mr. Robinson, of Cleveland, offered the following:

Resolved, That a Committee of seven be appointed by the Chair to consider and report on the subjects of Agriculture and Manufactures, and that all resolutions offered on these questions be referred to the same.

Mr. Randolph, of Chicago, asked if the attention of the Convention was not to be confined to matters included in the call.

Mr. Robinson thought that the topics of agriculture and manufactures were germane to the objects of the Convention, and disclaimed all design of interfering with its harmony.

Mr. Kennedy also advocated Mr. Robinson's motion at some length, as did Mr. Allen, of Buffalo.

The resolution was then passed.

Mr. Taylor, of Minnesota, offered the following:

Resolved, That the Boards of Trade represented in the Convention recognize the necessity of effective and organized measures to repress the practice of smuggling upon the extended frontier between the United States and British America, and will co-operate constantly and earnestly with the Finance Ministers of the respective countries for the suppression of such illicit trade.

Resolved, That we welcome the effort now making by commissioners under the direction of Hon. Hugh McCulloch, Secretary of the Treasury of the United States, to revise and present to Congress the best method for the collection of revenue, both internal and external, and that this Convention respectfully recommend that the Finance Ministers of the English Provinces on this continent shall be parties to such deliberations, with a view to uniformity of legislation on both sides of the international frontier, upon all questions relating to public revenue.

Mr. Taylor said that the Secretary of the Treasury had designated as Revenue Commissioners, Messrs. D. A. Wells, of Troy, New York, Stephen Colwell, of Philadelphia, and S. S. Hays, of Chicago — gentlemen who represented the business interests of the country, and one of whom, Mr. Hays, was not a political supporter of the Administration. The Commissioners expected and desired the hearty co-operation of Boards of Trade, and it would be fortunate if the Finance Ministers of the British Provinces would labor in concert with the Treasury Department at Washington to establish uniformity of revenue legislation on both sides of the international borders, thus effectually terminating the evil of illicit trade.

The resolutions were at first tabled, but subsequently referred to the Committee on Finance.

Mr. Thurston, of Pittsburgh, offered a resolution recommending that before the final voting upon any resolution before the Convention, such resolution be printed for distribution among the members. Laid on the table.

On motion, the Convention adjourned to nine o'clock to-morrow morning.

SECOND DAY.

WEDNESDAY, JULY 12—9 A. M.

The Convention met pursuant to adjournment.

Prayer by Rev. Geo. Duffield, D. D.

The President, by unanimous consent, announced the following additions to the Committee on Reciprocity.

Hon. Hannibal Hamlin, of Maine; H. P. Bridge, of Detroit; S. H. Dale, of Bangor, and Lorenzo Sabine, of Massachusetts.

Mr. Hamlin declined to serve on the Committee, and the name of Henry E. Prentiss, of Bangor, was substituted.

The President announced the following Committees:

ON COMMERCE.

J. H. Bowen,	Chicago.
T. G. Mitchell,	Cincinnati.
John Allen,	Buffalo.
Thos. Richeson,	St. Louis.
A. P. Grant,	Oswego.
A. E. Masters,	New York.
Delos DeWolf,	Oswego.
R. W. King,	Detroit.
F. A. Fisher,	New York.

ON FINANCE.

Hon. Lyman Tremain,	Albany.
J. S. T. Stranahan,	New York.

Col. W. S. Moseley, ...	St. Louis.
W. F. Coolbaugh, ...	Chicago.
Adolph Wood, ...	Cincinnati.
E. H. Tompkins, ...	New York.
John Derbyshire, ...	Philadelphia.
R. M. Richardson, ...	Portland.
Chas. A. King, ...	Toledo.

ON LAKE AND HARBOR IMPROVEMENTS.

Robert McChesney, ...	Chicago.
W. P. McLaren, ...	Milwaukee.
B. J. Brown, ...	East Saginaw.
Geo. W. Bissell, ...	Detroit.
C. Waggoner, ...	Toledo.
S. V. R. Watson, ...	Buffalo.
A. C. Mattoon, ...	Oswego.
P. P. Getty, ...	New York.
John Allen, jr., ...	Buffalo.

ON ORDER OF BUSINESS.

Col. Edward Hinken, ...	New York.
Franklin Moore, ...	Detroit.
J. O. Broadhead, ...	St. Louis.
Wm. L. P. Little, ...	Saginaw.
A. E. Bissell, ...	Detroit.

ON AGRICULTURE AND MANUFACTURES.

Hon. J. P. Robinson, ...	Cleveland.
E. B. Ward, ...	Detroit.
Henry Lansing, ...	Albany.
C. W. Willard, ...	Milwaukee.
J. I. Bennett, ...	Pittsburgh.
Hon. Lewis F. Allen, ...	Buffalo.
Wm. Hilton, ...	Boston.
W. H. Harris, ...	New York.
Jas. C. Osgood, ...	Troy.

Mr. Spaulding, of Ohio, offered the following resolution:

Resolved, That it is the duty of Congress to "regulate commerce with foreign nations" in such manner as to increase the resources of the Government for the payment of the national debt; to promote the independence and prosperity of the country, and effectually protect the labor and industry of the people of the United States against the conflicting policy of other powers.

The resolution was referred to the Committee on Agriculture and Manufactures.

Mr. Coolbaugh, of Chicago, introduced the following resolutions:

Resolved, That the action of the Convention in declaring that each Association represented in this Convention shall be entitled to but one vote, is a virtual declaration that the majority shall be controlled by the minority, entirely ignoring the great American doctrine of representation according to constituencies, and numbers in such constituencies.

Resolved, That the resolution giving to each Association but one vote be rescinded; that each Association be required to report to the Chairman the number of members of such Association, and any such Association shall be entitled to one vote for every one hundred members of such Association, and that a fraction over fifty members in any such Association be entitled to one additional delegate.

Mr. Coolbaugh said: If that resolution is in order, I beg the indulgence of the Convention to make a few remarks thereon. The delegation from the City of Chicago came here without any personal or ulterior purposes to subserve. They came here in good faith, under the call issued by the Board of Trade of the City of Detroit, to take part in the deliberations of the Convention, and to do what they could to promote the interests of the people and commerce of the West. We have found ourselves here, Sir, under the organization of this Convention, representing as we do, in common with two or three gentlemen from Cairo, the State of Illinois with two millions of people; the City of Chicago with two hundred thousand people, and its Board of Trade with one thousand eight hundred members.

After some temporary interruption, Mr. Coolbaugh resumed: I was stating that our delegation represented a Board of Trade of one thousand eight hundred members, and a domestic industry equal to, if not larger than, that of any other State in this Union. We find ourselves, under the rules of government of this Convention, placed on an equality, with no more power to shake the deliberations of this body than has the delegation from Bay City; no more than the town of Kalamazoo. In other words, the City of Chicago, represented here by more than fifty of her best business men, who, although they may not be able to talk quite as well as some of our Eastern men, are yet men of great commercial influence, possesses just one forty-fourth of the right to control the action of this body.

Under the rules of government adopted by this Convention, the States of Wisconsin, Missouri, and Illinois, representing, to say the least of it, an amount of commerce worthy the attention of this body, find themselves on an equality with the delegations here from the places I have named, and with no more power than they have. They have only the right to control one-twelfth or one-fourteenth of this Convention.

I think it is right we should have harmony and fairness here; but it does seem to numerous gentlemen belonging to the deputation to which I am attached, as though there were some ulterior purpose, else why should this manifest unfairness be carried out in its proceedings?

I beg the Convention to calmly consider the representations contained in that resolution. It has the entire sanction of our deputation. We desire harmony; we desire to do all we can to promote it, but we expect something like equal rights. We expect them; nay, we demand them. I am sure that the adoption of that resolution, or a similar resolution, will result in good to this Convention, and redound to the interest of our country.

G. F. Davis, of Cincinnati, rose and said: I am aware that some of our large commercial bodies complain that they have not a due amount of representation in this Convention. We would be entitled, by the operations of our Board of Trade, to as large a vote as they from Chicago. While the rule operates against us, as it does against Chicago, I hope the organization of the Convention will proceed without any further molestation. I hope, and I think I can speak fairly, without any accusation of being interested, because we received the same consideration as Chicago in the final vote.

Mr. R. P. Spaulding, of Cleveland—I cannot see how we are ever to transact our business in this Convention if we have to be continually called upon to make alterations in our members of committees, and our code of rules. We never can, upon any given subject, satisfy every man in a body so numerous as this, and therefore some of us must forego our private opinions. I think, Sir, with the gentleman from Cincinnati, that although the vote from Chicago may not be in proportion to their weight and importance, yet it would be better for them to accede to the arrangements made; and therefore I propose that the protest be laid on the table.

Mr. J. Y. Scammon, of Chicago—If it is intended that the deliberations of this Convention shall have any force whatever upon public opinion in this country, there must be that which is just and fair. Now, Sir, I state, without fear of contradiction, that the constitution of the Committee that went out to report upon organization, was such as to render it impossible to have the different portions of the people fairly represented, either in proportion to population or business. Now, the gentleman says that it would be better for Chicago to forego her rights. Chicago, with its one thousand eight hundred members of the Board of Trade—probably the largest in the United States—which represents an Association whose transactions in certain particulars are larger than any other body in the world, is placed upon an equality with Boards of Trade that have not had, and probably never will have, any connection with Canada. (Cheers.) Chicago has the largest direct trade with Canada. We are more interested in this matter than any other City; we raise more cereals; we produce more wheat; we have more transactions in lumber and in produce than any other constituency represented in this Convention; and yet, although the Committee on Reciprocity has been increased two or three times, the City of Chicago is not only ignored, but I say intentionally ignored, in the appointment of that Committee. (Great excitement.)

The President—I desire to state that the gentleman labors under a most gross misapprehension. The Chair has appointed from the Chicago delegation the heads of two of the most important Committees; and it would have afforded the Chair a great deal of pleasure to have placed upon the Committee on Reciprocity some gentleman from Chicago, if he had thought that he could have done so with justice. However, to allay any feelings of that kind, I ask the unanimous consent of the Convention that the Board of Trade of Chicago be allowed to place one name upon that Committee. (Cries of "no," "no," "no.")

Mr. Scammon—I will now state that Mr. Randolph handed up to the Chair the name of Mr. McChesney as a member of that Committee, and he understood it would be placed upon that Committee, but it was not.

The President—The Chair would say that the Committee, as first appointed, consisted of five members only. I came here prepared to appoint those members, and it was afterward changed to nine members. In the hurry of the moment I omitted to notice the name of Mr. McChesney. To make amends for that, I placed his name as Chairman on the Committee on Harbor Improvements, believing that Chicago had as high an interest in that as in any other Committee. I will ask that his name be placed upon the Committee on Reciprocity.

Mr. McChesney—It is too late for that now. I decline to serve on any Committee.

Mr. Pruyn's name was placed at the head of the Committee on Harbor Improvements in Mr. McChesney's stead.

The resolution to place a Chicago name on the Reciprocity Committee was then laid upon the table by a close vote, amid great confusion.

Mr. Kennedy—May we not amend our rules so that when the Chairman of any delegation announces his vote, he may state the number of votes he has? I move, therefore, to amend the rule requiring the vote to be taken *viva voce*, by saying that each person when he announces the vote of his delegation shall state the number of votes.

The President decided that the motion was not in order, inasmuch as he had already decided the question.

An appeal from the decision of the Chair was taken, but on its being put, the Chair was sustained.

Mr. Coolbaugh—In behalf of the delegation to this Convention from the City of Chicago, I ask leave to read a protest:

The delegates from the Board of Trade and Mercantile Association of the City of Chicago, representing a constituency of over one thousand seven hundred members, feeling that the decision of the Convention allowing to only nominal bodies the same voice in determining the action of the Convention as is allowed to one of the largest Commercial Cities in the Union, is a virtual disfranchisement of themselves and their constituents, enter their protest against the action of the Convention as arbitrary, unreasonable and unfair to the large bodies invited to send delegates to this body, and request that this protest may be entered upon the records of the Convention, while they withdraw from a body which in their opinion has refused them a fair representation, and deprived them of their numerical strength in its proceedings.

The delegation request that their protest may be entered upon the records, while they withdraw from a body which in their opinion has refused to give them those rights to which, in justice, they were entitled.

Mr. Able, of St. Louis, offered the following resolution:

Resolved, That each delegate shall have one vote for every twenty-five thousand people represented by it; provided, that each delegation shall have at least one vote.

Mr. Able said: I find, from the feeling of the Convention this morning, that if some change is not made, harmony cannot prevail in this body, and it would be very unfortunate that a deliberative body like this should be broken up. I feel that the great State of New York would be willing to do justice to Illinois in this matter of representation; and without saying anything as to the City which I represent, I do contend that the City of Chicago has a right to be heard upon this question of representation upon this floor. (Loud cheers.) And I trust there is no gentleman from any part of this broad Union, who will not give it that consideration to which it is entitled. I move the adoption of this resolution, in order to bring harmony and concord into the counsels of this Convention, and I trust that it will be adopted.

Mr. D. C. Littlejohn, of New York—The gentleman from Missouri has appealed to the State of New York to do justice to Illinois on this question. The City of New York, with a population of over one million, has been silent upon this question. We have been favorable to any rule of organization that would allow us to proceed, at the earliest moment, to the transaction of the business submitted to this Convention, which will undoubtedly influence the action of Congress thereon, and not to quarrel over matters of minor importance. When I came here, I foresaw difficulties in the way of the Committee, but for the sake of harmony in a Convention held at a critical moment, I was willing to submit to the report of the Committee, and proceed with business. We are to return home within a day or two. Already several members of the Convention are leaving by the first train of cars. I respect the great City of Chicago and its delegation. I know they are entitled to a larger vote upon the floor than the City that I represent; but I did suppose that when the great State of New York was silent, other States less populous might acquiesce; and I hope that if we cannot change this mode of voting, our friends from Chicago will withdraw this protest and return to their seats, and let us proceed in harmony, quiet, and peace.

Mr. J. F. Joy, of Detroit—I am more pained, perhaps, than any other gentleman in this house concerning this difficulty as to voting. I have had some agency in producing the report of the Committee. I was not in favor of that report; I opposed it at the outset; but when we were in the Committee, and we saw a large Convention waiting for the action of that Committee, with so many men distant from their homes, and when we considered the difficulty of ascertaining how there should be a fair and equal representation, as a choice of difficulties, we adopted the rule reported to the Convention. That was only a choice of difficulties—not because we deemed it perfectly fair; for no rule can be perfectly fair. Now, from the rest of the country we hear no complaint. I am sorry that we could not have a perfectly fair mode of voting, but it appeared to us that this was the best that could be done. Suppose we adopt the rule proposed, where would we be when the great State of New York comes in? She would have the power to almost overwhelm the Convention; yet it would be better to submit to this apparent injustice than to break up this Convention, and have any delegation withdraw. I am to a large extent a citizen of Chicago, and I regret beyond measure that the delegation from Chicago should have felt compelled to take such a step, and I still hope they will withdraw their protest.

The Chair—The Chair, deeply impressed with the necessity of giving harmony to the proceedings of this Convention, seeks a solution of the difficulty in this manner: I propose to appoint a Committee, to whom this matter shall be referred, with instructions to report in fifteen minutes, the decision to be left with the Committee, and accepted by all parties as final.

No objection being made, the Chair appointed as such Committee the following gentlemen:

Hon. H. Hamlin, Mr. Coolbaugh, J. F. Joy, D. C. Littlejohn, Mr. Stranahan, Samuel Treat, Hon. Mr. Merrick, of Philadelphia.

The Committee then withdrew, when Mr. Able rose to a personal explanation, and said: The gentleman from Oswego seemed to imply that I had made an attack on New York.

Mr. Littlejohn—Not at all.

The Chair—The Chair understood the gentleman as complimenting the State of New York. (Laughter.)

The Chair appointed the following gentlemen as members of the Committee on Miscellaneous Business:

J. V. L. Pruyn,	Albany
L. Worthington,	Cincinnati.
E. W. Coleman,	New York.
R. T. Lyon,	Cleveland.
J. L. Hancock,	Chicago.
John Johnson,	Milwaukee.
F. Bissell,	Toledo.
Mr. Marsh,	Buffalo.
N. W. Greenough,	Boston.

Mr. Alexander, of St. Louis, was subsequently substituted in Mr. Pruyn's place, and Mr. Trover, of Cairo, was added to the Committee.

Mr. Spaulding, of Ohio, offered the following:

Resolved, That it is the duty of Congress to regulate commerce with foreign nations in such manner as to increase the resources of this Government for the payment of the national debt, to promote the independence and prosperity of the country, and effectually protect the labor and industry of the people of the United States against the conflicting policy of other powers.

The resolution was referred to the Committee on Agriculture and Manufactures.

R. T. Lyon, of Cleveland, offered the following:

Whereas, The Chamber of Commerce of the City of Cincinnati, did cause to be circulated in the Fall of 1864 circulars to the different Boards of Trade in these United States, asking a report from these several Boards, to the effect that an expression of opinion of the several Boards of Trade be made to the Chamber of Commerce of the City of Cincinnati in regard to a more uniform mode for the disposal of produce, merchandize, fruit and spirits, and requiring of the said Boards of Trade their custom as to the disposal of property and the basis of measurement and weights of produce, merchandize, fruits, spirits, etc., to the end that said basis and custom may be made uniform throughout all the States composing our Union, and that the said intent of the Chamber of Commerce of Cincinnati was truly intended to rectify the inconvenient and improper custom that now exists, and has existed, in the diversity of modes and means of the disposal of the properties herein mentioned, of the sale of the same by the bushel, and parts of a bushel; and the difference in custom by the sale of spirits by inspection, varying in the instruments used, by and through the custom existing, and varying at the Cities composing our principal marts and centers of trade; and,

Whereas, The City of Cleveland, through the Board of Trade, did recommend, in answer to said circular, that there was no other mode of transacting the business between the said Cities except by an uniform weight and measurement that should be the law of all the States; and,

Whereas, The said Board of Trade of Cleveland did recommend to the Chamber of Commerce of Cincinnati, that the only mode of obviating the evils and inconveniences herein mentioned was, that all produce, merchandize, spirits, etc., be sold at a rate per 100, and tenths, or decimal system; and that they believed this to be the only true standard by which we, as an American people, can best remedy those evils, discrepancies and variations, in the transaction of business which now exist; be it therefore

Resolved, That a Committee of two from each State represented in this Convention be appointed by the Chair, to report to this Convention during the day, the most proper plan to obviate the inconveniencies that now exist in the disposal of property by the now existing custom, and that said Committee be instructed to report a plan that shall conform to the currency of our country on the decimal principle.

Resolved, That said Committee be instructed to report some plan by which the inspection of spirits and liquors be made uniform throughout the several States.

6

The resolutions were referred to the Committee on Miscellaneous Business.

Mr. Converse, of Boston, offered the following resolution, which was referred to the Committee on Commerce:

Resolved, That a Committee of one from each State represented in this Convention be appointed to consider and report upon the expediency of organizing a National Board of Trade, in order to promote by constant, systematic and permanent plans of action the various commercial, financial and industrial interests of the United States.

Hon. Hannibal Hamlin then announced that the Special Committee were ready to report.

The Chair—Please come forward to the stage.

Mr. Hamlin—No, sir. Perhaps our report will be attended with no better result than has attended the efforts already made. It is a question which has its difficulties and embarrassments. Yet we submit to the consideration of this Convention the following plan as the best which suggested itself to our minds in the few brief moments we have had to consider.

Resolved, That each State represented in this Convention shall be entitled to the same number of votes which it has in the Electoral College, first deducting one vote for each Association here represented.

And it is recommended that the Chairman of the delegations from the respective Associations from each State shall be a Committee to determine the manner in which said remaining votes for each State shall be given.

Mr. Hamlin—That proposition gives, first, to each Association a single vote. It gives to the various States the remaining votes which belong to the State in its electoral capacity. It is true that the State of New York may be represented here by some ten or more bodies, but we regarded them as representing the interests of the State. Illinois, I am told, is represented by two Associations. We regard those as representing the whole State of Illinois, as the greater number represent those of New York. So of the other States represented by a smaller number of Associations—we regard them as truly representing their whole State, and the vote in our Electoral College being the one known and recognized as one of equality—giving first a representation to the State, and then one to the locality—your Committee adopted it.

We omitted to make any provision in relation to the votes of our friends who represent the British Provinces. We did so because we understood that they had respectfully declined to vote in the Convention. [Hear! hear!] That was the reason. I am also instructed by the Committee to state, however, that any intimation from the gentlemen will receive prompt attention, and provision be made for their votes, if they choose to give them. [Applause.]

On motion of Mr. Able, the report of the Committee was accepted.

Mr. Coolbaugh—The delegation from the City of Chicago, which I have the honor to represent on this floor, have listened to the resolution read, and I have great pleasure in stating that they are satisfied [applause]; that while it does not meet their entire satisfaction, it approximates probably as near to a system of fairness as any which could be adopted. Therefore, I take great pleasure in stating that I am instructed to withdraw the protest entered by our delegation, and if we are permitted to withdraw it, we shall with pleasure remain to take part in the deliberations of the Convention.

The Chair—I will state for the information of the Convention, that as I felt myself particularly responsible in this matter, I had squelched the protest before the report came in. [Laughter.]

Mr. Pruyn asked to be allowed to withdraw his name from the Committee on Harbors, etc., and that Mr. McChesney might be placed there in his stead.

The President—The Chair remembered that the first great convention that ever was held in this country was held in Chicago, in reference to harbor improvements. The Chair believed there was no interest so near and dear to the citizens of the beautiful City at the end of Lake Michigan as this one of harbor improvements, and having failed to place the name of its representative on the Committee on Reciprocity, he thought it an honor to that city and that gentleman to place him at the head of the Committee on Harbor Improvements. Mr. McChesney will again be placed in that position.

Mr. Bowen, of Saginaw, moved that the Committee be increased by the addition of two members.

Mr. Able moved to amend by saying five instead of two, which was put and carried.

Mr. Lewis F. Allen, in reference to statements reflecting upon the exorbitant charges made by the State of New York, upon goods shipped from the West by the Erie Canal, said that the charge was false in its expression and unjust in its conclusions. [Cheers.] Forty-five years ago, in the year 1819, the men of New York conceived the grand project of uniting the lakes of the West with the Atlantic ocean by means of a canal. They addressed themselves to other States for the money which they could not at that time raise at home. Detroit was then a small village; Chicago was unknown. In 1825, the Erie Canal was opened. Michigan, Ohio and Indiana grew up to thrift and greatness, and Illinois had now risen to be the fourth State of the Union in production and population. If New York has done this, and had maintained this course in a way no other State could or would have done, exacting charges barely enough to pay the interest on the capital expended, surely they ought not to blame her. There was still a debt of $16,000,000 remaining on the canal, and the tolls had been laid as low as it was possible to make them. They did not demand gold, but were willing to take their pay in the currency of the country. New York was ready now to enlarge that canal to an indefinite capacity. [Cheers.] He had felt it no more than just to vindicate the action of New York in this matter, though he would not have taken any notice of it had it not been for the speech of the President, printed in the morning papers. He then adverted to the question of elevators at Buffalo, and maintained that they were all that could be desired, and their owners high-toned gentlemen.

Mr. Spalding, of Cleveland, did not feel that the Convention was wholly responsible for the address of the chairman of the Detroit Board of Trade. The imputation cast upon the State of New York was not by the Convention. He would however remind the gentleman from Buffalo, that last winter when the question of a ship canal was before Congress, gentlemen from Buffalo came to Washington to oppose the project. [Cheers.] Joint resolutions of the Senate and House of Representatives of that State were also brought against that great work. The gentleman from Buffalo might put this in his pipe and smoke it. [Laughter.]

Mr. Littlejohn moved that when the Convention take a recess the Chairmen of the respective State Delegations meet to adjust the mode of voting, so that they would be prepared to vote instantly upon the questions submitted. Carried.

Mr. Allen, of Buffalo, then entered into explanation respecting the action of the State of New York in reference to the ship canal bill.

Mr. Scammon asked Mr. Allen whether he had not

elevated his personal privilege a little high. (Laughter and cheers.)

Mr. Taylor, of St. Paul, announced that he had received a communuication from St. Paul concerning a railroad route from the head waters of the Mississippi to the head of Lake Superior. At his request it was referred to the Committee on Transit.

Mr. Brown, of Buffalo, suggested that inasmuch as the Committee on Credentials have been increased, there should be a corresponding increase of the number of gentlemen from Canada to appear before it.

Mr. Joy, of Detroit, said he was requested to state that the Canadian delegation have already placed all the matter before that Committee that they desired.

Mr. Kennedy complained that while New York had four members on the Committee of Agriculture and Manufactures, Pennsylvania had only one, and moved that said Committee be increased by the addition of five members. Carried.

The following gentlemen were accordingly added :

Messrs. Younglove, of Ohio; Plant, of St. Louis; Kennedy, of Philadelphia; Allen, of Buffalo, and Merrick, of Philadelphia.

Mr. Treat, of St. Louis, moved that all resolutions upon subjects referred to the Committees be sent the Chair, and be referred without being read. Carried.

Mr. Joy, of Detroit, moved that Prince Edward's Island, which was not represented before the Committees, have a member appointed to attend to their special interests. Carried.

The Chair appointed W. Herd, Esq.

The Committee on Manufactures was increased to fifteen, by the addition of Mr. Wood.

Mr. H. A. Hill, of Boston, introduced the following resolutions:

Resolved, That the widely extended and valuable commerce of Great Britain is principally owing to the liberal encouragement afforded by her Government to the ocean steamship lines, which her merchants have established upon almost every sea and along almost every coast upon the globe, and which have diverted to her ports and markets not only the traffic of the countries geographically approximate to and politically dependent upon her, but the trade of the Brazils and other Southern American sections, and largely, also, the Atlantic commerce which by every propriety belongs in part to the United States.

Resolved, That if we would participate in the ocean commerce of the world, and maintain our position as a mercantile power of the first class, it is indispensable that the Government of the United States, following the example of that of Great Britain, should grant wise and discriminating assistance to such steamship lines as may be established by our merchants to the Brazils, to ports on the Mediterranean Sea and to the British Isles.

Mr. Hill said;

Mr. President,—Among the subjects deserving and demanding the careful attention of this Convention, Ocean Steam Navigation is certainly not the least important. As citizens of the United States, we have constantly been in the habit, and justly, of pointing with pride to the extent and growth of our mercantile marine; to this we have been largely indebted for our national wealth, and this, perhaps more than anything else, has impressed other nations in reference to our resources and our enterprise. So long as the traffic of the ocean was carried on by means of sailing vessels, we not only maintained a respectable position before the world, but we were rapidly gaining upon all competitors, and the very first place seemed within our reach. The model and construction of our vessels, the intelligence and skill of our shipmasters, and the energy and character of our merchants, made the American flag known, respected, and admired on every sea. This was the state of things when the application of steam power to Ocean Navigation produced a change which was totally unexpected, and therefore unprovided for.

At the first, ocean steamships were built and used exclusively for the conveyance of the mails and of first-class passengers. This "packet service" regulated for its own requirements, as then understood, their construction and their management, and no provision was made for ordinary freight or for immigrant passengers. So long as they were the only steamers upon the ocean, there was little interference with sailing vessels; and so far from injuring these vessels, they increased their business by the added facilities afforded by them to general commercial intercourse. Up to that time, therefore, American shipping was benefitted by the establishment of steamship lines; and no such monopoly was threatened as would prevent a nation like our own from participating in the new traffic whenever it might desire to do so. Indeed, as soon as the voyages of the Great Western and the early Cunarders had demonstrated the feasibility and the value of this mode of navigating the Atlantic, there was a desire among the more enterprising citizens of our country to establish American lines to various European ports, and the attention of Congress was repeatedly called to the subject from 1841 and onward. The Cunard line commenced operations under a contract with the Lords of the Admiralty in 1840; but *our* first trans-Atlantic line, between New York and Bremen, did not start until 1847, the line from New York to Havre following the next year, or next but one. We were, from the first, at a disadvantage in this new competition on the ocean, and Great Britain was continually making her position stronger and more secure. The British companies were able to command an abundance of capital, and the comparative cheapness of material and labor in their country gave them opportunity to use this capital in the construction of their vessels to the best advantage. The Government grants — liberal, steady, and constantly increasing — superadded to the other facilities enjoyed by them, unquestionably laid the foundation for their subsequent stability and success. By these they were enabled to maintain themselves while making what was then an experiment, and a most costly one, and they gained time over us to our incalculable loss. Our Government rendered some aid to the Bremen and Havre companies just referred to; but it was inadequate, and was not given on a clearly defined and adopted principle, such as influenced the British Government in all its subsidies, from the time when the possibilities of Ocean Steam Navigation first became apparent. When the Peninsular and Oriental Company had taken full possession, as it were, of the Mediterranean, the Red Sea, and the Indian Ocean; when the Royal Mail Company had secured the monopoly of the Archipelago lying off our own coast, including also the Spanish Main, the Isthmus, and some of our Southern ports; and when the Cunard Company, by a weekly service alternately to Boston and New York, threatened to absorb the steamship traffic in the North Atlantic, Congress consented, for the first time, to give such assistance as was required to place an American line upon anything like an equal footing with its European rivals. The contract at length entered into with the Collins Company was more than liberal; the interest of the Federal Government, and of the people, was fully aroused to the importance of the undertaking; and a splendid opportunity was given to retrieve the apathy and the delay of the past. It was fully expected and believed that the New York line would develope to that success and permanent prosperity which the great companies under the British flag had attained; while our coastwise lines on the Atlantic and the Pacific gave encouragement to the friends of American commerce, which has not since been disappointed.

We cannot go at length into the causes of the failure of Mr. Collins and his associates, but they ought to be adverted to in a review of the past, and in making plans for the future, on this subject.

1st. The capital of the company was insufficient for the business which it was proposed to perform. It was stated during the debates in Congress in 1855—and the statement was not controverted—that up to that time, although the four vessels of the company had cost $2,944,142, its capital paid in amounted only to $1,200,000. It began, therefore, with a cumbrous debt of $1,744,142, which was secured by mortgages on its steamers, and which made a continued drain for interest and commissions. This difficulty, however, would not of itself have proved fatal, for the receipts of the company from the Government for the transportation of the mails during the first five years amounted to $3,413,966, or considerably more than the cost of its ships. Its receipts also for passengers and freight were very large.

But, 2d, the company was too anxious immediately to outdo those who, by perseverence and long experience, had become familiar with and skillful in the business. The Cunard Company had prospered because patient industry, caution, shrewdness, and economy had characterized its management from the very first; without these qualities the assistance it received from the English Government would have been in vain. Its success had been so complete, and the reasons for this success had been so obvious, that the Collins Company might well have been satisfied to emulate its example, and to use its experience. Instead of this, it was determined that the American steamships must be larger; that their fittings must be more luxurious; that their cuisine must be more elaborate, and that their speed must be far in advance of their staid, steady, but somewhat stolid rivals. On the very first voyage they were to demonstrate our superior genius and skill; and the uninterrupted, carefully acquired, and closely studied experience of ten years was to prove of no value to Cunard and MacIver in the contest. It would have been contrary both to principle and precedent, had such expectations been realized.

But, 3d, the danger of this rivalry was aggravated by its being made to exhibit itself mainly in reference to speed. The avowed object of Mr. Collins, from the first, was to outsail the British steamers, even if it were necessary to put all the capital at risk in order to do it. Nor was this enterprising gentleman the only one at fault in this respect. The speeches in Congress, by the friends of the line, were in the same strain; the newspapers encouraged it, and the people generally demanded for their mail steamers pre-eminence in speed, as in everything else. The result could not be otherwise than disastrous. To be sure, the object was attained, and the performances of the noble ships were brilliant, and for a long time unsurpassed. But at what cost? It was testified before a Committee of Congress that the saving of a day each way, in the trip from New York to Liverpool and return, cost the company $16,800, amounting at the end of the year to $436,800, more than half the cost of the Atlantic or the Arctic. Two items contributed principally to this enormous outlay—repairs and fuel. In reference to the former, Mr. Rainey, in his "Ocean Post," informs us that the repairs on the Collins ships for the first six years amounted to more than their original cost, or to about eighteen per cent. per annum; the usual cost on British mail steamers being about twelve per cent. This difference he attributes to the rate of speed attained by the Collins line. As regards fuel, few are aware how largely the consumption is increased by adding to the speed. It is an ascertained law that the resistance to bodies moving through the water increases as the square of the velocity; and the power (or coal) necessary to produce speed varies as the cube of the velocity. Thus, a steamship which, at the speed of ten miles an hour, consumes forty-one tons of coal a day, would, at twelve miles an hour, consume seventy-one tons, and at thirteen miles an hour ninety tons, or two and one-fourth times as much as at ten miles. With these estimates before us, and remembering the speed at which these boasted ships were driven, Mr. Collins's figures are by no means incredible. But they represent only a small portion of the sacrifices made to shorten the time between New York and Liverpool to the minimum. The swift passages of which the company and the country at large were so proud, were made on a most dangerous ocean, amid fog and ice, along a thousand miles of coasting, and in the track of the whole mercantile marine employed in the commerce between Europe and North America. It was not strange that, after many narrow escapes, two of the company's steamers at length perished in mid-ocean; the Arctic, in 1854, by collision in a fog with another steamer; and the Pacific, in 1856, probably by coming in contact with floating ice-fields. These disasters, attended with great loss of life, impaired the confidence of the traveling public, and of Congress, in the remaining vessels, and hastened, if they did not directly promote, the final ruin of the Company.

4th. One further consideration should not be overlooked. The Collins Company relied too much upon the support of the Government, and not sufficiently upon its own exertions. Feeling that it had the public purse to depend upon, it did not control its expenditures within the limits of a wise economy, or manage its affairs with that care and prudence which every commercial undertaking must receive in order to ensure its permanent prosperity. A Government subsidy, however liberal, will not sustain a line that does not possess the conditions of success within itself, nor is it desirable that it should do so. Whatever fault may attach to Congress in the matter, it should not be blamed for withdrawing the subsidy of 1852, which was a temporary and conditional concession added to the original contract amount; for its continuance would only have postponed, and, in all probability, have aggravated the catastrophe. It was evident that the company was disposed to live upon the Government, and the sooner the connection between the two was terminated, the better for the public morality and for the general interests of commerce. The failure of the costly enterprise was most humiliating to the nation, and its effect has been to discourage and retard our progress in Steam Navigation; but if we would not repeat the same experience, we must not hesitate to use candor and discrimination in judging of the causes which have worked us so much mortification and loss.

Two mistakes, as we apprehend, were made on the abandonment of the Collins enterprise, and which will account for the present unsatisfactory condition of our Ocean Steam Navigation. One of these mistakes was made by the Government, and one by the mercantile community. The mistake of the Government consisted in its throwing up in despair the whole subject of steam, and practically assuming that where Mr. Collins had failed no one else could succeed. In its relations with this favored company, it had been too easy and too liberal; it now swung to the opposite extreme, and from doing too much, came to do nothing. It was not politic to leave the steamship traffic of the Atlantic in the hands of foreigners, because one great experiment had proved abortive. A Special Committee should have been appointed by Congress to make a thorough investigation into the causes of this failure, and to propose a plan for the future. Judicious intervention at that time, on the part of the Government, would have encouraged new attempts, notwithstanding the disheartening effect of the misfortunes referred to. As a most important public interest, the subject should have received prompt and earnest consideration; the action of other Governments in fostering their respective steamship lines, laid the obligation upon our own to encourage our citizens to persistent efforts in the contest for the great steamship routes terminating on our shores; and our statesmen should have been no less sagacious and far-seeing in reference to the results of a liberal policy in this respect, than public men in other countries. Congress owes a duty to every source of national wealth; and it was a most serious error to permit one of the magnitude of Ocean Steam Navigation to fail from absolute neglect.

But, at the crisis alluded to, the mercantile community was also at fault, and our commerce is this day suffering in consequence. It was just at this time that screw steamers had begun to show their adaptation to ocean service, and were coming into general use with foreign companies. These are the steam vessels that have interfered with the business of sailing ships on the Atlantic Ocean; and as this business was largely in our hands, they have interfered seriously with us. They have diverted all the passenger and freighting business which our famous packets used to control; and as they are all owned abroad, this transfer of trade from canvas to steam has proved to be a transfer also from American to European tonnage. We have been strangely slow to the advantages offered by this class of vessels, although the experiment has been worked out under our very eyes, with the most abundant success. They cost less to construct, and less to sail, than paddle wheel vessels, while their capacity for freight and passengers is much more. We have it on the authority of Sir Samuel Cunard that the Arabia, of 2,400 tons, can carry only 400 or 500 tons of freight, while a screw steamer of the same tonnage, sailing at half the expense, will carry 1,800 tons. Their speed, also, has been proved to be fully equal, if not superior, to the side wheel steamers. Mr. Inman testified before the Select Committee on Ocean Steamships of the House of Commons, that, up to the advent of the Scotia, the vessels of his line, all screws, had beaten, on the average, all the Cunard vessels, and had beaten every vessel separately except the Persia. Subsequently, the City of New York, just before she was lost, beat the Scotia on the fastest passage ever made by the Cunard line; and during the month of June last, the splendid run of the China to Liverpool in nine days, and of the City of Boston to New York in about the same time, indicates that screw steamers are achieving a reputation for speed which promises to be permanent and uniform. This combination of economy, capacity, and rapidity has not only enabled ocean propellers to drive sailing ships out of the competition; they are also rapidly taking the place of the old-fashioned paddle wheel steamers. Of more than 73,000 tons owned by the Peninsular and Oriental Company, 60,000 tons are in screw steamers, although, up to 1852, all its tonnage was in side wheel vessels. The Cunard Company has for several years employed a fleet of screw steamers for freight and passengers both in the Mediterranean and in the Atlantic trade; it is now building this class of vessels for its regular mail service; its newest and most favorite ships are the China and the Cuba, and other similar steamers are in course of construction. There are other prosperous lines engaged in the trade between the United States and Europe, which have always employed screw steamers, as the well known and popular Inman line, and those connecting New York with Bremen and Hamburg. And yet, in this country, we are still indifferent to the merits of these steamships, and the ideas of most of our merchants cling to paddle wheel boats, which, to be sure, are well adapted for our river navigation, but which have lost pre-eminence on the ocean. Boston has built screw steamers for several of its coastwise routes, which have acquitted themselves well, both in the service for which they were designed, and in the employment of the Government during the war. In the great City of New York this class of vessels is not yet appreciated as it will be. We may be sure, however, that, with or without the assistance of Government, no American line which may be started in the trade with Europe will succeed, in a pecuniary point of view, unless the screw be adopted instead of the paddle wheel. Such a line will have to compete with screw steamers, skillfully managed and economically sailed; and for general commercial purposes, the paddle wheel cannot succeed against the screw. At the present time there are twelve steamship lines employed in the transit between Europe and the United States; of these, all except the new French line, and a portion of the Cunard fleet, are screw steamers. When to this fact it is added that none of these lines, trading as they do to American ports, belong to the American flag, there appears strong ground for the statement that the neglect of our merchants to apprehend and appreciate the advantages of the vessels referred to, and to adopt them for their use, has contributed in a most important degree to bring us, as a nation, to our present mortifying position in reference to the navigation of the ocean by steam.

To this two-fold mistake — of indifference on the part of the Government, and of slowness of comprehension on the part of the mercantile community — we attribute it that, at the opening of the civil war in 1861, there were only two or three American steamships in the European trade, and that for four years no American steamship in the merchant service has crossed the Atlantic. The departures from the port of New York, of trans-Atlantic steamers, are almost daily, but none of them belong to us. Two lines connect Boston with Liverpool, but they are both British. It is not pleasant to feel that we are indebted to the protection of a foreign flag for the safe transportation of our mails and our citizens on every ocean round the globe; but when we are obliged to have recourse to foreign steamers to convey us from our own shores across an ocean which, geographically, would almost seem to belong to us, the necessity is, to say the least, a most unfortunate one.

We cannot allow the present state of things to continue without seriously compromising our national dignity. If we would maintain the distinction upon the ocean to which we are entitled, we must perform our full share of the carrying trade, and to meet the existing requirements of this trade we must possess a large steam tonnage.

It should not be forgotten that, at the commencement of the rebellion, companies who had grown rich in connection with the prosperity of this country, refused, on the plea of neutrality, to bring supplies for the Government in the day of its trial. The advantages which would have accrued to the Government at that time from one or more well established steam lines to Europe, under our own flag, can hardly be estimated.

But the days of civil war have passed away, as we trust, never to return. It still remains true, however, that the position of our nation among the great powers of the world demands that we keep pace with all others in the developments of our mercantile marine. In former times, when our commerce was wafted under canvas upon every sea, it would have been thought most absurd to maintain that whether the carrying trade continued in our possession or otherwise was of little importance, so long as merchandise in sufficient quantity was brought to or taken from our shores. Such an opinion would have implied that there is little value in marine commerce, and that there is no special advantage in being a great commercial nation. This would have been held to be a concession to another power forever of the supremacy of the seas. But why, then, the anxiety always manifested by this nation to promote its foreign commerce? why its sensitiveness for the honor of the flag? why its jealousy for the protection of our seamen, the freedom of navigation, and the equality of our vessels with those of the most favored nations? The introduction of steam has not changed the principle upon which, as a nation, we have always acted; it has simply modified the conditions under which we must act for the future. In the very blood of our people we have the spirit and the ability to navigate the seas; our national energy requires that we maintain our position on the ocean, and our national history will lack consistency and completeness if we do not. And unquestionably we shall retrieve our position, and gain under steam all, and more than all, we have lost under canvas. We shall, doubtless, do our own carrying trade, just as we shall raise our own grains and staples, and manufacture our own goods; promoting all our great interests in harmony with and for the benefit of each other.

Our national wealth will be promoted in two ways by our participation in the Ocean Steam Navigation of the world. We shall, in the first place, receive the direct profits of ocean commerce, which now go abroad to build up and enrich foreign companies. For every passenger who travels to the old world, a sum of money in gold is withdrawn from our national resources. For every package of foreign merchandise entering into the consumption of the country, a certain amount of gold is remitted abroad for freight money. Even the postages on all our correspondence accrue to the benefit of other nations. Surely we cannot longer afford to employ foreigners to perform this service for us, seeing that we can do it equally well ourselves. All this capital we need at home for the establishment and support of our own steamship companies, and for increasing our ability to bear without inconvenience the national burdens.

But the indirect benefit to our wealth from successful Ocean Steam Navigation will be still more important. The statistics of British commerce show that with the opening of steam communication a new impulse is always given to the operations of trade. With the regularity of a natural law, frequent, speedy, and regular means of intercourse between nations invariably extend the exchanges of products, and add to the profit of such exchanges. The able and elaborate Memorial of the New York Chamber of Commerce, submitted to Congress in 1864, contains carefully prepared tables which fully establish this fact, and illustrate most clearly the benefit which other nations have derived from the multiplication of steamship lines, and, by implication, the opportunities for gain which we hitherto have failed to improve.

This subject is beginning to receive the thought and consideration to which its importance entitled it. Congress passed a bill in 1864, authorizing the Postmaster General to contract for a monthly mail service between some part north of the River Potomac and Rio de Janeiro, calling at certain intermediate ports. It is expected that the Brazilian Government will assist in the support of the line which will be established as the result of this legislation; and we may hope that the mails and market intelligence transmitted between the great and prosperous nations of North and South America will no longer be conveyed by way of England and English steamers, involving an unnecessary outlay and great loss of time. At its last session Congress passed a bill to encourage the establishment of a steamship line between California and China. This is a route which, by every right, belongs to the American people, and we should be culpable in the extreme if we failed to occupy it. English enterprise has long regarded it with interest, and an English company undertook the service two or three years ago, but, for some reason, did not continue it. We still have the opportunity, therefore, to open up this rich and promising trade for our own advantage; and, although it is the immediate and appropriate duty of our fellow citizens and our fellow merchants on the Pacific coast, to organize and promote this enterprize, it is no less our duty to assist it in every possible way, and to manifest on all favorable occasions that sense of its great value to the entire country which we cannot but entertain on an examination of the facts of the case. The merchants of New York are desirous to open direct communication by steam with the Mediterranean; and the Italian government, feeling anxious to be brought into closer contact with the United States, has proposed to guarantee a portion of the capital for a company, which shall assume this service. The advantages of such a line are very evident; and would have no direct conflicting line to contend with, a consideration which unfortunately for us, does not attach to many eligible steamship routes on the globe. In Boston, a company has been established by special charter, and has been regularly organized, which proposes to enter into competition with the Cunard line in the Liverpool trade. This company has been delayed in the fulfillment of its plans by the temporary effect of the war upon the currency, and by the requirements of the Government upon shipbuilders and merchants, but now that the price of labor and material is becoming more reasonable, it is preparing to build some large and powerful first-class screw steamers, suited to the export as well as the import trade, and adapted to the wants of an increasing immigration.

Thus it appears that the subject of Ocean Steam Navigation is beginning to awaken a new interest among us. This interest, however, is as yet too circumscribed in the community; our capitalists and business men are not fully alive to the bearing which an extended steamship commerce will have upon our general prosperity, nor do they realize the profitable character of this commerce when properly conducted. If it were otherwise, there would be much less difficulty in getting the stock taken up in the various steamship projects which are proposed. In part, the slowness which is exhibited to assist in these undertakings, may be attributed to the feeling of discouragement which has come over our people in view of our want of success in the past, and particularly in consequence of the failure of the Collins Company. But surely we are not prepared to admit our incapacity and inferiority upon the Ocean, and to confess that what we accomplished so easily and triumphantly in the days of canvas, we must yield to others, now that steam has changed the circumstances and conditions of Ocean commerce. If we were unable to explain the causes of our want of success hitherto in steamship navigation, there might perhaps be more excuse for our being dispirited and apathetic; but, as these causes are apparent on even a superficial examination of the history of American steamship lines, there is no reason whatever why our attempts should not be made with all confidence in their complete success in every respect. For this reason only the Collins Company is more particularly referred to at this time than might otherwise be desirable; not that there is any satisfaction in dwelling upon its misfortunes, but because the misapprehensions which have so widely prevailed in reference to them, have worked a serious injury to our national trade, and have made us weak on the Ocean, where we ought to and might have continued to be strong.

Shall it not be the emphatically expressed conviction of this Convention, that Ocean Steam Navigation under the American flag must henceforth be accepted as of the first national importance, and that its promotion must be the aim of all our enterprising citizens? Shall we not recommend it as entitled to the encouragement and assistance of local Chambers of Commerce and Boards of Trade; and as worthy of the careful consideration of those who, while making judicious investments for themselves, would be glad at the same time to subserve the public good? The time has gone by for this interest to be called simply a commercial or a seaboard question. It is a national question, involving the national honor as well as the national wealth; and as such it cannot but warmly commend itself equally to the West and to the East, which have so nobly vied with each other in zealous regard for, and in vigorous and potential effort to maintain whatever is essential to the dignity of the Flag and to the honor of the Republic. The old paddle wheel steamer was available, to a certain extent, for the importation of merchandise from Great Britain and continental Europe; but for the exportation of our products, it was of no service whatever. Now that Ocean steamships have been perfected for the export, no less than for the import trade, the agricultural interest in our country, as much as the commercial, is concerned in them, and it can no longer be a matter of indifference, either to the West or to the East, whether the Ocean lines, which under the new order of things will run from our Eastern seaports, and which will simply serve as the continuation of the great railway routes traversing our broad domain, bringing St. Louis Chicago and Detroit in close communication with Liverpool, Manchester, Havre, Genoa and other trans-Atlantic marts and markets, shall be controlled and managed abroad, with reference solely to foreign ideas and for the benefit of foreign owners. So far from this, we hope, in the American steamship lines now going into operation, to see Western and Eastern names side by side, not only in the stock subscriptions, but in the lists of directors and managers, believing, as we do, that such an arrangement will insure the broadest, most comprehensive, and most truly national administration of the affairs of these Companies.

May not this Convention also respectfully memorialize Congress to mature and adopt a policy which shall protect and promote American steamship navigation? As already stated, measures have been passed to encourage a movement on one or two of our routes; but we fear that as yet the importance of this subject is only in part appreciated at Washington; or we should certainly see more determined and hearty action. A spirit of hesitancy and distrust appears in the legislation which has taken place, and there is a want of energy and will, such as we should like to discover. The subsidy for a line to Brazil is dependent upon the course of the Brazilian Government, and will fail unless a corresponding amount be granted by that power. In the matter of the proposed Italian line, our Government has as yet taken no action, nor in reference to the Boston and Liverpool line, which has a company to compete with, enriched and made powerful by the long continued and most liberal patronage of the British Government. It is not likely that the new American steamship lines will need assistance beyond a proper compensation for carrying the mails, for any length of time; nor is it desirable that they should be organized in the expectation of receiving permanent aid; but it seems necessary that in view of all the circumstances of the case, such public aid and encouragement should be offered as will induce our capitalists to enter upon this department of enterprise, and to assist in building up an interest which has too long been permitted to languish. We care not how carefully guarded, in all its provisions, such legislative aid may be made, or how strict the requirements may be in reference to the character of the vessels to be employed, and the method of their management. But it certainly becomes Congress to foster our steamship enterprises until they have had opportunity to develop themselves and to gain a footing similar to that of the foreign companies which now control the trade. We have succeeded far beyond any other nation in our inland and coastwise navigation; and in the ocean steamers which we have built in the past, we have shown a skill in modeling and in constructing which all our rivals have recognized and admitted. With judicious and timely assistance from the Government, and with prudence on the part of our merchants, we believe ourselves able to re-commence an amicable contest for the carrying trade of the Ocean; and notwithstanding the start, which by our misfortunes and mistakes others have secured, if we are true to our past achievements, we shall, in due time, see the American steamship where the American sailing packet formerly was in the estimation of the world, and where it was in our own regard—the peer of all competitors, and the worthy representative on every Ocean of the National genius and prosperity.

The resolutions offered by Mr. Hill were referred to the Committee on Commerce.

Mr. Walker, of Illinois, offered the following:

Resolved, That the West and the East have an interest in common in cheap transit, and will in future use all reasonable means to open all channels available to extend the commerce of the country—nationally and internationally—and will insist that highways opened for commerce shall reduce the tolls thereon to a rate only sufficient to pay interest on the capital invested, and expense of keeping the same in repair, thereby giving the producer and consumer a fair participation in the benefit to be derived therefrom.

The resolution was referred to the Committee on Transit.

On motion, the Convention took a recess until 3 o'clock P. M.

AFTERNOON SESSION.

The Convention was called to order by the President at 3 P. M.

Mr. Micken, of the Committee on Order of Business, submitted the following partial report:

1. Reading of Minutes.
2. Reports of Committees, which will be received in the following order:
   - I. Reciprocity.
   - II. Transit and Transportation.
   - III. Improvement of Rivers and Harbors.
   - IV. Commerce.
   - V. Finance.
   - VI. Agriculture and Manufactures.
   - VII. Miscellaneous Business.
   - VIII. Resolutions and Motions.

Mr. Robinson, of Cleveland, from the Committee on Agriculture and Manufactures, submitted the following report on the resolution offered by Mr. Spaulding:

The Committee to whom Mr. Spaulding's resolution was referred, recommend the adoption of the following resolutions:

Whereas, Owing to the heavy taxation necessarily levied upon the people of the United States, to meet the interests and expenses of the Government, it has become more imperative upon the Government to nourish and encourage the industrial pursuits of the nation; therefore,

Resolved, That Agricultural, Mechanical, Mining, Manufacturing, and all other branches of American Industry should be alike secured in the enjoyment of a permanent and remunerative recompense, inasmuch as American labor and its products are the main source upon which the Government must rely for its needed revenue to meet the annual demands upon its Treasury, and its only safe dependence.

Resolved, That in order to perform this duty, as well as a financial necessity, a discrimination in favor of those productions upon which American labor depends for its permanent prosperity, should be expressed by the Government when imposing duties upon foreign imports, because when American industry and labor languish, their ability to respond to the excise demands must be correspondingly impaired.

Resolved, That such action is now more the absolute duty of the Government, inasmuch as her hosts of heroes, who have on the battle field vindicated her honor and maintained her flag, are returning to those varied pursuits which they left to defend the country, and to which they now again look for their livelihood, and which the Government, in justice to their patriotism and its own wants, should render as remunerative as possible.

Mr. Robinson, in submitting the report, spoke as follows:

We presume it is not necessary to take up time here upon the subject matter of this resolution; we presume that every man will see the necessity of it. I, sir, for one, am willing to abide by the conditions of that resolution, for under the exigencies by which we are now surrounded it is necessary for us to take care of our own citadel, to take care of our own family, (cheers,) and now, as these noble men have protected us in the field, it is our duty to protect them in the resumption of their original occupations, and with God's help we would yet wipe out this debt. (Cheers.)

Gen. Ord was here discovered to be present, and was escorted to a seat upon the stage, and presented by the President to the Convention, who received him with six hearty cheers.

The report of the Committee on Manufactures was then submitted to the Convention and carried.

Mr. Seymour, of Troy, raised a question of order as to the method of voting.

Upon explanation by Mr. Hamlin, it was decided that the questions were correctly put.

The roll was called, on motion, and the basis of voting among the American delegations was fixed as follows:

Board of Trade, Albany, New York,	5
Board of Trade, Buffalo, New York,	6
Board of Trade, Bay City, Michigan,	1½
Board of Trade, Boston, Massachusetts,	6½
Mercantile Association, Bangor, Maine,	3½
Corn Exchange, Boston Massachusetts,	6½
Board of Trade, Chicago, Illinois,	6
Mercantile Association, Chicago, Illinois,	4
Chamber of Commerce, Cairo, Illinois,	5
Chamber of Commerce, Cincinnati, Ohio,	10
Board of Trade, Cleveland, Ohio,	5
Board of Trade, Detroit	4
Board of Trade, Erie, Pennsylvania,	5
Michigan Central Board of Trade, Kalamazoo,	1
Chamber of Commerce, Milwaukee, Wisconsin,	8
Chamber of Commerce, New York City,	7
Commercial Association, New York City,	7
Board of Trade, Oswego, New York,	4
Board of Trade, Philadelphia, Pennsylvania,	6
Corn Exchange Association, Philadelphia,	5
Coal Exchange, Philadelphia,	4
Board of Trade, Portland, Maine,	3½
Board of Trade, Pittsburgh, Pennsylvania,	6
Board of Trade, St. Paul, Minnesota,	4
Board of Trade, St. Louis, Missouri,	11
Board of Trade, Springfield, Ohio,	2
Board of Trade, East Saginaw, Michigan,	1½
Board of Trade, Toledo, Ohio,	4
Board of Trade, Troy, New York,	4
Burlington, Iowa,	1

The President then made the following announcement:

The Great Western and Detroit and Milwaukee Railroads, and John Hutchings, Esq., each have kindly tendered the use of a steamer for the purpose of an excursion on the river, for the Delegates of the

Convention; the Board of Trade and citizens of Detroit have provided an excursion for Delegates and citizens, on which occasion those three boats will be employed. A collation will be served, as also some other entertainment on board the steamers. All the Delegates and the representatives of the press are respectfully invited to be present. Tickets of admission to the Convention will admit a gentleman and his ladies. Tickets will be furnished to friends of delegates who may be strangers in the City, on application to Mr. Ray Haddock, one of the Secretaries of the Convention. The steamers will leave the Detroit and Milwaukee Railroad dock at 3 o'clock tomorrow (Thursday) afternoon.

The invitation was accepted amid applause.

The Secretary then read the following letter, which was vociferously applauded:

LONDON, ENGLAND, JUNE 10, 1865.

Joseph Aspinall Esq.:

DEAR SIR—I am much obliged to you for the invitation to your approaching Commercial Convention to be held in the month of July.

If I were on your continent, I should avail myself of your friendly offer to be present at your deliberations, and if I could not add to their usefulness I could learn much from them. But to me Detroit seems a long way from England, and, unfortunately for me, I seem never to be able to steal three months from my many engagements here, to enable me to pay a long hoped for visit to the United States, and now I feel it quite out of my power to avail myself of your tempting invitation.

The project of your Convention gives me great pleasure. I hope it will lead to a renewal of commercial intercourse with the British North American Provinces, for it will be a miserable thing if, because they are in connection with the British Crown, and you acknowledge as your Chief Magistrate your President at Washington, there should not be a commercial intercourse between them and you as free as if you were one people and living under one Government.

I have felt that when your people, so free and so instructed, apply their minds to any questions of commerce, they will soon discover what is true and adopt it, and in this faith I shall look with confidence for the most beneficial results from the discussions into which you are about to enter. Whatever tends to promote harmony and commercial dealings between the United States and the Canadas will be favorably regarded by every intelligent statesman in this country.

Wishing you the happiest results from the Convention, and thanking you for your most kind letter, I am, with great respect, very sincerely yours,

JOHN BRIGHT.

The following letter was also read and referred to the Committee on Harbor Improvements:

OFFICE U. S. LAKE SURVEY,
Detroit, July 10, 1865.

J. Aspinall, Esq., President Board of Trade, Detroit, Mich.:

DEAR SIR—Believing that the commercial men of the country do not fully realize what is being done for the benefit of commerce by the Lake Survey, and that the meeting of the Convention which is about to assemble in this City, is a favorable opportunity to bring the matter directly before them, I take the liberty of addressing you, and of requesting—if you agree with me—that you will bring the matter before the Convention in such way as you may think best.

It would give me pleasure to have members of the Convention visit my office, that they may see for themselves the labor that is expended to furnish perfectly reliable charts of the Lakes.

I have the pleasure of sending you herewith a set of the charts as far as published. I would say, however, that the published charts give a very imperfect idea of the work of the Survey. They are of necessity of too small a scale to show the works in detail.

Each one of these charts is but the reduction of many others drawn on a large scale, and which show perfectly every foot of the ground, and every danger to navigation. Not one-tenth of the soundings that are taken, can be shown on the published charts; and it is only by an examination of the original manuscript maps, that the work can be fully appreciated.

Besides the duty of map-making, the survey has for several years past carried on an extensive system of meterological observation, which promises valuable results. The existence of lunar tides in the lakes has been demonstrated; the effect of the winds is being elucidated; and there is good reason to believe that if the observations are continued, storms can be predicted in season to enable vessels to avoid their fury.

The Astronomical Department of the survey is also of great interest in a scientific point of view. The most careful observations are made for both latitude and longitude, and all published charts are projected with reference to the exact position upon the earth's surface, thus making them the only authentic data for correct geographical knowledge of the lake region.

Very respectfully, your obed't serv't,

W. F. RAYNOLDS,
Col. U. S. A., Sup't.

The following resolution was offered in reference to this matter by R. W. King, of Detroit, and passed:

Resolved, That the letter of Col. Raynolds, of the Lake Survey, addressed to this Convention, be referred to the Committee on Lake and Harbor Improvements, and that Committee, together with the Committee on Commerce, be requested to visit the office of Col. Raynolds, examine the charts of Lake and River Surveys, and, after consultation, report to this Convention such recommendations as in their judgment they may deem advisable in the premises.

The President presented the following communication, which was read and accepted ;

DETROIT, July 5, 1865.

Mr. Jos. Aspinall, President of Detroit Board of Trade :

DEAR SIR — In behalf of the Board of Directors and Members of the Detroit Young Men's Society, I have the pleasure of tendering you, and through you to the members of the Commercial Convention, the use of the Library and Reading Rooms of the Society during the Convention. Hoping that the Rooms will be freely used by all,

I am, yours truly,

EDWARD LEFAVOUR,
President of Detroit Y. M. Society.

The President presented the following letter, which was read and laid on the table :

DETROIT, July 10, 1865.

To the Honorable the President :

SIR — I have caused to be made a skeleton map of Michigan, which I herewith present to you, designed more particularly to exhibit, at a glance, the commercial advantages which nature has afforded to the Peninsular State, but at the same time intending to call the attention of strangers, who are about to visit the City, under the auspices of the Board of Trade, to the many and vast internal resources of the region of country yet undeveloped, which is embraced within the boundaries of this State.

The leading and important natural productions, already developed, and entering largely into the trade and commerce of the State and the country, are indicated in a tabular form upon the margin of the map, and to those who are at all familiar with the statistics of trade in this locality, this simple catalogue, copper, iron, salt, plaster, marble, coal, timber, speaks volumes for the wealth, both present and prospective, of a State which, in the progress of the settlement of the Great West, has been to a great extent passed by, inasmuch that its undeveloped territory, rich and valuable as it proves to be, at present embraces nearly two-thirds of its whole surface.

May we not, then, at this time, and under these auspices, with some degree of pride, call the especial attention of our guests and friends to these facts, for although we do not possess the soil and the prairie, which has given the tide of emigration to our western sister States and Territories, yet now we find compensation in the fact that after a few years of culture, our soil is equal in many respects and unsurpassed in others, and that the prairies must look to us for timber, and out of our vast and almost unbroken forests we now supply the necessary and increasing demand for material both for fencing and building.

Our copper, iron, plaster, salt, coal, are, we may suppose, inexhaustible, and need only continual development to increase the abundance of their product and value.

The forest, however, with its wealth, is gradually but surely melting away, and before many years, as in other localities formerly producing large quantities of timber and lumber, but now entirely exhausted, we shall have reason to appreciate the value of timber lands.

Very respectfully, your obed't servant,

GEO. S. FROST.

Hon. D. C. Littlejohn, Chairman of the Committee on Transit, submitted the following:

Whereas, The annual increase of the productions of the States bordering upon and tributary to the Northern Lakes has exceeded the capacity of transportation of all the avenues to the Atlantic, demonstrating the urgent necessity of enlarged water facilities for communication between the West and East; and,

Whereas, The canals and various lines of railroads, leading to and from said Lakes, while they have contributed vastly to develop the resources, increase the wealth and promote the permanent union of our whole country, are wholly inadequate to the demands of the immense and rapidly growing commerce; therefore,

Resolved, That this Convention regard the construction of a ship canal around the Falls of Niagara, a national work of great military and commercial importance, alike demanded by military prudence, the necessities of commerce and political wisdom, and that its early completion by the General Government is required by every consideration of sound political economy.

Resolved, That such a canal, of a capacity to pass the largest steam or sail vessels, which now or hereafter may navigate the lakes, will afford the cheapest and most expeditious water communication for the transportation of the products of the great producing waters of the West and Northwest, by bringing into use the most easterly of the entire chain of lakes on our Northern frontier, from which these annually increasing products may be distributed by short, enlarged canals, and by railway to the Hudson and New York, by sailing into New England and Pennsylvania, and by the St. Lawrence River direct to the ocean.

Resolved, That the State of New York, geographically located on the highway of commerce between the great chain of lakes to the seaboard, and having within her borders her metropolis of the nation, is bound by every consideration of interest and true policy, and by the comity she owes her sister States, to improve and enlarge the shortest water communication between the lakes and tide-water. Failing to do so, she must not complain if a portion of her great inland commerce shall be diverted through other cheaper channels of communication.

Resolved, That we hail with satisfaction the proposed enlargement of the Welland and St. Lawrence Canals, and other proposed improvements through the Provinces, affording other cheap outlets through which the commerce of the States, tributary to the Lakes, may seek our Eastern markets, as well as the markets of the Old World.

Resolved, That in the event of the negotiation of any treaty of reciprocity between the United States and the British Provinces, our Government should be careful to secure in such a treaty a guarantee of a sufficient depth of water to enable Ocean steamers of not less than 1,000 tons cargo carrying capacity, to pass from Port Colburn, C. W., to tide-water.

Resolved, That this Convention congratulate the merchants and citizens generally residing in the Towns and Cities, and especially those of the great City of St. Louis, bordering upon the banks of the Mississippi, upon the termination of the rebellion, by which they are permitted to resume and enter upon the immense commerce which is forever to float upon the bosom of the Father of Waters, and that we recognize that river as a national highway, watering, as it does, the shores of many popular and thriving States, and recommend such legislation by Congress as will best develop its usefulness and resources.

Hon. D. C. Littlejohn, also submitted the following preambles and resolution:

Whereas, Heavy and oftentimes disastrous losses result to shippers in consequence of the delays and irregularities which attend the transportation and delivery of merchandise and produce on the great railroad routes between the East and West; and,

Whereas, In the opinion of this Convention, there is no reason why the same certainty and regularity which attend the transit of passengers should not also exist in the transportation of freight by rail; therefore,

Resolved, That the question of *time* should enter into all contracts for the delivery of freight by the principal railroad lines, and that it is equally for the interests of railroad companies themselves, and of the community at large, that a system of management be immediately arranged and adopted, which shall enable shippers to rely upon the delivery of freight at its destination within a definite and specified time.

Mr. Prosser, of Buffalo, a member of the Committee, submitted the following minority report:

Dissenting from the conclusions of the majority of the Committee to whom was referred the subject of channels of transit between the West and the Sea-board, so far as relates to the Niagara Ship Canal, I submit the following minority report:

Whereas, A large portion of the surplus products of the great grain-growing States of the Northwest are annually exported to foreign countries through the State of New York, thus furnishing the means to pay goods imported into this country, as also furnishing the means to pay to the National Treasury the import duties thereon, and in the opinion of this Convention, this trade is substantially national in its character, and hence entitled to the encouragement, protection, and fostering care of the United States.

Whereas, For the last ten years the said trade shows a rapid and steady increase, with every reason to expect a like continuance for a long time to come, in proportion to the increasing population in those States, while the residue of the arable lands therein, now only about one-eighth under cultivation, shall be cultivated, and,

Whereas, During the prolific years of 1860, 1861, and 1862, when the shipments East from Buffalo and Oswego reached nearly 3,000,000 tons, accompanied by great difficulty in the transit through the State of New York, together with onerous rates of freight upon her canals, in consequence of an inadequate capacity therein to pass the same without delay, thus to a considerable extent diminishing the ability of the Western States to export their surplus products with profit to the producer, and,

Whereas, By a recent survey and estimate by the proper authorities of the State of New York, it is shown to be entirely feasible and practicable, and comparatively cheap, within two years to enlarge the locks upon her canals, with very slight improvement in a small portion of the channel, so as to admit the passage of boats carrying

550 to 600 tons, instead of 220 tons now, thereby increasing their capacity to at least 10,000,000 tons annually eastward, and diminishing the cost of transportation fully one-half, thus furnishing a cheap and ample outlet to an eastern market whenever and wherever it can be found, for at least 200,000,000 bushels of grain *more* than was forwarded through those canals in the prolific year of 1862; and,

Whereas, This Convention, not unmindful of the still undefended condition of the commerce upon the lakes, and the unprotected Towns and Cities upon their borders, though reluctant to call upon the General Government for aid in the present state of our National affairs, yet feel it a duty to call their attention to an Act passed by the Legislature of the State of New York, April 24, 1862, entitled "An Act to adapt the Canals of the State to the defense of the North-western Lakes; therefore,

Resolved, That Congress be, and is hereby requested to make the necessary appropriation, without delay, to carry the said Act into effect, and thus, while protecting these inland seas, and the great and rapidly increasing commerce thereon, from foreign aggression not only, but opening a channel of transit to the Ocean, and the City of New York, alike ample and cheap, sufficient to meet the wants of the great grain-growing States of the Northwest for a century to come.

Mr. Alexander, from the Committee on Miscellaneous Business, to which had been referred the resolution offered by Mr. Lyon, of Cleveland, on the subject of a uniform system of weights and measures, together with the resolution offered by Mr. Converse on the subject of a National Board of Trade, reported back said resolutions, and recommended their adoption. The resolutions were then adopted.

Mr. Randolph, of Chicago, moved the adoption of the report of the majority of the Committee on Transit.

Mr. Allen, of Buffalo, moved that the other report be also adopted. (Laughter.) I can understand this laughter. I knew from the first that there would be a majority report, and I do not intend to be factious. (Laughter.) I see no impropriety, however, in adopting them both together. The State of New York now has a canal from Buffalo to Albany. This other proposed canal does not exist yet, and may not exist for some years. We are not the Congress of the United States, and cannot determine that the Erie Canal shall be made; but it has been determined by survey that, at a comparatively small cost, and within two years, it can be enlarged so as to admit vessels of six hundred tons burden, which is more than the average of the vessels on the lakes. Then you have two distinct propositions, on one of which action can be taken at once; on the other of which no action can be had for many years to come. I submit it to the sagacity of this Convention whether it would be wise to put the former out of sight, in order to favor an extremely problematical scheme. Look at the scope of this majority report. By it you propose to the Canadian Government to enlarge the Welland Canal to an enormous capacity. Well, I have no objection to that. You also propose, when you get into Lake Ontario, that they should enlarge their side canals running parallel with the St. Lawrence. Nor do I object to this; but when all that is done, where are you? That all points to the Atlantic Ocean, and avoids New York and New England. If you get into Lake Ontario, you have then to take advantage of the Erie Canal to get to New York, and have still nearly two hundred miles of a New York canal to go through. You may talk of going through Ogdensburgh by rail, and of distributing your grain by driblets by way of Lake Champlain into Boston or Connecticut, but surely that won't satisfy you. Say that the minority report is the only one that can be acted on for the next five years, and perhaps for the next twenty. Now, the question of Reciprocity, Sir, is being brought into this Convention in almost every way. Let us just look at it a little now. As for Reciprocity, I avow I am against it from the beginning to the end. We have been wheedled and deluded into the idea that it is of great advantage; but I say the Reciprocity Treaty is a treaty for the benefit of the surplus products of Canada, and for the benefit of her manufactures, but not for ours. With all respect to the highly respectable delegation from the British Provinces, I must say that I regard them as a foreign nation. We have heard it said that they live on the opposite side of the same river; but I reply that they might as well be on the opposite side of the Atlantic for that matter. There is no fraternity amongst us in this particular; it is a business matter; and though we may dine and take tea together in a friendly way, yet we know a bargain is a bargain. (Laughter.) It is all very well for Canadians to come and say, We want to unite our bans with yours, but we have seen a good deal of the feeling both of Canada and the mother country during the rebellion. (Hear.) If they did not make war upon us, at least they gave aid and comfort to our enemies. (Applause, and "No, no.") Say what you will, facts are facts. Your report should be, not that you want Canadians to deepen their canals — what they do is none of our business — but that you desire the deepening of the New York canals; and I think it would be wrong in a Convention of this kind to consider a proposition like that in the minority report, as of no account.

It was moved to take up the majority report by sections, and vote upon each resolution separately. Agreed to.

Mr. Randolph, of Chicago, desired, so far as possible, that the Convention be united in any measure they might recommend to the attention of the National Congress. This was why Chicago had not pressed on the Committee the consideration of its own great work; they had yielded it because it might generate opposition, and had united in recommending what they believed to be a National work. The Niagara Ship Canal, he was sorry to say, had met with some opposition in the Committee, the same which it met with here. As touching the Reciprocity question, he thought the resolution ought not to be considered as expressing views favorable or the reverse, and he would only vote for it on the understanding that it did not pledge the Convention to a decided opinion on that point.

Mr. Younglove, of Cleveland, believed he spoke correctly when he said that Ohio was favorable to the Niagara Ship Canal, and he did not think any of the delegates from that State would vote against it, though there were opinions in the report he was not in favor of. So far as it had a squinting towards the Reciprocity Treaty, he did not approve of it, and it did not meet the approval of the other delegates from his State. The gentleman from Chicago said well, that the Convention, in adopting the report, was not to be considered to pledge itself to Reciprocity.

Mr. Littlejohn, of Oswego, said the Committee did not design to give any opinion on the question of Reciprocity in reporting these resolutions, but had taken the ground as having charge of the question of communication and transit over this whole wide country, that if a treaty should be negotiated, one condition should be that the Government controlling the St. Lawrence should deepen the navigation through the St. Lawrence and to the Gulf of St. Lawrence, which was one of the outlets of the Great Northwest. If the Convention preferred to state the case otherwise he would say that the Committee were, as it were, advising or giving a suggestion to the Committee on Reciprocity.

Mr. Younglove — I accept the explanation, but the report has been understood as lugging in Reciprocity, upon which we are not now called upon to express our views.

Mr. Martin J. Townsend, of Troy, believed the questions brought before them in the reports just submitted the most important that could be submitted to the Convention. He desired to see the object contemplated by the majority report accomplished. The most far-seeing men of a few years ago never dreamed of the hundredth part of the prosperity that had grown up in the Great West, and which now called for such improvements as those foreshadowed in the report. But these measures, if attained, were to be attained only by calm and deliberate consideration of the varied interests involved. Contracted local interests, heated feeling and excited antagonisms would never accomplish the objects they had met to promote. The great object now under consideration was the providing of an easy and cheap water transit from the Great West to the Atlantic Sea-board. It was not enough now, as it once was thought to be, to provide ways and means of getting a limited quantity of produce from Chicago to the East. There was now a Great New World far to the west of Chicago. In getting communication with Chicago they would only have begun to touch the real Western trade. What was to be done with Minnesota? What was to be done with Iowa, now coming up close to a million of inhabitants? and what were they to do for the trade of Colorado, of Nebraska, and of Kansas? What were they going to do to provide conveyance eastward for the immense wealth of produce that could be poured down to the mouth of the great Missouri, and was Missouri to be left with the only resource of sending her products down the Mississippi, and away round by New Orleans, nearly five thousand miles, to New York. He was surprised that the Committee should have overlooked the fact that there was a considerable portion of the American World now to be found west of Chicago. Chicago was a great place, certainly, but was not the only great place out West. He heard Artemus Ward lecture a short time ago down in Troy; speaking of his visit to Utah, he remarked that Salt Lake was a City, and Chicago was a City, too, although she lacked confidence in herself. (Laughter.) Now, he, (Mr. Townsend,) was getting to be an old man, and he desired to put it on record that it was blind economy and short-sighted patriotism to forget that the best portion of the United States was to be found west of Chicago. (Hear, hear.) In looking to the Eastward it should not be forgotten that right on their way stood the great State of New York, whose interests for some reason or other had not been popular in the Convention. (Laughter.) But after all they could not get along without New York even so well as the West could get along without Chicago, and they could not get along much longer, he was satisfied, without the long-talked-of enlargement of the Erie Canal. (Hear, hear.) He hoped they would cease talking about running around New York. He owned a great deal of property in New York, and was taxed as heavily in proportion to his property as most men, but he was quite willing to be taxed to the fullest extent for the enlargement of that Canal, or to build a new Canal all the way to New York, to carry the western trade to the Atlantic. Suppose they build that great Ship Canal around the State of New York to carry the commerce of the Great West into Lake Ontario; what then?

What did they think they would accomplish by getting Western produce into Lake Ontario? Were they going to hand over the commerce of the Great West into the hands of the Canadians? He was a pretty patriotic sort of an American citizen, himself, and had talked strongly and felt as badly hurt as anybody could with regard to the occurrences that had taken place in Canada of a hostile character to the United States. He would take occasion to say, too, in the hearing of his friends from the other side of the river, that in times of threatened difficulty he had spoken as hard of "old John Bull" as anybody, and he held to the opinion that that gentleman was the only individual whom the people of the United States found ready to put himself in hostile attitude to their country on the slightest provocation. He knew that the people of Canada sympathized largely with the rebels, and had aided and abetted them in their dastardly designs, and had given them a constant refuge; but now that the war was over, it was not in good taste that they should on that account refuse to treat them in a gentlemanly manner. Nobody would pretend to say that they should cease to have social or commercial intercourse with them because they had assisted the rebellion. He thought it was a little unfortunate, however, that they should have been called to meet together just now in Convention. A little of the heat of war was still attached to them, and after the great victory they had achieved, they all felt a little extra patriotism animating them, and were in a little danger of going too far. If they had the opportunity of considering these matters by themselves they might approach their consideration in a more cool and deliberative mood. He might mention that as a result of Reciprocity the fishing trade of Massachusetts had more than trebled since the adoption of the Treaty. (Hear, hear.) The town from which he came was doing an immense business in lumber, every foot of which was cut in Canada. While he felt that that Treaty was not all that it should be, he could not deny that it had been of great benefit to the Eastern States, and to all the States bordering on Canada. It was now dead or about dying, and he hoped it would be renewed upon such a basis that every intelligent American could feel that its adoption would promote the best interests of his country, and not otherwise. (Applause.) He hoped to see an expression of the Convention made in favor, at least, of the enlargement of the Erie Canal, if not, of a Canal to the Mississippi.

Mr. Littlejohn remarked that he would, as Chairman of the Committee from which the report under consideration had emanated, and as a citizen of the Empire State, proceed without heat or temper to lay before the Convention the reasons actuating the Committee in coming to the conclusions reported. He differed widely in some respects from the gentleman who had just sat down. The Committee on Transit represented different sections of the nation and was called upon to recommend some means to the Convention of cheapening and facilitating the transportation of the products of the West to the East. The Committee first agreed upon the proposition that the products of the West should be allowed to follow nature's highway to the nearest point to New York, possible before breaking bulk. [Hear, hear.] They then sought to discover nature's own course of transit, and thought they had found it. Before the days of Clinton and the Erie Canal, the commerce between the East and West found its way up the Hudson River to Troy, and along the Mohawk, and with a little help overland, down the Oswego River to Lake Ontario. Then it was conveyed in batteaux up the Lake to Niagara Falls, the great barrier nature interposed between the Lower and Upper Lakes. Then the back of the poor Indian came into use over the portage around the Falls until the Lake Erie vessels took it from his shoulders. The Committee thought it of the utmost importance that they should go back to that route, as being the best and cheapest that could be opened up between the Sea-board and the West. A great portion of the Erie Canal had been stretched along parallel with the south shore of the Lake at an average distance of about fourteen miles, and the trade had thus been diverted from its natural highway. The distance from Buffalo to Albany was 345 miles, and New York State levied a canal toll of six mills per mile upon every ton of merchandise transported, which was six and one quarter cents upon every bushel of wheat carried through. The Committee proposed to remove the barrier interposed upon trade by the Falls of Niagara by a ship canal, and thus bring the produce of the West down to within 160 miles of tide-water at New York without breaking bulk. This would reduce the toll imposed by the State of New York one-half, making a reduction of three cents per bushel in the cost of transportation. With the aid of the ship canal, too, it was proposed to float down vessels of 1,000 and 1,500 tons to Lake Ontario, laden with the corn and wheat and oats of the Great West, all the way from the heads of Lakes Michigan and Superior. At present, only vessels of about 450 tons could be sent through the Welland Canal. By doing this, the cost of transportation would be still further reduced to the extent of two cents per bushel, making a total deduction of five cents, and rendering the products of the West proportionately more valuable. It ought to be kept in mind, too, that when that was accomplished they would be able to bring produce from 100 or 200 miles farther West than at present, taking in a large belt of country about the head of Lake Superior, and extending much farther back than formerly into the whole country bordering on the lakes all the way around to the City of Erie, at the foot of Lake Erie and the mouth of the Ship Canal. If nature had not interposed that great barrier, did anybody suppose that an artificial mode of transit by way of Buffalo and Rochester would have been constructed? Not at all.

He claimed that it was a self-evident proposition, requiring no argument that the nearer they could bring the works of art to those of nature, in the matter of transportation, the cheaper and better would the transportation be found. In his State no opposition to the Ship Canal came from any other quarter than from the Western portion, and especially from Buffalo. At the last session of the New York Legislature, a vote of nearly three to one was given in the Assembly for providing for constructing the canal, and the bill was sent up to the Senate, a majority of the members of which were known to be in favor of its adoption. But as soon as it had passed the Lower House the toll-gate of the State sent a deputation eastward, which induced the Canal Board to pass resolutions adverse to the Ship Canal, which resolutions were sent to the Senate, and were instrumental in defeating the bill for that session. Two Senators from New York City, both of whom were in favor of the bill, were instructed to oppose it, and the question never came up for consideration in the Senate at all. This was the history of the efforts in behalf of the Ship Canal around Niagara Falls, in his State. A bill had been passed in Congress, providing that the President should take means to purchase the right of way along the proposed route, and then give to any company that might be formed the right to construct and use the canal. There could be no question that the construction of that canal would greatly cheapen the cost of transportation and give a great impetus to the trade of the West, and the Committee were confident the saving would not be less than five cents per bushel. While they were talking of this project their enterprising neighbors in the Northwest were also stirring themselves with a view of diverting to themselves a trade that was worth to New York more than all the gold of California. Running from the Georgian Bay to Montreal was a great natural channel which would furnish water navigation over 400 out of the 430 miles of distance between those two points. Vessels of 1,000 tons burden could easily be made to pass over that route at a speed of ten to twelve miles per hour, and would bring tide-water, by way of Montreal, 500 miles nearer Chicago than New York could possibly be brought. (Applause from the Provincial and Western delegates.) He warned the citizens of New York against allowing Provincial authorities a premium upon the construction of the proposed Ottawa Ship Canal. That constructed, it would be too late for New York to think of trying to control the "lion's share" of the Western trade. The proposition was that a new canal should also be constructed through the State of New York from Lake Ontario to the Hudson River, by way of Oneida Lake. They were well aware of the great objection urged to the Niagara Canal, that the trade of the West would go away from them down the St. Lawrence. But he could assure them that if New York could not hold and control the trade by a short cut of 130 miles from Lake Ontario to the

Hudson River, she could never hope to hold it by the long route of 345 miles from Buffalo to Albany. (Hear, hear.) He did not care from what part of New York his hearers might have come, he would state to them that, knowing as they did that their facilities were not sufficient to take to the market the products of the West — that the closing of the war had rendered it necessary to make new arrangements for business — that thousands of emigrants from the Old World were coming over to people the prairies of the West, stimulated thereto by the power which the Government of the United States had shown in suppressing the great rebellion — that not one acre in twenty of their vast Western domain had yet been brought under cultivation. In view of this he asked this Convention, and he particularly asked his friends from New York, what they were going to do if they did not resolve that a new outlet, a new avenue, should be opened up, and that speedily. (Applause.) He was asked what New York was going to do when the Ship Canal was built. He would say that New York would take care of herself, and would get the bulk of the trade that came within her reach. If the State did not provide for taking the products of the West from Lake Ontario to the Hudson River, private enterprise would very speedily do it. The nearest point on Lake Ontario to the Hudson River was Sackett's Harbor, and next Oswego. From one or the other of those points private enterprise would soon construct a double track railway to Troy or Albany. A propeller of 1,500 tons could leave Chicago and reach the lower end of Lake Ontario in six days. A train could be loaded up by an elevator from the vessel and despatched every two hours, which would take from 200,000 to 250,000 bushels to the Hudson River in every twenty-four hours. The cost of transferring the grain from the vessel to the cars would be but a quarter of a cent per bushel, and the law of gravitation would carry it into the barge at Troy or Albany, and another day would put it on board the ship for Liverpool. A vessel could then arrive in port from Liverpool and proceed to unload her cargo, while her owner, sitting in his office in New York, puts his finger to the wire, and, with the aid of electricity, taps his granary at Chicago; in eight days he has a cargo of wheat on board as the last package of Liverpool freight is taken off, and the ship sets sail for the other side of the Atlantic. (Applause.) It had been stated that New York State would be a loser by the shorter transportation, in getting only three instead of six cents. But the increased trade would amply compensate for the apparent loss, and Boston would be a gainer by a cheaper transit to the Hudson River, the railway from Troy to Boston would get all the business it could possibly transact, while the Ogdensburgh and Boston road would get its share from Lake Ontario direct. Portland, too, would be in the same position, and would share in the benefit. And where would Pennsylvania stand? The shortest and cheapest route for Pennsylvania coal to the West would be by a line of railway already built to Lake Ontario, but not much used, from Scranton to Oswego. Those princely inland ships, after bringing down grain, would take back coal for ballast at a cheap rate to the very heart of the Northwest, and give a new impetus to the mining interests of Pennsylvania. (Hear, hear.) The Committee had taken a broad and liberal view of the whole question, and sought to devise such a plan of improvement as would facilitate trade with a large number of the States at the same time, and materially cheapen the communication; and they claim that they have done their duty in the best manner that circumstances would allow. (Loud applause.)

Mr. McLennan, of Montreal, said:

The delegates from the British Provinces had accepted the call of the Detroit Board of Trade to their Convention to discuss commercial subjects. They felt the presence of many sympathies which called them to meet with the American delegates, and the common interest they had in the great Continent, and its noble waters now flowing past their feet. They had come, however, to discuss the matters apart from political feeling or connection. He apprehended that the West was very largely concerned in this question of transit. During the last eighteen months this country had been comparatively sealed up from the European markets, yet the prices of grain there had been maintained at a range at which they had seldom been maintained for so long a time before. The nations on the Baltic, the Adriatic, and the Black Seas had all been exerting themselves to cheapen their route of communication to the great central market of the world, and this rendered it all the more necessary for the West to have cheap channels of communication with the Sea-board. (Applause.) Some cheaper avenue than at present exists must be found for the millions of bushels that are already produced, and the still greater number of millions that are expected to be produced. (A Voice—"Louder. We can hardly hear the gentleman.") Well, Sir, when we follow the course of the St. Lawrence we follow the course which nature has pointed out as that which these products ought to follow in their travel from the lakes to the Atlantic Ocean. We find that, even as it is, we have been able, by that route, to give no inconsiderable relief to the producers of the Western country. In the year 1863, when the largest crop ever grown here was moved—when Chicago handled forty-five millions of bushels—we, in the City of Montreal, helped forward to a market eleven millions. During the same period we consumed a large quantity of the corn grown in the Western States, while the Eastern and Central States of the Union took from us, for their own benefit and economy, an equal quantity of our wheat, barley, and oats. All were mutually assisting each other to reach, with our products, the most accessible market by the simplest possible route.

(Applause.) We came here without power to negotiate with this great Convention for a treaty. We came to discuss these questions in a neighborly spirit. This we are anxious to do, especially at this early beginning of our intercourse.

Hon. Malcolm Cameron, of Quebec, said:

I am sorry that my friend who was addressing you had not stronger lungs, because he was much better prepared and much better capable of speaking on the details of the subject now before you than I am, for I have not of late given my attention to matters of commerce so much as formerly. It affords me, however, great gratification to see this assembly of commercial men, assembled in the City of Detroit. My acquaintance with this City extends as far back as 1834. I was then a merchant in St. Clair, and had transactions in this neighborhood of many hundreds of thousands of dollars. This City I then knew to have merchants of as much integrity, and of as perfect honesty and as extended views, as could be found in the British Isles. They have struggled and labored on, and seen their City rise to the magnificence it now exhibits, and to the highest honor of all — the honor of having this Convention of commercial men from all parts of the Union and the British Provinces held in their midst. (Applause.) I assert, then, that the feelings of the people on the frontier — the people of Sarnia, of Lambton, Kent, Huron, and so on — have been with you at all times in your great struggle. We have done nothing to deserve the aspersions thrown out by some gentlemen here to-day. (Applause.) I was happy to hear the gentleman from Buffalo speak so vehemently as he did, for after he had done with us, and given us our dressing, he said he had near neighbors in his own City, in the State of New York itself, who had given him a dreadful amount of trouble. (Laughter.) Now, there happened to be in Canada an immense majority who entirely sympathized with the Northerners in their struggle; but there were others who thought at first that the North were not sincere in the matter of slavery, and afterwards that they could not succeed in conquering the South; but those were no worse, after all, than the friends and neighbors of the honorable gentleman from Buffalo. (Laughter.) When you got to know what you were about yourselves, and we began to understand your objects, then you had no lack of sympathy among us. You put your trust in God; I believe your cause was right, and I rejoice that you were successful. (Applause.) But while the Canadians generally rejoice that your glorious flag, which was raised some seventy-nine years ago, and, I think, by a Scotchman, one Paul Jones — yes, it was Paul Jones who first held up the thirteen little stripes on the Bay of Delaware — and I may say the greatest minds of England sympathized with you even then — we cannot forget ourselves. Nothing changes the respect we owe to our institutions, and we are not going to forget that if you, the sons of Britons, have held your noble flag aloft for nearly eighty summers, we have a banner that for a thousand years has braved the battle and the breeze. (Cheers.) We do not forget that England is the home of liberty and true freedom. (Renewed applause.) Let the venerable gentleman, who was so severe on Canada, remember that while the Press shows the sentiments of the majority of the people, and while the most influential portion of our Press was friendly to the North, there is not a gentleman here who will not admit that the Government of Canada has done its duty to the United States fully and completely. Poor as we are, we have spent a million of dollars in protecting our honor on your frontier. (Cheers.) If I wished to retaliate upon the gentleman from Buffalo, I would remind him of 1837. I wonder if there were no sympathizers in those days. (Laughter.) I believe General Scott — I met him then on the frontier, for I, too, carried my musket then — I believe, I say, that he was an honest man, but he sent arms to an arsenal near the lines for our protection, and the next morning they were in the hands of our would-be invaders. (Hear, and laughter.) Excuse me, Sir, for saying this, but I know there is a little buncombe to be done on these occasions as on others, and I wish to show that even that game is one that two can play at. (Laughter.) Now, we have a good opinion of Uncle Sam's sharpness, but we wish to tell you at once, and you may see it instantly, that we do not come here expecting mercy at your hands. We do not expect you to listen to a tale of difficulties, from which we expect you to relieve us. (Canadian cheers.) We and you are two peoples, living under two different flags in the same country — that is, in the valley drained by the St. Lawrence — and it is your interest as much as ours — it is our common interest — that we should work together. Now, you should remember — as, indeed, one of yourselves has said — that we are a fighting people. (Cheers and laughter.) We are a pugnacious set, and if you cross us and say, You shan't navigate Lake Michigan, which you claim to be yours, we may say, You shan't come into the St. Lawrence. (Loud cheers, and shouts of laughter.) Our friend Littlejohn, just now, has made a splendid Canadian speech. He has said a great deal about the Sea-board, but it seems, curiously enough, that he thinks New York is the only Sea-board town in the world. (Laughter.) I think, Sir, however, that there is a little smell of salt water down about the Gulf of St. Lawrence. (Cheers.) Now, the people of these Western States will soon number fifty or sixty millions, and will produce food enough to feed the whole of the people of the British Isles. Build a Ship Canal down the course of the Ottawa, enlarge the canals beside the St. Lawrence, and the whole of the agricultural portion of the Continent may be changed, and much changed, for the better. It is our business, I am sure, to live at peace with you. As a member of Parliament for twenty-eight years, I have always gone for any measure that would bring us nearer together, such as the repeal of the Alien Laws — for we don't distrust Americans; we can live beside them, and learn to make nutmegs and hams, and all that kind of thing, as well as they. (Vociferous cheers and laughter.) I do not believe that we will ever go to war for any cause with which we have anything to do, and I would not spend one shilling for fortifications. (Applause.) I dare say this may be reported to our Government, and I have a very nice, snug berth under the Government, and I may for this be put out of it; but I say we want no defences, except twelve and a half or fourteen feet of water in the canals. (Shouts of applause and laughter.) We have already laid out twenty millions of dollars on our canals, and if we got twelve or fourteen feet of water in them we would feel we had done all that could be required for the defence of the country against the United States. (Cheers.) United States property, then, would not stay at Oswego, but must go to Montreal. You, in sending off your produce to follow nature's lead to the ocean, carrying it the way Providence intended, should go by the great St. Lawrence. We wanted those great ships to be loaded at Chicago, and carry the Western produce right to the European markets, to fill the poor Irish and Scotch who have been referred to, with the best and finest of your wheat, while they, on their part, send back their manufactures for the myriads of people who are filling up the West and Canada. He wished to tell the people of the United States that she had the control of that route, and that she wished to use it in bargaining with you, and a hard bargain she will make with you if she can. (Laughter.) And, let me say, you have not acted very fairly with us about Reciprocity. If we send over a pack of shingles it is all right, but if a shaving has been taken off it becomes quite changed in its character. (Laughter.) It is all right to send hay, but if it happens to be pressed — oh! then it is manufactured; for it has been squeezed, and our respectable friends, the Consuls, get two dollars for a certificate to certify it was squeezed. (Laughter.) Gentlemen, it is your business to look into these details. I, for my part, believe in Reciprocity, and I trust you do the same, without caring what politicians may say or do about it. (Hear, hear.) It is for you, gentlemen, on behalf of the farmers, to look into this question of Reciprocity, as concerning alike the United States, England, and Canada, and put it in a proper shape, so that we can best effect an exchange of our various products. One point to be looked at is this: that we raise, in several instances, the very thing you have, but not in the same place. Lumber is an instance in point; and I ask, Would it not be a narrow-minded system of protection if you were to legislate so that the people of Michigan should pay twenty per cent. on their lumber, and New York the same, to the people down below? We want to have all these matters carefully considered, and that you should look at the liberality with which Great Britain and the Colonies have offered to deal with you. In 1850 I went to Washington on this very subject, and among others I met was the gentleman I have the pleasure of meeting now again, the Hon. Mr. Hamlin, and I must say he was one of the hardest knots I met. (Much laughter.) You have seen from what has taken place in the Convention to-day that he is one not easily moved from his own view of any matter. Well, I found him very difficult to deal with in this matter of lumber, because he comes from the State of Maine, where they have a great many pine sticks. (Laughter.) Since then he has been in a larger sphere, and I hope has now more expanded notions. (Laughter.) At that time the question of the navigation laws was on the *tapis*, and the result was that the liberal ideas of men like Bright and Cobden prevailed, and England admitted American ships on a fair footing. But, in this rebellion, it became dangerous for your ships to navigate the seas, and what could you have done but for the English principle of Free Trade? We want you to grant us the same privileges as we have granted you for years past, with reference to the St. Lawrence navigation. We feel that there is room for all the channels of communication that can be opened. When the railroad from Manchester to Liverpool was projected, those interested in the Bridgewater Canal got alarmed, and sent in politicians representing that their traffic would be ruined, and that the large capital they had invested would be destroyed The result was that whereas they had done comparatively little business before, they got a large traffic, and now that canal is one of the most prosperous enterprises in England. And so it is with the question now before the Convention. You are always telling us about the boundless extent of your Country, and the vast trade there will be in the future, and that you have not avenues enough to convey it; and yet some of you would shut up the natural avenue of one thousand five hundred miles you have through our territory, although we are willing to work fairly with you, and to remain good friends to the end of time — desiring, however, that the people of each Country should hold their own views as to the Constitution they shall live under. (Hear, hear.) I have always told my friends on our side not to be alarmed by any little thunder they may hear from this side about John Bull, and rumors of war about supposed offences. Four or five years ago I was in Detroit when the son of her Majesty came here on a visit, and I ask Canadians to remember that he was as well received in this City as he was on the other side. (Hear, hear, and cheers.) And why was this? Because the people here had learned, like us, to respect her who is placed at the head of our nation, and who has won the respect not only of her own people, but of the people of the world, on account of the way in which she has purified her Court, elevated its honor, and contributed to the spread of pure and liberal principles all over the earth. (Cheers.) And I think she has shown, lately, not only the good feeling of a Sovereign, but the sympathy of a woman, with the suffering widow of your late Chief Magistrate. (Loud cheers.)

Mr. Stranahan moved that the Convention adjourn till half-past seven.

The motion for adjournment was put and lost.

Mr. Mitchell, of Cincinnati, opposed the taking of a vote before ten o'clock. It would devolve on him to cast the Ohio vote, and he had not sufficient opportunity for consulting his colleagues. He had been told by some Detroit gentlemen that it was all a foregone conclusion, and that they might just as well adopt it first as last; but if so, there was no necessity for their having come together at all. He did not take it upon himself to differ from the gentlemen urging these resolutions as to the magnitude and importance of the enterprize which they had recommended; the only objection that he had was that in the present state of the country he thought it would be very unwise to take this course. He did not see why the ship canal round the Falls of Niagara was of more importance at this moment than re-establishing the broken routes of travel between the North and South, or the improvement of the navigation of the Ohio river. The people in the central part of the country seemed, in some respects, to be unfortunately situated. They had not reached sunset, like those in some other sections, or acquired confidence in themselves. (Laughter.) It was probably for this reason that Cincinnati was not represented on the Transit Committee. Having placed an Oswego member on it, the President announced that all the great Commercial Cities in the country were now represented on that Committee. (Laughter.) In that matter the interests in the central valley of the country—which he thought was as much a regular route for transit according to the laws of nature as the route through the lakes and the St. Lawrence—had been quite ignored. He understood there had been some little kicking on the part of St. Louis in the Committee, but matters were made pleasant for St. Louis. The pill was not changed, but it was sugared over by the addition of a resolution that some time or other, when the convenient season arrived, they would have such legislation as might hereafter be considered necessary—(laughter)—but, meanwhile, this natural barrier at the Falls of

Niagara must be cut away, without reference to the amount of the national debt or the interests of other parts of the country. He believed if there was any one duty now incumbent on the people of the United States, it was to cultivate a spirit of national unity—(cheers)—and if any apple of discord, more serious than another, could be thrown among the people, it would be by commencing on the frontier a system of extravagance by undertaking local improvements, which, however laudable in themselves, had no special claim on the national treasury. To single out one enterprise of this kind, however important in itself, and ask the general Government to step in to the aid of a particular State and create that improvement, was a thing which could not have his vote. By one gentleman from New York State the idea was repudiated that the general Government should step in, and spend a paltry two or three millions in enlarging the Erie Canal, but another gentleman from the same State had urged that idea. He could not understand what harmony there was in that sort of discussion. He did not intend, however, to enter on the subject at length. He was sure nothing he could say would change the fixed convictions of gentlemen on this floor, if, as they had been told, the matter was now all settled; but that they might make their record clear, and as it had not been expected the vote would be taken this afternoon, he did think it should be postponed, and he therefore moved that the Convention adjourn till half-past seven.

Mr. Littlejohn said the gentlemen from Cincinnati had referred to this report as requiring aid from the general Government. The Committee reported the Niagara Falls Ship Canal as both a Military and a Commercial work. With the Erie Canal it would connect the New England States on the East with the several States of the Union on the West. It was a work entirely national in its character, and the necessity for which was shown by the fact that at present they had a chain of lakes which could not be reached by a single gunboat for military defence.

On motion, the Convention adjourned to 9 o'clock to-morrow morning.

THIRD DAY.

THURSDAY, JULY 13.

The Convention met at 9 o'clock, and was opened with prayer by Rev. Mr. Freeland, of Detroit.

The President laid before the Convention a lengthy communication from Thomas Clark, Esq., of Superior, Wisconsin, advocating the construction of a railway from the Upper Mississippi to Lake Superior.

Mr. Taylor, of Minnesota, moved that Mr. Clark's communication, together with that of the Board of Trade of St. Paul, presented yesterday, be ordered to be printed, with the official records. Agreed to.*

NIAGARA SHIP CANAL.

On motion, the Convention proceeded to the consideration of the regular order, viz: the majority report on Transit. (Mr. Littlejohn's.)

Mr. Prosser, of Buffalo, said he rose to withdraw the minority report, and he would also move the adoption of an amendment to the majority report, as follows:

Whereas, By a recent survey and estimate, by the proper authorities of the State of New York, it is shown to be entirely feasible and practicable, and comparatively cheap, within two years to enlarge the locks upon the canals, with very slight improvement in a small portion of the channel, so as to admit the passage of boats carrying 550 to 600 tons, instead of 220 tons as now, thereby increasing their capacity to at least 10,000,000 tons annually eastward, and diminishing

---

*See Addenda.

the cost of transportation fully one-half, thus furnishing a cheap and ample outlet to an Eastern market, whenever and wherever it can be found, for at least 200,000,000 bushels of grain more than was forwarded through those canals in the prolific year of 1862; therefore,

Resolved, That the Governor of the State of New York be and is hereby respectfully requested to recommend in his next annual message to the Legislature that authority be granted to proceed without delay with the said improvements, and a suitable appropriation made therefor, so as to complete the work at the earliest day practicable, thereby opening a channel between the lakes and tidewater, alike ample and cheap, sufficient to meet the wants of the great grain growing States of the Northwest for a long time to come, and as the trade increases, enabling the State of New York to reduce the tolls on her canals in a corresponding proportion.

Resolved, That the Secretary of this Convention be requested to send a copy of the foregoing preamble and resolutions to the Governor of the State of New York.

Mr. Littlejohn accepted the amendment as part of his report, but disclaimed the idea of binding the action of the Convention by such acceptance.

Mr. Thurston offered for adoption the following:

Resolved, That the Ohio river, the great highway — one of the most important communications of the country, connecting with more than 15,000 miles of inland river transportation, needs, to enable the country to fully enjoy the benefits of the middle national highway of commerce, such improvements as will enable its waters to be navigated at all seasons by large boats from its mouth to Pittsburgh. Therefore, we recommend to Congress such legislation at the proper time as will best develop the resources and usefulness of this important national highway, whose waters wash the shores of six important Western States, and are essential to the inland navigation of all others.

Said resolution was referred to the Committee on Rivers and Harbors.

The question was on the adoption of the first resolution reported by the Committee, as follows:

Resolved, That this Convention regard the construction of a ship canal around the Falls of Niagara a national work of great military and commercial importance, alike demanded by military prudence, the necessities of commerce and political wisdom, and that its early completion by the General Government is required by every consideration of sound political economy.

Mr. Mitchell offered the following as a substitute for the resolution:

Resolved, That this Convention deem the construction of a ship canal around the Falls of Niagara a national work of great commercial importance, alike demanded by the necessities of commerce and political wisdom; and that its early completion is required by the country; but that in the present condition of the national finances we cannot demand its construction by the General Government.

Mr. Littlejohn stood opposed to the amendment proposed by the gentleman from Ohio, for the reason that the entire frontier of the United States is exposed to aggression on the part of Great Britain. She owned to-day over a hundred gunboats that can be sent across the seas and put upon the chain of lakes. The United States had not a single gunboat upon the lakes, at all. The Government has given notice to suspend that treaty which confined each nation to a single gunboat. Our Government was now in an attitude to place proper defenses on these lakes: and whenever there was a war with Great Britain, (and such a war was possible) gunboats could be sent to the St. Lawrence. We wanted it so that we could send our gunboats through the entire chain of lakes for purposes of defense. If there ever was a measure that commended itself to our attention it was this one. We could not forget that when this war commenced, four-fifths of the people of the North were beaten by the rebels; and as in the outset of the war our enemies had the advantage; so in a war with England, they would have the advantage at the outset, and would destroy our Cities on the Sea-board and interrupt our commercial transportation. He would ask if the people of this country would stand such a result as that the corn of the West should be cut off for six or eight weeks from reaching its markets? Gentlemen protested against the expenditure, by our Government, of so much money as would be required for a Ship Canal. All that the fifteen States bordering upon the lakes desired was a loan. The Canal would not cost over $6,000,000, and all that was asked was a loan of $2,500,000 to complete this great undertaking, because private enterprise could do the rest. When the volume of trade was increased, it would enable them to do the business at a very low rate of taxation. This Ship Canal would increase the volume of trade 100,000,000 of bushels in three years, and save five cents a bushel on the whole of the grain shipped. That would give $5,000,000 of money saved to the producers of the Northwest.

Mr. Allen, of Buffalo, asked what would be the expense of the Canal, and what would be its length?

Mr. Littlejohn — The length of the Canal would be seven miles, and it could be made for $6,000,000. If the National Government would loan the money asked, it would save $4,000,000 or $5,000,000 a year, which in fifteen or twenty years would amount to quite a large sum. It was the duty of Government to make such a loan.

Mr. Pruyn, of New York — We are asked to recommend the construction of a Ship Canal around the Falls of Niagara, first as a military necessity, and secondly, for commercial purposes. Now, as a military necessity, he ventured to say that it would be worth nothing at all. (Cheers.) For six months in the year it could be of no service whatever, and for the residue, let us see what it would be worth. For the purpose of carrying munitions of war around the Falls, the means employed were sufficient, and they could be increased to any desirable extent. If a war occurred with England, (which God forbid,) he ventured to say that both nations would require all their gunboats to take care of their coasts and harbors. The work of constructing gunboats for the lakes must be a separate and independent work. By the supplementary treaty of Ghent, it was provided that neither should retain in these lakes any force except a revenue cutter. They dedicated these lakes to the great idea of commerce. (Cheers.) Let us not talk of war in connection with them. Let the lakes and the country surrounding them be so indefinite and intangible in this respect that a man for miles would not know whether he traveled in Canada or the Northwest. (Loud cheers.) If it be insisted that we must build gunboats, we could do it in these lakes; we could build them in Lake Michigan, which was not belonging to any other country but this. He would ask how the business of Lake Ontario was conducted?

Mr. Littlejohn — On Lake Ontario the tonnage of English vessels is ten to one as compared with those of America.

Mr. Pruyn — We do not think Great Britain can make any such preparations as could be made by our statesmen. (Cheers.) He ventured to say that the capacity of the New York, Pennsylvania and Ohio Railroads was amply sufficient to carry all the produce of the West to the Seaboard for years to come. It might be desirable at a future day to construct a Canal around the Falls of Niagara, but looking at the wants of the present and the future it was not needed now. Not more than half the canal boats in the Erie Canal were employed, and during this whole season the work of transportation had been done at a loss. That that was true no one could deny. These works had never been tested to their full capacity. Mr. Allen had made some very pertinent remarks in reference to the expense the State had been at the construction of these works, and it was true that that Government had not derived any profit from the Canal for many years, and even for the last few years had only received some $200,000 a year from it. They were willing and would be happy to see the Canadian Canals enlarged, and the State of New York was in favor of a Reciprocity Treaty which should be fair and just to both parties. (Cheers.) It was not necessary for New York to incur an expense of $25,000,000 when the Canadian Canals were open to us. On the other hand, if Canada was to be annexed to us, we certainly did not need a Canal on the American side. If we were not to be cut out from the St. Lawrence we cannot see the necessity of building this Canal simply for the purpose of taking a portion of the produce of the West to the Seaboard. If ever a Convention was assembled on this continent which should be peaceful in its objects, it was this one. (Cheers.) Nothing was said in the case by the Detroit Board of Trade of any war measures. It was a Convention for matters of commerce and peace. Do not talk of war, then, but let that subject be laid aside. (Cheers.)

Mr. Townsend opposed the idea urged by Mr. Littlejohn, that this was a war measure. If the Canal was only seven miles in length, let us stretch an imaginary line and test the Canal as a war measure. There was not a single mile of it which could not be reached by the guns of an opposing power on the opposite shore; and it would be the most utterly worthless thing that could be imagined. The gentleman said that it was impossible to pass gunboats from Lake Ontario to Lake Erie without this Canal. If a war were to take place how would the United States get her gunboats into Lake Ontario? He doubted if England, in such a case, would be as liberal as we were when the Trent affair happened, and we let her pass her troops through Portland to Canada. Such courtesy could hardly be expected in times of war. This Canal might do all very well in times of peace, but it would be utterly worthless in times of war.

Hon. James F. Joy, of Detroit, said:

I quite agree with those who say, that the allusion to military necessity ought to be stricken out of this resolution. We are here to consult and deliberate upon the business interests and necessities of the country alone, and all talk of war with any power has no place here. The commercial necessities of the country are not only amply sufficient to justify, but absolute require at the hands of the General Government, the construction of the canal around the Niagara Falls of dimensions to accommodate vessels of twelve to fifteen hundred tons burden. Nay, it is a work of such imperative necessity, and demanded by such vast interests, that it will admit of no delay. Of this, I think that all will be convinced.

But it is alleged, that we are at the end of a great civil contest; with the finances of the country disturbed; an immense debt resting upon its resources, and that, in the present state of affairs, it is neither politic nor expedient for the Government to undertake a public work which will add to that debt, and increase the burdens already resting upon the country. It is to this question that it is my wish to make a few remarks. In so doing, I will say that I am not of those who cast censure upon New York and Pennsylvania, or their public works. These States are great States — filled with enterprise, talent and wealth; and characterized by public works of various kinds, which do them great honor. I am proud of these States — the one, long designated as the Keystone, and the other as the Empire State of the Union, and well deserving the names given. The whole country may well be proud of them as members of this great confederacy of States. But while we accord them all honor, and grant the fullest meed of praise, we must have regard to the necessities of other parts of the country. And since even these States have acquired the designations which they have so long borne, and to which I have alluded, an Empire of a thousand miles in extent has grown up west of them; filled with a teeming population, and of unparalleled fertility and productiveness — whose varied productions, even now, crowd all the passages to the Seaboard, and with whose progress, and whose necessities, these States and all their enterprise and ability, have been unable, and will continue to be unable, to attain and maintain parallel progress in providing avenues to the great markets of the world. I think I hazard nothing in saying that the break in the lines of transit through New York, by the floods last spring, only for the period of three weeks, occasioned a greater loss by far to the holders of Western produce, seeking the market, than this proposed Canal would cost, even though it should reach $25,000,000 of money. How important, then, that the avenues to market should be multiplied, even if in ordinary times they would suffice? But it will be, and is apparent that they are by no means, even now, adequate. Let me, for a moment, call your attention to the progress of the West and Lake States and their productions, as compared with those of the great States named, and all New England and her six States added to them. I will go back only for a period of twenty-five years. The statement will arrest the attention of all, and convince all of the necessity of this Canal, and of all outlets to the Ocean for the business of the Western world. In 1840, the great States of New York and Pennsylvania, and all the New England States together, had a population of some more than six millions of people. [I omit in all my statements, for convenience, the thousands, stating only the millions.] At that time, the States of Ohio, Indiana, Illinois, Iowa, Missouri, Minnesota, and Michigan, had a population of about two millions. In 1850, the Atlantic States named had increased from six to eight millions of people, while the Lake States had increased from about two to five millions. In 1860, the Atlantic States named had acquired ten millions of people, while the Lake States had acquired eight millions. At the same comparative rates of increase, the two are at this time nearly equal, and in the next ten years the Lake States will far surpass the great Atlantic States named, in population.

Now, let it be borne in mind, that the great Cities of the country are in the East, as yet, and that its Cities and Towns probably contain nearly half of the inhabitants; while in the Lake States, hardly a million of the ten millions, which people these States, are found in Cities or large Towns. They are almost entirely devoted to agriculture, to the extent of the remaining nine millions. And the Cities and Towns are not built up by manufactures, as it is in the East, but by the purchase, and handling and trade in the productions of agriculture; and by distributing, as merchants, the manufactures of the East and of the world, among the people spread over this vast region of country.

Contrast, now, the progress of agriculture between the two sections. All the Atlantic States named, in 1850, produced twenty millions of bushels of wheat, and in 1860, had increased the production only two millions, and risen to twenty-two millions. In the same years the Lake States had produced forty millions and eighty-eight millions of bushels of wheat. Of corn, the Atlantic States produced in those years forty-seven and fifty-seven millions of bushels. The Lake States named, produced in 1850, of corn, 185,000,000 bushels, and in 1860, 319,000,000, and at the same rate of increase, will, in ten years more, produce near or about 200,000,000 bushels of wheat and 600,000,000 bushels of corn. I might enumerate the increase of cattle, swine and other productions in the West, as compared with the East, showing the same rapidity of increase, but it would only occupy time. I will merely mention the increase of cattle and hogs which came to Chicago, to market, within the last four years alone. In 1860, there came to the market of that City, about 400,000 hogs. In 1863, the number had risen to near 1,700,000. Of cattle, in 1860, which came to that market, there were 177,000, and in 1863, there were 343,000. This is for a single market, but it strikingly illustrates the progress of the West. Now, there are ten millions of people interested in these productions, and to them the matter of access to market is of the first and last importance. Are they, for the next twenty years, to depend upon two or three railroads and a small canal, when a freshet may cause more inconvenience and loss than, I had almost said, all the canals and railways are worth? But it is not the possibility of getting to market, through the avenues now open, but the expense of so doing which is involved. Every additional avenue both adds to the facilities and diminishes the expense. On this point, I may say a word by and by, when the Reciprocity question comes up. At present, none can fail to see that the Ship Canal around the Falls is a necessity, as an outlet for the productions of a people spread over the Great

West, numbering ten millions. All can see, and none can fail to see, its value and importance. When shall it be built? Shall it be built now, or forty or fifty years hence? When will the debt now resting upon the country be paid? That is to be paid, every dollar, I assume; and palsied be the tongue which shall lisp the sentiment of repudiation of any part of it. But, in the meantime, is the world to come to a stand-still? Is the West to stop in its progress? Are we to be paralized for half a century? Suppose the canal cost $5,000,000 or $10,000,000 or $25,000,000. What is it? It is but as dust upon the balance compared with the importance of increased facilities to market, for the Great West, and for the East, also. It is not worthy of a moment's thought. Look for a moment at what the Government has done towards improvement, even during the war? It has undertaken the great road to the Pacific coast, granting a subsidy of $16,000 per mile for its whole main line, and the same amount for two or three branches, each more than three hundred miles long. I am glad of it. Let us bind the East and West together by every possible tie. But that road, as important as it is deemed, is not by any means of the same importance as is an easy access to market from the West. There is not so large a population whose interests and welfare are to be affected by it. With the millions of the West, the avenue to market is a vital question — when close upon the Mississippi corn is burned for fuel, because the expense of sending it to market is more than it is worth — when from Illinois, on an average, it costs the farmer three bushels to get the fourth to market in New York, and much more to lay it down in Liverpool — when from all the Lake States it costs half of all the flour and wheat to the farmer to get the rest into the markets of the world — it has become high time for the Government to look a little to the protection of his interests. And there is and can be no higher duty for it, than to open this Canal of such size and dimensions as will accommodate ships of large tonnage, as one step in the progress of a line of communication which shall reach from Lake Superior and Lake Michigan, by the way of the St. Lawrence, for ships of the same kind to the Atlantic Ocean and the great markets of the world. There should be no delay. The exigency will not admit of it. As to the financial expediency, it may be said that the additional revenue which may be derived simply from the increased productiveness of the West, which will be caused by it, will enable the Government to redeem the bonds, if this may be necessary to secure its construction. In a case like this, in an emergency like this — for it is an emergency of no ordinary kind — it is not possible to suffer a delay of even ten, much less twenty years or half a century, until the public debt is removed and its burdens made easy. All the expense sinks into insignificance in comparison with the necessities of the case; and since there is no possible way in which Government can protect our railroad interests by tariffs or otherwise — since the farmer must send his productions on to the great markets to compete with the productions of all the world — it is but little the Great West asks when it asks that the barriers which obstruct the avenues to those markets shall at least be made passable for the ships to be freighted with the fruits of her labor and her fertile soil, on their way to the markets of the world.

Mr. Randolph, of Chicago, moved to lay the amendment on the table, and called for a division.

Mr. Stranahan, of New York, moved that the delegate from the State of Iowa, on the floor of the Convention, be allowed to vote.

Mr. Armstrong raised the question that that motion could not now be made, as the Convention was in the midst of a special order, taking the vote.

The President stated that the Convention had yesterday held that the delegate from Iowa was entitled to a vote under the report of the Committee of which Mr. Hamlin was Chairman.

The question was taken on the motion to lay on the table, and carried by the following vote:

	AYE.	NO.
Mercantile Association, Bangor,	3½	..
Board of Trade, Portland,	3½	..
Board of Trade, Boston.	13	..
Chamber of Commerce, New York,	7	..
Commercial Association, New York,	7	..
Board of Trade, Albany,	..	5
Board of Trade, Troy,	..	4
Board of Trade, Buffalo,	..	6
Board of Trade, Oswego,	4	..
Cincinnati,	1	9
Cleveland,	5	..
Toledo,	4	..
Springfield,	..	2
Detroit,	4	..
Kalamazoo,	1	..
Bay City,	1½	..
East Saginaw,	1½	..
Board of Trade, Cairo,	..	5
Board of Trade, Chicago,	7	..

	AYE.	NO.
Mercantile Association, Chicago,	4	..
Chamber of Commerce, Milwaukee,	8	..
Board of Trade, Philadelphia,	..	6
Corn Exchange, Philadelphia,	..	5
Coal Exchange, Philadelphia,	..	4
Board of Trade, Pittsburgh,	..	6
Board of Trade, Erie,	..	5
Minnesota,	4	..
Missouri,	9	..
Iowa,	8	..
	96	59

So the substitute of Mr. Mitchell was laid on the table.

Mr. Kennedy then moved to amend the resolution by striking out the word "military," so that it would read:

Resolved, That this Convention regard the construction of a Ship Canal around the Falls of Niagara a National work of great commercial importance, alike demanded by the necessities of commerce and political wisdom, and that its early completion by the General Government is required by every consideration of sound political economy.

Mr. Kennedy thought if the construction of the Niagara Canal was put forward as a military work, the improvement of communications in the West would be prejudiced, as they could not be urged on any other than purely commercial grounds.

Mr. Robinson, of Cleveland, sustained the motion. He thought it a poor time to talk about military necessity when property consigned to the Seaboard was liable to deterioration before it could be got to market, at the rate of twenty dollars per barrel for pork which sad experience had fallen to his lot. The talk about the slow progress of freight on the Erie Canal did not cover the whole ground. Why not talk about the ability of the New York Central Road?

Mr. Pruyn — The ability of that Road is well understood.

Mr. Robinson — Yes; that is so, as I know to my sorrow. Only give the West adequate transit, and the country will soon be in a condition to be ready for England or any other power.

Mr. Kennedy's amendment prevailed by the following vote:

	AYE.	NO.
Mercantile Association, Bangor, ...	..	3½
Board of Trade, Portland, ...	..	3½
Board of Trade, Boston, ...	..	13
Chamber of Commerce, New York, ...	7	..
Commercial Association, New York, ...	7	..
Board of Trade, Albany, ...	5	..
Board of Trade, Troy, ...	4	..
Board of Trade, Buffalo, ...	6	..
Board of Trade, Oswego, ...	4	..
Cincinnati, ...	10	..
Cleveland, ...	5	..
Toledo, ...	4	..
Springfield, ...	2	..
Detroit, ...	4	..
Kalamazoo, ...	..	1
Bay City, ...	..	1½
East Saginaw, ...	..	1½
Board of Trade, Cairo, ...	5	..
Board of Trade, Chicago, ...	7	..
Mercantile Association, Chicago, ...	4	..
Chamber of Commerce, Milwaukee, ...	6	2
Board of Trade, Philadelphia, ...	6	..
Corn Exchange, Philadelphia, ...	5	..
Coal Exchange, Philadelphia, ...	4	..
Board of Trade, Pittsburgh, ...	6	..
Board of Trade, Erie, ...	5	..
Minnesota, ...	4	..
Missouri, ...	11	..
Iowa, ...	8	..
	129	26

The question recurring on the adoption of the first resolution, as amended, it was carried by the following vote:

	AYE.	NO.
Mercantile Association, Bangor, ...	3½	..
Board of Trade, Portland, ...	3½	..
Board of Trade, Boston, ...	13	..
Chamber of Commerce, New York, ...	7	..
Commercial Association, New York, ...	7	..
Board of Trade, Albany, ...	..	5
Board of Trade, Troy, ...	..	4
Board of Trade, Buffalo, ...	..	6
Board of Trade, Oswego, ...	4	..

	AYE.	NO.
Cincinnati,	1	9
Cleveland,	5	..
Toledo,	4	..
Springfield,	..	2
Detroit,	4	..
Kalamazoo,	1	..
Bay City,	1½	..
East Saginaw,	1½	..
Board of Trade, Cairo,	5	..
Board of Trade, Chicago,	7	..
Mercantile Association, Chicago,	4	..
Chamber of Commerce, Milwaukee,	8	..
Board of Trade, Philadelphia,	6	..
Corn Exchange, Philadelphia,	5	..
Coal Exchange, Philadelphia,	4	..
Board of Trade, Pittsburgh,	6	..
Board of Trade, Erie,	..	5
Minnesota,	4	..
Missouri,	10	1
Iowa,	8	..
	123	32

The second resolution (see page 64) was read and adopted.

The third resolution (see page 65) was read.

Mr. Seymour, of Troy, moved to strike out the last clause, commencing with the word "Failing." This clause embodied a reflection on the great State of New York, and ought to be stricken out.

Mr. Scammon, of Chicago, moved to lay the amendment and resolution on the table.

Mr. L. F. Allen, of Buffalo, said that the Empire State, with one arm on the lakes and the other on the Ocean, commanded the route to the Seaboard, and was not to be insulted. He (Mr. A.) was the "mildest, mannered man that ever cut a throat," but he warned the Convention, and warned gentlemen that that Great State would not tamely submit to such insults. You may go around her, but when you attempt to go *through* her, you ought to deal gently. It had become quite obvious if the gentleman from Oswego did not succeed in forcing the commerce of the West to come to Oswego, he would soon be battering at the gates of —— well, he wouldn't say where. The State of New York had expended $60,000,000 on her canals to accommodate the commerce of the West. He thought it out of character for her citizens to be now bringing their family quarrels before the country.

Mr. Scammon — If the State of New York does stand with one arm on the Lakes and the other on the Ocean, I deny that she commands the route of the Great West to the Seaboard. That doctrine went under when New Orleans and Vicksburg fell.

The motion to table the amendment and resolution was lost.

Mr. Seymour's amendment was lost.

Mr. Able, of St. Louis, moved the indefinite postponement of the resolution.

A delegate expressed curiosity to see if the gentleman from Oswego, (Mr. Littlejohn) would be found voting for a direct insult to his own State.

Mr. Littlejohn — With a proper sense of regard for the honor of New York, I shall vote against the indefinite postponement of the resolution.

The question was taken on the motion to indefinitely postpone, and lost by the following vote:

	AYE.	NO.
Mercantile Association, Bangor,	..	3½
Board of Trade, Portland,	..	3½
Board of Trade, Boston,	..	13
Chamber of Commerce, New York,	7	..
Commercial Association, New York,	4	3
Board of Trade, Albany,	5	..
Board of Trade, Troy,	4	..
Board of Trade, Buffalo,	6	..
Board of Trade, Oswego,	..	4
Cincinnati,	..	10
Cleveland,	..	5
Toledo,	..	4
Springfield,	..	2
Detroit,	..	4
Kalamazoo,	..	1
Bay City,	..	1½

	AYE.	NO.
East Saginaw,	..	1½
Board of Trade, Cairo,	1	4
Board of Trade, Chicago,	1	6
Mercantile Association, Chicago,	..	4
Milwaukee Chamber of Commerce,	..	8
Board of Trade, Philadelphia,	6	..
Corn Exchange, Philadelphia,	5	..
Coal Exchange, Philadelphia,	4	..
Board of Trade, Pittsburgh,	6	..
Board of Trade, Erie,	5	..
Minnesota,	..	4
Missouri,	11	..
Iowa,	..	8
	65	90

The resolution was then adopted.

The fourth and fifth resolutions, (see page 65,) were also agreed to.

The sixth resolution, (see page 65,) was read.

Mr. Mitchell moved to strike out all after the word "Resolved," and substitute therefor the following:

Resolved, That this Convention congratulates the merchants and citizens generally, residing in the Towns and Cities, and especially those of the great Cities bordering upon the Mississippi River and its tributaries, upon the successful termination of the Rebellion by which they are permitted to resume and enter upon the immense commerce, which is forever to float upon the Western waters, and that we recognize those rivers as National highways, watering as they do the shores of many populous States, and entitled to the legislative aid of Congress to the same extent precisely as the waters of the Lakes and of the Ocean.

After debate, the motion to strike out prevailed, and as amended the resolution was adopted.

Mr. Prosser's preamble and resolutions, which had been made part of the majority report, were read and adopted.

The preamble and resolution No. 7, (see pages 65 and 66,) were adopted.

The question then recurred upon the preamble to the resolutions of the majority, which were read and adopted.

The question was then put upon the whole of the preambles and resolutions and they were declared adopted in the following words:

NIAGARA SHIP CANAL.

Whereas, The annual increase of the productions of the States bordering upon and tributary to the Northern Lakes has exceeded the capacity of transportation of all the avenues to the Atlantic, demonstrating the urgent necessity of enlarged water facilities for communication between the West and the East; and,

Whereas, The canals and various lines of railroads, leading to and from said lakes, while they have contributed vastly to develop the resources, increase the wealth, and promote the permanent union of our whole country, are wholly inadequate to the demands of the immense and rapidly growing commerce; therefore,

1st. *Resolved*, That this Convention regard the construction of a Ship Canal around the Falls of Niagara a National work of great commercial importance, alike demanded by the necessities of commerce and political wisdom, and that its early completion by the General Government is required by every consideration of sound political economy.

2d. *Resolved*, That such a canal, of a capacity to pass the largest steam or sail vessels, which now or hereafter may navigate the lakes, will afford the cheapest and most expeditious water communication for the transportation of the products of the great producing waters of the West and Northwest, by bringing into use the most easterly of the entire chain of lakes on our Northern frontier, from which these annually increasing products may be distributed by short, enlarged canals, and by railway to the Hudson and New York, by sailing into New England and Pennsylvania, and by the St. Lawrence River direct to the Ocean.

3d. *Resolved*, That the State of New York, geographically located on the highway of commerce between the great chain of lakes to the Seaboard, and having within her borders her metropolis of the nation, is bound by every consideration of interest and true policy, and by the comity she owes her sister States, to improve and enlarge the shortest water communication between the lakes and tide-water. Failing to do so, she must not complain if a portion of her great inland commerce shall be diverted through other cheaper channels of communication.

4th. *Resolved*, That we hail with satisfaction the proposed enlargement of the Welland and St. Lawrence Canals, and other proposed improvements through the Provinces, affording other cheap outlets through which the commerce of the States, tributary to the lakes, may seek our Eastern markets, as well as the markets of the Old World.

5th. *Resolved*, That in the event of the negotiation of any Treaty of Reciprocity between the United States and the British Provinces, our Government should be careful to secure in such a treaty a guarantee of a sufficient depth of water to enable Ocean steamers, of not less than one thousand tons cargo carrying capacity, to pass from Port Colborne, C. W., to tide-water.

6th. *Resolved*, That this Convention congratulates the merchants and citizens generally residing in the Towns and Cities, and especially those great Cities bordering upon the banks of the Mississippi and its tributaries, upon the successful termination of the rebellion, by which they are permitted to resume and enter upon the immense commerce which is forever to float upon the Western waters, and that we recognize those rivers as national highways, watering, as they do, the shores of many populous States, and entitled to the legislative aid of Congress to the same extent precisely as the waters of the lakes and of the Ocean.

IMPROVEMENT OF THE NEW YORK CANALS.

Whereas, By a recent survey and estimate by the proper authorities of the State of New York, it is shown to be entirely feasible and practicable, and comparatively cheap, within two years to enlarge the locks upon the Canals, and with very slight improvement in a small portion of the channel, so as to admit the passage of boats carrying five hundred and fifty to six hundred tons, instead of two hundred and twenty tons now, thereby increasing the capacity to, at least, ten million tons annually eastward, and diminishing the cost of transportation fully one-half, thus furnishing a cheap and ample outlet to an Eastern market, whenever and wherever it can be found, for at least two hundred million bushels of grain *more* than was forwarded through those Canals in the prolific year of 1862; therefore,

Resolved, That the Governor of the State of New York be, and is hereby respectfully requested to recommend in his next annual message to the Legislature of that State, that authority be granted to proceed with the said improvement, and that a suitable appropriation be made therefor, so as to complete the work at the earliest day practicable, opening up a channel between the States and tide-water, alike ample and cheap, sufficient to meet the wants of the great grain-growing States of the Northwest for a long time to come, and as the trade increases, enabling the State of New York to reduce the tolls on her Canals in a corresponding proportion.

Resolved, That the Secretary of this Convention be requested to send a copy of the foregoing Preambles and Resolutions to the Governor of the State of New York.

TIME CONTRACTS FOR THE DELIVERY OF FREIGHT.

Whereas, Heavy and oftentimes disastrous losses result to shippers, in consequence of the delays and irregularities which attend the transportation and delivery of merchandise and produce on the great railway routes between the East and West; and,

Whereas, In the opinion of this Convention, there is no reason why the same certainty and regularity which attend the transit of passengers should not also exist in the transportation of freight by rail; therefore,

Resolved, That the question of *time* should enter into all contracts for the delivery of freight by the principal railroad lines, and that it is equally for the interests of railroad companies themselves, and of the community at large, that a system of management be immediately arranged and adopted, which shall enable shippers to rely upon the delivery of freight at its destination within a definite and specified time.

Mr. Davis, of Ohio, offered the following resolution, which was referred to the Committee on Miscellaneous Business.

Whereas, There now exists great irregularity in the time and manner of making up the trade statistics of the various Cities of the country; and,

Whereas, Accurate information about such matters is yearly becoming more essential to the successful prosecution of business; be it

Resolved, That it shall be considered a part of the duty of this Convention to endeavor to bring about greater uniformity in the yearly reports of the Commerce and Manufactures of the various Cities of the country, and in the manner of compiling the statistics.

THE RECIPROCITY QUESTION.

Mr. Joy, of Detroit, from the Committee on Reciprocity, presented the following report:

The Committee to whom was referred the question of the Reciprocity Treaty and reciprocal trade between the United States and the British Provinces of North America, have directed me to report to the Convention that it has considered the questions referred to it as fully as the limited time would admit of; that the gentlemen from the various British Provinces have been before the Committee, and all the statements deemed important by them to be made, have been heard, and that the Consul General of the United States in Canada has also been before the Committee, and his statements heard; that the questions submitted in all the aspects presented have been freely discussed in the Committee, and that, as the results of that discussion, they have adopted two resolutions which they have instructed me to present to the Convention, and recommend their adoption. They are hereto appended:

Resolved, That this Convention do approve of the action of the Government of the United States in giving the notice to the Government of Great Britain of its wish to terminate the Treaty of Reciprocity of June 6, 1854.

Resolved, That this Convention do respectfully request the President of the United States to enter into negotiations with the Government of Great Britain, having in view the execution of a treaty between the two countries for reciprocal commercial intercourse between the United States and the several provinces of British North America, including British Columbia, the Selkirk Settlement, and Vancouver's Island, based on principles which shall be just and equitable to all parties, and which shall also include the free navigation of the St. Lawrence and the other rivers of British North America, with such improvements of the rivers and the enlargement of the canals as shall render them adequate for the requirements of the West in communicating with the Ocean.

The question being upon the adoption of the first resolution, it was carried unanimously.

The question then being on the adoption of the second resolution.

Mr. McChesney, of Chicago, offered the following as a substitute:

Resolved, That in the still unsettled condition of some of the States recently in rebellion, and the state of the finances of the Government, as well as the immature state of our system of taxation, any action tending to a renewal of a Reciprocity Treaty may wisely and appropriately be left to the respective Governments by which it would be negotiated.

A resolution to lay the substitute on the table was made and withdrawn.

Hon. Hannibal Hamlin, of Maine, spoke as follows:

I am deeply sensible, from the earnestness which I witness all around me, or perhaps I may say, from the enthusiasm which shall I see manifested, that it may be utter folly on my part to present to this Convention the views which will control the vote which I give on this question. But all the way here with my colleagues, from the most eastern of the States of the Union, I would be faithless to the gentlemen who sent me here, were I to fail to present to this Convention the views I entertain, and which will at least control my vote. You are an intelligent body of men, merchants, princes of merchants, who occupy a position of proud pre-eminence, and as such I ask you to pause in the action you are about to take, and to weigh deliberately what you are about to do. Let us do nothing hastily; let no mere local and sectional interests control the action of wise men. (Cheers.) Let us deliberate calmly, and be guided by the dictates of cool and deliberate judgment. I am for the resolution submitted by Mr. McChesney, because I believe it wisest and best. (Cheers.) I do not believe it is wise that this body should assume to itself the duties that belong to the Executive of this country. (Cheers.) I do not think that it reflects credit upon the high character of the mercantile associations met here, to do it. I can call to my mind no instance in the history of my country, when any body of men have undertaken to advise the Chief Magistrate of this country in reference to his executive acts.

Mr. Sabine, of Massachusetts — Thousands of them.

Mr. Hamlin — We reach our Executive through other than such channels as these. That is my recollection; but my friend before me says thousands of such instances have occurred. He has a statistical mind. I have not. We have adopted the resolution unanimously in this body declaring that we need the revenues of this country, derived from all sources, for its maintenance and support, and for the payment of the debt which is hanging over us. I stand by that resolution; and if you are going to adopt the course suggested, what becomes of the resolution you unanimously adopted here yesterday? Now, I hold that our national debt must be paid to the last mill. (Cheers.) And I hold that a wise statesmanship would dictate that the revenues to do that should be drawn from all sources, and that you shall not select a few articles, and make your revenue system one of special protection. I was educated in the school of Free Trade. Not Free Trade in slices. (Cheers and laughter.) I affirm that that is the most obnoxious system of legislation that can be devised by man.

I am for Free Trade. I want it for ourselves, and I want to give it to our colonial brethren. But what do I mean by Free Trade? Not that system which selects a few articles and makes them entirely free, rendering it necessary that you should impose additional revenues upon other articles, in order to make up for the deficiency. That is Free Trade in slices, and it cannot be defended upon any principles of political economy ever enunciated by any man. (Cheers.) It is not true, and you cannot make it true. You cannot find an author on the whole catalogue of writers upon that subject who has adopted that principle. I want to see our revenue placed upon a basis in which every interest in our broad land shall be represented and protected under the ægis of our Government. (Cheers, and cries of "good.") In the Eastern States, from which I come, where we raise nothing but fish, some few potatoes, and some men, that I see around me here to-day, from Wisconsin, Illinois, and Michigan, standing as we do upon the very confines of the Union, weak and feeble though we are, we feel that we have a right to come here and ask that our interests shall be protected, preserved, and cared for, as are those of the people of this great country in the heart of this Republic. (Cheers.) And, as the best evidence of the spirit which animates us, while we are divided upon this question of Reciprocity, because the great commercial men have special interests to take care of, yet I ask you to-day to say if we have not aided in expressing the opinion that you should have proper channels from the great West to the Ocean. We have an interest in it as well as yourselves, and we have steadily pursued that course. What will my friend say if I ask him to let in the whole commerce of Great Britain side by side with that of our own country? That would affect his peculiar interests at home, and would, in effect, be Free Trade in slices, from the peculiar circumstances by which we are surrounded. I make these remarks because I think it is wiser and better to leave the whole of this subject in the hands of the executive powers that have to negotiate a treaty, if one is to be negotiated. There is another proposition which comes from the gentlemen on the other side of this hall, and whom we are glad to meet here. What is their proposition to this Convention? They have observed a masterly silence (laughter); and allow me to say, gentlemen, there is wisdom in that silence.

Mr. McLennan, of Montreal — We have made no objection to the Reciprocity Treaty as it stood, and as it stands at present. It was the United States that made objections. We came here to learn what those objections were that were made to it, and to try if we could meet them.

Mr. Hamlin — They have wisely executed their trust. (Loud cheers and laughter.) In a very plain manner, which you will all understand, they have come here and asked us to show our hand, and we have done it, but they have not shown theirs.

Mr. Bloodgood, of New York, rose to explain that the Committee had held three sessions, and the Canadian gentlemen had been present and stated their views, and that they had expressed themselves willing to make great concessions to this country in any future treaty. They stated their views fully, and asked us for our objections, which we had to give.

Mr. Hamlin — The gentleman has given me no information; none whatever. He has simply stated what the report said, that the Committee had listened with great pleasure to the matter so very ably and eloquently presented by Canada. But what of that goes to the public? What was there stated that is published to the world? I only meant to repeat, in the language of the proposed amendment, that I did not believe it was wise, and I do not now, and that controls my action fully. I do not believe it is wise, in the present condition of the country, for us to make a proposition to our Government to propose to the English Government a renewal of the Reciprocity Treaty. I think you are more certain to get poorer terms by doing so than you are by doing as the gentlemen do on the other side. I read a pamphlet as I came over the Grand Trunk Railway, very fairly written, and fairly representing the views of the writer, in which it was said that the colonies sought no Reciprocity in trade with us. It had been all against them; but they were willing to receive overtures from the United States. It had the imprint of Ottawa upon it, and was a very fair and just statement of the case in the mind of the gentleman who wrote it. I allude to it for the purpose of showing that in our extreme case it will be very unwise for the preservation of local interests, and for the great interests of our country, to make a proposition for the renewal of that treaty. I could go into a discussion of the benefits and evils which have flowed from that Treaty. That, however, is not now the question, and I shall do no such thing; but if you are wise, you will leave this matter in the hands of the Executive of your country. (Loud cheers.)

Hon. Lorenzo Sabine, Secretary of the Boston Board of Trade, spoke as follows:

Mr. President — As I rise to urge the appointment of a joint commission to revise the Reciprocity Treaty, between the United States and Great Britain, of June, 1854, my thoughts are on the past. Twenty-eight years of my life were passed on the Northeastern frontier, where I mingled daily with colonists, as freely as with my own countrymen. To-day, in this City of historic interest, on another border, I greet those who still bear allegiance to a common — though sometimes to us, we think — a wayward, mother. Enough. The time of this Convention is far too precious for exordium, and I enter at once upon my subject. Except to illustrate a single point, I shall use no statistics. I stand here, indeed, in defence of the interests of my own dear country, but that defence, as I understand the case before us, consists in the advocacy of continued progress in commercial freedom; and, of direct consequence, progress in the sublime doctrine of human brotherhood, as enunciated to the Athenians on Mars Hill.

Mr. President, I pray the members of this Convention to recommend to the several Chambers of Commerce and Boards of Trade, which they represent on this floor, the appointment of a joint commission, to attempt, at least, the revision of the Reciprocity Treaty of 1854. Sir, in my very nature, I abhor the word *restriction*, in commercial intercourse between the United States and British America. I know, sir, that Colonies become Nations as surely as boys become men, and by the same natural law. But, how sad to recall the fact, that, unlike the transition at the fireside, separation has been accomplished only by dissension, and the desolation and horrors of war. I do not honor the name of Cromwell, for he was neither a wise statesman nor a respectable merchant, else he would not have signed the so-called celebrated—but to me, infamous—Act of Navigation. As concerns Charles the Second, who perpetuated that Act, he was so unconditionally dissolute, that, his simple presence in a fashionable brothel, in our day, in London or Washington, would excite disgust. And yet, in politics, as I have read history and consulted State papers, the Act of Navigation contained not only the germ, but was the direct occasion of the American Revolution: and, alas, of the expenditure of more than five hundred millions of dollars, on which the people of England are paying interest at this very hour: and sadder still, the loss of one hundred thousand lives, in storm, in prison, and in battle.

While our fathers were British subjects, they were smugglers from one end of the thirteen Colonies to the other: *emphatically*, *smugglers*, and of necessity. The "three pence the pound on tea," is well enough for the fustian of an oration on the Fourth of July; but, to the close student of history, it was precisely and unconditionally, a question between the British Government and Colonial smugglers. The contraband trade was not confined to tea, but extended to rum, wine, sugar, and nearly every product of foreign countries. I repeat, distinctly and without qualification, that merchants, anterior to 1776, were smugglers. Just one quarter part of the signers of the Declaration of Independence were bred to commerce or to the command of ships; and were concerned in the illicit trade of the time. John Hancock was the prince of contraband traders, and, with John Adams as his counsel, was on trial before the Admiralty Court, in Boston, at the exact hour of the shedding of blood at Lexington, to answer for a half a million of dollars penalties, alleged to have been incurred as a *smuggler*. This brief mention of the commercial policy of Cromwell, the canting Puritan hypocrite, and of the licentious Catholic Stuart, the worst of a race that was a curse to America, will suffice for the occasion.

Would that I could relate that *restriction* ended with the war of the Revolution. A few still survive who were personally concerned in some part of the controversy between the two Governments, which, with more or less intensity, lasted for a period of forty-seven years. In 1783, it was proposed to allow the United States to participate in the trade of the remaining Colonies in this hemisphere, on terms of equality with England herself; but the English merchants who enjoyed that trade in monopoly were alarmed, and defeated the measure. Two years after, Mr. Adams, our first Minister at the Court of St. James, was instructed to renew the proposition; and was curtly answed that it could not be entertained even as a subject of negotiation. A third effort was made in 1789, with no better success.

A quarter of a century elapsed without a change of policy, or, as far as I know, without serious effort on our part to obtain concessions. But, in 1815, by an Act of Congress, we relaxed our policy of discrimination in favor of our own flag, to such nations as should reciprocate; and the terms proposed were adopted in the commercial treaty concluded with Great Britain the same year, which, after repeated renewals, is still in force. And this was the beginning of "Reciprocity." Our Government wished to place the Colonial trade on the same footing; but the overture was declined. Yet, intercourse was permitted between the United States and the Colonies, by British legislation and by Orders in Council. Subsequently, efforts to adjust the question by negotiation failed; and, in 1817, an Act of Congress restricted importations in foreign vessels to articles of the growth, produce, or manufactures of the country to which such vessels belonged. The measure was retaliatory. In the year 1817, also, Lord Castlereagh proposed to our Minister in London, to allow our vessels of one deck a limited trade with a portion of the Colonies, under the "Free Port" arrangement: our Government not only refused to accept the proposition, but retaliated a second time, and more severely than at first. A few years later, so hostile had become the relations between the two countries, that the ports of the United States were entirely closed against the British Colonies and West Indies; and, lest British vessels coming to these ports under the "Reciprocity Treaty" of 1815, should evade our laws, bonds were exacted at their departure, obligatory not to land merchandise in either of these interdicted possessions. *To countervail, an order of the King in Council, followed; and non-intercourse on both sides was established.*

In 1824, an Act of Congress declared the suspension of all discriminating duties to the several European nations and their possessions, which had reciprocated the provisions of the Act of 1815, and gave the President authority to extend the exemption to such other powers as should, thereafter, meet the United States on terms of equality; but the British Government refused to accede to stipulations suggested by Mr. Rush, our Minister at the Court of St. James, and negotiations were again interrupted. On the 5th of July, 1825, however, Parliament passed an Act, under which hope was entertained that an end had come to the policy of which we speak, to allow free intercourse with the Colonies; and an unsuccessful attempt was made in Congress, soon after, to meet its provisions with corresponding legislation. The result was another order of his Majesty in Council, declaring the cessation of trade between the United States and the greater part of the Colonial ports, on a certain specified day. At this juncture, Mr. Gallatin, who had succeeded Mr. Rush, was instructed to accept, by treaty, the same terms, substantially, as were offered to the last named gentleman, in 1824; but the determination of the British Government to decline all further endeavors to conclude a Convention, was promptly and definitely announced.

Meantime, the question of the "Colonial Trade," had become political, and the debates in Congress were long and acrimonious; while the newspapers and the people blamed or praised President Adams and his advisers, according to their party proclivities. In the winter of 1827, the President submitted the whole subject to Congress; and, after much discussion, a bill to countervail the last Order in Council, failed; but after the session had closed, the President issued a proclamation which accomplished the object designed by those who supported his administration. The King, in still another Order in Council, recited the nations that had met the provisions of the Act of July 5th, 1825, and excluded from its benefits such as had refused, and among them, of course, was our own country. Mr. Gallatin, who was still in London, however, renewed his efforts to place the Colonial Trade on a satisfactory footing by legislation rather than by treaty, in a dispatch to Lord Dudley. His Lordship did not even reply. So, subsequently, when our Minister addressed Mr. Canning, the curt answer was surprise that any doubt could exist as to the final determination of the British Government on the subject.

After the decease of Mr. Canning, Mr. Gallatin, in a communication to Lord Dudley, asked whether, if Congress complied with the recommendations which the President was prepared to make, the United States would be permitted to avail themselves of the Act of July 5th, 1825; and, in a conference with Mr. Huskisson, our Minister was evasively answered on this point, and told, moreover, that Great Britain considered the trade with her Colonies as exclusively under her own control, and that whatever terms might be granted to foreigners was a concession. Thus, then, after twelve years of negotiation, nothing whatever had been accomplished, save indeed, the official declaration just recorded, that any relaxation of the principles of the original "Navigation Act" of England, as related to her Colonies, was to be deemed a mere "boon." And yet, during these twelve years, the diplomats of both Governments had almost always conceded that the interests of all parties would be promoted by "Reciprocity." Thus stood the controversy at the beginning of the administration of President Jackson; for Mr. Barbour, in January, 1829, Minister at the Court of St. James, advised Mr. Van Buren, Secretary of State, that he was induced to believe that no change of policy in favor of the United States was meditated by his Majesty's advisers. Such, in truth, was the general opinion; but a change soon occurred.

Mr. McLane, who succeeded Mr. Barbour, in 1830, made an "Arrangement,"—known by his name—which took effect in October of that year, and which was undisturbed until 1854, when the existing "Reciprocity Treaty" was concluded. Embarrassed in the Department of State, Mr. Van Buren retired, and accepted the mission to England. As already remarked, the question of the Colonial Trade had been mingled with the politics of the time; and we may now add, that it helped to defeat President Adams. The friends of his successor, President Jackson, had, in a manner, pledged themselves to the country, to obtain speedy and satisfactory concessions. It was accordingly known that Mr. McLane had been specially directed to open negotiations with Lord Aberdeen; but it was not known until after Mr. Van Buren had gone abroad, that, in his instructions of July 20, 1829, he had used these remarkable words:—"*To set up the acts of the late administration*," he said, "*as the cause of forfeiture of privilege which would otherwise be extended to the people of the United States, would, under existing circumstances, be unjust in itself, and could not fail to excite their deepest sympathy*." Such a statement to a foreign power of "the relations of our domestic parties," was thought so very objectionable, that the Senate refused to confirm Mr. Van Buren as Minister to England. He returned a *martyr;* and, in due time became President. And it is possible that some yet live, who think that the utterance of the sentiment I have quoted—with such a result, was so extremely unfortunate, as to have had an adverse influence over our public affairs down to this very hour.

Such, rapidly drawn, are the outlines of the controversy relative to the Colonial Trade, which preceded the "McLane Arrangement." For nine years I was myself in and of that controversy. I was bred, Sir, on the Northeastern frontier, to evade the navigation laws of my country. The merchant with whom I served my apprenticeship, was the greatest ship owner within one hundred and fifty miles of the American side of the boundary, and to obtain the advantages of both Flags, some of his vessels wore the Cross of England, while others hoisted the Stars and Stripes of the Union. "Anything to make money," was the motto of everybody. Church members and deacons were smugglers. Ministers preached in smuggled clothes, and were paid in money earned in contraband trade. And, then, Sir, the *fun* of catching, and tarring and feathering an "informer," of which—for a young man—I had my full share.

Do the members of this Convention desire the return of this state of things along sixteen hundred miles of frontier? Abrogate the Reciprocity Treaty of 1854, and that wish will be surely gratified. Nay, more: put an end to that compact, and another long and angry dispute will certainly follow. I am to be told, perhaps, that the condition of the United States and of the Colonies are so changed that these predictions cannot be verified. To this I reply, that there has been no change in the nature of man; and that, the Proverbs of Solomon, though written two thousand years ago, are still of yesterday, to guide and admonish us.

Abrogate, Sir, and controversy inevitably ensues; and, legislation on both sides will become, possibly, quite as barbarous as at any previous period. And upon this point it is pertinent to remark that, on our part, we shall be compelled to deal not with the Imperial Parliament, as at first, but with the different Colonial Assemblies, and with each according to its own pleasure, and distinct power of annoyance. The Colonies, in truth, are now nearly independent of England. Lord Durham, who came out as Governor General of British America, during the Rebellion in Canada, made a Report of what he himself did, of what he intended to do, and of what should be done, for the Colonies; which, though stigmatized in Parliament and in the "Quarterly Review," as "a gospel of treason," has been adopted by her Majesty's advisers, in almost every essential particular; and, these bold and comprehensive reforms accomplished, the Colonists are nearly free. In a word, the policy indicated by Sir James Mackintosh, the philosopher and statesman, as far back as 1828, prevails, even to the extent of his own lofty sense of wisdom and justice.

Mr. President, full well do I know the hazard of prediction, but, at my age, and living as I am, with the fires of ambition utterly extinguished, I can well afford to the ill-natured the remark, that "what a man fortells, he wishes, in his pride of opinion, may be accomplished." I know, too, that "In the silence of retirement, nothing seems more melancholy than the spirit of the world." But, in my "retirement," I bear in my memory another long and bitter quarrel which the Treaty under consideration alone hushed, and as I have ventured to hope, until lately, forever terminated. I refer, Sir, to our rights to the fisheries in the British Colonial bays and seas. I stand here to speak the simple truth, even though truth is sometimes humiliating to us of the Union, who weary every foreign ear with constant boasts of our boundless resources in material wealth. We are so constituted as to seek, nay, to absolutely crave, variety in food. The human family, the world over, are fond of, indeed, need, the different kinds of sea and fresh water fish. The latter we can propagate to the extent of our wants, as is already done in France; but, the cod, the haddock, the hake, the halibut, the herring, and the mackerel, except for consumption when fresh, are not to be found in any of our waters. For these, and for other sea fish, we are, and from the peace of 1783, ever have been, dependant upon treaty stipulations. *In a word, Sir, the United States do not exercise sovereign jurisdiction over a single fishing ground in all America.* In the wars between England and France for the mastery of this hemisphere, which, with inconsiderable intervals lasted almost a century and a half, our fathers, in successive generations, and as Colonists, fought everywhere for the fisheries of Nova Scotia, of Newfoundland, and other British Possessions; and I claim that they, and they alone — those that belong to Canada excepted — annexed them to the Crown of England. But, as I have first said, we have no rights of ownership, and catch and cure the sea fish I have mentioned on terms defined by compact. Be it as some would have it, that our fisheries are no longer "nurseries of seamen," and that the "bounty" to our fishermen should cease. I may still appeal to every American citizen in this Convention to preserve our rights by Treaty, simply to continue a healthy variety in food. True, *we* of the East secure, pickle, or dry, or smoke the several sea luxuries of the table; but, are not *you* of the West as deeply concerned as we are in the preservation of this branch of industry, which, toilsome and perilous to *us*, gives *you* all its fruits in exchange for productions of the soil, without the perilling of life on stormy, uninhabited and inhospitable coasts? Some of *our* people — as we say in pleasantry — are born "web-footed," and seem to care nothing for the dangers and hardships of their calling. To such there is a charm in the Ocean itself, and in the casting of the line, the net and the seine, else, I cannot but think, thousands would long ago have abandoned the employment. Way back in the first Congress under the Constitution, the pure and gifted Fisher Ames, in pleading for these half amphibious men, said, "the fishermen of Massachusetts are too poor to go, too poor to stay." If the remark has lost its original force I have still to aver that I know of no class of American citizens, who, in a course of years are so poorly rewarded for their labors and their dangers, as those who search for "the wealth of seas."

Mr. President, the avocation of these hardly worked, poorly paid men, ever has been, now is, and always will be essentially national; and, in the most earnest tones, I ask for the influence of this Convention in their behalf, by a vote to recommend the appointment of a joint Commission. Bear with me, Sir, while I rapidly state my reasons. The Treaty once abrogated, our right of fishing in British Colonial waters would depend entirely on the unfortunate Convention of 1818, with the certainty of disputes, collisions, and probably of bloody contentions. On this point, the past is full of warning.

At the close of the war of 1812, our Government was firm in the opinion that the rights stipulated in 1783 remained entire. It was assumed in England and in the Colonies, however, that this principle was in contravention of public law, and claim was made to exclude our vessels from the fishing grounds, and even to seize them when found there. In accordance with the British view, his Majesty's ship *Jasseur*, in June, 1815, made prize of eight American vessels in a single day. This outrage, and the order that our fishermen should not come within sixty miles of the Colonial coast, caused a long negotiation, which terminated in the Convention of 1818, and which I again pronounce unfortunate. The capture of twelve other vessels followed. In 1819, Parliament passed an Act regulating the fisheries of Newfoundland, Labrador, and other possessions of the Crown, to meet the provisions of the Convention of the preceding year; but the Colonial authorities in due time took the ground that this Act excluded our flag from the great "bays." For four years, there was a degree of quiet and security; but, in 1823, the ship of war *Argus* (captured from us in the war of 1812) and the *Sparrow-hawk*, spread alarm among our fishermen employed in the Bay of Fundy, and elsewhere in the waters of New Brunswick and Nova Scotia; and though the *Charles*, of York, Maine, was the only prize, fifty other vessels were molested, and the voyages of several of them utterly ruined. A year later, Captain Hoare, of his Majesty's brig *Dotterel*, pursued a course which drove hundreds of our fishermen from the "bays" of the two Colonies just mentioned; and I myself saw, on more than one occasion, the arrival of sixty or seventy of these vessels at one port, on a single day. After the loss of a week's time, perhaps, the boldest of the masters ventured to go to sea; but the report that the vigilant Hoare had been seen in close proximity a day or two previously, caused a second flight to some harbor on the American side of the frontier, with another loss of time. In a word, the zeal of Captain Hoare "in guarding the coast from the intrusion of foreign fishermen and smugglers," gave rise to great excitement on the eastern border of Maine, which finally attracted the attention of Congress; when the United States schooner *Porpoise* was despatched to the Bay of Fundy, to protect the "craft" that wore our country's flag. So, too, subsequently, as the *Dotterel* continued to annoy our fishing vessels, the sloop-of-war *Lexington* was ordered to cruise in the interdicted "bays."

During these troubles, I, in common with hundreds of other persons, witnessed the re-capture of two of the "Dotterel's" prizes by a party of armed men; an affray which, in the correspondence that followed between a Charge d'Affaires and a Minister of England, on the one hand, and Mr. Adams and Mr. Clay, successively Secretaries of State, on the other, was deemed by the representatives of royalty "an outrage;" and one for which they required an "acknowledgment." A period of quiet followed. Early in 1836, however, Mr.

Bankhead, the British Charge d'Affaires, at the instance of the Colonial authorities, called the attention of Mr. Forsyth, Secretary of State, to "*repeated* acts of irregularity, committed by fishermen of the United States;" but, strangely enough, the papers which accompanied his note specified a *single* encroachment only, namely, that of the schooner "Bethel," of Provincetown, Massachusetts. In less than three months, Nova Scotia passed an Act of extreme, and in some of its provisions, of inexcusible severity; and, in 1837, an elaborate Report was made to the Assembly of that Colony, in which it was proposed to maintain their pretensions by the employment of steamers on the part of England, and of a preventive force on the part of her Dependencies. The latter recommendation was adopted. And Nova Scotia, not content with this, transmitted an Address to the Queen, in 1838, complaining of the habitual violation of the Convention of 1818 by our countrymen; and praying for a naval force to put an end to the alleged aggressions. The appeal was successful, for Lord Glenelg, Secretary for the Colonies, announced that during the fishing season, ships of war would be stationed on the coast, "to enforce a more strict observance of the provisions of the treaty by American citizens."

The early part of 1841 is fruitful of events which show the progress of the controversy, and the development of Colonial plans and pretensions. On the 20th of February, Mr. Forsyth, Secretary of State, addressed Mr. Stevenson, our Minister at London, a letter of definitive instructions, in which he reviewed the points in dispute, and stated that he was directed by the President to convey his desire that a representation should be made to her Majesty's Government, immediately on receipt of the despatch, earnestly remonstrating "against the illegal and vexatious proceedings of the authorities of Nova Scotia towards our fishermen;" and requesting of the Ministry, "that measures be forthwith adopted" to remedy the evils arising "from the course of the Colony, and to prevent the possibility of the occurrence of similar acts." Mr. Stevenson's attention to his instructions was prompt; but we must omit all mention of his communication to Lord Palmerston; and my limits compel me to omit, also, several incidents necessary to a full understanding of the gravity of the case at that time.

I renew my narrative, however, at the moment when Mr. Everett appeared as the Envoy of our country at the Court of St. James. Seemingly, such were the complications at this juncture, that the "Fishery Question," hardly admitted of solution. The hostile action of Nova Scotia had been continued; Lord Falkland, the Governor, had transmitted several documents to the Ministry, and among them a paper containing "Seven Queries"—so called, subsequently—for an opinion by the great law officers of the Crown; which, if answered affirmatively, would not only drive our Flag from the "bays," but deny it the shelter which, in peace, is allowed by one civilized power to another, all over the world. These "Queries" were considered with commendable promptness; but fifteen months elapsed before Lord Stanley acquainted Lord Falkland with the result. To the amazement of well informed persons in the United States, the legal advisers of the British Crown decided that our fishermen, under the Convention of 1818, must keep three miles from the shore, and that this distance should "be measured from the headlands or extreme points of land next to the sea of the coast, or of the entrance of the bays." By this decision, as will be seen, the only fishing grounds which could be used by American vessels were those of the open Ocean. Rapidly enough did the Colonists avail themselves of this remarkable judgment of the Queen's Advocate, and of the Attorney General of England. The schooner "Washington," of Newburyport, Massachusetts, was seized while "fishing broad," in the Bay of Fundy, in consequence; and, in June, 1843, Mr. Upsher, Secretary of State, in a despatch to Mr. Everett, spoke of the "obvious necessity" which existed, "to put an end to proceedings on the part of the British Colonial authorities, alike conflicting with their conventional obligations, and ruinous to the fortunes and subversive of the rights of an enterprising and deserving class of our fellow-citizens."

Of the occurrences between the years 1846 and 1851, I need mention only the capture and total loss of several American fishing vessels, and of four annual reports to the Assembly of Nova Scotia, on the question of depriving our countrymen of the use of the Strait of Canso, and thus compelling them to make the long and dangerous passage around Cape Breton, an island so large as to have been a colony of France, and, for a considerable time, of England. And yet, the controversy was then fast approaching a crisis.

On the 19th of July, 1852, Mr. Webster, Secretary of State, made the startling declaration that vessels of war of her Majesty were expected to arrive upon the coasts of British America during that month, "when," he said, "no doubt seizures will begin to be made;" that the "Coral," of Machias, Maine, had already been captured by the cutter "Nettle;" that Canada had fitted an armed vessel, to be stationed in the Gulf; that Nova Scotia had four cruisers in commission, "ready to pounce upon any American vessels who may accidentally, or otherwise, be found fishing within limits defined by the Crown officers of England;" that New Brunswick had agreed to place a cutter in the Bay of Fundy; and that the steam frigate "Devastation" had been ordered to act under the instructions of the Governor of Prince Edward Island. This official statement attracted immediate and universal attention, and by opponents of the Administration was severely criticized. On the 23d of July, Mr. Mason, Chairman of the Committee on Foreign Relations, offered a resolution in the Senate — which was agreed to unanimously — requesting the President to communicate all the correspondence touching the fisheries since the Convention of 1818, and wishing to be informed whether any of the naval forces of the United States had been ordered to the seas adjacent to the British possessions. The debate which preceded the passage of this resolution was highly animated. The newspapers discussed the condition of affairs with warmth, and the whole country soon became excited. On the fishing grounds, apprehension and threats of combination to capture the "Devastation" by boarding continued throughout the season. The fact that the two Governments were negotiating the "Reciprocity Treaty" had a sensible influence upon our fishermen, and probably prevented collisions and the loss of life.

Such is an outline of the controversy relative to our right to the fisheries of British America, which, beginning in 1815, lasted thirty-nine years, and until 1854. Members of Congress who favor the abrogation of the Treaty, dwell on the fact that, during this long period, few vessels were captured and condemned. True, the number of seizures was not large; but we have shown that the interruptions were many and serious. For twenty-eight years, I was a constant observer of, and often a party to, the troubles here related, and therefore speak from personal knowledge of the losses incurred. The fishing months are few; and year after year hundreds of vessels were driven from the fishing grounds, and were detained in ports of refuge by fog and storm, so frequently as to lose nearly one-fourth of the season. The aggregate loss in these thirty-nine years may be estimated by millions.

Abrogate the Reciprocity Treaty of 1854, and the "headland" construction of the Convention of 1818, which I not only again pronounce unfortunate, but deliberately denounce as the greatest blunder in the whole diplomatic history of our country; abrogate that Treaty, Sir, and the "headland" construction will be revived, and insisted upon, in a moment. And I pray, in all soberness, to ask what we of the United States can say or do in the premises? As I have already remarked, the Crown lawyers of England have passed in judgment upon the case; her Majesty's Government have adopted their opinion, and our Government must submit to it, or appeal to force. The question of "free fishing" in the seas of America is almost as old as Protestant civilization in this hemisphere; and yet, strangely enough, our flag, in the lapse of a few months, as matters now stand, will disappear in all the "Bays" of the British possessions, and be seen only on the open Ocean. I warn the country, on this floor, of right, and in duty. The late lamented President of the United States, without a word of solicitation on my part, was pleased to appoint me Commissioner of the Fisheries, in the expectation that her Britannic Majesty and the Emperor of France would join; and that thus representatives of the three countries would endeavor to come to a good understanding upon several points of difference, which, at any hour, *may* disturb the common peace. Nothing whatever has been done, for the reason that neither power has accepted our overture for a joint commission. I forbear a word of comment.

Mr. President: Young men will call me an alarmist. Be it so. The first treaty of commerce and navigation between the United States and Great Britain was concluded on the 19th of November, 1794, and bears the signatures of John Jay, and the Earl of Grenville. Here, except with merchants, it was so unpopular, that Washington himself was assailed in terms of bitter reproach and unconditional malignity. His decision to send that instrument to the Senate, was one of the greatest and most patriotic acts of his life. Its ratification sheathed the scalping knife, and gave the first impulse to the growth of the West. There had been eleven years of nominal peace; but, we had never been in possession of the country bordering on the Lakes, and the very city in which we are now assembled, had continued a British post. On the question of an appropriation of money to carry that Treaty into effect, Fisher Ames, in one of the most eloquent speeches ever delivered in the House of Representatives, uttered words which seem to me somewhat applicable at the present hour. "The consequences of refusing to make provision for the Treaty," said he, "are not to be foreseen. By rejecting, vast interests are committed to the sport of the winds. Chance becomes the arbiter of events, and it is forbidden to human foresight to count their number or measure their extent. Before we resolve to leap into this abyss, so dark and so profound, it becomes us to pause upon such of the dangers as are obvious and inevitable."

Sir, "the consequences of refusing" to negotiate for the continuance of the *last* Commercial Treaty with Great Britain, in my judgment, "are not to be foreseen." I regret to believe that the only constant agents in political affairs, are the passions of men; regret to declare my conviction that passion exists in this very case, and eagerly waits for the termination of Reciprocity. It is the malady of the public mind in times of civil confusion, to prefer charges of hostility and conspiracy against a whole people, because of the declarations or the acts of a few. Men whom "no King can govern, and no God can please," write and speak in favor of strife, in all free countries; and, animated by the spirit of revenge, will not be quieted by the possibility of profit, commercial or otherwise. To such, discord is heaven, and slaughter, a desirable sport; and inconsiderable difficulties between nations, a cause of war. Had I no other reason, I would negotiate, simply to disappoint the miscreants of England, of the Colonies and of my own country.

But, in the matter before us, the *principle* of Reciprocity is to be advocated on its own intrinsic merits. The policy of prohibition, from the restoration of the Stuarts down to the dismemberment of the British Empire — and the immediate political cause of it; prohibition and non-intercourse from 1783 to the "McLane Arrangement," in 1830, are enough for me, I confess. If insufficient for others — look at Spain, the most melancholy example of fallen greatness in modern times — Spain, poor, distracted, miserable; and why? Because the only free traders are the smugglers, and the smugglers' dogs. "I freely admit," said Burke, "to the East Company their claim to exclude their fellow-subjects from the commerce of half the world." We all honor the memory of that great man; but what of such a declaration from a statesman now? On the question of human progress, of commercial freedom, as presented to this Convention, reasoning — I had almost said — is folly; for the brain in vain essays to state the premises or the conclusions; the argument is in the pleader's pulse, and in his heart. As concerns our trade with British America, I hold this distinct proposition that we should deal with the Colonists precisely as we do with one another. I well understand that, at times, and owing to particular and transient causes, the pendulum of traffic will have an irregular swing — if I may use the figure — but, what then? Is it not precisely so among ourselves? Recall the recent price of cotton, tobacco, and other staples of the South, as an illustration. The case, to me, is too humane, too Christian, *as relates to consumers*, for logic; and is to be determined only in the affections. And yet, addressing myself to the American merchants of this Convention, I ask, in all sincerity, why each one of you have not the same, precisely the same interest — both personal and national — in the prosperity of Toronto, Montreal, Quebec, St. John, and Halifax, and in every other City in the Colonies, and in every branch of Colonial industry, as you have in the ability to pay, and in the increasing wealth of your individual customers? I know the *politician's* answer, for I have heard it often. Can you, *as merchants*, reply that there is any difference in principle, or, "in the long run," in results, in dealing with persons of the two flags? If not, then, the problem is solved by the laws of trade alone.

In conversations with gentlemen of different parts of the country, I have found a general assent to Reciprocity, as a *proposition;* but, frequent dissent from it, in *operation*, and as touching the personal or sectional purse. Thus, Vermont, though a buyer of Canadian flour, objects to competition with Canadian wool and butter. Maine, with the same keen economic eye to cheap bread, stands fast for her timber lands, as sufficient, without interference from New Brunswick and Canada. And so, too, you gentlemen of the West, peering across the Lakes, insinuate — much as Yankees do — and some even "guess," thus betraying your origin — that Illinois, Wisconsin, and the rest, can feed the whole family of Jonathan, without any help from "rebel sympathizers," specially, or, the children of John, generally. All this in gentle tones. The outright grumblers are in Massachusetts and New Hampshire. You need not, however, heed the mutterings of the mother of the North, for, every body has heard that, she is never perfectly happy, except when she is utterly miserable. Yet, I must tell you that she, and the Granite Hills, scold about Reciprocity, because the spindles and looms of Lowell, of Lawrence, Nashua, Manchester, and Dover, are not allowed to move for the Colonists more freely.

In this condition of things, it is wise for all to remember, what, in advocating the particular productions of our respective sections of country, we sometimes forget, namely, *that we are both producers and consumers, and that, we gain as eaters and wearers, much in the ratio of our losses as sellers.* In the words of the old saw, none of us "can have our cake and eat it, too," so let us make the best of everything, and continue our interchange of commodities. The old Bay State, forgetful of her own short-comings, will scold others by day and "caudle" others by night, and so, ye men of the West, close your ears; but give us cheap food, in order that we may pay you in cheap clothing, and our many "notions"; always allowing, however, that we leave to Connecticut the fame of making, vending and warranting the modern time-piece, and the wooden spice. But enough of playfulness. Merchants, some members of Congress, mourn the disadvantages of Reciprocity; but, cannot you respond with me, in the sentiment of Sir James Mackintosh, that, "Happy is that people whose commerce flourishes in the ledger, while it is bewailed in orations; and remains untouched in calculations, while it expires in pictures of eloquence." And here, I must be permitted to say, that I am amazed to hear from Mr. Morrill, of Vermont, the declaration in a speech which, under his own *frank*, has been very extensively circulated, that, "By the treaty, the ancient laws of trade have been subverted," and that, especially, our Canadian neighbors "*sell to us, but go elsewhere to buy.*" I repeat, that I am amazed. On what authority does he make this extraordinary statement? The late Secretary of the Treasury, in a communication which was referred to the Committee on Commerce, February 1, 1864, informed the country that during the ten years ending in 1863, our exports to Canada amounted (in whole numbers) to $170,635,000; and that our imports from that Colony for the same period were of the value of $152,051,000; or that our sales exceeded our purchases in the sum of $18,584,000. With these figures what becomes of the assertion that the Canadians "sell to us, but go elsewhere to buy?" The truth is, that, under "Reciprocity," and until the late rebellion, Canada *bought more of the United States than of all of the rest of the world besides!* As thus: total imports from every country from 1855 to 1860, (both years inclusive,) $215,982,776, of which $114,259,345 were from *our* ports; *showing a balance in our favor against all other nations, in these six years, of $12,535,914, or of more than two millions of dollars, annually.*

While I respect, as much as I should do, the utterances of public men at Washington, I prefer, in matters of trade, as the wise Mackintosh did, to make an appeal to the counting-room, to the "leger," and to the members of this Convention.

Mr. President, I have purposely refrained from expressing any opinion whatever relative to the provisions of the existing treaty. I advocate on this floor the *principle* of Reciprocity and negotiation. *If a joint commission cannot agree, we have abrogation as the last resort. I plead, here, simply for negotiation.* No matter for the changes since 1854—they are all in my mind. I deem it fit, as concerns myself, individually, and as one of the delegates of the Boston Board of Trade, to stand to-day for the appointment of Commissioners, and for that alone. Merchants do not possess the influence which belongs to them in the councils of the nation. Too many, like John Randolph, sneer at "counting-house administrations." I have the courage to say, that, if there was a little more of the "counting-house"—a little more practical knowledge of commercial affairs, in Congress, the country would not suffer in consequence. Our Chambers of Commerce, and our Boards of Trade, are merely recommendatory.

I have occupied far more time than I intended to do, and should now take my seat. If, however, I may be allowed to proceed, I desire to say a few words more on the topic of the little share which we "middle men," as political economists call us—we who stand between the producer and the consumer—have in legislation. My reflections have convinced me that there is but a single remedy—namely, a National Board, with a President, a member of the Cabinet, as in England.

I do not accuse the Government of the United States of willful neglect of the commercial interests of the country; but, with all deference, I do say, that as now constituted, the Treasury Department cannot devote to these interests either the time or the attention which they imperatively demand. We commenced our career as a nation with half the ports of Europe shut against our unknown flag, with but two hundred thousand tons of navigation, and with exports of only twenty millions of dollars; and the care of our commerce, rapid as was its growth, was an easy duty until after the lapse of a generation. But now, when we own millions of tons of shipping, and, in peace, send off annually surplus products of the soil, the sea, and of the shop and the mill, worth two hundred and fifty millions of dollars; when our territories and population, and means of transportation inland, have multiplied in the ratio of ships and exports; I may venture to remark, that the fiscal operations of that Department, in which there has been a corresponding increase, require the attention of its officers, without any concern whatever in navigation and trade, save in matters of revenue; and that of consequence it has become the duty of our statesmen to form another Department, which shall relieve the Treasury, and possess, as closely as the nature of our institutions will allow, the powers of the Board of Trade of England. And, in the most respectful tone, I will add, that the merchants and ship owners of the United States have a right to ask that the Government assume and bear much of the labor and expense which, under existing circumstances, local Chambers of Commerce and Boards of Trade are obliged to incur in order to be useful in their respective sections of country; and for the very conclusive reason, that many of the questions which these Associations are required to entertain are, either incidentally or directly, national in their character. It is not just, I think, that merchants, who are borne down by the cares of private business, should be compelled, as they are, to devote the time which they need for rest or recreation, to concerns which, though of interest to them professionally, affect still more the humanity of the age, and the commerce of the world.

But while I suggest a new Department in the Government, with the powers indicated, I would not dispense with local Chambers and Boards, since these and similar Associations are necessary to ascertain and remove evils in trade with which a National Board could hardly be expected to interfere: necessary, to devise ways for safe, speedy, and cheap transportation inland, to produce uniformity in commercial customs and charges of factorage, and to form and to concentrate commercial opinion. Nay more: just one-quarter part of the signers of the Declaration of Independence, as I have once remarked, were bred merchants or ship-masters, and men of these classes, retained in Congress after the adoption of the Constitution, helped materially to shape the policy of the country; but as neither are hardly represented in the public councils now, the abolition of these Chambers and Boards would deprive us of our principal remaining power in legislation. For this reason alone, then, I would not only maintain existing organizations, under whatever name, but would earnestly recommend the formation of others.

Finally: merchants, I repeat, are entitled to greater influence in the councils of the country. Sir, the noble Burke did us justice. "I have known merchants," he said, "with the abilities of great statesmen; and I have seen persons in the rank of statesmen, with the conceptions and characters of peddlers."

Mr. D. L. Seymour, of New York, said:

I regret that this important question—second to no other in its business relations between our country and the people on the other side of the Lakes — should have come up for the consideration of this Convention at this hour, so near the time when we are invited by the hospitable people of Detroit to participate in an excursion upon their beautiful river. I consider this question of the utmost importance to the people of this country in every point of view, and I beg the indulgence of the Convention for a few moments, while I give my views upon it. I may not be able to compress into the limited time allowed, the remarks which ought to have been made by others, but I shall endeavor to compress them into a very little space. In the first place I wish to call the attention of this Convention to what was the original scope of that which was known as the Reciprocity measure or Treaty, and I trust I may be permitted to say here, without arrogating to myself anything improper, that I know something about that Treaty. Now, Sir, it has been supposed very generally, by the people of this country, and I have no doubt some gentlemen here may have looked upon it in the same light, the measure only extended to the interchange of commodities between the British Provinces of North America, and the United States. That is a very small part of it. Let me call the attention of this Convention to the circumstances that existed at the era of the Reciprocity Treaty in 1853. At that time there were various questions agitating our country as well as the people of the Provinces, and one of them was the fishery question. We all know that it has been regarded as a very important question by the United States. There has not been a Treaty made between this country and Great Britain from 1783, at which time the independence of the Union was conceded, to this Reciprocity Treaty in 1854, which has not referred to or embraced within its proposition something in reference to the fishery question. These fisheries have yielded a revenue of millions of dollars to the United States. They have always been considered as of the highest national importance, and more than once the people of the United States have recommended to Congress the encouragement of these interests, upon the ground that they were the best nurseries for seamen that we could have. We have tried the experiment, and we have found that in this great emergency, when we were called upon to man and equip large fleets, they answered that purpose. We have known the results, and we are deeply indebted to those hardy mariners who had as their daily employment and their means of education a life spent in this seafaring business.

Now, Sir, at the period this Treaty was formed, there were important questions being agitated on the other side. A Convention had been made between Great Britain and the United States in 1818, and in that Convention it was declared that American fishermen should not be permitted to fish upon the coasts of British North America, within three miles of the coast. The question of what should be the proper construction of that language was very much agitated in this country and Great Britain. The diplomatists on both sides had the matter in charge; lawyers—the ablest in the realm—and it was referred to them by the Crown—gave a construction which the British Government afterwards insisted upon, that the language of that Treaty restricted us to a line three miles outside of the extreme limits of the land—that the three miles should be measured from the extreme point of projection. The result of it was, that the American fishermen were excluded from all the large bays and harbors, and in a few years this important interest declined, and it became known to the people of the United States and to many of our most eminent statesmen—among whom I may name Seward, Everett and Daniel Webster, that these restrictions cut off the American fishing interests from the harbors and bays, and deep indentions of the coast. Here, then, were important questions between the two Governments, and for a few years, each side maintained its own view of the Treaty, and by-and-by, we found how imminent was the danger of hostilities between us, and if you will refer to the history of 1853, you will find that both parties went out to their fishing grounds in these vessels, each armed to defend itself against the other. The British Government sent out ships of war to protect their fishermen, and the American Government, in imitation, and as a matter of duty, sent out ships of war to protect its fishermen, and the spectacle was witnessed of a fleet of fishermen with a squadron of ships of war on each side of them for protection.

Hon. Israel T. Hatch, of Buffalo, said:

Reciprocal trade with the Canadas and other North American British Provinces has received the sanction of the leading statesmen of all former political parties in this country.

The territory of the Provinces is extended on a boundary indented with our own across the continent. Climate, soil, and the cost of labor—the main elements of value in cereal productions—are nearly alike in both countries. These similitudes, no doubt, suggested the idea of reciprocal trade and commerce, and the discussion, legislation, and diplomacy of the country finally gave it a practical application in the adoption of the so-called Reciprocity Treaty. The principle of the Treaty itself was to permit the interchange of products between the countries, free of duty; and equivalent benefits were expected to follow to each. It was a formal movement in substantial Free Trade. The belief entertained by an American Congress that its spirit and its substance had been disregarded by the leading British Provinces, no doubt, led to its abrogation by the last Congress, and the refusal to authorize any negotiations for its renewal. The Treaty expires in a few months, under the notice given by the

President for its termination, and our commercial intercourse with British Provinces, so far as the Reciprocity Treaty affected or changed it, is again open for discussion and legislation or diplomacy.

A brief reference to the history of our commercial relations with the North American British Provinces, and a review of the leading features of the statistics of trade with them for the last eight years, furnish the only safe guides to conclusions which should govern the action of this Convention. The examination will disclose grievances, if any exist; and mutual explanations, made in a fraternal spirit, may lead to the removal of the cause, and the restoration of those free commercial relations, (so soon to terminate,) upon a more enduring basis.

The commerce between the United States and the British Provinces, reviewed from the central point, upon the chain of our most magnificent inland seas, where this Convention now sits, now reveals to us the anomalous spectacle of two border nations with an array of custom-houses extending along their whole conterminous frontiers, sustained at an expense to this Government, heretofore exceeding the revenue they collect, whose principal occupation is to enter and register the free products of Canada on their way to our free markets; while on the opposite shore, often separated from us only by a bridge, a ferry, or a boundary line, is found an equally extended cordon of Imperial customs buildings, collecting large revenues on our taxed products, as a tribute which the unfriendly legislation of Provincial Parliaments has exacted from us in exchange for the commercial freedom we have granted to the Canadas. These exactions have been justified on the ground that no special provision against them was inserted in the Treaty, although its avowed object was to carry out the principle of Reciprocity, and "especially to regulate the commerce and navigation between her Majesty's possessions in North America and the United States, in such manner as to render the same reciprocally beneficial and satisfactory."

Official Canadian reports show that in 1859 the amount of duties collected by the Canadas on imports from the United States, was, in 1859, \$1,825,135; in 1860, \$1,759,928; and in 1861, \$1,584,892. During these three years the whole value of property imported into this country from the Canadas, upon which duty was levied, was only, in 1859, \$434,532; in 1860, \$358,240; and in 1861, \$227,859. The average amount of duty annually levied and collected on these imports, in these three years, would probably not exceed \$75,000.

The average annual value of property entering Canada, from the United States, in the eight years preceding 1863, upon which duties have been imposed, is \$8,401,481, while Canadian goods entering the United States during the same period only paid duty on an annual average value of $467,238. It will thus be seen that duty is paid on goods of the United States entering Canada to the average annual excess in value, over those of Canada entering this country, of $7,934,241.

The value of free goods imported into Canada from the United States, for the last eight years, has been $73,215,623. The export of free goods from the Canadas into the United States for the same period has been $115,548,880. The result has been the exoneration from duty of goods imported from Canada to the value of $42,333,-257 more than the value of the goods imported from the United States into Canada in the eight years which have been referred to.

On closer examination it will be seen that a large proportion of the duty paying articles imported from Canada consist of commodities not produced in that country. In 1858, the dutiable importations from Canada were only $313,953, of which iron, hardware and salt, (articles not produced in Canada for exportation, in any appreciable quantities,) alone furnished $193,595. Of the remainder a considerable portion was also of foreign origin. As the same reasoning applies also to other years, the following tabular statement for the term of four years, ending June 30, 1859, is added:

	1856.	1857.	1858.	1859.
Total amount of duty paying articles imported into the United States from Canada.......	$640,375	$691,097	$313,953	$504,969
Iron, Hardware and Salt......................	503,995	531,011	193,595	319,555
Amount of Canadian and other goods charged with duties in the United States..........	$136,370	$160,086	$119,358	$184,414

This statement demonstrates, that during these years we have not collected, annually, duties on much more than $100,000 in value of merchandise, actually produced in Canada, which, contributing an average duty of 20 per cent., produces only $25,000 towards defraying the immense yearly expense incident to our custom-house system, along a frontier of inland coast 6,000 miles in extent.

The Canadian duties have been increased from time to time since the adoption of the Reciprocity Treaty; and during the five years commencing in 1855 and ending in 1859, duties were exacted on the declared value of chief articles of consumption, as exhibited in the following table:

VALUE OF CHIEF ARTICLES OF CONSUMPTION.

ARTICLES.	1855. Per Cent.	1856. Per Cent.	1857. Per Cent.	1858. Per Cent.	1859. Per Cent.
Molasses	16	11	11	18	30
Sugar, refined	32	28	25	26½	40
Sugar, other	27½	20	17½	21	30
Boots and Shoes	12½	14½	20	21	25
Harness	12½	17	20	21	25
Cotton Goods	12½	13½	15	15	20
Iron Goods	12½	18½	15	16	20
Silk Goods	12½	13½	15	17	20
Wool Goods	12½	14	15	18	20

Almost every year a new tariff has been enacted in Canada, each inflicting higher duties upon the chief productions of American labor.

The tariff of 1859 was avowedly based upon an exclusive policy. It was supported on this ground alike by ministerial organs of the press, by petitions in its favor, and by members of the Colonial Parliament. After securing our free market for all Canadian productions, its advocates argued that it was the interest of Canadians to become independent of all other countries, and to employ their own ships and their own people; thus, to employ their own language, "keeping in the country all that is now paid the United States."

No justification for the annual increase in these rates can be found in the assertion that the then present rates did not exceed our own. When the Treaty was ratified our tariff exceeded theirs, and the consideration given to them was not an equality of tariffs, but an interchange of the produce of both countries, and certain privileges in navigation. A liberal policy towards our manufactures was promised and had been before adopted; and thus the commerce and navigation of the two countries, it was expected, would be placed on "terms reciprocally beneficial and satisfactory." Justice to our people demanded that future Canadian legislation should conform to the letter and spirit of the Treaty.

Certainly the spirit of the Treaty has not been thus observed, and the increase of Canadian duties has not only affected our trade and commerce injuriously, but the manner in which they were levied has increased the burden, and now operates as a system of differential duties against us.

Canada now endeavors to deprive us of all the benefits of reciprocal trade by levying duties on the value of goods at the place of purchase. The people of Western Canada were accustomed to buy their wines, spirits, groceries, and East and West India produce, besides many other commodities, at New York, Boston, or Montreal. The former system admitted American Cities to competition — the duties having been specified and levied on the weight, measure or number of articles wherever they were purchased. Thus no greater duty was charged on imports *via* Boston or New York to Toronto or Hamilton, than *via* the St. Lawrence to Montreal. The present system forces the people of Canada to discontinue their business connections with our merchants, and buy from the Montreal or Quebec importer. Thus the productions of China, Brazil, or Cuba, if brought to Canada *via* the St. Lawrence, pay duty on their value in the country of their origin, but if purchased in our Atlantic Cities, must pay duty on that value increased by interest, freight over the Ocean, and the various other expenses and charges of the insurer, shipper and merchant. This is not only legislation against our carriers, but against all our mercantile interests. The "increase of duty" has been carefully estimated to be 20 per cent. on goods imported into the United States and thence into Canada, in excess of the duties levied upon goods carried *via* Montreal. The distance from Cuba to Toronto *via* the St. Lawrence, (a river closed half the year,) is about three times as great as through the United States. Thus Canada vainly strives to conquer the laws of arithmetic, climate and geography.

The Committee appointed by the Canadian Legislative Assembly in 1855, unhesitatingly affirm in their report, (*page* 3,) that the St. Lawrence Canals were constructed at a large public expenditure, for the purpose of drawing the trade of the Western States to the ports of Montreal and Quebec.

The people of the United States are entitled, under the Treaty, to use the river St. Lawrence and the Canals in Canada, as the "means of communicating between the Great Lakes and the Atlantic Ocean, subject only to the same tolls and other assessments as now are, or may hereafter be exacted of her Majesty's subjects." (*See Article IV. of Treaty.*)

But as we are the chief carriers through the Welland Canal of wheat, flour and corn — almost the only freight of our vessels by this route — a discrimination against us is made by imposing the same tolls on these articles on their passage through the Canal, (a work twenty-eight miles in length, and forming the only means of communication for lake vessels between the upper and lower lakes,) as if they passed through the Canadian Canals. Yet we carry twenty-five tons on the Welland Canal for every single ton we carry on the others. If the cargo is not delivered to an American port, but delivered to a Canadian port, the shipper, upon the presentation of an official certificate of the latter fact to the Custom House Officer at Port Colborne, receives a drawback of 90 per cent. upon the tolls paid upon his cargo.

Exports of American goods to Canada show a marked decline during these eight years, falling from $6,790,333 in 1854, and $8,759,000 in 1855, to $1,560,397 in 1862, and $1,468,113 in 1863. It is thus demonstrated that the Canadian supply of foreign goods is no longer purchased in the importing cities of the United States as before the Treaty. The statistics of bonded goods entering Canada confirm this proof, and establish the fact that the foreign supplies of the Colonies are principally passed through Portland.

Although no duties avowedly discriminating are levied on American goods, the influence of the provincial tariff produces the same effect, for the manufactures most readily adopted by Canada must be like our own. The climate, price of materials, interest on money, wages of labor, and various causes, determining the kind and prices of manufactures on both sides of the frontier, are nearly identical, when no legislation intervenes to arrest or alter the laws of trade.

If these views in relation to the injurious effects caused by the changes in levying duties upon our trade and commerce needed confirmation, it can be found in the arguments and expectations of the authors of those changes.

Mr. Galt, Finance Minister of Canada, in his report of March 1, 1860, at page 36, states as follows:

"By extending the *ad valorem* principle to all importations, and thereby encouraging and developing the direct trade between Canada and all foreign countries by sea, and so far benefiting *the shipping interests of Great Britain* — an object which is partly attained through the duties being taken upon the value in the market where last bought — the levy of specific duties for several years had completely diverted the trade of Canada in teas, sugars, etc., to the American markets, (our Atlantic Cities,) and had destroyed a very valuable trade which formerly existed from the St. Lawrence to the Lower Provinces and West Indies. It was believed that the competition of our canals and railroad systems, (*via* Portland,) together with the improvements in the navigation of the Lower St. Lawrence, justified the belief that the supply of Canadian wants might be once more made by sea, and the benefits of this commerce obtained for our own merchants and forwarders. Under this conviction, it was determined by the Government to apply the principles of *ad valorem* duties."

At page 38 he adds:

"Any increase of duty which has been placed on English goods is quite indemnified by the decreased costs at which our canals, railways, and steamships enable them now to be delivered throughout the Province, and that if the question were one of competition with Canadian manufacturers, the *English exporter* is quite as well off as before, while, as compared with the *American*, his position is greatly improved."

The history of the increase of taxation on American manufactures will disclose the fact, (as is asserted by the organs of the Government,) that the increase was made necessary by Canadian expenditure in carrying out their system of internal improvements. That a large amount has been thus expended is shown by the following quotation from the Report of the Select Committee appointed in 1858, by the Legislative Assembly of Canada, to inquire into the course of trade between the different Atlantic ports in America and Great Britain, etc., (*page* 3):

"The public debt of Canada has increased from year to year to about fifty millions of dollars, twenty-five millions of which have been created since 1853, principally in the construction of railways yielding no income." (*See Public Accounts*, 1857, *p.* 223.)

Mr. Galt, in a report issued by him in England in support of a Canadian ministerial scheme, admits the insufficiency of the commerce of Canada to support her public works, and expressly states that, whilst possessing the most magnificent canals in the world, she is "*without any trade to support them*, except her own," and adding that the canals of Canada have failed to divert trade from the channels it had already formed; a system of railroads had also been constructed for the purpose of competing with American interests.—(*See Report entitled* "*Canada*, 1849 *to* 1859, *by Hon. A. T. Galt, Finance Minister of Canada*, 1860.") He then proceeds to state that, after deducting a sinking fund for the redemption of the Imperial guaranteed loan, the direct public debt of the Province amounts to £8,884,672, or $43,001,812; adding, that of this sum, debts incurred in consequence of the canals and other works connected with the navigation of the St. Lawrence, and railway advances, furnish £8,861,400, leaving only £22,272, or $107,796, as the total direct debt of Canada made for any other purpose. These large Canadian expenditures in the construction of railroads and ship canals, were not made for their local traffic, as will be seen from ministerial statements, but to compete with our carrying systems in the transportation of property from the West to the Seaboard.

To close these canals to our vessels would not only be an act of folly on the part of Canada, but would be contrary to the objects of their creation. The State of New York might with more wisdom close the Erie Canal against the commerce of the Western States. That canal passes through the central portion of a State possessing a much larger population than Canada, and from thence derives immense local traffic for its support, while the canals of Canada are lateral, and depend almost entirely upon the commerce of the United States.

Of nearly all the articles named in the Treaty, a surplus is common to both countries; and we have an abundant supply, and a surplus for export, of every article named in it.

Canada has no crop so cheap and profitable for various manufacturing and other purposes as the corn bought from us, which was admitted free before the Treaty. Wheat, the staple crop and chief export of Canada, was also admitted free before the Treaty, for the benefit of Canadian millers and ship-owners.

For other grains, barley, rye, oats, animals, etc., we furnished for Canada the only market worthy of mention.

The Western States had from an early day looked upon the free navigation of the St. Lawrence as affording a natural and cheap outlet for their products, and believed that benefits arising from the concession of this national privilege, would more than counterbalance any incidental injuries to other interests.

Sir H. L. Bulwer, a former British Minister to this country, after pressing upon our attention the spirit evinced by Canada towards our manufacturers, and promising on behalf of the Canadian Government to carry a liberal policy out still further, presented the free navigation of the St. Lawrence, with the adjoining Canals, as the consideration to be paid by that Province for the free interchange of all natural productions with us, and for the navigation of Lake Michigan. The provisions of the Reciprocity Treaty were comprehensive, and included a satisfactory solution of the perplexities then existing in regard to all the commercial relations between this country and the Provinces.

Official reports upon our foreign and domestic commerce give us the number of clearances from Western ports to Foreign ports for the last eight years, forty-four, and the number of entrances thirty-two. In 1863 only one vessel cleared and entered, so that the concession of the free navigation of the St. Lawrence practically has proved not worthy of consideration. The co-operating efforts of the two Governments have been unavailing in making it an outward channel to the Ocean in preference to the canals, lakes and railroads of the United States.

To contrast the privileges the United States had hoped to gain in exchanging the free navigation of Lake Michigan for the free navigation of the St. Lawrence, with the substantial advantages derived from our concessions in this particular, it is only necessary to state the shipments from one port on Lake Michigan, Chicago, to Canadian ports in 1862.

The shipments from Chicago for 1862 to Canadian ports were: Flour, 420,544 barrels; wheat, 3,098,424 bushels; corn, 6,005,661 bushels; oats, 187,252 bushels; rye, 200,659 bushels; barley, 71,919 bushels; reaching, in estimated amount, about one quarter of the total export of these commodities to Canada from Lake Michigan.

The aid of foreign and rival lines of transportation, entering within our territory, no doubt has cheapened freights, but it well may be questioned whether the loss to our carriers has inured to the advantage of the American producer. The value of the crop at home is actually established in its ultimate market, and the added supply derived from Canadian production must most materially decrease prices.

Our intercourse with Canada has been characterized upon our

part by an amount of liberality and forbearance that is rarely exhibited by one neighboring nation to another. It was enacted by Congress, March 3, 1811, that "no goods shall be imported from one port in the United States, to another port in the United States, in a vessel belonging wholly or in part to a subject of a foreign power." Whilst the United States has prohibited the transportation in foreign vessels from one American port to another, it has permitted Canadian railroads to transport property from one American port to another across their territory, although this mode of transportation is in manifest rivalry with the enterprise, labor and capital of our citizens. All other means of transportation in the struggle to control the inland carrying trade of our country, are of minor character compared with the gigantic efforts of the Grand Trunk Railroad, owned by British capitalists. This road is one of the greatest works of modern enterprise. Few equal it in magnitude or importance. It reaches from an American port upon the Atlantic Ocean through subsidized American railroads, to the very centre of the grain-growing regions in the valleys of our lakes and tributary rivers; and is to-day, and upon our soil, the most powerful competitor with all our various carrying systems for the supremacy over our inland commerce.

The recent movement in Great Britain to aid in widening and deepening the Canadian Canals, for the passage of ships of the largest burden to our inland seas, and the revival of the project of an inter-colonial railroad, cannot have escaped the attention of our people, and are deserving of the gravest consideration. In 1858, said Mr. Roebuck in Parliament:

"The present state of the North American continent was a matter of great interest to England. That continent was divided among three possessors. The southern and most important portion belonged to the United States of America, which ran up to where they met the dominion of England, which stretched from the Atlantic to the Pacific. England possessed the larger part of the continent, which proceeded northward until it reached, upon its western frontier, the territory belonging to Russia. We heretofore had planted Colonies in the southern division that he had named. We had planted thirteen Colonies in that country; those Colonies had declared their independence, and had since increased to the number of thirty-five or thirty-six free States. We had created a power there which, if something were not done by England, as a counterpoise to the United States of America, it would overshadow not only England, but the Earth. He believed that, in the northern part of the continent, we had the means of establishing the counterpoise which he sought."

"Taking the Western side of Lake Superior to the Rocky Mountains, they would cut the new Colony which the Right Honorable Secretary for the Colonies proposed to establish, and he believed plans had been laid before the Right Honorable Baronet for carrying a railway completely across the Continent, so that a direct communication would be established between England and Vancouver's Island, by way of Halifax."

This was a magnificent scheme.

"The accomplishment of such a scheme would unite England with Vancouver's Island and with China, and they would be enabled widely to extend the civilization of England. When he referred to the civilization of England, he wished it to be compared with the civilization of America, and he would boldly assert that the civilization of England was greater than that of America."

The Colonial Secretary, Sir E. B. Lytton, in the same debate added, that this project would be "an essential arch, as it were, to that great viaduct by which we hope one day to connect the harbors of Vancouver with the Gulf of St. Lawrence." These ambitious views have, in late years, been expressed from time to time by British statesmen, and certainly are not referred to here to awaken any traditional prejudices, but to call attention to the fact that there is an attempt to give them a practical application upon this Continent, recently shadowed forth in the negotiations of the British North American Provinces with Great Britain.

The past history of Great Britain leaves no room to doubt, as to the attempted consummation of any scheme for the extension of her Imperial sway; for no power in the earth or on the earth, material, physical or elemental, has ever arrested the march of her empire around the globe. She seeks to grasp in the North, the great commercial prize of the age: Supremacy over the inland commerce of the North American continent. This gigantic rivalry is worthy of Imperial ambition, for our artificial and water lines of transportation now almost extend into the center of the continent, and soon must be connected by railroads with the Pacific. Over these transit lines are now passing the industrial and agricultural wealth of the West to the Seaboard, and American and European emigration from the dense population of the East towards the Pacific. They lie, too, between those parallels of latitude in which the human race is ever moving in its exodus from the East to the West.

The extraordinary commercial struggle now going on between ourselves and our Colonial neighbors must end in colossal consolidations of American capital and enterprise, in some degree equaling theirs, or the field must be abandoned to a foreign rival.

The whole modern system of Canadian-British internal improvements originated in the freedom conceded to the trade and commerce between the two countries by the adoption of the Reciprocity Treaty. Without such concessions British capital never would have found investment in such immense works, nor could those works to-day find anything like adequate support, except upon the basis of our bonded system, and the liberal exercise of official authority under the act of 1799, and the warehousing act of 1854, (and certainly under the most liberal construction of the Act of 1799,) permitting the transit of foreign and domestic goods first through our territory, then through Canada, and afterwards to their ultimate destination in this country. The law of 1799 was enacted at a time when its framers could not have foreseen any such application of its authority as to permit the productions of American origin to be taken from one section of the United States through a foreign country, by foreign means, to another section of the United States, duty free.

No wise or even national policy permits such foreign rivalry. The argument seeking to sustain it would find its parallel in an attempt to defend the course which, through the past years, has driven our ships from the seas, and surrendered into alien hands three-quarters of that foreign trade, once so much the object of our national pride.

The trade of the United States with other North American British Provinces than Canada, is upon more favorable terms, but in amount is of minor importance compared with the trade with the latter. Our exports to those other Provinces are made up of wheat, flour, Indian corn, corn meal, and rye. The fisheries of the coast Provinces furnish a natural market for our provisions and breadstuffs, which can never be supplied so cheaply from Canada as the United States. Most of those articles, if not all, are necessities of Provincial consumption, and many of them were admitted, (as they were into Canada,) free from duty before the adoption of the Reciprocity Treaty.

The exports of these smaller Provinces to the United States are mainly made up of coal, lumber, and fish. The coal comes directly in competition, in our market, with the products of the coal mines of Pennsylvania and Maryland; and the lumber, with the lumber of Maine, Michigan, and New York. The product of the mine must become, on both sides, a rapidly increasing class of our exchanges. Hitherto the balance has been much in our favor. Extensive regions, rich in mineral wealth, exist in Canada West; but her geological formations are destitute of coal, and, as the forests are cleared away, an incalculable amount of fuel from the limitless coal fields on the south side of Lake Erie will be required in her northern climate. The coal of Ohio, Northern Virginia, and Pennsylvania, supplies advantageously the means of smelting the ores of Canada West. It will never be politic, nor will it scarcely be possible, for the Government of Canada again to tax this indispensable necessary of life; and if the Treaty expires, Canada would yet be compelled to buy it from us in increasing quantities. Its abundance in our territory, and its absence in the geological formations of Canada West, exhibit, in the greatest degree, a natural adaptation to the system of reciprocal benefits.

The average annual value of imports from these Provinces, paying duty for the eight years during the operation of the Reciprocity Treaty, was $216,172, while for the five years preceding the average annual value paying duty was $1,751,000.

Upon the fishery question, New England authority must be regarded as most reliable. The Hon. Mr. Morrell, M. C. from one of the New England States, and among the ablest of her public men, says:

"To go back to the Treaty of 1818, as the worst possibility that might happen, would subject American fishermen to the inconvenience of keeping off three marine miles from shores to which that Treaty gives us no privileges, leading to occasional disputes, and might prove an injury to the mackerel fisheries; but these evils are not wholly insurmountable, and by no means of the weight of the general considerations exacted of us as equivalents. These would be the proper subjects for Treaties, and would be readjusted in some subsequent Convention. It is no longer doubtful that our fishermen lose more from the free admission of fish from the Provinces than they gain from the privilege of fishing inside of the line of three miles from certain shores. When the catch is short, they make nothing; and when abundant, the glut from provincial competition steps in between them and all legitimate profits. Besides the near-shore fishermen lose their hardiness and become idlers. Thus our people, renowned for their aptitude and success in securing 'the wealth of the seas,' behold their empire passing to the hands of strangers."

In presenting this summary of the results of commercial intercourse with the British North American Provinces, the exhibit of minor details has been omitted. The only object has been to bring before the people of neighboring countries the precise state of our past and present commercial relations to each other, and exhibit fairly, though briefly, the advantages and disadvantages resulting to each, under the Treaty and laws which now govern their intercourse. The proximity and natural adaptation of the United States and the British North American Provinces to give and receive reciprocal benefits, easily and without humiliation conferred by neighbors on each other, have long been recognized by American and British statesmanship. Great Britain has expressed no official desire for the prolongation of the so-called Reciprocity Treaty.

The Committee on Commerce made a very elaborate report in our House of Representatives on the Reciprocity Treaty, (February 5, 1862,) wherein they argued that the grave faults already developed in the Treaty should be remedied by a greater extension of the same system, even to the extent of the German Zollverein.

It would seem, from the Canadian reply, that too much Reciprocity was regarded as a "dangerous thing." Our offers were altogether too liberal, and Mr. Galt, in a report upon the action of the Committee of our House of Representatives upon the Reciprocity Treaty, made to the Governor General in 1862, disposes of the proposition as follows:

"The undersigned can have no hesitation in stating to your Excellency that, in his opinion, the project of an American Zollverein, to which the British Provinces should become parties, is one wholly inconsistent with the maintenance of their connection with Great Britain, and also opposed on its own merits to the interest of the people of these Provinces."

Notwithstanding such objection to a freer, or too free an intercourse with us, a Treaty no doubt might be made so comprehensive in all its details that neither party could be mistaken as to its results, or be capable of evading either its spirit or substance; or, our future intercourse might be left to reciprocal legislation, to be changed from time to time, as the varying interests dependent on our international relations might demand, or the violation of reciprocal obligations by either party might require.

Mr. Broadhead, of St. Louis, said:

There have been but two objections urged to the Resolutions of the Committee:

First. That any action of this Convention is an improper interference with the Treaty-making powers of the Government.

Second. That the adoption of the principle of Reciprocity will curtail the revenue of the Government, so much needed now for the payment of the public debt.

It is true that the President and the Senate are the departments of our Government whose peculiar province it is to make treaties with foreign powers. Yet, it is not a singular fact in the history of our country, that the people, in their primary assemblies, should discuss and recommend the adoption of treaties. The gentleman will recollect that, many years ago, the subject of the boundary between this country and the British Possessions of the Northwest was much agitated throughout the country, and many meetings of the people had, which passed resolutions in favor of 54:40 or fight. Such questions have always been discussed before the people when any question of great public interest was under consideration; and generally our public officers are glad to have an expression of the public sentiment of the nation upon these questions. The Congress of the United States, at least the lower branch of it, is no part of the treaty-making power; and yet on the 18th of January last, the Congress of the United States passed an Act requiring the President to give notice of the abrogation of the Treaty.

As to the question of revenue, I do not understand that this resolution proposes to commit the nation to any policy which is to curtail its revenue. The Treaty is proposed to be reciprocal, and for the mutual benefit of each nation; the articles proposed to be admitted duty free are not named. How then can it be said that the revenue of the Government is to be curtailed by any such measure?

The honorable gentleman from Maine says he has always been an advocate of free trade, but not free trade *in slices.* Now, I affirm that there has not been an Act passed, from the origin of our Government down to the present time, providing for raising a revenue from duties upon foreign importations which did not give us *free trade* in slices. It was always the case that there were certain articles admitted duty free; so that we do not, by the adoption of the proposition contained in the resolution, violate, in any respect, the long established principles adopted by our Government.

How, in what particular, our finances are to be affected by the adoption of a Reciprocity Treaty, such as is recommended in this resolution, has not even been indicated. The arguments seem to be directed to the provisions of the treaty which has just been abrogated; and yet I am at a loss to conceive how even that treaty affected the finances. The articles admitted free of duty under that treaty were generally such as were produced in abundance in our own country; and the effect of a duty upon these articles, or most of them, instead of adding to the revenue, would only serve to give to the producers of those articles a monopoly of the market. If those productions were raised in quantities less than sufficient to supply the demand, the producers could command their own prices; if more than sufficient, those very producers would be shut out from the markets of Canada and the British Provinces; for it is not to be supposed that if we levied duties upon their productions, they would not also levy corresponding duties upon ours.

But, Sir, it has been well said that we look to the internal revenue system of taxation for the means of paying off our national debt; the wealth and resources of the country are to be taxed for that purpose. The $3,000,000,000 of national debt, which now hangs over us represents so much as taken from the capital of the country, and we want to find the best market and the cheapest transportation for all our productions, in order that we may restore that lost wealth. This is the true system of political economy for us to adopt. And we who lie west of the Mississippi — the commercial men and the agriculturalists of Missouri and Iowa, and Kansas and Nebraska — want the gates of commerce thrown wide open, that we may get the benefit of the markets of the world.

We have a great country, Sir, west of the Mississippi and north of the thirty-sixth parallel of north latitude; rich in agricultural resources, rich in minerals, with mountains of iron, just now beginning to be worked. A country larger far than what has heretofore been called the Northwest; embracing those young Empires heretofore almost untrodden, except by the foot of the wandering savage or the daring hunter — just bounding into life, and ready to pour their wealth down the waters of the Missouri into the markets of the world. A large portion of these productions are handled by the commercial men of St. Louis, and a large portion by our sister City of Chicago.

You would hardly believe it, if I were to tell you, that for the two years past thousands of tons of merchandise are transported every Spring from the City of St. Louis, a distance of over three thousand miles by water to Fort Benton, on the Missouri, and thence by land transportation to the mining districts of Montana. This trade is increasing and will increase more than fifty fold each succeeding year, as those Territories become settled up by the advancing tide of emigration, which is sweeping across the Western plains.

St. Louis is the natural commercial emporium of this trade. To supply the wants of these emigrants, she wants all the lines of communication with the Atlantic and with Europe opened to her. And having the interests of the country as well as her own at heart, she wishes the most friendly relations cultivated with our neighbors across the frontier. Missouri knows how much commerce has done to bury national animosities, and advance the interests of civilization. She knows how to appreciate the blessings of peace, because she has felt so much of the horrors of war; for, in the terrible struggle through which we have triumphantly passed, her loyal people have suffered more, perhaps, than those of any other State. In that struggle she has performed her part — as many of her sons, in proportion to her population as of any other State, have followed the gallant captains of our armies to battle and to victory. A few years of peace, and she will be ready to bound again, like a young giant, along the pathway of progress.

I have felt it my duty to say thus much on behalf of the St. Louis delegation, as indicating the views which they entertain upon the subject of reciprocal trade with the British Provinces of North America.

Mr. John Johnston, of Milwaukee, said:

We have come together, representatives of the Boards of Trade of the leading Cities in the United States, and of the British North American Provinces, for the purpose of considering, in that calm, frank and liberal spirit which always marks the true business man, questions of trade which are of the most vital importance to all that vast region stretching from the Western boundary of the Mississippi Valley to the shores of the Atlantic Ocean.

I believe, Sir, we have, here, no old scores to settle, no spiteful feelings to gratify, no revenge to inflict on any, because they may not, at all times, have said and done just as we think they ought; but we have come together in conformity with the spirit of advancement which marks our age, to consider how we can best promote the interests of trade, and help on the people of these great countries in the paths of prosperity and progress.

It is now over ten years since the Plenipotentiaries of the United States and Great Britain, being desirous to regulate the commerce between their respective territories and people in such a manner as to be mutually beneficial and satisfactory, agreed upon the Reciprocity Treaty.

Whether the means used were the best or not, I presume there is no one here but will say that the accomplishment of so laudable an object was in the highest degree desirable. The geographical situation of the two countries is such as to call for the closest commercial intercourse, and makes the progress and prosperity of the one of the greatest benefit to the other. Speaking the same language, both friends of freedom and constitutional government — equally enterprising, energetic and industrious, it was but proper that the fetters of trade should be unloosed, and an interchange of commodities encouraged all along their borders.

One of the first effects of the Treaty we notice is the great impetus it gave to trade between the United States and the Provinces. During eight years previous to the treaty, it amounted to $150,000,-000, while, during eight years since the treaty, it has reached the enormous sum of $400,000,000. Now, Mr. Chairman, I am one of those who believe that Americans will not continue to carry on a trade of $50.000,000 per annum, year after year, if they are losing by it. The Reciprocity Treaty compels no man to buy or sell the Canadians one dollar's worth, and I am convinced no American does buy or sell one dollar's worth unless where he considers that it pays to do so. There are some who think that in every trade between two nations one or the other must lose. I do not believe it. I think two nations may carry on a large trade for years and both grow rich by it. In fact, it must be profitable to both or it will be abandoned. Now, the very fact that trade has increased largely under the Treaty, is to me a strong evidence that it is highly advantageous to both.

There are those who think that, while the closest commercial intercourse with Canada is desirable, yet hope by stopping that intercourse for a few years, to compel the Canadians to sue for annexation. Vain delusion! Every link between the United States and the Provinces that is severed tends to strengthen the connection between the latter and the mother country. Annexation will never be brought about by force in matters of trade. Why, the independent existence of this great country arose from the attempts of Britain to coerce the Colonies in this very respect. No, Sir, if we wish to annex the Provinces we have to assimilate them by unrestricted intercourse to our habits and our manners of action and feeling — we have to Americanize them. That will assuredly be done far sooner by reciprocal trade and by Conventions like this than by non-intercourse. Every railroad that is built, every telegraph that is erected, every ship that passes between the two countries, tends to bind them closer in the bands of brotherhood.

The opponents of Reciprocity tantalize us by parading the millions of revenue which we would have obtained from the articles now being imported from the Provinces had they not been made free by the Treaty. They forget to tell us that this great trade would not have existed had it not been for the Treaty; and even had it existed, and a large revenue accrued from it, we would have been the persons who would have enjoyed the privilege of paying the duties, and not the Canadians, for it is the consumers of commodities who pay the imports upon them. But, think you, would the people of these Northern States be more able to pay their taxes after this immense and profitable trade is destroyed than they are now? Would it not be a sad spectacle to witness this great Convention of commercial men vote to dry up the mighty streams of traffic which unceasingly flow across our vast frontier merely to enable the Government to collect a few thousand dollars more revenue?

The State of Wisconsin, which I have the honor here in part to represent, has many varied interests, but those of our farmers far exceed all others. Wisconsin produces more wheat, to the population, than any other State, Territory or Province on this continent, and whatever benefits the farmer, is for the benefit of the *major* interests of Wisconsin. We have lumber, milling and shipping interests, but these are minor interests. It is asserted that the Treaty cheapens lumber, which I grant. It is of the highest importance to the great majority of the people of my State to have cheap lumber. Every farmer that builds a barn or a fence, every merchant or mechanic that builds a house, is interested in having lumber cheap. I know there are hundreds waiting now for lumber to fall in price, till they build. But the lumbermen of Wisconsin are *not* suffering through the Treaty. They have ample markets on the broad prairies, down the Mississippi, and in our growing cities and villages. The whole imports, *of all kinds*, west of Buffalo, under the Treaty have only been about $1,000,000 per annum, so that the imports of lumber cannot have been very large. These figures are from the tables of the Secretary of the Treasury. Whatever figures I may hereafter give are taken from the same source.

The shipping interests oppose the treaty, because Canadian vessels compete for the carriage of our wheat. The more competition there is, the lower will freight be, and the higher will be the price which the farmer gets for his products; so that in this also is the major interest of Wisconsin benefitted by the Treaty. But the shipping interests of Wisconsin do *not* suffer; for it is a fact that in the last few years, vessels have been known to pay for themselves in one summer. These immense profits come out of the pockets of our farmers by lessening the price of their grain.

It is said that the Canadian farmers compete with our farmers in the markets of our country, while the privilege of importing breadstuffs to Canada is only such as it would be to "carry coals to Newcastle." But is not the privilege accorded to Canada of importing breadstuffs to the United States also like that of carrying coals to Newcastle? We have a surplus of ten times what the Canadas have, and by throwing the two markets into one, is not the smaller surplus likely to be overwhelmed by the larger? I believe, however, that it is absurd to speak of the balance of trade between two countries in a commodity of which both have a surplus. The question is one of transportation, and that alone. The Canadas lie between the Western States and the markets of Europe, and the Eastern States lie between Canada and those markets, and is not the true policy for the two countries to grant an unimpeded passage for each other's products through their respective territories?

There is some exchange of breadstuffs between the two countries. Canada East consumes largely of flour made from the spring wheat of Wisconsin and Illinois, while New England consumes largely of the fine wheat and flour of Canada West, so that the exchange is a reciprocal advantage to both. Shall we step in and prevent New England from buying the finer flour she desires, or shall Wisconsin and Illinois be prohibited from selling their coarser article to those Lower Canadians who desire to buy it? I would here state that there is no more reliable market for our breadstuffs than the Maritime Provinces. Since the Treaty came into effect they have taken from us $30,000,000 worth, while they have sent us comparatively no agricultural products, save a few potatoes and oats.

It is said that one reason why the treaty should be repealed and no new one made is, that we cannot tax our flour, inasmuch as it would give the Canadian flour, which paid no tax, the monopoly of the market. Now I ask you — farmers and millers — are you seriously going to advocate the abrogation of this treaty, so that your flour may be more effectually taxed? How will you then compete with Canadian flour, which pays no such tax in the markets of the Old World?

Any one who examines the Secretary of the Treasury's reports cannot but be struck with the great advantages arising from the Treaty. Since its formation we have sent the Provinces more than we have received:

Of Flour,	$8,797,468
Of Meat,	7,881,239
Of Tallow,	2,500,000
Of Fruit,	1,900,000
Of Coal,	2,800,000

One of the Senators from Vermont—Mr. Morrill—recently delivered a speech on Reciprocity, and gave a number of statistics, which I have compared carefully with those of our Treasury Department, and I find them very incorrect and unfair. In the first place he, for the most part, gives only the statistics of trade with Canada, ignoring that with the Maritime Provinces, and whenever he selects the trade of a single year, he invariably chooses that year when it appeared most unfavorable to the United States. This course is worthy of a tricky politician, but would be spurned by a candid man of business. Mr. Morrill, to show the injurious workings of the Treaty, states that the domestic exports from Chicago in 1856 were $1,345,223, and in 1861 they were $352,000; "surely," says he, "we have no reason to look on such a trade with favor." Now the exports of domestic produce from Chicago in 1861 were, according to the Custom House Books and Secretary's Report, not $352,000, but $3,522,343. What confidence can be placed on reasoning based on such erroneous statistics as these? Mr Morrill's speech was widely circulated, and may have had some weight against the Treaty, with those who did not examine the figures for themselves, but with any one acquainted with its operation, his assertions have no more weight than the passing wind.

I have great faith, Mr. Chairman, that this Convention will take no retrograde step, or do anything to destroy the great and prosperous trade which has sprung up between us and the neighboring Provinces. It would indeed be a disgrace to the intelligence of this mighty nation, to see its leading business men go back half a century and recommend a course to our Government of restriction, retaliation and non-intercourse worthy of China and Japan. Far, rather, let us recognize the vast influence which commerce has ever had in elevating the minds, refining the manners, and enlarging the hearts of men, so that what Gibbon says may still prove true, that "the merchant is the friend of man."

Who can estimate what Commerce has done in the past to promote civil and religious liberty, to provide for the material wants of the people, to elevate the nations and bind them into one civilized family. She is even lifting the dark gloom which enshrouds the untutored tribes of Africa, and is locating in fixed habitations the hordes which roam the Steppes of Central Asia, and I believe that though many years may come and go till that happy day arrives, and many barriers lie between, yet the time will come when Christianity and its handmaid, Commerce, will so assimilate the Nations that "men shall beat their swords into plowshares, and their spears into pruning hooks; when Nation shall not lift up sword against Nation, neither shall they learn war any more."

Shall we, the ministers of Commerce, do ought to retard that happy day? God forbid!

It being now $1\frac{1}{2}$ o'clock P. M., and the hour for the excursion being fixed at 3 o'clock,

Mr. Joy moved that the excursion be postponed to 5 o'clock.

Mr. Randolph moved that the citizens of Detroit be requested to postpone the excursion until after the final adjournment, but this motion was subsequently withdrawn.

Mr. Joy's motion was carried.

Mr. Seymour then attempted to resume his remarks, but could not proceed owing to the number of delegates who were leaving the room.

An adjournment was then again moved, and finally a recess of half an hour was taken.

AFTERNOON SESSION.

The Convention was called to order by Mr. Davis, of Cincinnati, one of the Vice Presidents.

A delegate from Bangor hoped that the ten minutes' rule in reference to the debate, would be rigidly enforced.

Hon. D. C. Littlejohn, of Oswego, moved that the vote be taken on the question under discussion at 4 o'clock, that other business before the Convention might be cleared off by 5 o'clock, and the Convention then adjourn *sine die*.

Mr. Treat, of St. Louis, stated that two of the most important Committees had not yet reported, and he objected to this unseemly hastening of business. The

Convention should not hurry through these important questions.

Mr. Littlejohn withdrew his motion.

Mr. Fraley, of Philadelphia, moved that each State be called and first heard through some delegate, selected for the purpose, and that then the debate be opened to the Convention at large, each speaker to only consume ten minutes. This was to secure to each State an opportunity of being heard on this important question, instead of the representatives of one section consuming the whole time.

The motion was put and carried.

Hon. Lyman Tremain, Chairman of the Committee on Finance, by unanimous consent of the Convention, submitted the following report:

The Committee on Finance respectfully report that, having heard the explanations submitted by the Hon. J. W. Taylor, of Minnesota, they report favorably, for the consideration of the Convention, the resolution referred to the Committee, which is in the following words:

Resolved, That the Boards of Trade represented in this Convention recognize the necessity of effective organized measures to repress the practice of smuggling upon the extended frontier between the United States and British America, and will co-operate constantly and earnestly with the Finance Ministers of the respective countries for the suppression of such illicit trade.

Resolved, That we welcome the effort now making by the Commissioners, under the direction of Hon. Hugh McCulloch, Secretary of the Treasury of the United States, to revise and present to Congress the best method for the collection of revenue, both internal and external, and that this Convention respectfully recommend that the Finance Minister of the English Provinces of the Northwest shall be parties to such deliberations, with a view to uniformity of legislation on both sides of the international border, upon all questions relating to public matters.

The attention of the Committee has been directed to the subject of the National Debt, existing against the Government and people of the United States, and to the Internal Revenue Laws, which have been established to defray, in part, the expenses of the Government. While the Committee could not ignore the existence of imperfections in these laws, yet they regarded them as the necessary incidents of a system of legislation novel in the history of the country, and adopted by Congress, for a temporary period, under the pressure of a great emergency. Feeling confident that all the errors and irregularities which experience had disclosed would be remedied at no distant day, by future legislation, the Committee did not regard the present as a proper occasion to consider them specifically, or in detail.

The Committee, however, were unanimously of the opinion that the present was a fitting occasion for the great commercial classes of the country, represented in this Convention, to express their judgment concerning the sacred character of the debt thus existing. This debt was the necessary result of the war forced upon the people by a gigantic and wicked rebellion. At a time when the capitalists of the Old World were unwilling to purchase our national securities, our citizens themselves, including our bankers, merchants, business men, farmers, and mechanics, rallied to the rescue of the Government, and loaned it whatever money it required, voluntarily and cheerfully assuming the risks and hazards of advancing money to a Government that might be overthrown in the pending conflict. Every consideration of honor, duty, and good faith demands that every dollar of this debt, principal and interest, should be faithfully paid. He knows but little of the American people who doubts that the statesman or the party which breathes the word Repudiation will be indignantly repudiated and condemned by the people of this country.

The Committee recommend the adoption of the following preamble and resolutions:

Whereas, The war for the preservation of their national existence has resulted in the creation of a large National Debt against the Government and people of the United States; and,

Whereas, Experience has developed many imperfections and inequalities in the system of Internal Revenue Taxation established by Congress; and,

Whereas, This Convention, entertaining the confident belief that such defects will be amended in any new legislation, which it is believed may be found necessary; and,

Whereas, Said debt is the price which the nation has been compelled to pay for the protection of its integrity, its honor, and its life;

Therefore, this Convention, in behalf of the commercial classes represented by it, doth

Resolve, First, that it be respectfully recommended to the Government, that in any future re-adjustment of our Tariff and Internal

Revenue Laws, the burdens of taxation, direct or indirect, may be made to fall, so far as possible, on the vices and luxuries of the people, thus relieving the laboring and industrial classes.

Second, That regarding such national debt as a pecuniary obligation most sacred in its character, this Convention declares its conviction that all sacrifices will be cheerfully borne that may be necessary to maintain the national credit unimpaired, at all times and under all circumstances, and that every dollar of such debt, principal and interest, can and will be discharged, without retarding, in the slightest degree, the onward progress of the nation in its career of prosperity, greatness and glory.

The report was accepted, and the accompanying preamble and resolutions were unanimously adopted.

On behalf of the Harbor Commissioners of Montreal, J. L. Beaudry, Esq., Mayor of that City, presented charts of the St. Lawrence from Montreal to the Straits of Belle Isle, to the President of the Convention, and to the Boards of Trade of Buffalo, Toledo, Cleveland, Detroit, Milwaukee and Chicago.

The Chair announced that Hon. D. L. Seymour, of Troy, had the floor.

Mr. Seymour then resumed his remarks:

He alluded to the timber interests affected by the Treaty. A large section of the State of Maine had no convenient mode of sending its lumber to market but by the St. John river; but that river lay for the greatest portion of its four hundred miles in length in the Province of New Brunswick. That Province imposed an export duty, as it had a perfect right to do, of which, however, the people of Maine complained and asked to be relieved. The people of the West at the same time began to find out that they would require some more easy and enlarged mode of transit to the Seaboard than through the Erie canal and over the New York railways, and they, too, asked the General Government to procure for them the free navigation of the Welland and St. Lawrence canals. On the other hand, the British Provinces decided to have their goods carried through the United States from the English markets to their shores in bond, and they desired a less restricted general trade with the United States. In 1859 the United States Government passed a law permitting goods to go over their railways and canals to Canada in bond, and the result had been most satisfactory to the United States, through the increased carrying trade obtained and the profit made upon that trade. Having derived so much advantage from this extension of trade with the Provinces, the people of the United States could not reasonably refuse to accede to the request made by the British Provinces for additional commercial intercourse through a Reciprocity Treaty. The United States desired fishing privileges, desired a free transit for their lumber through New Brunswick, and desired the opportunity afforded their people of sending vessels down the St. Lawrence, through the British Canals, constructed at immense cost, on the same terms as the people of the Provinces had the use of them. The British Government met their demands in a spirit of liberality, and granted all they asked, getting in return only some advantages in the way of the abolishing of duty, on both sides of the line on certain articles, and the free navigation of Lake Michigan; but this enlargement of trade had been of a reciprocal character. Vessels brought certain Canadian wheat to their harbors, and took back American goods. They brought the fish, and gypsum, and coal of the lower Provinces to Boston, and took back the manufactures of the Eastern States. He asked the attention of Western merchants to the fact that they had passed a resolution, calling upon the Government to aid in constructing the Niagara Ship Canal, and to the necessity of following that up, by asking for the Niagara Canal, and to the necessity of following that up by asking that the Reciprocity Treaty be continued, so that their vessels can reach tide water through the St. Lawrence, without breaking bulk. They had been able to make but little use of the privilege they had obtained of freely navigating the St. Lawrence, for want of a ship canal, and now that there is some prospect of the construction of that great work, it became all important that the St. Lawrence should remain free. If the Reciprocity Treaty were abolished, the United States Government would have to obtain for their people the right to fish, and the right to the navigation of the St. Lawrence, and use of the canals, either by negotiation, or by war. They could not get along with any degree of comfort without those privileges. He then referred to statistics to show how vastly the trade of the United States had been developed along the great lakes under the operation of the Treaty, and to show that a very large excess of goods had been shipped to the Provinces from the United States over the amount the Provinces had shipped to them. During the ten years the Treaty had been in operation, the exports of the United States to the Provinces had amounted to $250,350,000, while the imports were $200,399,000, thus shewing a trade of over $450,000,000 between the two countries, to be affected by the withdrawal of the Treaty, which had worked so satisfactorily, experiment as it was. It was a trade that ought not to be whistled away by such a resolution as that proposed in the amendment to the report. But he must say that the Canadian people had added to the duties on American manufactured goods to an extent they had not expected when the Treaty was made. Articles that then were taxed but twelve and a half per cent. had lately been put up to twenty and twenty-five per cent., and this had caused dissatisfaction. They had also adopted some sort of discriminating duty against American vessels passing through the canals, of ninety per cent in favor of British vessels.

Hon. Mr. Ryan, of Montreal explained that a remission of a portion of the Canal Tolls had once been made as an experiment on all vessels going through both the Welland and St. Lawrence Canals, but had been abolished for several years past.

Mr. Seymour was very happy to be corrected; but these and other things he mentioned, such as the raids from Canada, had tended to excite a feeling of hostility to the Provinces in the minds of the people of the United States, but for which feeling he had no doubt the action towards repealing the Treaty taken by Congress would never have been thought of in that body, much less carried out. Now that that the action had been taken, however, he thought it would be a wise plan to fully consider the subject, and see if they could not construct a Treaty that would confer larger advantages on both nations. Mr. Seymour sat down amid loud applause.

Hon. S. H. Blake, of Bangor, Maine, said:

I have listened with pleasure to the gentleman from New York; but the advocacy of the interests of the fisheries the gentleman might, perhaps, in good taste, have deferred to some one who lived nearer the sea, and might be supposed to understand as well the condition and wants of this great branch of business.

The gentleman is in favor of a Reciprocity Treaty, because the fishing interest demands it. The corner stone of the edifice he has erected rests upon the fisheries. He is in favor of a renewal of the Treaty because the fishermen want it. Now, Sir, the fishermen on the Atlantic coast do not want a Reciprocity Treaty, admitting Provincial fish free into our markets in competition with their own, and for the best reason in the world — that it is against their interest. They prefer rather the exclusive right of fishing on our own coast, and the right of fishing on the Banks and the Ocean in common, and the exclusion of foreign fish, except upon payment of such duties as it may be to the interest of our revenue to impose. The State of Maine is very largely engaged in the fisheries. It has a sea coast of three hundred miles, and that coast is dotted all along with fishing establishments, owned and carried on by a shrewd and intelligent people, and they understand their interests quite as well, they think, as gentlemen who live so far in the interior that ocean gales never waft them the smell of salt water; and I feel well assured that the number, in that long stretch of three hundred miles, who could be found favorable to the Reciprocity Treaty of 1854 would be very small indeed. There is a little eddy at Portland, to be sure, in the great sweep of the commerce of that coast, favorable to Reciprocity. It grows out of the fact of its being the terminus of the Grand Trunk Railway. Just as there is an interest here at Detroit, for the same reason, in favor of it, against the general interest, I think, of the State of Michigan. The Legislature of Maine, of 1862, passed resolutions condemnatory of the Reciprocity Treaty by a vote unanimous, with one vote only excepted; and the Legislature, I have no doubt, truly reflected the then and present sentiment of the State upon the subject. The fishermen of Maine do not want such a Treaty, nor does the capital of Maine invested in the business want it; and I think the fishermen of Massachusetts, and the very great capital there engaged in the fisheries, take the same view of their interest as do the fishermen of Maine. Mr. Sabine, of Boston, says, "No." Then why have we not had memorials from there at Washington against rescinding the Treaty? Why has Marblehead, and Salem, and Gloucester, been silent, and New Bedford, whose merchants are princes, and whose daughters have royal incomes? Why have they not had influence enough to be heard upon the floor of Congress against the termination of a Treaty so beneficial to them? There are other interests in Massachusetts in favor of the Treaty; I cannot believe the purely fishing interest is so.

But there is a greater interest in Maine that is affected most injuriously by the Treaty. We have large tracts of forest in Maine, and to them we look very much for our growth and prosperity. The Kennebec, upon which is our little, though beautiful, Capitol, and the Penobscot, upon which nestles the growing City that I, in part, represent here — these rivers, as they extend their arms northward, hold a territory of forest out of which you might carve a State as large as Massachusetts, and two such States as Rhode Island. We manufacture annually some 200,000,000 feet of lumber on the Penobscot, and all this lumber, when sent to Boston, or Baltimore, or elsewhere, to market, in the United States, comes in direct competition with similar lumber from New Brunswick and Nova Scotia; just as does the lumber from Michigan, Wisconsin, and Minnesota come in competition at Albany, St. Louis, and elsewhere, with lumber from Canada. And is this interest local? So is every other interest local that goes to make up the aggregate of the enormous products of the whole country. And it is the leading interest of four great States. Cotton, sugar, wheat, are also local products; and no one of them should be sacrificed upon the altar of courtesy to our neighbors. So, too, are the fisheries of Maine, New Hampshire, and Massachusetts local. This lumbering business is local. Add all the other local interests of the country, and you have that great aggregate that makes up the whole of our annual products. Now, will you admit any and all foreign products, duty free, in competition with any and all the items of this aggregate? If not, why discriminate in favor of one foreign product, and consequently against the same product of domestic growth or manufacture? Why admit Canadian products of the farm, or forest, or water, of all which we have a surplus, and hence to come in direct competition with our own, and not admit Canadian whisky, or Canadian anything else, also, in competition with our own? Sugar, or cotton, or brandy, or any other product of any other country — why not admit them in competition with our own of like kind, also? True, it would seem to be against the interest of the American producer to do so, but then it would increase the volume of trade, and thereby might add to the *local* interest of the Erie Canal or New York Central. No, Sir; the proposition to admit Provincial products free, and leave American manufactures, which we pay for them with, to be taxed by the Provinces at their pleasure, will never, I trust, receive favor this side the line.

Again, we cannot now enter into a Reciprocity Treaty if we would, for the reason that our system of taxation is not yet so adjusted to the objects capable of revenue, that we can know before the system is perfected, what, if any, articles can be spared from its embrace and still leave enough to raise the sum of $240,000,000 annually to pay the interest upon our debt; nor do we now know that any leading articles can ever be spared from taxation. Our debt is nearly $4,000,000,000, and we may need every source of taxation, without solitary exception, to pay it, as we shall to the last farthing, and to meet its interest promptly. But if we admit Canadian wheat free, we cannot tax American flour, for if we do we shall give Canadian flour an advantage to the extent of the tax. If we admit provincial lumber free, we cannot tax American lumber, for if we do the Provincial can undersell us just so much, and thus monopolize our markets and drive our lumber out of them.

The lumber manufactured in the States exceeds $100,000,000 yearly, thus reaching a sum one-half as large as the entire annual domestic exports of the whole country had reached prior to 1854, the date of this treaty. And why should not this product of $100,000,000 be left in a condition that it can contribute its proportion toward the revenue annually necessary, as well as any other manufacture, whether of cloth, or boots and shoes, or whisky? And corn and flour, that as the fat and virgin soils of the West are opened to cultivation, increase so fast that statistics can hardly keep pace with their yearly value — why should not their hundreds of millions of dollars also be so left, unfettered by treaty, that the revenue of the country may be swollen by their increasing volume of contribution? Is it policy, and is it fair to the other interests of the country, to exempt these or any products from their rateable contribution to the revenue, and thereby necessitate an increased and heavier taxation upon other manufactures or products?

Again, Canada has recently sent Commissioners to Great Britain to discuss the question of confederation, frontier defences, etc., and these Commissioners have returned, and I see by the morning papers that confederation has been agreed upon by the Home Government, and the Maritime Provinces are to be persuaded into it, if possible; that a fortress is to be constructed at Point Levi, opposite Quebec, and that the Canadian frontier upon the Lakes is to frown upon us with its forts, and that the inter-Colonial Railroad is to be undertaken as a Governmental measure.

Mr. Chairman, I do not like the looks of this matter. If a Confederacy is to be established here to the North of us, greater in territory than our own, and hereafter to vie with us in its resources and power, why should we treat with it upon terms more favorable than we grant to other most favored nations? Does it lie adjacent to us, and is that any reason why we should modify our internal policy toward it? The contiguity does not change its character as a foreign nation, nor reduce the amount of taxation necessary to carry on one Government and pay its debt. Mexico is adjacent to us, and the Home Government of our friends here to the left is separated from us only by a ten days' passage, and does that constitute any reason why we should make a Treaty with either, more favorable than our interests would dictate, or than if they were more remote?

The Province of New Brunswick has recently granted a subsidy of $10,000 a mile towards the construction of a railroad to connect Nova Scotia and New Brunswick with Maine, thus making a continuous railroad from Halifax to Boston — a project eminently calculated to develop the resources of these Provinces, to facilitate European travel, and to add to the trade alike of Maine and New Brunswick, of Halifax and Boston, and to bind in close friendly relations the Maritime Provinces and the States. Now, Sir, if the British Government had given assurance of aid to this road, instead of the antagonistic project of an inter-Colonial road, on which freight and passengers will be like angels' visits; or if, instead of proposing military works upon the Canadian frontier, it had offered its credit to deepen the Welland Canal and improve the rapids of the St. Lawrence, that Western produce might have a better outlet to the Atlantic, it would have looked much more like inviting to a reciprocity of trade and good offices, than this hostile programme in the morning papers that comes to us from the London Spectator.

T. C. Hersey, Esq., President of the Portland Board of Trade, spoke as follows:

MR. PRESIDENT: — My voice is feeble and I will ask for no privilege beyond the ten minutes, if I can have the attention of the Convention.

It was far from my purpose to say a word in this Convention, and I should not have been heard did I not feel that the State of Maine, and especially the City of Portland, which I in part represent, had been misrepresented on this floor. It is with no little embarrassment I appear here to follow the distinguished gentlemen from Bangor, who have addressed you. The Hon. Vice President said he "desired in the consideration of this question that local and sectional feelings should be entirely set aside." What do the gentlemen represent? The City of Bangor, a noble City of Maine, which has sent here some of her most distinguished lawyers and judges to represent a single interest — Lumber, and to overawe the Convention. They claim to represent Maine, and the last gentleman has alluded to Portland, the Commercial Metropolis of Maine, in no very complimentary terms, and this is not the first time that remarks and acts emanating from the same source have endeavored to ignore all other sections of the State, and especially that portion west of Bangor. Perhaps I may say that these gentlemen do not represent the whole of the interest of Maine, not even in fact all the lumbering interests, for her citizens to a great extent, are engaged in lumbering in the British Provinces, and in a Reciprocity Treaty they will ask for no privileges not granted to our own lumbermen. The gentleman has thrown out some unjust and ungenerous reflections upon the representatives of the British Provinces here. I feel it to be my duty, Sir, to disclaim any participation in this feeling. I have had an opportunity since this rebellion broke out of visiting Canada and the lower Provinces, and more courteous and gentlemanly treatment I have never met with in any quarter. I have found to a very great extent warm sympathy with the North in our struggle.

Maine borders on New Brunswick, and we don't want better neighbors. Maine may have pronounced against the old Reciprocity Treaty, and so has this Convention unanimously, but Maine is not opposed to a more perfect and enlarged Reciprocity Treaty.

The gentleman who last addressed you, said that the fishing as well as lumbering interests were opposed to a Treaty. That gentleman has undertaken a subject he very little understands, as must be apparent to this Convention. The fishing interests of Maine have prospered beyond precedent under the Reciprocity Treaty. A gentleman from Maine, very largely interested in the fishing business, was to have attended this Convention, as an advocate of the Treaty, but was unfortunately detained. The terminus of the Grand Trunk Railway being in Portland, has been assigned as one reason for advocating the Treaty. Mr. President, we are in Maine, not Portland alone, interested in the prosperity of the Grand Trunk Railway. It is one means for the transportation of the productions of the Great West which we want to keep open, and it comes with ill grace from a gentleman of Maine to make unkind allusions to the road which brought him here in safety, and which he may desire to use again.

Maine is a consuming State, and should favor all modes of communication, calculated to cheapen the transportation of the surplus productions of the producing sections, and, besides this is of immense advantage to Maine, as being the most direct and expeditious mode of transportation.

Mr. Blake said he alluded to the termini at Detroit and Portland as creating necessarily a feeling in favor of Reciprocity. In traveling with a free ticket over the Grand Trunk, and being feasted with champagne, he was almost in favor of annexation to Canada. He then paid a compliment to the gentlemen from Canada.

Mr. Hersey — The Portland delegation was not thus favored.

I will not say more if my time is up, (Chair, two minutes more) but I want to briefly refer to the points made by the worthy Vice President, that a body of merchants (especially in Convention) have no right to advise their Chief Magistrate. I am a plain, simple business man, and don't pretend to know much about Conventions and their rights — we brought no lawyers from Portland to plead our cause — but as merchants, believe we have a right to be heard and to make our wants known to the Government. I would say to our friends on the right (the Provincials) that if they ever contemplate that "closer alliance" which has been so often referred to, that this is a Government of the people, and I trust they will not join us, unless with the clear understanding that in our Government the people rule.

It is a strange doctrine that the wishes of an intelligent body of merchants cannot be made known to the Executive. I know the Government would be gratified to have such a Convention assemble to discuss business questions. I am willing to trust the negotiations of a Treaty with the present head of the State Department. Gentle men seem to be afraid that in the negotiation of a Treaty we shall be overreached.

This terrible strife we have just passed through has developed noble soldiers, and I trust, statesmen too, far in advance of some who have preceded them. The great argument used to defeat the opening of negotiations is that without a Treaty, we shall have a "closer alliance." Now, Mr. President, when I was a young man, if a gentleman desired an alliance with a young lady, he made his advances through the mother, and I think if we desire a "closer alliance," we'd better keep in the family, and make a Treaty as broad and generous as possible. If we can not have all we want at first take the nearest we can get to it.

Mr. President, as I shall not be likely to speak again on this floor, permit me in the name of the citizens of Portland to invite the first meeting of the "National Board of Trade" to meet on Casco Bay, where we will do what we can to make their stay pleasant.

Hon. James F. Joy, of Detroit, said:

Having been the Chairman of the Committee on the Reciprocal Trade and Treaty between this Country and the British Provinces of North America, it may not be improper for me, at this stage of the debate to state some of the reasons which induced that Committee to recommend the last resolution which it has brought before the Convention.

In so doing it is not my intention to go fully into the merits of the present Treaty. It has been in existence now ten years and more. In consequence of it, a very large trade has sprung up between this Country and the British Provinces, amounting in the aggregate to some $500,000,000, within the eleven years during which the Treaty has been standing, and in which aggregate trade the balance has been in favor of the United States, some $115,000,000, exclusive of the value of the fisheries in British waters, which has become very large, and amounting in value annually to upwards of $4,000,000, and involving a very large outlay of capital invested in ships, and giving employment to nearly ten thousand hardy and enterprising men. It is now proposed by those who are opposed to the formation of a new Treaty, upon fair and just principles, and which should not be unjust to any interest, to strike a death blow to this large trade, and disturb, if not destroy, to a great extent, this large fishing interest. It is difficult to imagine a motive strong enough to induce fair men to come to such a resolution. This trade has been doubtless profitable to both sides, but far the most so to the United States, in whose favor the aggregate balance has always been, and whose citizens, in addition, have had the benefit of the British fisheries, to the extent, as I have said, of upwards of $4,000,000 annually.

Now, why should this trade, so beneficial to both parties, be disturbed? And why should not this Convention recommend the negotiation of a new Treaty having reference to the present condition of the country—just and fair to all interests, and which shall continue these benefits to both this country and the Provinces? I will briefly allude to some of the arguments of those who oppose the negotiation of a new Treaty upon this floor.

First, The late Vice President, whom I very highly respect, and who has rendered very great and valuable services to his country, says that it is not the province of this Convention to give advice to the Chief Executive of the Country. That it might be proper to approach thus the other Departments of the Government, but thus to approach the Executive is a thing most extraordinary, and, *at this time, unwise;* upon both of which points, I beg leave to differ with him, and to say that his position is indeed a strange one, and totally new in the ears of the American people. What, Sir, is it presumption in a Convention made up of representatives from all the interests of the Country, when it perceives that large trade and other interests are to be disturbed, to meet together and consult upon the subjects involved, and make known their judgment relative thereto? For what was the Government established, pray, except to protect, foster and develop the commerce, agriculture and manufactures of the country, and promote the general prosperity of the whole people? And how shall the Government become acquainted with all those interests and their necessities, if the conclusions of business men may not be communicated to it, and influence its actions? Who can best judge of the interests of business, if not those whose lives are devoted to it? And what is this Convention made up of but the representatives of all the great leading business interests of the Country?

But to approach the Executive, and to suggest a policy to it, is most extraordinary, says the gentleman from Maine! Ah, indeed! what is the Executive of this Republic? Is he the master of the people, so high that he may not be approached by them, that it is sacrilege to look him in the face and proffer an humble request or petition? Are these the notions that gentleman has imbibed by or from the high positions he has occupied? Or is the Executive of this Country but the servant of the people, appointed to execute its will, as its name indicates? Sir, in this Country, there is no Sovereign but the people, and all who are placed in office by them, from the Chief Magistrate down, are but their servants, and there are none so humble in all this broad land that they may not approach boldly the highest official, and respectfully proffer their petitions. The right of petition in this country, is a sacred right.

But, it is unwise for this Convention to act upon the matter, says the gentleman. His judgment would have carried more weight with it if he had given us the reasons upon which it is based. Why is it unwise? When great commercial and other interests which have been settled for years are to be disturbed, when questions which were once the subjects of angry national disputes and conflicts are about to be re-opened, and which may lead to national difficulties, and certainly will lead to irritation and anger, and possibly to war and a total disruption of all commercial intercourse between two great Nations, is it not high time for those whose interests are involved to meet together and take measures to bring their sentiments and their judgments in the matter before every Department of the Government? When is it wise to speak if it be not when the disturbance and the difficulties are immediately before our eyes, and may now be obviated with honor and without passion? I do not think that the Convention will agree with the distinguished gentleman that it is not wise to declare our convictions upon this subject and lay them before the Executive.

That gentleman says, the delegations from the Provinces have been shrewd; they have not shown their hands, but have lain by while we have shown ours on this subject. What does the gentleman mean by this remark? He knows that this subject could not come before the Convention for debate until the report of the Committee should be made, and that, therefore, they could say nothing upon the subject until now. He knows that a Committee from those delegations was appointed by the Convention to go before that Committee, where they have been open, frank and manly in expressing their views. That gentleman is a skillful politician, and knows how powerfully a prejudice acts upon the minds of a body like this, and I hazard nothing in saying that that remark was made by him, not to enlighten your judgments, but to lead them astray; not to enable them to decide justly, but to turn them away from true wisdom in this matter.

Having said all I desire to say as to the value of this or some just and fair Treaty as it affects the commercial interests of the Country, I desire to speak of it now as a Western man, as it affects Western interests. I have alluded in my remarks to the resolutions relative to the Ship Canal around the Falls, to the comparative progress of the Atlantic and the Lake States, showing the population of the Northwest now to be equal to the Atlantic States, including New York and Pennsylvania, and that ten years hence they will far surpass them. I stated the rapid increase of the productions of agriculture — great almost beyond conception — and that in ten years more all present avenues to the Seaboard would be crowded beyond their utmost capacity. I may now state, and I do it without any doubting, that there is but one avenue which, at that time, will be at all adequate to the necessities of the West, after crowding all the Canals and Railways leading to the Atlantic coast, and that is the one provided by the Almighty — the River St. Lawrence. A comparatively small expense will enlarge the locks and Canals, which are short and small around the rapids in that great river, and deepen its bed in one or two places sufficient to enable it to float vessels having twelve hundred to fifteen hundred tons burden. With that improvement, it will be profitable for Western merchants and dealers to ship from Detroit and Chicago, and other lake ports, the grain of the West, the staves and other of its productions, direct to all the markets of the world, including those of the Atlantic coast. A ship, with its fifteen hundred tons cargo, may reach Quebec as quick as a canal boat of from two hundred to five hundred tons can reach Albany. It will avoid the slow time of about a mile an hour on the Canal, making five, eight, or ten miles on the lakes and rivers. It will be many hundred miles nearer Europe than at New York. It will avoid the exactions of elevators at Buffalo, so much complained of, whether justly or not; it will avoid canal tolls through New York, also all charges in the City of New York, paying tolls only on the short Canals around the Falls and rapids, and with a large ship and full cargo, the charge for transportation will be much less. It is very safe to say that the productions of the West may be laid down in Liverpool at much less cost than they can now be in New York, and I think for about half very often; and that the saving to the Western farmer will be from ten to twenty cents, and often much more, upon every bushel he has to sell. Compute the amount that will be saved upon a hundred millions of bushels of grain alone and all will see the importance each year to the Western producer.

Now, when we consider that every other great interest is or may be to some extent at least protected by the legislation of Congress, and that the Iron interest, and the great manufacturing interests have been, and are now, fostered by the Government, and that they are all shielded to a considerable extent from the free competition of foreign manufactures of the same character by the operation of tariffs, and that it is not within the power of the Government to create any protection for the productions of the farm, that they must go forth into the foreign markets of the world burdened with all the charges consequent upon transportation; all can easily see how important to the Western farmer is the question whether he shall have the most direct and least expensive road to the market which fixes the price of his produce all over the world, or whether it shall be a straitened route, disturbed by breaks, the charges enhanced by numerous transhipments, until half his flour, three-fifths of all his corn, and similar proportions on other productions shall be absorbed in order to to lay down the portions which may be left him in the market where it must be sold?

It is this consideration which makes the question of the Reciprocity Treaty of immense importance to the whole Northwest, and brings it home to the very door of the ten millions of people already inhabiting this great and fertile region, and soon to be double that number. The interests of that great population, it is not in the power of the Government to protect by tariffs. They must compete freely with all the world; with the Pole, the Russian, the Egyptian, as well as the Englishman in the markets of England and France, and their productions must not only go to the Seaboard, but across the Atlantic to meet that competition. Who can estimate then, the importance to the West of an open trade and unobstructed highway to the Ocean, ample for ships of the proper dimensions to render cheap transportation profitable? Those who can appreciate this may know the importance of the Reciprocity Treaty to the Lake Country, which shall secure this object. The statesman who does it will merit the gratitude of a countless population in all coming time, who will be relieved and enriched by his statesmanship.

And now I have a word to say to the antagonist interests which appear in this Hall to this great interest of the West, one of which is represented by the gentleman from Bangor. He says Bangor cuts two hundred millions feet of lumber, and that Maine embraces timber regions out of which you might carve a State like Massachusetts, and two or three like Rhode Island. Let us admit this for a moment, and let us admit that it shall be an antagonistic interest, which ought not to be, and will not be under any just and fair Treaty. Which is the most important, that interest, great as it may be, in the hands of a few rich men, or the interest of a population of ten millions, devoted to agriculture, and whose prosperity depends upon an easy and cheap access to market. Let me tell that gentleman that if he places that great interest across the highway to the markets of the world from the Northwest, he and his friends and all their interests will necessarily go to the wall. And the same may be said of any other great interest. With the population now in the West, and soon to be there, its interests are now, and will become more so, paramount to any other; I had almost said to all others. They will have a power which nothing can stand against. But this is not the light in which to place this question. And we do not advocate a Treaty which shall sacrifice any interests, but which shall be in harmony with them all, and which shall be reciprocal so far as possible, and shall secure what is of the greatest importance to the Western millions, viz: an ample, broad, unimpeded highway to all the markets of the world. In doing this we bid the great States of New York and Pennsylvania to be of good cheer. *It will be only the overflowings of the exuberant West* which will go down the St. Lawrence. There will then be ample enough to crowd all the avenues to New York and Philadelphia to their utmost capacity.

I have said enough upon the importance of this matter, and now I must allude to an argument which may influence some minds, and which is put forth almost with the importance of official statements, which is, that if no Treaty is formed, Canada will suffer so much, that in the course of a few years her government will be revolutionized and she will come into the Federal Union. This is possible; but I reason differently. Men, and particularly whole people, do not like to be coerced. The more likely course of events would be that which took place before the present Treaty was made. All the questions connected with the fisheries would be thrown open. Collisions would again take place upon the fishing grounds. Irritations would beget irritations. A blow would be struck one side or the other, and the people of the Provinces would rally around the flag of their country, and we should have acquired a war instead of an addition of States. Who, for a moment, during the late civil war, entertained the thought, that had a war broken out between us and Great Britain, which would have suspended all treaties and stopped all trade, that Canada would have joined us in the contest? Who does not know that such would not have been the case? Besides, a policy adopted from such a motive is unworthy of a great Nation. I have but little sympathy with Great Britain. Her conduct merits but little at our hands; but I would not imitate her. I would adopt no policy designed to foster dissensions or create revolutions in her Provinces. If such a policy could, by possibility, be entertained by the American people, it would be the amplest, fullest and most complete justification of all the conduct of Great Britain during the late unhappy war. Our mouths would be, and should be, in that case, forever closed against all censure for her conduct. We should ourselves be equally guilty without the same sympathy to lead our judgments astray.

One other thing I may allude to which affects many minds, and that is the sympathy which the rebellion has found in England and in Canada. I, myself, attach no importance to this, because it could not be otherwise, with human nature as it is. You cannot see a street fight where the feeling of the bystanders will not become enlisted on one side or the other; and, generally, it will be on that of the weaker party. In this instance, before we let such feelings guide us, we should look back a few years to the rebellion of 1837 in Canada. I myself awoke in the morning and saw the boats at the landing, and the town across the river in flames. A band of desperate men, calling themselves patriots, had crossed the river in the night, had a skirmish, some were killed, the inhabitants were driven away, and the town fired. All who lived here at that time remember the attack on Amherstburg, and the difficulties all along the frontier. In all such matters let none throw a stone at a neighbor unless he be without sin himself.

Mr. Chairman, I have said all I desire upon this subject to-day. This Convention will, I am sure, realize the important Western interests involved, and that they can scarcely be overestimated, and will pardon much of the earnestness with which we press them, and I think will sustain and maintain our interests by its decision. They are not only the interests of the Northwest, but of the East as well as the West; in fact, of the whole Country, almost in equal degree, because that which is so important to so large an extent of it, cannot but involve the prosperity of all its parts.

Mr. Hamlin rose to explain that three gentlemen who had spoken here had represented him as having stated that the people of this country had no right to address the Executive on such questions as the one before the Convention. He took no such position, and held no such doctrine; but there were times when we might be silent, and this he took to be one of them. He did not think it wise to treat this matter in public. It had also been stated that he had said something derogatory to our friends across the border. That was not so; he had meant to compliment them on their superior wisdom. They had shown vastly more than ourselves. (Cheers.)

An invitation was received from the State University and the authorities of Ann Arbor to visit that City and Town. Accepted.

Mr. Scammon, of Chicago, moved that when the Convention adjourn, it be to 9 o'clock Friday morning, and that the further discussion of the Reciprocity question be taken up at 10 o'clock, when the Convention would listen to Mr. Howe, of Halifax.

A delegate from Milwaukee stated that he understood many gentlemen proposed leaving to-night. In that case he hoped that a final vote would be reached before adjournment.

The Chair called upon the members of the Convention to remain until this, the most important matter of all, should have reached a conclusion, and stated that he did not doubt that, under the circumstances, they would do so.

Mr. Howe signified his willingness to speak immediately if the Convention so desired. Loud cries were made of "To-morrow," and Mr. Scammon's resolution was put and carried.

The Convention then adjourned till Friday morning at 9 o'clock.

FOURTH DAY.

FRIDAY, July 14, 1865.

The Convention was called to order by the President at 9.20 A. M., and its proceedings were opened with prayer by Rev. J. M. Buckley, of Detroit.

Mr. Bloodgood, of New York, asked permission to present the statistics he had prepared on the question of a Ship Canal from the St. Lawrence to the Hudson. Permission was granted accordingly. The following is Mr. Bloodgood's statement:

The extension, as well as the continuance, of our commercial intercourse with the British North American Provinces is, I believe, a subject fully within the scope of our present deliberations; and while the main question, undoubtedly, is that of Reciprocity, there are topics which bear upon it with a large influence, not unworthy of our deliberate consideration. It is not with the expectation of doing more than keeping an important subject alive — for, obviously, the times are not as favorable for its adoption as I hope they will be in a few years hence — that I will endeavor to draw your attention for a few minutes to a commercial project that has had powerful support at various periods for more than twenty years, and is essentially calculated to facilitate and cheapen transportation, and thus favor the growth and prosperity of our Western world. The return of the revolted States to our Union, with the difficult labor of reconstruction on the one hand, and the projected change of the political system in the British North American Provinces on the other, would seem to test all the skill and energy of both countries, and absorb all their attention; and yet I venture to hope — yes, even to predict, that the day is not distant when the St. Lawrence and the Hudson Rivers will be united by a Ship Canal, and the noble craft which ply on these magnificent lakes may pursue their voyage, without interruption, to the Harbor and City of New York. And, if you will have the patience to listen to me, I think I shall be able to demonstrate the feasibility and the advantage of this connection. It is not a new idea; it has long attracted the attention of many leading minds, has drawn forth the opinions of eminent public men, and been approved, after rigid scrutiny and calculation, by distinguished and practical civil engineers. Perhaps of all the opportunities offered for the exercise of skill, with but a moderate outlay of money, there is not within our reach a greater improvement, at less cost, or which can be more readily accomplished, and will conduce more to the extension of our commercial relations and future friendly intercourse with our Northern neighbors, than this. And when I look at our own map, and see how the Great Lakes have thus far been wisely connected; how Lake Superior has been opened to the lower Lakes; how Ontario and Erie are now practically one, by means of that admirable work, the Welland Canal; how the St. Lawrence Canals have opened the vast trade of the interior to the Ocean; and then when I also perceive one of the most beautiful of this series of Lakes, with a ship navigation of one hundred and twenty-five miles, lying near, though disconnected from, its fellows, and isolated from the commercial world by very slight natural barriers, I neither regret that Providence had not originally deepened its outlet, or that its improvement had not, from the first steps in that direction, received the earnest attention of the Governments in whose territories it reposes. If Champlain bore to the St. Lawrence River and Lake Ontario the same relation that Erie does to the Huron, who does not see the immense advantages that would have followed? What an extended coast, and what valuable markets could have been added to those now enjoyed; and if we go further, and look at the terminus of the voyage merely, what a saving of expense, and what a port of delivery would such a voyage have secured! It seems to be eminently proper that Lake Champlain should be included in the commercial system of the Lakes, or else it almost seems to have been created in vain. Certainly but a very small portion of the skill and labor of man, so well applied hitherto in works of internal improvement in both countries, is necessary to complete this chain of waters, and connect them by perpetual ties.

I say a small portion of the skill and labor, for nature has interposed but trifling obstacles to their exercise. Lake Champlain has once witnessed large and hostile fleets, engaged in conflict on its crystal waters, for the first and last time, I trust, in our history. Let us of the present day endeavor to draw thither fleets of a different character, engaged in the more blessed pursuits of peace and commerce, not laden with cannon and armed with fighting men, but freighted with the rich products of Western and Canadian fields seeking the readiest markets, a sincere welcome and certain returns. Already the value of this uninterrupted water communication, in a small way, is appreciated. At the North, the Canal of Chamblee does its useful work; at the South, the Canal of Champlain unites the Lake and the Hudson River; and, indeed, at this moment, it is practicable for a vessel of one hundred and twenty tons to clear from Chicago, or Sarnia, or Detroit, and reach the Hudson River without moving its cargo. And, even as far as it has been accomplished, this important navigation has been of essential advantage to Canada and the United States. This connection is briefly this:

The waters of the Lakes flow into and join the St. Lawrence at Sorel, fifty-seven miles from St. John. The Champlain Canal connects its waters with the Richelieu River, thirty-three miles from its outlet, which admits the passage of vessels of from three hundred and fifty to four hundred tons, drawing between six and seven feet of water, and to make it navigable for vessels drawing twelve feet it will be only necessary to raise the present lock and dam, at St. Ours, to a corresponding height. Our Canadian friends, particularly the merchants and public authorities of Montreal, have long understood this subject, and have for many years endeavored to warm it into life. In 1849, at their instance, a Convention was held at Saratoga Springs, in the State of New York, at which the gallant Gen. Wool presided, and there, if I mistake not, upon the report of Mr. Ryan, of Montreal, the plan was fully endorsed of constructing a Ship Canal of the character alluded to.

Still later, in 1855, the then Canadian Commissioner of Public Works, Mr. Chabot, under authority from the Executive Council, approved by the Governor in Council, prepared instructions for new surveys of routes between the St. Lawrence and Lake Champlain, by an experienced and skilled American Engineer, John B. Jarvis, well known in the State of New York for his connection with the Erie Canal, and subsequently with the Croton Aqueduct. His report — one of the many of his able productions — established the fact that a Ship Canal between the St. Lawrence and the Lake was practicable, at a moderate expense, by several routes, and it must always be high authority on this subject. While the route of the Chamblee, even to the unprofessional observer, is evidently an easy one, others, especially that known as the Caughnawaga, were surveyed. The total lockage of the former is but seventy-four feet, the latter more generally regarded as the best of any Ship Canal entering the River St. Lawrence, near the foot of Lake Louis, and using a portion of the enlarged Chamblee, would require about eight locks, each of a moderate lift of about twelve feet. It is not my purpose to occupy your time with an examination as to the comparative value of these routes. The report of Mr. Jarvis is minute and conclusive; it was verified by that of a Canadian Engineer, Mr. Swift, in 1852, and from that we learn that the enlargement of the present Canal, or the construction of a new one, adequate to the navigation of vessels of from five hundred to seven hundred tons, would cost, in round numbers, from two to four millions of dollars, not as much as we see almost every day put into a silver or copper mine, or even a Petroleum Company! And yet who would venture to compare them in real importance? We have, therefore, a right to assert that the

Canadian part of this enterprise is of such moderate dimensions, has been so thoroughly examined and understood, and requires so little capital for its execution, that we may call upon our friends in that country to renew their exertions in this direction, and persevere until they are successful.

Now as regards our share in this great work. Lake Champlain, fortunately, part is already finished, and is so safe of navigation as to be considered, in the calculation of the Engineer, as part of the Canal itself. Between the Lake and the Hudson River is our present Champlain Canal, admitted to be entirely too small, even for the existing local trade, and calling for enlargement at the hands of the State. On the breaking out of the rebellion, the feasibility of enlarging the Champlain, so as to admit the passage of gunboats, was agitated in the New York Legislature, and the State Engineer, W. B. Taylor, was directed to make a report on the subject. This Canal, about sixty-six miles in length, ascends fifty-four feet from the Lake to the summit level, and one hundred and twenty-five thence to the Hudson River. The Engineer reported that the expense of changing it into a Ship Canal for gunboats, one hundred and fifty feet in length, and twenty-five feet beam, and eight feet draft, would be $3,770,000. So that we may safely calculate that, with a slight enlargement from the plan of Mr. Taylor, $5,000,000 would change the Champlain to a first-class Ship Canal. Mr. Jarvis estimated the cost, of this improvement and that of the Hudson River for twenty miles below Troy, altogether, at $8,000,000, but since then, moderate appropriations have been made for this improvement, which are going on with every probability of success, and would leave the Champlain enlargement to stand on its own merits, and come within the estimate already given. In a report of the New York State Engineer, in 1863, it was made evident that the channel of the Hudson might be permanently improved at a moderate cost, upon the plan so successfully adopted in the Clyde. I do not propose to advocate this project merely as a question of revenue, though it would not be difficult to do so. The total tons which came from the present Canal to the Hudson River from 1835 to 1860 was about 9,500,000, and the amount in the years of 1863 and 1864 was 1,287,661 tons, of which the products of the forest were more than half. More than one-quarter, as it will thus be seen, of the tonnage of the Erie Canal (4,794,345 tons,) in the same year, passed over the Champlain in two years.

Now let us see how the subject has been regarded in Canada. In 1846, two years before the completion of the St. Lawrence Canals, Mr. John Young, of Montreal, advocated this project in a series of letters, which appeared in the Montreal Gazette. In 1847, he made a personal examination of the Caughnawaga route, in company with engineers, and satisfied himself of its practicability, and a report to that effect was made by J. B. Mills, Esq. In 1848, the Board of Trade of Montreal, always distinguished by its intelligence and enterprise, memorialized the Provincial Government in its favor, and in 1849 a bill was passed by the Canadian Parliament authorizing a company to construct the work. Upon a subsequent report, made by a Committee on Public Works, the Chamblee route was finally preferred, and Mr. Young assented to it. As tolls and freights stood at the time, it was ascertained that the cost of taking property from Chicago to Troy was, *via* Buffalo Mills, per mile, $4 85 ; *via* Oswego, $4 01, and by the new route it would be $3 90. Mr. McAlpine, an eminent American Engineer, came to the same conclusion. He declared that, with the Caughnawaga Canal, even if the Erie was enlarged, the cost of transportation by the new route, from Chicago, would be less than any other. We give an extract from his tables:

From Chicago to New York by the way of the Lake to Buffalo, by the Erie Canal and Hudson River to New York,—by sailing vessels, 1,418 miles, $5 30, and by steamers $6 98.

By the way of the Welland Canal and Oswego, 1,410 miles; by sailing vessels, $4 46; by steamer, $6 36, per ton.

From Chicago to New York by the Lakes, Welland Canal, the St. Lawrence and Caughnawaga and Champlain Canals and Hudson River, 1,632 miles; by sailing vessels, $3 76; by steamers, $6 21. The cost of transportation by this route, with the Champlain Canal as it is now, is given by Mr. McAlpine as follows:

	Per ton.
Chicago to Whitehall, 1,451 miles, at two mills per mile, ...	$2 83
Expenses on the Canadian Canals, Caughnawaga included, 96 miles, at three mills,	29
Transfer of cargo at Whitehall, ...	20
Transportation on present Champlain Canal, ...	58
	$3 90

So that the figures would stand thus: *Via* Buffalo to Troy, $4 85; Oswego, $4 01; and Caughnawaga, $3 90.

It will thus be seen that in regarding this part of the subject, I have treated it purely on general principles, without regard to the interests or prejudices of any locality, especially those of my own country and State, and probably what I say may not be entirely acceptable. But in this, as I trust in all other cases, I am disposed to act on the principle of the fact: "*Tros, Tyriusve, mihi nullo discrimine agetur*," which, very freely translated, is, that neither Trojan nor Oswegoan makes any difference, in my opinion.

There cannot be any doubt that the prolific and enterprising regions of the Northwest are producing on such a scale as to require more outlets for their products, and that the want of these will check their industry. Certainly, the inducement to raise grain for its people will diminish, if the grain cannot be readily and cheaply transported to market. If the cost of transportation is to eat up all the profit of production, production will cease. Again and again have the Boards of Trade in this region shown in their very able and satisfactory reports, the extent of this production, and the necessity of its passing a safe and cheap transit to the Atlantic Coast.

In numerous official tables the fact is demonstrated that it is of vital consequence to the Great West, that these facilities should be increased. The Erie Canal, due to the genius and perseverance of the great Clinton, built up these new States on and beyond the Lakes. At first, an enterprise of modest proportions, it was soon found that its capacity was too small for its objects, and it has been enlarged to its present dimensions. Naturally enough, since the results have outstripped the calculation of its early and most sanguine friends, it has been again proposed to increase its size to that of a Ship Canal, able to float vessels from the Lakes of over a thousand tons.

The practical difficulties in the way of this project are three:

First, That it will incur a vast expenditure, which the State of New York is at this time unable to undertake without great hazard.

Second, That if it could be accomplished, the supply of water would become very doubtful, as it appears by the testimony of Mr. Hutchinson, a civil engineer connected and familiar with our Canal Works, and to be found in a report of the Committee of the House of Representatives, January 8, 1863, on the naval defenses of the Great Lakes. In his communication on the subject then under discussion, he said that on the one hundred and twenty miles of the present Canal, extending from near Seneca river to the feeder east of Little Falls, there is not now a full supply of water during the business season, and that, notwithstanding that section had the advantage of eleven millions and sixty-four thousand acres of reservoirs, of nearly three thousand millions of cubic feet, and one-half the Black River Canal and Erie Canal Feeders' reservoirs, and also various intersecting streams, any addition to the dimensions of the present locks alone would require large additional supplies. To enlarge the prism of the Canal would also be necessary, and to maintain an adequate supply of water, even in the levels, would seem impracticable, to secure the passage of vessels with any increased draught.

Third, To enlarge the Erie Canal to the proposed size, would not secure the supposed advantages. The largest Ship Canal now known in Europe is the Caledonia, connecting the German and Atlantic Oceans, between the Murray Frith and Cantyre, opening by means of lakes and narrow arms of the sea, an interior navigation of two hundred and fifty miles, and large enough to float a thirty-two-gun frigate, and yet is an entire failure. Though it saves a large distance of navigation around the North of Scotland, by the Orkneys, it is scarcely used, it does not pay its expenses, much less the interest on the cost of construction, and is proposed to be abandoned. The open navigation of the Sea, though somewhat dangerous, is found cheaper and more convenient. Again, the fact may be demonstrated that the movement of a large vessel, especially a steamer, through a long Ship Canal would be slow; it would involve the absurdity of carrying a very heavy weight of machinery, which would be useless on the voyage, displacing, by just so many tons, more valuable and paying freight for the time, with a loss of the advantage of the machinery at the same time. Indeed, it might be said that with boats of the present size used upon the enlarged Canal, of two hundred tons each, may be tracked more economically than one large vessel of equal burthen. These are certain principles which are well understood by engineers, and have been made the subject of exact calculation. It would also require a much larger sum to construct one vessel of this size than an equal tonnage of smaller vessels carrying the same amount of freight.

But if it be true that our Canals are worked up to their capacity, which does not appear from the official reports of the Canal Boards or their engineers, then it is most clear that all that remains is to open and improve the other channels of trade, and especially those which Nature has given us, which may be constructed and taken advantage of. No words can do justice to those magnificent Lakes, on the shores of one of which we are now assembled. No one can have visited these Lake Cities, Chicago, Milwaukee, Detroit, Buffalo, Hamilton, Toronto, Oswego, without being impressed by their prosperity, their commerce, their industry. No one can have crossed these waters without being amazed at the numbers of the craft and the magnitude of the business. Here we see thousands of miles of almost free navigation, and competition of the most valuable character. To extend these advantages and add to this free navigation is the object which I present for your consideration. It seems to me, therefore, that the plan I have suggested is a step in the right direction, that Canada should lead off in the work by the enlargement of Champlain and the construction of the Caughnawaga. Compared with the other works which Canadian enterprise has carried out, it is a small one. And here let me say, that we have not always done full justice to our neighbors. The Welland Canal saved the navigation of the Lakes, and it is a memorable example of perseverance over the most discouraging difficulties. The Suspension Bridge is a still greater wonder, without a parallel on the globe for the grandeur of the design and the skill and boldness with which it was executed. It is as great a marvel of Art as the Falls of Niagara are of Nature, and competes with them for our admiration. It is a link of commerce and travel suspended in mid-air, which binds together the State of New York and the beautiful Peninsula of Canada West, and pleads this day for friendship and Reciprocity. So, too, the St. Lawrence Canals are unrivalled works of their kind, and do everlasting honor to the country which constructed them; and, once more, the Victoria Bridge is another of the wonders of our times, executed in a commercial spirit, by the most far-seeing enterprise. Surely the people that have produced these works are able to finish such as remain to complete the system. Should, for some years to come, Burlington and Whitehall only be the terminus of that part of the international system, the results would still be beneficient both to the Western States and to the Provinces. In tolls, in transhipment, and in time, the saving would be large.

I have not entered here upon the question of income. I well know that the St. Lawrence Canals produce but little revenue, but three-fourths of one per cent., according to Mr. Kingford, Civil Engineer of Toronto, and over the Welland but two and a half per cent. on its cost, about $6,000,000. But if the Ship Canal between the St. Lawrence and the Hudson was made, the benefit would accrue of more business on these Canals. The Champlain takes care of itself with an annual business of 658,000 tons, and a revenue in tolls of $163,000.

It is very certain that the public men of Canada have entertained this scheme in high estimation. Such men as Mr. Young have long given it their support. The Commissioner of Public Works, in his official report for the year 1864, says: "In the existing state of our navigation, the cargo of a vessel arriving at Montreal loaded with grain for the Eastern States, cannot be portaged to Lake Champlain, except at such an increase in the cost of transport as to nullify all the advantages of the St. Lawrence navigation. The connection," he adds, "would also facilitate the large export of sawed lumber from various points along the Canada frontier by costly and often circuitous routes, and would enable it to be laid down at the minimum of transport charges at the great lumber mart of Albany. *It would also form a direct route for that portion of the staple product of the Ottawa Valley required for the American market.*"

And this question of lumber — next almost to grain — is one which concerns us much in New York. At least one thousand more houses are this day required in the City of New York, but the price of lumber prevents their construction, and will until there is an approximation to former rates.

As I have said before, I have not intended to advocate this work on the ground of its offering a profit as an investment, but purely as an international work. At many public meetings and Conventions in the State of New York it has been advocated for many years past. The Press has supported it, and Governor Seymour, in his last message, brought it to the notice of the Legislature of his State. It has also been the subject of official inquiry, and there it stands. The approbation of this most respectable body, with an unusual share of influence and talent, may give it a fresh start, or at least, which is my principal object, "keep it before the people."

In concluding these remarks, I would add that the presence of so many distinguished delegates from the neighboring Provinces is, I trust, but the assurance that not only our reciprocal commerce may be maintained, but in objects of mutual interest, co-operation may be confidently anticipated. I maintain that our commercial interests are almost identical, and mutual interest is among the strongest of human ties. We watch with deep sympathy their future, and trust their present political attempts may end in increased prosperity.

It seems to me, and I say it without the slightest intention of reproach or incivility, that these canals and international works of improvements, these international bridges and connecting railways are a better defence for Canada, than any fortifications wherever placed, or however costly. I will go further and say that in my opinion a suggestion made in the recent report of the New York Chamber of Commerce on the subject of the Reciprocity Treaty, is worthy of some attention. Let the Provinces retain their loyalty of feeling towards and their connection with the mother country. We have learned at vast expense to know the virtue and the value of this principle of loyalty. Let them accept their chief executive if they like from among the experienced statesmen of that country, and cultivate all friendly relations with her, but nevertheless it would be better for both, if the Provinces were never called on to take part in foreign wars. An arrangement by which this could be effected would settle all Canadian anxieties forever. The differences between the United States and Great Britain have always arisen and always must arise from opinions and events, diplomatic and otherwise, over which Canada can exercise no control, and she should not suffer therefrom. In the time of James II., when the American colonists were engaged in border wars with the French, in the time of Dongan, Andros and De Nouville, a treaty was made between France and England, by which the colonies were declared to be neutral, and this state of things lasted until the abdication of James II, and the change in the government. I do not see why the precedent may not be followed with the greatest propriety at this very time. Confederate, assume even closer connections with the Imperial government if you please, but ask that where you are not the cause of war, nor an aggressor, nor an enemy, that you shall not be compelled to take part in it. This would save a world of anxiety, and millions of money. Fortresses and fleets, on both sides, at a vast expense, would be avoided, and the Canadas and these portions, scenes of deadly strife in former years, would know such grief no more. This suggestion has, I am happy to say, recently received some attention in England, and a recent letter from a distinguished member of Parliament, who has on one occasion alluded to it in a debate, states that if the United States could be expected to sanction such a neutrality, a strong party would be formed in England at once to press it to a favorable termination. Certainly this simple yet conclusive plan would settle a very difficult and unpleasant agitation now going on as to what Canada has to expect from England, and which has brought out very strong opinions on both sides, and from the ablest men. It is not unworthy of consideration that the idea is gaining ground that free trade in its growth is everywhere loosening the ties of Colonial dependence, as is explained in a recent work of some reputation, by Viscount Bury, called the Exodus of Western Nations. The writer is well known in Canada, is connected himself with a leading Provincial family, and is considered in his own country as very good authority with regard to the British American colonies. He openly says that an amicable separation of these from the mother country is unavoidable, and preparation for it should begin. And going further than any other writer as yet, he exhibits a treaty of separation in eleven articles drawn with much care, securing the independence of the Provinces, establishing with them diplomatic relations, remitting all moneys due the Imperial Government, and guaranteeing friendship and support against an external enemy. It is a document which speaks volumes and indirectly fortifies the suggestion of neutrality already made.

If the people of Canada have any idea that there is in the United States any plan of the Government or any large number of the people who wish to possess themselves of the Provinces, they are, I honestly think, mistaken. The party of annexation was the party of secession, and both principles are extinct. Our vast territories on the Pacific with their pasture lands, mines and minerals are quite enough to employ all our care for a century to come. Friendly intercourse, enlarged commerce, and peace forever established, express my own wishes toward Canada. Still further, a friendly Confederacy at the North would be a pleasing contrast to that which attempted the life of our nationality, and failed in the effort. And, therefore, speaking as one of the New York delegation, I sincerely trust that the Convention we have been holding here, on ground once the scene of hostility, and to us of mortification, will have brought about a full and entire harmony between the commercial interests of the two countries, and their only future object will be, not to sever, but to extend their present friendly relations, and perpetuate them on a solid and reciprocal basis.

Mr. Brown, of East Saginaw, called the attention of the Convention to the acceptance of the invitation to Ann Arbor. The citizens of Ann Arbor being desirous of knowing how many they might expect, and when ?

The President stated that the Michigan Central

Railroad had placed at the disposal of the Convention cars to convey delegates and their ladies, and suggested that those delegates who felt desirous of going should rise in their places.

At a subsequent period several members rose, and the Chair directed the Secretary to telegraph to the Mayor of Ann Arbor that two hundred visitors would leave Detroit for Ann Arbor at 3 o'clock P. M.

Mr. Brown, of East Saginaw, from the Committee on Lake and Harbor Improvements, submitted the following report, which was accepted, and the accompanying resolution passed:

The Committee appointed to consider the subject of River and Harbor Improvements, respectfully beg leave to report: The time afforded them has been quite too short to give to that subject the consideration its importance demands. While this may be regretted, the Committee feel that the finances of the Government will not warrant appropriations at present. An expression of this Convention, recognizing the national character of such improvements, and the duty of the Government to make them when the condition of the Treasury will permit them to again enter upon the work of international improvement, is all that we can now hope to accomplish.

Recent events have demonstrated the military necessity of such rivers as the Mississippi, Ohio, Illinois and Missouri, and the National character of that of the Hudson, now long since recognized by appropriations for and improvements made on that river, both above and below the City of Albany. The navigation laws having been extended to the Lakes, the Custom House regulations are a recognition of the duty of the government to provide light houses and harbors for the protection of shipping and Commerce, for which the Government is in receipt of large revenue, and in common justice cannot refuse appropriations necessary for its continuance and extension. Your Committee, therefore, beg leave to recommend the adoption of the following resolution:

Resolved, That the Convention recognize the National character of navigable Rivers and Lake Harbors which afford facilities for conducting the Commerce of the Country from which the Government derives a large revenue, and it is the sense of this Convention that it is the interest, as well as the duty, of the General Government, to make such improvement in such navigable Rivers and Lake

Harbors, from time to time, as the necessity for it may be developed, and as the condition of the Treasury will justify appropriations for such work.

Mr. L. J. N. Stark, of New York, offered the following resolution:

Resolved, That a Committee of Seventeen be appointed by the President for the purpose of calling another Convention of this character, to name the time and place where it shall be held, and to make such arrangements for the same as shall be necessary.

It was suggested that the report of the Committee on the resolution, offered by Mr. Converse, of Boston, which was still on the table, covered the matter, and Mr. Stark therefore withdrew his resolution.

The resolution of Mr. R. T. Lyon, of Cleveland, in reference to weights and measures, was taken up and passed. It was as follows:

Resolved, That a committee of two from each State represented in this Convention, be appointed by the Chair, to report to this Convention during the day, the most proper plan to obviate the inconveniences that now exist in the disposal of property by the now existing custom, and that said Committee be instructed to report a plan that shall conform to the currency of our country on the decimal principle.

The Chairman called upon the various States to name two members of the Committee, with the following result:

Missouri,	J. H. Alexander, J. F. Driller.
Illinois,	H. McClellan, G. P. Scudder.
Michigan,	H. P. Bridge, Geo. W. Bissell.
Wisconsin,	W. E. McLaren, John Johnson.
Massachusetts,	J. F. Ropes, W. Greenough.
Maine,	F. H. Sabine, N. M. Rich.
Ohio,	J. A. Gano, R. T. Lyon.
New York,	S. D. Bloodgood, P. S. Marsh.
Pennsylvania,	J. I. Bennett, G. L. Busby.
Minnesota,	N. P. Harwood, J. P. Ford.

Mr. Bentley, of New York, moved that as Canada was equally interested in this matter, the Provinces be also represented in this Committee. Carried.

The resolution upon the National Board of Trade, offered by Mr. Converse, of Boston, was taken up and passed. It is as follows :

Resolved, That a Committee of one from each State represented in this Convention be appointed to consider and report upon the expediency of organizing a National Board of Trade, in order to promote by constant, systematic and permanent plans of action the various commercial, financial and industrial interests of the United States.

The Chair appointed as such Committee the following :

Massachusetts,	J. C. Converse.
Michigan,	H. P. Bridge.
Illinois,	J. Young Scammon.
Missouri,	Thomas Richeson.
Ohio,	S. Lester Taylor.
Maine,	T. C. Hersey.
Pennsylvania,	John Welsh.
Wisconsin,	Thos. Whitney.
New York,	L. J. N. Stark.
Minnesota,	J. W. Taylor.

Mr. Bowen, of Chicago, Chairman of the Committee on Commerce, submitted the following report :

The Committee of Commerce, having had under consideration the various subjects referred to them, as well as matters pertaining to the domestic and foreign commerce of the country, beg leave to present the following report:

That the large and rapidly increasing magnitude of our domestic commerce demands from the legislative councils of the various States of the Nation the most careful consideration and fostering protection.

Every facility should be extended that will cheapen freight, remove annoyance, invite competition, develop our resources, enlarge our communications, and promote transactions between the various portions of the country so as to secure ample remuneration to all participants in our commercial movements.

To this end the Committee regard the construction of the Illinois

River and Niagara Ship Canals, and the Fox and Wisconsin River improvements, as measures largely calculated to promote the commercial interests and develop the broad area of our land, and in case of inability on the part of the General Government, that private corporations may have authority, with national favor, to construct these improvements.

They also consider that the State of New York should at once proceed to enlarge its Canals to ship capacity, and adjust the tolls thereon as much in favor of Western productions as the interests of the State will permit, not discriminating in favor of one point over any other, to the detriment of producers, shippers, or consumers.

The Committee also express the necessity of close attention being given to the rates of freight, as well as the shipping capacity of the principal lines of railway leading from the Seaboard to the West, so as to prevent combinations or excessive *freight tariffs*, thus levying burthens upon our commerce, and, by short capacity, causing great delay in the shipment of property both East and West.

We also suggest to the Internal Revenue Commission the fitness of removing such taxation from shipping and railroad interests as may be consistent with the claims of the Government, and at the same time extend such fostering aid as may be just and due to so large a national interest in support of the GREAT DESIDERATUM, CHEAP TRANSPORTATION.

We also ask from the United States Government such legislation and regulations as will give to our shipping interest the benefit of a perfected system of surveys and soundings, together with custom-house and light-house provisions adapted to our increasing commerce and changing condition; and such early improvement of principal Western rivers and harbors as will relieve the various Cities and Towns from heavy expenses now needful to guard against constant disasters, as well as to give additional protection to the shipping upon our Lakes, Rivers, and Bays.

The Committee also, with reference to our foreign commerce, express the belief that the true interests of the United States Government will be greatly advanced by extending considerate and judicious encouragement to regular lines of steamships to the various countries upon this Continent, as well as to foreign ports, that we may secure our due and proper share of the trade of the Cities upon this Continent and Europe, which traffic and business can only be secured by the intervention of the rapid communication of steamships and vessels, and thus open increased markets for our productions of every kind.

We also commend to the Congress of this Government such legislation regulating commerce and the carrying trade with the Canadas and foreign countries, as will best promote the general interests of the United States, including the work of our merchants, farmers, manufacturers, and shippers, that we may most successfully move forward in this true and great destiny of this vigorous Nation.

The Committee omit statistics for want of time, as the data and items bearing upon these considerations are quite familiar to all. We desire that this body should give the weight of its influence in favor of the up-building of our common country, and at the same time secure the prosperity of its agriculture, manufactures, and commerce, enabling us to liquidate our national debt, and cement the bonds of Union and Peace.

The report was adopted.

The Chair then announced the following gentlemen as constituting the Committee of Conference on the part of the Canadians, on the subject of weights and measures :

Mr. Irvine,	Hamilton.
Mr. Rose,	Kingston.
Mr. Spratt,	Toronto.
Mr. Leonard,	London.
Mr. Grant,	Quebec.
Mr. Currier,	Ottawa.
Mr. Lyman,	Montreal.
Hon. John Steeves,	New Brunswick.
Mr. B. N. Salter,	Halifax.
Mr. Braken,	Prince Edward's Island.

Mr. Randolph, of Chicago, moved that when the Convention adjourn, at this session, it be *sine die*. Carried.

The Chair announced that the time for the special order had arrived, and introduced to the audience, the Hon. Joseph Howe, of Halifax:

Hon. Joseph Howe, of Nova Scotia, took the floor and made a long and eloquent speech. He said:

I never prayed for the gift of eloquence till now. Although I have passed through a long public life, I never was called upon to discuss a question so important in the presence of a body of representative men so large. I see before me merchants who think in millions, and whose daily transactions would sweep the harvest of a Greek Island or a Russian Principality. I see before me the men who whiten the Ocean and the Great Lakes with the sails of commerce —who own the Railroads, Canals and Telegraphs, which spread life and civilization through this great country, making the waste plains fertile, and the wilderness to blossom as the rose. I see before me men whose capital and financial skill form the bulwark and sustain the Government in every crisis of public affairs. (Cheers.) On either hand I see the gentlemen who control and animate the Press, whose laborious vigils mould public sentiment — whose honorable ambition I can estimate from my early connection with the profession. On those benches, sir, or I mistake the intelligence to be read in their faces, sit those who will yet be Governors and Ministers of State. I may well feel awed in presence of an audience such as this; but the great question which brings us together is worthy of the audience, and challenges their grave consideration.

What is that question? Sir, we are here to determine how best we can draw together, in the bonds of peace, friendship and commercial prosperity, the three great branches of the British family. (Cheers.) In the presence of this great theme all petty interests should stand rebuked — we are not dealing with the concerns of a City, a Province or a State, but with the future of our race in all time to come. Some reference has been made to "Elevators" in your discussions. What we want is an elevator to lift our souls to the height of this argument. Why should not these three great branches of the family flourish, under different systems of government, it may be, but forming one grand whole, proud of a common origin and of their advanced civilization? We are taught to reverence the mystery of the Trinity, and our salvation depends on our belief. The clover lifts its try-foil leaves to the evening dew, yet they draw their nourishment from a single stem. Thus distinct, and yet united, let us live and flourish. Why should we not? For nearly two thousand years we were one family. Our fathers fought side by side at Hastings, and heard the curfew toll. They fought in the same ranks for the sepulchre of our Saviour — in the earlier and later civil wars. We can wear our white and red roses without a blush, and glory in the principles those conflicts established. Our common ancestors won the great Charter and the Bill of Rights — established free Parliaments, the Habeas Corpus, and Trial by Jury. Our jurisprudence comes down from Coke and Mansfield to Marshall and Story, rich in knowledge and experience, which no man can divide. From Chaucer to Shakespeare our literature is common inheritance. Tennyson and Longfellow write in one language, which is enriched by the genius developed on either side of the Atlantic. In the great navigators from Cotterel to Hudson, and in all their "moving accidents by flood and field," we have a common interest. On this side of the sea we have been largely reinforced by the Germans and French, but there is strength in both elements. The Germans gave to us the sovereigns who established our freedom, and they gave to you industry, intelligence and thrift; and the French, who have distinguished themselves in arts and arms for centuries, now strengthen the Provinces which the fortune of war decided they could not control. But it may be said we have been divided by two wars. What then? The noble St. Lawrence is split in two places—by Goat Island and by Anticosti—but it comes down to us from the same springs in the same mountain sides; its waters sweep together past the Pictured Rocks of Lake Superior, and encircle in their loving embrace the shores of Huron and Michigan. They are divided at Niagara Falls as we were at the Revolutionary War; but they come together again on the peaceful bosom of Ontario. Again they are divided on their passage to the sea; but who thinks of divisions when they lift the keels of Commerce, or when drawn up to heaven they form the rainbow or the cloud? It is true that in eighty-five years we have had two wars; but what then? Since the last we have had fifty years of peace, and there have been more people killed in a single campaign in the late civil war than there were in the two national wars between this Country and Great Britain. The people of the United States hope to draw together the two conflicting elements and make them one people. And in that task I wish them God speed! And in the same way I feel that we ought to rule out everything disagreeable in the recollection of our old wars, and unite together as one people for all time to come. I see around the door the flags of the two countries. United as they are there, I would ever have them draped together, fold within fold, and let "their varying tints unite and form in heaven's light, one arch of peace." (Applause.)

He thanked the Board of Trade, and the people of the City for the hospitality extended to the Provincial Delegates, and proceeded as follows to the general exposition of his subject:

The most important question to be considered at this great meeting of the Commercial Men of North America, involves the relations which are to subsist between the inhabitants of the British Empire and the citizens of the United States. Before we can deliver a rational judgment upon that question it becomes us to consider what those relations are now. The British Government controls the destinies and regulates the trade of two hundred and fifty millions of people, distributed over the four quarters of the Globe, and the British Islands alone, the machinery in constant running order, does the work of eight hundred millions more. Now in what spirit has the British Government, controlling this great Empire, dealt in commercial matters with the United States? It has extended to them all the privileges of the most favored Nation, and has opened up to them, on the most easy terms, the consumption of everything that they can produce; all of these people. Millions of emigrants, and hundreds of millions of money have flowed in here without any attempt by unwise laws to dam up the streams of industry and capital. Leaving those of her Provinces that have Legislatures free to regulate their own tariffs, Great Britain restrains them from discriminating as against the productions of this country, even in favor of her own. Though burdened with an enormous debt, and always compelled to confront the military Monarchies of Europe with a powerful force by land and sea, the people of England prefer to pay direct taxes to burthening commerce with heavy import duties. Year by year the highest financial skill of the Nation has been employed to discover how its traffic could be simplified, port charges reduced, obsolete regulations removed, and year by year, as trade extends and revenue increases, taxes are reduced or abolished upon articles of prime necessity, consumed by the great body of the people. I notice that some writers in the West complain that wheat is sent into this Country from Canada, duty free; but it should be remembered that the surplus of all the cereals, ground or unground, is not only admitted to the British Islands duty free from the United States, but to almost, if not to all, the ports in our widely extended Empire. It is some times said that because this country admits breadstuffs from Canada, manufactures free of duty should be taken in return. But Great Britian and the Provinces take annually an enormous quantity of breadstuffs and meat from this country, but do not ask from you the privilege that some persons would claim from us.

In three departments of economic science, Great Britain has made advances far outstripping in liberality the policy of this or of any foreign country. France and the United States continue to foster and extend their fisheries by high bounties, but she leaves her people, without any special encouragement, to meet on the sea, and in foreign markets, the unfair competition to which they are subjected by this system.

Great Britain throws open to the people of this country the coasting trade of the entire empire. A ship from Maine, or Massachusetts, or from any State in the Union, may not only visit and unload at the port to which she has been cleared, but she may go from port to port, and from Province to Province, until she has circumnavigated the Globe, the discretion of her owners being the only limit to the extent of her transactions. The Government of the United States gives to British subjects no participation in her coasting trade. Whether they find a market or not, they must break bulk and sell at any port they enter. With our fifty colonies spread over the face of the Globe, your shipowners participate in the same privileges as our own. And when I speak of the shipping interest, it must be admitted to include many interests — the lumber interest, (and an important one it is;)

the industry of the blacksmith, of the caulker, the rigger, the rope-maker, and of the man who works in copper. All these branches of industry are represented in a ship, and fostered by this policy of Great Britain. (Cheers.)

Mr. Younglove, of Philadelphia — I would ask the gentleman if the rights he speaks of, on the part of the shipping interest, are dependent on the Reciprocity Treaty?

Mr. Howe — Yesterday our worthy friend, Mr. Hamlin, talked about Reciprocity in "slices," and I am now simply showing you how many slices we gave you before the Reciprocity Treaty was negotiated. (Loud cheers and laughter.) I assert that Great Britain, with a liberality which would do honor to any Government, has thrown open this whole trade without any restriction. She says to us, if not in so many words, "You are all children of mine, and are dear to me. You are all on the other side of the Atlantic, possessing a common heritage; make the best of it." (Hear, hear.) Your vessels are permitted to run to Halifax, from Halifax to St. John, from St. John to British Columbia, and from British Columbia to England, Scotland, or Ireland. They are allowed to go coasting around the British Empire until they rot. But you do not give us the privilege of coasting anywhere from one end of your Atlantic coast to the other. And now I hope that our friend from Maine will acknowledge that in granting this privilege, with nothing in return, Great Britain gave you a pretty large slice. (Cheers and laughter.)

The citizens of this country may build in any of its ports, steamers, or sailing vessels, and clothe them with the character, and invest them with the privileges of British ships, by registering them in any part of the Empire. In peace, this is a great privilege, and gives to the ship builders of Maine and Massachusetts a very decided advantage over those on the opposite side of the Bay of Fundy. In war, assuming Great Britain to be a neutral, it is a protection. I trust I have shown — 1st, That the British Empire is sufficiently extended, populous, and powerful to be independent of the hostility or fiscal errors of any foreign State; 2d, That her commercial code is characterized by principles of liberality so broad as to invite exchanges with all the world; and that, altogether independent of the Reciprocity Treaty, she has granted privileges to this country for which no equivalents have been asked or given.

The Reciprocity Treaty was a special arrangement, forced upon both countries by a long frontier, by the proximity of rich fishing grounds, and by the difficulty of drawing accurate and recognized boundaries upon the sea. I need not enter upon the history of this question, which has been most accurately given by Lorenzo Sabine, Esq., in his very able reports to the Boston Board of Trade. It is sufficient for us to know that, for forty years, the use by American citizens of the in-shore fisheries upon the coasts of British America was in controversy between the two Governments; that every year American fishing vessels were seized or driven off, it being impossible to define accurately a sea line of five thousand miles; that disputes were endless, tending ultimately to the employment of naval forces, with evident danger of hostile collisions and of war.

On the other hand, the Canadians, seeing the great staples of the United States freely admitted into every part of the British Empire, naturally claimed that their breadstuffs should pass with equal freedom into the United States, the greater portion being only *in transitu* to the Mother Country. The Maritime Provinces, admitting breadstuffs from the United States duty free, and all their manufactures under low import duties, not exceeding ten to twelve and a half per cent., naturally claimed that their own unmanufactured staples should be admitted free into this country. They as fairly claimed that their tonnage should be entitled to the right of registry in the United States, and to participate in its coasting trade.

The Reciprocity Treaty was a compromise of all these claims and interests. For the Provinces, it was an unfair compromise. The right of registry and to trade coastwise was not conceded. The free interchange of the produce of the soil, the forest, and the mine, was satisfactory. The right to navigate Lake Michigan was perfectly fair to both countries.

But the retention of bounties gave to the fishermen of the United States an unfair advantage, and for the free navigation of the rivers and canals of British America no equivalents were given. To the Maritime Provinces, the concession of the in-shore fisheries, with the right to dry and cure fish upon their coasts, was particularly distasteful. So long as American fishermen were kept outside of a line drawn three marine miles from the headlands, as fixed by the Convention of 1818, the mackerel, herring, and ale-wife fisheries were secure from intrusion within those limits, and the codfishery within the great bays of Newfoundland was a close preserve, while the protection of the revenue in all the Provinces gave the Government but little concern. But the moment that American fishermen obtained the right to fish in all the bays, harbors, and estuaries of British America, the line of operations was doubled in length, and the privilege, if they choose to use it, of carrying on illicit trade with the inhabitants of the sea coast, and of sending goods into the interior free of duty, gave them facilities extremely difficult to control. A very large amount of spirits and manufactures have in this way been introduced into the Maritime Provinces free of duty, within the past ten years, that it would not be easy to trace in the regular trade returns. So distasteful was this great concession, without equivalent, to the people of the Lower Provinces, that it was denounced by some of their ablest public men as an unrequited sacrifice of their interests.

In this connection, it is but right to show that, whether the Treaty was fair or unfair, in the working of it, the citizens of this Country have had advantages not contemplated when it was signed. The arrangement was completed on the 5th of June, 1854, but it was not to come into full effect till ratified by the Colonial Legislatures. Mr. Marcy requested that, pending the decisions of the Provinces, the American fishermen should be permitted to enter upon the in-shore fisheries in as full and ample a manner as they would be when the Treaty came into force. The concession was yielded, and the British and Colonial cruisers withdrawn. When the Colonies claimed the free entry of their products, pending the ratification of the Treaty in return for this concession, existing revenue laws were pleaded, and this very reasonable claim was denied, so that at the outset the citizens of the Republic enjoyed the chief advantages of the Treaty for nearly a year before the Colonists were practically brought within its scope and operations.

Again, when the civil war broke out, one-half the Seaboard of the United States was blockaded, and all the advantages of the Reciprocity Treaty, so far as the consumption of the ten millions of people in the Southern States was a benefit to the Provinces, were withdrawn. Assuming that the treaty runs over ten years, it will be seen that for the whole of that period the people of this Country have enjoyed all the benefits for which they stipulated, while the British Americans, for one year of the ten, have enjoyed no benefit at all, and for four years have lost the consumption of one-third of the people with whom, by the Treaty, they were entitled to trade. Recognizing the political necessities of the period, British subjects have made no complaints of this exclusion, but it ought to be borne in mind, now that the whole subject is about to be revised.

Let us now look at the working of the Treaty, and estimate, if we can, in a judicial spirit, its fair and legitimate fruits. We must confess that, as a measure of peace and National fraternity, it has been most successful. It has extended to the Gulf of St. Lawrence and to the North Alantic, the freedom and the security enjoyed by the Great Lakes under a kindred arrangement. There have been no more intrusions, warnings, captures — no rival squadrons guarding boundaries not possible to define. This Treaty settled amicably the last boundary question, about which the Governments of Great Britain and the United States could by any possibility dispute. This was a great matter, had no other good been accomplished, and he is no friend to either country who would desire to throw open this wide field of controversy again. Looking at the industrial results of the Treaty, any fair minded and dispassionate man must admit that they have far surpassed, in utility and value, all that could have been hoped by the most sanguine advocates of the measure in 1854. The trade of the United States and of the Provinces, feeble, restricted, slow of growth, and vexatious before, has been annually swelled by mutual exchanges and honorable competition, till it is represented by a grand total of $456,350,391, in about nine years. This amount seems almost incredible in the figures by which this trade will be expressed, but who can hazard an estimate of ten or twenty years hence, if this wise adjustment of our mutual interests be not disturbed? If there be any advantages in a balance of trade, the returns show that the citizens of the United States have had it to the extent of $55,951,145. But in presence of the great benefits conferred upon both countries by the measure, it would be a waste of time to chaffer over their distribution. In the interests of peace and honest industry, we should thank Providence for the blessing, and confidently rely upon the wisdom of our statesmen to see that it is preserved.

Mr. Chairman, let me now turn your attention to some of the topics touched by other gentlemen in the course of this three days' debate. Some gentlemen seem to be apprehensive that if this Treaty is renewed, it will lead to illicit trade along the frontier. For a long time your duties were lower than ours. Mr. Sabine said he was once a smuggler. At that time he could not carry on trade or business at Eastport and be anything else. The traders on the whole coast of Maine were engaged in the same business, and so was Massachusetts; and small blame to them. The smuggler is a check upon the extravagance of a government, or the increase of taxation. (Cheers.) Any country that raises its tariff too high, or increases its taxation too far, will be kept in check by smugglers. The boot was formerly on your leg; it is now perhaps on the other. You have been driven into a war, which has created a large expenditure and increased your taxation. It would perhaps pay at this moment to smuggle some articles from the Provinces into this country. You are entitled to defend your revenue. But at the same time bear this in mind, that one of the main objections in the Maratime Provinces to this Treaty was, that it gave to your people the power of smuggling. And that power you possess and may use to any extent you please. (Laughter.) Over thousands of miles of coast we cannot afford to keep revenue officers. Down come cutters from Maine, with flour, pork, salt, &c.; but who can tell what they have in the salt? (Great Laughter.) Why, Sir, we sometimes laugh at Yankee Notions, one of those is what is called white-eye in the Provinces—a life destroying spirit which these coasters bring, and with which they deluge our coasts; and it comes in the salt. (Laughter.) So in like manner tea, tobacco and manufactures. Some fishermen can land on any part of our 5,000 miles of coast, and when challenged by our custom-house officer, withdraws, and the white-eye is landed. And I will tell you what we do to adapt ourselves to the circumstances. We are free-traders, and we maintain our Government, have an overflowing treasury and carry on our public works, with a tariff of ten per cent. (Hear, hear.) The only way we can keep out smuggling is to keep our tariff so low as to make it not worth while for any one to smuggle. Let me now draw your attention for a moment to the value of these North American Fisheries. You have behind and around you here, boundless prairies, which an all-bountiful Creator annually covers with rich harvests of wheat and corn. The Ocean is our prairie, and it stretches away before and around us, and Almighty God, for the sustenance of man, annnally replenishes it with fish in myriads that can't be counted, having a commercial value that no man can estimate. The fecundity of the Ocean may be estimated by the fact that the roes of thirty codfish annually replace all the fish that are taken by the British and French and American fishermen on the Banks of Newfoundland. In like manner the schools of mackerel, herring and of all other fish that swarm in the Bays and trim around the Shores, are replaced year by year. These great store-houses of food can never be exhausted. But it may be said, does not the free competition, which now exists, lower the prices? No. Codfish have never been higher in the markets of the world than they were last summer. Herrings are now selling in Baltimore for $13 a barrel. Thirty years ago I used to buy No. 1 mackerel in Halifax for $4 a barrel. They now cost $19, and I have seen them selling, since the Reciprocity Treaty was signed, for $22. The reason for this is, that, relative to other employments, fishing is a perilous and poor business, and that, with the progress of settlement and growth of population in all these great States and Provinces, to say nothing of the increased consumption in Spain, the Mediterranean, the Brazils, and the West Indies,—all that your fishermen and ours can catch will scarcely supply the demand. I placed before the Committee a paper, signed by two American merchants, carrying on trade in Prince Edward's Island, which proves, that under the Treaty your mackerel fishery has flourished and expanded to an extent unexampled in its former history. Taking two years prior to the existence of the treaty, and contrasting them with the two last years, they show that your mackerel fishery has grown from 250 vessels, measuring 18,150 tons, valued at $750,000 and manned by 2,750 men, and securing a catch worth $850,000, to 600 vessels, measuring 54,000 tons, employing 9,000 men, and securing 315,000 barrels, worth $4,567,500. So with the herring fishery, it is equally prosperous. I have seen two American seine boats take 500 barrels of herrings, at Baltimore prices worth $6,500 on the coast of Labrador, in a summer afternoon. The net fishing is also profitable. The Bank earns and Mill grinds while the Banker and Miller sleep. The fisherman sets his net at night; and finds in the morning that a kind Providence, without a miracle, except the "wealth of seas," that standing miracle, has loaded his net with a liberal hand. These fisheries, Sir, are sufficient for us all. The French, who are anxious to build up a powerful navy, maintain 10,000 men by their bounties in these North American waters, and it is most creditable to our fishermen, that in the face of these bounties and of yours, they have been able, by strict economy and hardy endurance, to wrestle for a share of these Ocean treasures, to maintain their families and increase their numbers.

A gentleman asked: — But had we not the right to fish on the Banks of Newfoundland before the treaty?

Mr. Howe—Yes, but not in the great bays of Newfoundland, and along the coast lines, where the people of Newfoundland, who frequent the Banks but little, catch all their Codfish. Some of these bays are twenty or thirty miles in width and deeply indent the Island, being broken into numerous fiords or smaller bays, where fish are plenty. By the treaty American fishermen can now use all these bays, as well as those upon the coast of Canada, Nova Scotia, New Brunswick and Prince Edward's Island. The command of the inshore fisheries gives to your people the opportunity to supply themselves with bait, whether they resort to banks or fish around the coast.

I trust I have thus shown you, Mr. Chairman, that the fisheries are inexhaustible, and of inestimable value; that free competition does not lower the prices, and that your fishermen and the French have special aids to stimulate their industry. But my great objection to the abrogation of this Treaty, is that it throws open again a wide field of controversy. Who can measure by the eye a mile even upon the land? And how are your fishermen to measure accurately three marine miles at sea even in fair weather? In a fog it is impossible to do so. And the naval officers who may be sent down to guard our mutual rights, will be as much mystified and puzzled as they were before.

But it may be said you gave us your inshore fisheries when we gave you ours. You did, but they were of comparatively little value. This was the objection that we took to the Treaty in Nova Scotia, in 1854. Let me illustrate. Suppose a farmer, living on a poor farm, exhausted by excessive cropping, were to say to a neighbor having a rich soil, let us save fencing and throw our farms into one. (Laughter.) That was your proposition, and it was accepted. Now mark the result: that while your vessels have swarmed in our waters for the last nine years, carrying off enormous values every year, we have never sent a vessel south during all that time, or caught a single cargo of fish on the coast or in the bays of the United States. (Hear, hear.)

Let me ask your attention to another matter which requires to be explained. Mr. Seymour, of New York, who made an excellent speech in favor of the resolution, took exception to the high tariff of Canada. Now, in the Provinces our people are naturally anxious to improve their internal communications, and bring them up to a level with other portions of the continent. Yielding to this pressure, the Government of Canada has expended large sums in the construction of railroads and canals; and let me say, that for every pound expended this Western Country has, either directly or indirectly, derived some benefit. But the money being spent, of course the interest has to be paid, and that that might be done, changes have been made in the tariff, from time to time. But you have been compelled to raise your tariff, and although I have not the two to compare, I assume that yours is much higher than that of Canada. Of this we do not complain. Why should you? Both countries must maintain their credit and pay their obligations. I was very much amused by a speech made by Mr. Morrill in your Congress, who assumes that "the magnificent Railway improvements of Canada have been made with the profits derived from the Reciprocity Treaty." But Mr. Morrill ought to know that out of about £13,000,000, expended upon the Grand Trunk Railway and the Victoria Bridge, £10,000,000 were subscribed by a body of British Capitalists, who have never got a shilling in return for their outlay. I was even more amused at the gentleman from Maine who took exception to the construction of the Intercolonial Road. He ought to remember that a very large amount, for which Canada pays interest, has gone to improve and re-stock the road running through Maine to Portland and to pay interest to the American proprietors from whom it was leased. As respects the road from Halifax to Bangor, I am happy to be able to inform him, that the Governments of Nova Scotia and New Brunswick have made 160 miles of that road since the Treaty was signed, while the State of Maine has not yet made a single mile to meet us. It ought to be remembered that Canada is spending, at this moment, a million of dollars on her frontier. For what? To keep her own people from coming to injure you? Why there is not a man would ever come. It is to keep the people from your side, who abused the rights of hospitality, from injuring or compromising us.

The necessities of Canada from these large expenditures compelled her to raise her import duty. And after all, Canada cannot levy a tax upon your manufactures that she does not also levy on those of Britain, so that you may be easy on that point. We are no more fond of taxation than you are, and there is no more popular cry for a man to get up in our Legislature than that of reducing taxation.

Passing from the subject of Railroads, let us speak of Canals. I candidly confess that when I came to this Convention, I was ignorant on the subject of Western extension, but I listened with great pleasure to the speeches made here, and especially to that of Mr. Littlejohn, and I began to feel the importance of the question. But this has been felt in Canada for many years. Has not Canada always been in advance of her means in trying to improve the course of navigation?

I know that a large portion of her debt has been expended in these canal improvements to accommodate the great West, and I know there is no question at this time which engrosses the attention of Canadians more than how they can best extend these highways of commerce. (Cheers.) And let me say, that from what I have heard here, when New York, Pennsylvania and Canada have done their best, and made their Canals as efficient as they can, there will be business enough to occupy them all, and the produce of the Great West will still crowd all those avenues. (Loud cheers.) The complaint that Canada has given drawbacks and discriminated has been fairly met by my friend, Mr. Ryan. There is no complaint against the Maritime Provinces, as the Boards of Trade of Boston and New York acknowledge with great candor. Newfoundland takes nearly all her breadstuffs and pork from this country free, and all your manufactures, under a very low tariff. As Spain, the Mediterranean and the West Indies all take codfish, she has very little to send in return. Prince Edward's Island sends you barley, oats and eggs, and takes from you by far the largest portion of her whole import from other Countries

My friend, Mr. Hamlin, seemed reluctant that any expression of opinion should go from this body. When any expression goes, it must go from American citizens. All we can do is to express an individual opinion. It is for American citizens to judge of what their own rights are. That is for you and not us to determine. But I do not believe that any expression of opinion from any body of men in this Country, will be looked upon as an interference with the authority of this Government, if I know the men at the head of your affairs, and understand your system. (Applause.) I may say that I believe this whole matter might be safely left in the hands of the very able man who presides over your State Department. (Cheers.) I have no hesitation in saying, as a British subject, that the manner in which he has dealt with the variety of vexed questions between the two Countries, for the last four years, gives me a fair assurance that upon this question, as upon all others, he will deal with these important interests as an intelligent, able and experienced statesman. (Loud cheers.) But I quite agree with Mr. Hamlin, and other gentlemen, that in making this Treaty you must have regard to the revenue you have to raise. I know that to be perfectly true. You have had a large expenditure, and I entirely approve of the spirit in which this assembly recognizes the duty of the Government to sustain the credit of the Country and maintain its obligations. We know you must do that. Why, if you do not, we should share in the disgrace; we should feel as a part of the British family, that when you had issued your bonds and sent them largely into foreign Countries, we should be disgraced as well as you if you did not sustain them. (Cheers.) But I believe that the resources of this Country are so vast and varied, and the development of its industry is so rapid and extensive, that you will be able to master the debt, maintain your credit, and deal with your neighbors in a kindly spirit beside. Why, Sir, if it was said by your Minister that this Treaty could not be renewed in consequence of your financial wants, there is not a man in the Colonies, who would not take that answer. (Cheers.) But if it were done in any other way, we would say, "it is not done from necessity — it is not done for revenue — it is done in temper, and it is an indication of the feeling which we must endeavor to eradicate." If Mr. Seward tells us that they cannot retain this Treaty and have a revenue, we shall be satisfied, and will live beside you and be good neighbors, and wait till your finances are in a better condition. (Loud cheers.) Now, I quite admit the general principle laid down by Mr. Hamlin, that it is not wise to enter into Treaties that shall withdraw large portions of produce from the operation of general revenue laws. But there may be circumstances that will render it expedient to make exceptions to that rule. We have a large debt in England. But, nevertheless, one of the most singular illustrations of this principle was that great achievement by that noble man whose loss is deplored by all parties, and who was in all respects a representative Englishman; I mean Richard Cobden. (Great applause.) The Treaty that he concluded with France was justified by the public necessities and the importance of that trade. And the exception to the rule in the case of the Reciprocity Treaty is justified in the same way. The French Treaty was essentially a Reciprocity Treaty, and has rapidly developed the commerce of the two countries, and has bound with ties of amity and peace the people of two great Countries who for centuries thought they ought to be natural enemies.

Among the interests represented here is the lumber interest. Now, I know something of the lumber trade, although the Province I came from is not very largely interested in it; but the Provinces of Canada and New Brunswick are. The gentleman from Maine seems to be afraid of the competition of Colonial lumber. I wish I had all these gentlemen on the River St. Croix. On the one side of that river is built the town of Calais, and on the other the town of St. Stephen's. They are connected by a bridge, and they have a railway for the transportation of lumber. It is about twenty miles long, and it accommodates the lumber of the two Countries. The merchant from Calais is loading a vessel at his wharf, and he has not got lumber enough to make up his cargo. Down goes from the other side a few loads of lumber to make up the cargo, and the next day down goes American lumber to load a British ship.

These two are thus made one by that Reciprocity, and I do not believe, in the case of a war, that there is a single man in St. Stephen's who would shoot a man in Calais. (Laughter.) They are kept together by this Treaty, and why should it not be so with reference to these Western States? If there be more lumber in Michigan than in Canada, why should it not go there; and if there is more in Canada than on your prairies, why should not our lumber go out upon the prairies? Why would any one refuse to the poor settler the privilege of buying the cheapest lumber he can get? (Loud cheers.)

But it is said that there is danger of the price of your lumber being affected by the introduction of ours. There is no evidence of this. The price of lumber last year was very high, and I know that since the Treaty has been in operation the people of Bangor have all got rich. But let us reassure them. There are causes at work over the face of the Continent that must always keep up the price of lumber. Nobody plants a pine tree except for shade, and everybody is cutting them down. Many of the States are almost cleared of pine, from the Seaboard back to the Lakes. There are millions of axes cutting down trees, and millions of firesides burning them up, to say nothing of Railroads in every section of the Country in want of fuel. These are our securities that the price of lumber will never get too low. It has passed away or is before the pioneer. Every poor German or Irishman who goes into the backwoods and destroys the timber helps to keep up the price of lumber, and no man in the State of Maine believes that the price can come largely down. But even if it would is it not better that it should be so? When a hundred logs are thrown into a river the Almighty furnishes the trees and the means to bring them down free. Why, then, should we divide the river and the forest by restrictive regulations? But we do not own all the timber in our possession. In all the Provinces we have abolished our alien laws. The American citizen can come and buy mines, and land, and timber wherever he likes. And I know of men in Maine and Massachusetts who own as much as twenty thousand acres in one block in Nova Scotia. A large portion of the lumber of our Province is owned by the citizens of this Republic. Take the case of the river St. John, and you will find that American lumber comes down there paying no taxes, and the whole of that river is alive in the summer with your lumber taken off our land and worked by enterprising Americans. If there is an American vessel there she carries it to your own ports, or to England; and so the lumber, twisted and intertwined as it is, is a trade owned in fact by the two Countries.

A word with regard to coal. I was amused at the exception taken to the action of a gentleman from Philadelphia, and at the statement made by some speaker that he could see nothing but coal and iron. Well, they are very good things to see, and I am happy to say that in Nova Scotia we have them both in large quantities, and we have them near the sea, therefore I have great sympathy with a Pennsylvanian who does not undervalue coal and iron. But let me say this, that I have just done what I never had an opportunity of doing before — I have seen the front, and rear, and centre of this State of Pennsylvania. I have seen there what reconciles me to all the misfortunes that may happen to her if this Treaty should go into effect. Pennsylvania is so rich in a fertile soil, so rich in honest industry, so rich in iron and coal, so rich in fruits, and in all that can embellish or give animation to industrial life, that she need care nothing about this Treaty. God has been good to her, and her thrifty sons have made the best use of the blessings that have been bestowed upon them. As I passed over that State and saw her fertile fields, I should have fancied I was in one the richest districts of England, but for the wooden fences. I visited her great workshop, and I saw a City that has no rival on this continent — a City only matched by three or four in Europe. There Pennsylvania stands in her beauty and power, and she need not fear competition from any of our Provinces. But as with timber, so with coal. Do you think we own all the coal in Nova Scotia? I think not. There is hardly a steamer comes down from New York or Boston that does not bring American capitalists to invest money in our coal.

Now a few words in explanation for the gentleman from Buffalo, who asked me if the Provinces had not received some compensation by blockade-running, for the loss of the Southern Trade, and I answer, certainly not. We have fifty seaports where we maintain officers, and from whence we carry on foreign trade. But one out of fifty has had anything to do with blockade-running. Now, then, if fifty citizens of this Country had the option to do a thing, and but one had done it, it would be rather hard to bring a charge against the whole lot for the wrong done by one. But who has carried on this blockade-running? Not our Nova Scotia merchants. Has anybody put Nova Scotia capital into this business? I do not believe £5. Then where did the capital come from? It came from your own Country, either in the form of gold brought there, or it came in the shape of bills drawn on the cotton loan in England, by your own people. A gentleman from New York, or Portland, or Boston, or anywhere else, comes down to Halifax, and says to one of our merchants, I want you to buy 100 barrels of pork. He buys it and ships it to whatever place he is directed. Our merchant receives his commission, and that is all he has to do with it. Even in this I know of very few merchants who have touched it at all. There are a few, a very few, but whether they have made a profit by it, I do not know. It has not amounted to anything as a business, as compared with the general volume of our Colonial trade. I have not been home lately, but I should not be very much surprised if, when I get there, I find that the rebellion caved in so rapidly that some of these bills have not been paid in England.

Mr. Allen—I did not inquire from any captious motives. I have no doubt that American traitors are as deeply concerned in it as Canadian speculators. (Great applause.)

Mr. Howe—I believe you did not; and let me say, also, Mr. Chairman, that no gentleman from the Provinces has taken offence at anything said or done in this assembly. We are accustomed to free debates at home, and let me assure Mr. Hamlin that none of us felt aggrieved at his banter yesterday, which we accepted as a compliment to our shrewdness.

Mr. Chairman, I must now touch upon a subject of some delicacy and importance. It has been urged by Mr. Morrill, in Congress, and by the people of the United States, that the Treaty ought not to be renewed because it had bred no friendship towards them across the Lakes—that in their struggle the sympathies of the Provinces were with the South. Well, if that were true in its fullest extent, which it was not, if you had not had one sympathiser among the native people and British residents of the Provinces, it could be fairly plead in response that when Great Britain was at war with Russia the sympathies of the American People were very generally with the latter Country. I was in the United States at the time, and was perfectly astonished at the feeling. Russia was at that time a Country full of slaves, for the serfs had not been emancipated, and England was at war with her to prevent her aggressions upon weak neighboring Countries. How the American people could sympathise with Russia was a perfect puzzle at first sight, and could only be explained in the same manner that much of the sympathy for the South on the part of the British subjects can be explained. And when the Canadians once had a rebellion within her borders, where were the sympathies of the American people then? Were they with the Canadian Government or with the Rebels? Why, you not only sympathized with them, but I am sorry to have to say it, gave them aid along the frontier in many ways, and to a very large extent. I am happy to be able to say, that during the whole four years of the late rebellion in the United States there has not been developed a particle of èvidence to show that a single citizen of any British North American Province put a hostile foot on your soil. (Loud applause.) Everything of which complaint can be made has been the act of your own people, in violation of hospitality and right of asylum everywhere extended to them on the soil of Great Britain and her Dependencies. I make these remarks in no spirit of anger, or of excitement, but to show how unfair it is to hold any Government or people responsible for the actions in it of a few evil disposed individuals, as well as how natural it was for sympathy to be aroused in the minds of people on one side or another. In our rebellion, when its attention was called to their acts, the United States Government exerted itself to keep its own citizens within its bounds, and all that could have been asked of the Provincial authorities has been freely done to prevent any cause of complaint against them. It is something to be able to say that during the four long disastrous years of war just ended, not a single act of which complaint could be made has been committed by a Canadian. Notwithstanding the false reports that were circulated, I do not believe there was a single intelligent citizen, of my Province at least, who did not believe the capture of the Chesapeake, off the coast of Maine, by rebellious citizens of the United States, was nothing less or more than an act of piracy. And so of the St. Albans raid. The Government of Canada acted most promptly and nobly in connection with that affair, and has repaid the money which rebellious citizens of the United States had carried into their territory from the State banks. (Hear, hear.) As to their harboring the rebels and extending to them the right of asylum, is there a single American here who would have his Government surrender that right? (Applause.) There is not an Englishman, an Irishman, a Scotchman, nor an American who would not fight these wars rather than give up that sacred right. (Applause.) How many excellent citizens of the United States are there from this Country at this moment, and how many were there who helped them to fight their battles, who dare not go back to their own native lands across the Ocean on account of political offences? The American people would not give these men up to their respective Governments and thus surrender their right of asylum; they would every man of them fight first. (Applause.) It is very proper that criminals should be given up, and a Treaty for that purpose has been made between England and the United States. We may sympathise with political offenders, but not with criminals. When Abraham Lincoln fell by the hand of the assassin, the act was reprobated from end to end of the British Empire. (Hear.) But admitting that a large number of people in the Provinces sympathised with the rebels; what of that? Did not a very large number of people in the Northern States sympathize with them? Nobody ever saw two dogs fighting in the street, or two cocks fighting in a back yard, wthout having his sympathies aroused, he scarcely knew why, in favor of one or the other of the combatants, and generally the weakest. (Laughter.) Suppose some feeling was excited in the British Provinces, was that any good reason for refusing to allow us to trade with you across the Lakes? The sympathy expressed for the South may be well balanced by the young men whom you have drawn from the Colonies into the conflict. (Hear, hear.) For one ton of goods sent to the Southerners, and for one young man sent to aid their cause, we have sent fifty tons and fifty able bodied soldiers to the North. The people of the Provinces might lay the charge against you of having seduced their young men away from their homes, and left their bodies bleaching on Southern plains or rotting in Southern prisons. Only a short time ago I met three British Americans, going home on a single vessel, after having served three years in the war, and having left scores of their companions behind to enrich the soil. At Washington I met with a brave nephew of one of my late colleagues in the Legislature of Nova Scotia, who had held the rank of Lieutenant in a Massachusetts regiment, with only one leg to take back to his home instead of two. (Loud cheers.) I met another veteran from my Province who had fought in twenty battles, and was on his way home. In my own family and person I have suffered not a little by this unhappy rebellion. I have five boys, and one of them took it into his head to enter your army. He has now been for nearly two years in the Twenty-third Ohio Regiment, and has fought in all the battles in which that regiment has been engaged during that period. He was in both the great battles under General Sheridan, in which General Early's forces were scattered, and the Shenandoah Valley cleared. (Loud and long continued applause.) All the personal benefit that I have derived from the Reciprocity Treaty, or hope to derive from its renewal, will never compensate me or that boy's mother for the anxiety we have had with regard to him; but when he produced the certificates of his commanding officer showing that he had conducted himself like a gentleman, and had been faithful and brave, it was some consolation for all our anguish to know that he had performed his duty. (Enthusiastic applause, during which the speaker's feelings nearly overcame him; as this subsided, a gentleman proposed "three cheers for the boy," which were given with great vivacity.) I know that it has been asserted by some, and I have heard it said since I came to the Convention, that if the Reciprocity Treaty is annulled the British Provinces will be so cramped that they will be compelled to seek annexation to the United States. I beg leave to be allowed to say on that point that I know the feeling in the Lower Provinces pretty thoroughly, and believe I am well enough acquainted with the Canadians to speak for them also, and speak for them all, with such exceptions as must be made when speaking for any entire population, when I make the assertion, that no considerations of finance, no question of balance for or against them, upon interchanges of commodities, can have any influence upon the loyalty of the inhabitants of the British Provinces, or tend in the slightest degree to alienate the affections of the people from their Country, their Institutions, their Government, and their Queen. There is not a loyal man in the British American Provinces, no man worthy of the name, who, whatever may happen to the Treaty, will become any the less loyal, any the less true to his Country on that account. There is not a man who dare, on the abrogation of the Treaty, if such should be its fate, take the hustings and appeal to any constituency on annexation principles throughout the entire domain. The man who avows such a sentiment will be scouted from society by his best friends. What other treatment would a man deserve who should turn traitor to his Sovereign and his Government, and violate for pecuniary advantage all obligations to the Country which gave him birth! You know what you call Copperheads, and a nice life they have of it. (Laughter.) Just such a life will the man have who talks treason on the other side of the lines. (Applause.) The very boy of whom I have alluded as having fought manfully for the Stars and Stripes, would rather blow his own father's brains out than haul down the honored flag under which he has been born — the flag of his nation and of his fatherland. (Cheers.) I do not believe there is a young Canadian in the Army who does not honor his own flag as you honor yours, and they would be despised if they did not. If any member of the Convention harbors the idea that in refusing Reciprocity to British America, they will undermine the loyal feelings of the people of those Colonies, he is laboring under a delusion, and doing injustice to a people whose sentiment of loyalty is as indelible as your own. (Loud and continued applause.)

Some gentlemen from Maine asked me if we were not building fortifications in the Provinces. Well, after so many threats from Northern newspapers that so soon as the rebellion was put down and Mexico was attended to, the face of the army would be turned towards Canada, it was not to be wondered at that the mother country should become a little anxious about her children so far from home, and send out an experienced officer to report upon the situation. The officer did not report any armed force in sight, but reported that if they did come, Canada was in a very poor condition to receive them, and it was resolved to build further fortifications at Quebec, and there has been some talk about places further westward, but no action has been taken. But what do we see on the other hand? I passed down the Penobscot river a few weeks ago, and what did I see there? A great frowning fort, of the most approved pattern, looking as new and as pretty as if it had just come from the mint. (Laughter.) At Portland, also, I observe some extensive fortifications in progress, and have been informed that you are at work in the same line at other points, so that nothing need be said if Canada does invest some money in costly fortifications. But I have no faith in fortifications. I do not rely on military defences:

We need no bulwarks,
No towers along the steep;
Our march is o'er the mountain wave,

And our homes are in the mart, on the mountain and the prairie, wherever there is good work to be done, and God's gifts to be appropriated. I have faith in our common brotherhood—in such meetings as this—in such social gatherings as that magnificent demonstration which we all enjoyed so much last night. I sincerely hope that all thought of forcing annexation upon the people of Canada will be abandoned, and that if not, you will seek a more pleasant sort of annexation for your children and your children's children. It was a novel mode of attaching them that the people of Detroit adopted, in lashing a fleet of their steamers together, and getting up such a grand entertainment, and there was no question that it had a strong tendency to promote one kind of annexation, especially among the young people. (Laughter.) As a measure of self-protection, I put myself under the wing of a pretty little New Brunswick woman, and charged her to take good care of me until we got safe ashore. (Laughter and applause, twice repeated.) I fear I am detaining you too long. Cries of "go on" from all parts of the house.) In conclusion let me say, that in dealing with this great subject, I have spoken in an open, plain manner, and kept back nothing that ought to be said upon it, considering the limited time at my disposal. My friend Mr. Hamlin wished us "to show our hands"; we have done so, and shown our hearts also, in all sincerity. The subject is of vast importance to us all. Though living away down East, I take a deep interest in the Great West, and I trust God will spare my life long enough to permit me to explore its vastness more thoroughly than I have yet been able to do, that I may the better discuss the great interests created by its commerce. British America has a great West, as yet almost entirely undeveloped, out of which four or five States or Provinces may yet be formed, to pour their wealth down the great Lake Huron into Canada, and through the Straits, past the city of Detroit, to the Ocean, while the manufactures of the United States, of England and of the Provinces go back to supply the wants. The moment Providence gives me opportunity, I will return to the West and examine its rescources, and understand its position, in order that I may lay before my own people, and the people of the Provinces generally, and the capitalists of the Mother Country, an adequate idea of its importance, with a view of promoting a more active settlement and development of the territory on both sides of the boundary line, for the trade would be as valuable to the world on one side as on the other.

Thanking the Convention for the courtesy of so extended a hearing as had been granted him, the Honorable gentleman left the platform, amidst deafening and long continued applause.

J. Young Scammon, of Chicago, said:

After listening to the eloquent speech of the very able gentleman from Nova Scotia, I should not rise at this time to address any remarks to this Convention, did not I feel it a duty incumbent upon me to say a few words in behalf of a class of people in this country, who have as yet had no representative upon this floor.

We have heard from the pine forests of Maine; we have heard from the gentlemen engaged in transportation, and from the great carrying interests of New York; we have heard from the fisheries of the maratime border; but we have not heard from the men who stand at the handle of the plow, and produce the grain to feed the millions of this country.

In behalf of them, I wish to speak a few words. The commercial motto of the great State of Illinois stands over the portals of this hall, in these words: "The Great West seeks to extend her commerce to all parts of the World, and demands the opening of all communications to the Seaboard." I had the honor to be sent by the Government of Illinois, the summer before last to wait upon the Governor General and the authorities of Canada, and present for their consideration the grounds upon which we asked the Canadian Government that they should give us broader and deeper avenues to the Atlantic Seaboard through the great channel the Almighty had made for the Northwest. (Cheers.) It would ill become me, whatever my opinions and those of my constituents might be on the subject of Reciprocity, to refuse to give my assent to the resolution which was reported here from the committee, asking the authorities of this country to enter into negotiations with the authorities of Great Britain in order to see whether a treaty could not be formed that should be just and equitable to all parties, and which should secure greater avenues to the Ocean, for the West. I should act against the unanimous decision of the Board of Trade of Chicago, if I should not vote in favor of that proposition. And now, after having gone to the Govèrnor General of Canada, and having submitted to him, in writing, these views, to submit to the Parliament of Canada, and the Government of England, as representative from Illinois, as representing the Chicago Board of Trade, under whose authority I proceeded to Quebec, if I should refuse to give my sanction to this negociation for a treaty, upon fair and equitable principles, which would secure this outlet to the Atlantic coast, I should be very inconsistent. So far as the opinion of the people I represent is concerned, I believe they are opposed to the present treaty, and I believe they decide correctly; for I find that all our friends across the border vote unanimously for the treaty, and therefore I think with my friend from Maine, that they are getting two slices to our one.

But in reference to this matter of opening up communication from the West to the East, there is, I think, no difference of opinion. In addressing the Governor General, we said to him:

"We have come briefly and respectfully to present to you, and through you to the Provincial Parliament and the British Government, the importance both to Great Britain and the United States of so opening and perfecting the navigation of the St. Lawrence, as to afford to the commerce of both countries a cheap communication between the shipping ports on the Northwestern Lakes and Great Britain."

"The future prosperity of these States, bordering on the Great Lakes, depends in a great measure upon cheap transportation to foreign markets; hence, they are vitally interested in the question of opening the St. Lawrence, the great national thoroughfare to the Ocean, through and by which the people of England may enlarge their supplies of breadstuffs and provisions, greatly exceeding the quantity heretofore received from the United States, at one-fourth less cost than it has heretofore been received.

"From actual experience, derived from shipment of Indian corn from Chicago to Liverpool, it is shown that the freight charges often cover seven-eighths of the value of a bushel of corn at Liverpool. More than one-half of the cost of wheat is also covered by the present very inadequate means of transportation.

"The Northwestern States furnished one-third of 16,094,914 quarters of grain imported into England in the year 1861, a season of extremely high freights on the Lakes and Canals, as well as upon the Ocean.

"It is our opinion that the cost of transportation may be reduced to ten shillings per quarter, or thirty cents on a bushel. One-half of this sum added to the incomes of our farmers, would give a remarkable stimulus to the production of grain, and would lead, within a few years — five years at the farthest — to the production of a surplus, exceeding the total of grain imported into England from all countries.

"The interior of North America is drained by the St Lawrence, which furnishes for the country bordering upon the Lakes a natural highway to the sea. Through its deep channel must pass the agricultural productions of the vast Lake Region. The commercial spirit of the age forbids that international jealousy should interfere with great national thoroughfares, and the Governments of Great Britain and the United States will appreciate this spirit, and cheerfully yield to its influence. The great avenue of the Atlantic, through the St. Lawrence, being once opened to its largest capacity, the laws of trade, which it has never been the policy of the Federal Government to obstruct, will carry the commerce of the Northwest through it."

Having said this to the Governor General of Canada, under authority of the State of Illinois, it ill becomes us to refuse to pass resolutions which have been reported by the Committee on Reciprocity. And now, then, as I don't wish to take up the time of the house, I will call attention to the difference between the resolution proposed by the Committee and the one proposed as a substitute.

In the one reported from the Committee nothing is said about the old Treaty, to which objection has been made. We merely declare that we are in favor of negotiations, with a view to forming a Treaty which shall be entirely just and equitable, and shall, at the same time secure us what is stated over the portals of this hall.

Now, what is the other resolution? It refers all these matters to the Government. The difference is that in the one case, we say that it is our desire that the government should enter into negotiations to see whether a treaty cannot be formed, and at the same time secure these great channels of communication for the productions of the Northwest. Now, I think that the men who toil at the plow-handle, who produce the bread that feeds the Eastern States, a large portion of Canada, and other parts of the World, are entitled to be heard here, and that it is due to these men to see if our Government cannot afford them some relief; they are entitled to present their views, and receive due consideration. (Cheers.)

After some debate as to points of order, and who was entitled to the floor, the Chairman awarded the privilege of speaking to Hon. Fred. Fraley, of Philadelphia, who spoke as follows:

I will not trespass upon your time by ornamental language, but I had the honor of being a member of the Committee on Reciprocity. I heard the arguments and explanations of our friends from the British Provinces. I tendered manfully and openly the terms upon which Pennsylvania was in favor of a Reciprocity Treaty. Those were the same terms that Pennsylvania enjoys under the Constitution of the United States in trading with New York, or any other State of this Union. I tendered to them the same law of registry and coasting, and everything going to make a similarity of interests, a similarity of pursuits, a similarity of all matters between the British Provinces and the United States. Could Pennsylvania have tendered them more? On the other questions discussed in this Convention — those of agriculture, and mining, and manufactures — Pennsylvania has stood upon the same ground that she has always occupied, and she thanks this Convention for the unanimous vote whch has been given in favor of these interests. In regard to questions affecting transit and transportation, Pennsylvania has voted solidly for every proposition to open all possible avenues of trade to the Great West. She has not only voted so here and there, but for upwards of a half a century she has voted so everywhere; and I challenge any man to show me the record of an open, honest hearted Pennsylvanian who has ever gone against the widest system of internal improvement in any part of the United States. (Cheers.) I thank the gentleman from Nova Scotia for the noble tribute which he has paid to the Keystone State, and what we wish is that our friends in the West will pursue the policy of Pennsylvania, and make their markets at home; that instead of the transit from the farm to the Ocean, they they shall make the transit from the farm to the manufactory. (Loud cheers.) It is that which has made Pennsylvania rich. We are self-supporting, and while we stretch out our iron arms and our water arms to all sections of the world, we believe in the policy of protecting domestic industry, and making the market of the farmer upon the same ground as the workshop.

Now, with reference to this particular question, I have to say that while the delegation from Pennsylvania were prepared to support the substitute to the original resolution offered by the Committee, yet they have authorized me to say that, with a slight modification in the original resolution, they are disposed to go unanimously for that — that is, with a word or two put in to define what we mean by just and equitable principles. That is what I understood to be conceded by the gentleman from Nova Scotia as the financial interests of our country.

At the conclusion of his remarks, Mr. Fraley moved an amendment to the original resolution, by inserting after the words "just and equitable to all parties," the words, "and with reference to the present financial condition of the United States."

The Chair, (Mr. Randolph, of Chicago,) ruled that the question was on Mr. McChesney's substitute, and not on the original resolution, and, therefore, Mr. Fraley's amendment was not in order.

Mr. Hamlin stated the Parliamentary Law in reference to the matter, and the Chair reversed his previous decision.

Mr. Fraley's amendment was then carried.

The Chair then stated the question to be upon the passage of the substitute of Mr. McChesney.

Mr. Bowen, of Chicago, stated that Mr. McChesney had returned home on account of sickness in his family, but that as his representative here, and by the

25

advice of a fellow member of the Committee, he would withdraw the substitute. (Applause.)

The question was then taken on the original resolution, as amended, which was as follows:

Resolved, That this Convention do respectfully request the President of the United States to enter into negotiations with the Government of Great Britain having in view the execution of a Treaty between the two Countries for Reciprocal Commercial Intercourse between the United States and the several Provinces of British North America, including British Columbia, the Selkirk Settlement and Vancouver's Island, based on principles which shall be just and equitable to all parties, and with reference to the present financial condition of the United States, and which shall also include the free navigation of the St. Lawrence, and the other Rivers of British North America, with such improvements of the Rivers and the enlargement of the Canals as shall render them adequate for the requirements of the West in communicating with the Ocean.

The resolution was unanimously adopted by the following vote:

	AYE.	NO.
Mercantile Association, Bangor,	3½	..
Board of Trade, Portland,	3½	..
Board of Trade, Boston,	13	..
Chamber of Commerce, New York,	7	..
Commercial Association, New York,	7	..
Board of Trade, Albany,	5	..
Board of Trade, Troy,	4	..
Board of Trade, Buffalo,	6	..
Board of Trade, Oswego,	4	..
Cincinnati,	10	..
Cleveland,	5	..
Toledo,	4	..
Springfield,	2	..
Detroit,	4	..
Kalamazoo,	1	..
Bay City,	1½	..
East Saginaw,	1½	..
Board of Trade, Cairo,	5	..
Board of Trade, Chicago,	7	..
Mercantile Association, Chicago,	4	..
Chamber of Commerce, Milwaukee,	8	..
Board of Trade, Philadelphia,	6	..

	AYE.	NO.
Corn Exchange, Philadelphia,	5	..
Coal Exchange, Philadelphia,	4	..
Board of Trade, Pittsburgh,	6	..
Board of Trade, Erie,	5	..
Minnesota,	4	..
Missouri,	11	..
Iowa,	8	..
	155	..

The various votes, as called out, were heartily applauded, and the announcement of the result was received with great cheering.

Mr. Converse, from the special committee on the subject of a National Board of Trade, presented the following report:

Every year the mercantile community feel more and more the necessity of some closer bond, to unite all the mercantile interests of the Union, than any which does now exist. The only connection now existing are political ones, established purely for political and administrative purposes, and only incidentally designed to assist the large section of the country devoted to trade, commerce and manufactures.

Many plans have been suggested to establish some such bond, by the organization of an association or creation of some office especially devoted to the mercantile interests of the country. All of them, however, can be divided into two classes—one based upon a political board or department, the other upon a voluntary association of the commercial and mercantile interests for their own protection and benefit. Without paying much attention to the innumerable details which a plan founded on either of these great leading principles would comprise, this paper will present briefly some of the considerations naturally presented by these two rival methods for attaining what it is so generally acknowledged that we need.

The relations between the Federal Government and the mercantile classes has thus far not been very intimate. Up to 1861, our revenue was derived almost entirely from the customs, and even the imposition of import duties was governed but little by broad views of the great mercantile interests of the country which paid them. The tariff was to a great extent a political and sectional question. The minds of legislators were biased, if not settled beyond influence, by the accidents of party and local connections. A representative from many parts of the country would not throw a vote on this subject during a whole session, that might not have been surely foretold before he took his seat; for it was universally known that had he not held the views ascribed to him, and held them, either from principle or policy, most tenaciously, he would never have found his way to Washington as a member of Congress. As local and political reasons thus controlled questions of pure political economy, so they divided the mercantile classes, and often very difficult would it have been to convince a business man from one part of the Union that it was for his best interest to yield many of his own claims to those of men in his position in other States. It was easy for a free-trader to see that the protectionists themselves would be in the end benefitted and enriched by a free trade policy, but to have proved to him that however true his principles might be as a general rule, it was of the greatest importance to him to bear a troublesome and unpopular duty on some commodity for the purpose of assisting other and different branches of trade struggling with adversity, five hundred or a thousand miles distant, would have been difficult indeed. Fortunately, however, for many years, the political interest in mercantile questions has steadily declined, and just now they are of comparatively little importance as party issues; and if, in raising the great revenue which we shall now have to levy, broad, national and sound principles actuate our rulers, we may hope to see subjects so vitally affecting our prosperity, taken almost entirely out of the arena of politics. The inquiry, therefore, presents itself. How can this be done?

For a long time it has been felt by reflecting men that the relations between the government and the merchant are not exactly what they ought to be. While our revenue came solely from duties on imports, those relations were confined almost entirely to the Seaboard, and to those three or four great ports where most of these duties are collected. Frequent was the complaint that the laws were framed as if all the trading class was prepared to cheat the government, and administered in a spirit which placed the government and the merchant in antagonistic positions. On the other side the official declared that the most high-minded business man possessed no conscience where the government was concerned, and that the most rigid severity was necessary to prevent frauds that would be ruinous to the revenue. This state of things is no longer confined to the sea-coast. The heavy excise duties everywhere bring the assessor and collector in contact with the merchant, farmer and manufacturer, and loud complaints, once confined to one region and one class, are heard throughout the land.

This, clearly, is not as it should be. As the interest of the government and the trader are one, so their unity should be more apparent, or it may cease in time to be real. When the trading classes really perceive that the General Government is disposed help them, to listen to their complaints, and to do everything in its power to increase trade and commerce, and apportion the public burdens equitably, they, in their turn, will discourage all attempts to defraud the revenue — attempts which, when successful, injure the honest merchant much more than the sovereign authority.

All communications between the government and the trader are carried on through the Treasury Department. Formerly, when the revenue was small and derived from one source, the Secretary of the Treasury was able to give something like proper attention to every question under his jurisdiction. Now, however, this great minister must barely find time to perform the higher duties of his department, and upon all minor matters he must from necessity be governed by the judgment of subordinates, on account of the impossibility of being able himself to give time to independent investigations. This, in reality, deprives the merchant of an appeal to the Secretary of the Treasury, which the law gives him. Nor are these smaller questions of no importance. On the contrary, we are inclined to look upon them as of the most serious consequence. As the London *Spectator* wisely said, in speaking of our ability to bear our public burdens, we are like a powerful horse, which cares nothing about the weight of his rider, but will nevertheless become ungovernable, if the saddle galls him. Our capacity is beyond question, if the burden is only placed so as not to irritate and fret us; and any danger that there may be in this respect is confined to the impatience which a harsh administration of the laws, and "the insolence of office" may tend to create. It is therefore essential that for all complaints of this nature there should be a tribunal, ready and willing to listen, and prompt to give relief when injustice has been done.

We think that, from these reflections, it will be perceived that a Department of Trade and Commerce might be established with great advantage to the Government and the Merchant. Such a Department exists in all other great Countries. The leading Powers of the European Continent each has its Minister of Commerce. Great Britain possesses her Board of Trade, with a President and Vice President, and Secretaries, besides subordinate officers; and by watching the administration of this Department of the Imperial Government for one session of Parliament, any one will see the immense benefit it is to both Sovereign and People. It matters not whether it is a Commercial Treaty, or the burning of a steamer, or a railway disaster — whatever question comes before the English Board of Trade receives an attention which it would be impossible for it to obtain were no such Department in existence. Besides, the information and statistics collected by it are of the utmost importance to the Chancellor of the Exchequer in preparing his Budget, and to enable Parliament to legislate with all the assistance derived from knowledge and experience.

The old Committee on Ways and Means, in the House of Representatives, has been divided, and its duties distributed among other and new Committees, rendered necessary by the changes in our finances and fiscal system. The division of the Treasury Department into two or more Departments is likely to follow very soon; some think, this coming session of Congress. This presents an excellent opportunity for organizing a Department of Trade. To such a Department would naturally be transferred the charge of the Customs, with custom-houses and light-houses, and perhaps the care of the Internal Revenue, which, in its details, would fall properly within it. This would enable a high Government officer to superintend the administration of these bureaux in a far more efficient manner than the overworked Secretary of the Treasury can ever hope to do; and such a superintendence cannot fail to be of infinite service to the Government, even if the actual saving in money consequent thereon should not be, as we believe it would be, sufficient to meet all the expenses of the new Department. The authority of such an officer would be far more telling and effective than the authority of a subordinate Commissioner, Assistant Secretary, or Chief of a Bureau. As the care of Trade would fall to this Department, the collection of mercantile statistics and information; the examination of new projects for increasing Commerce and Trade, and opening up new channels for them; the protection and encouragement of new and struggling enterprises, and the harmonizing, as far as possible, of conflicting interests, so as to make the commercial interests all over the Country identical, would each and all require close attention from it, and, if these various and vital questions were properly attended to, would prevent the officers in it from being very idle.

The present English Board of Trade was established by the second William Pitt in 1786. It is, in fact, a Committee of the Privy Council; for, except the President and Vice President, the members of it are all heads of other Departments of Government, who, however, only assemble on important occasions. The President and Vice President are both Privy Councillors, and must have seats in Parliament; and the former is generally a member of the Cabinet. The salary of each is two thousand pounds. There are also two Secretaries, who do not sit in Parliament, and who are permanent officers, unlike the President and Vice President, who, being political officers, are changed with each change in the Administration. Some of the duties of this Board — such as the Superintendence of Railways, the charge of a School of Design, and of a Committee on the Fine Arts — in our country do not fall within the province of the Federal Government. Other branches of its duties — the inspection of steamboats and other ships, the charge of the coast and light-houses — administered by the subordinate corporation known as the Trinity House — would naturally devolve upon a similar Department at Washington, should one be created. In higher branches of service — such as the negotiation of Commercial Treaties, the distribution of custom duties, and the details of all commercial legislation — the Board of Trade always gives invaluable aid to the other Departments of the Government, and the most comprehensive and valuable statistics in the world are those contained in its various reports to Parliament. It is not saying too much to assert that the prosperity of the commercial interests of Great Britain, and the colossal proportions to which her trade and manufactures have grown, are owing in no small measure to the ever watchful, wise, and jealous care bestowed upon them by the Board of Trade. The closest intercourse, by correspondence and interviews, is kept up between its chiefs and the innumerable branches of mercantile pursuits all over the United Kingdom, and the vast information derived therefrom has extraordinary influence in moulding the commercial policy of the Empire. The result is perceived too frequently by those who have to compete with Englishmen in any branch of trade.

The very fact that Great Britain, France, and other great foreign nations cherish and protect so eagerly their own merchants, renders it necessary for our self-protection that the Federal Government should pay closer attention to our mercantile community, and endeavor, as far as it is compatible with the true objects for which the Federal Government was formed, to protect and foster them, to take care that taxation be not inequitably distributed, and that Congress shall have the most exact information, and be enabled to apply the most enlightened principles, in its commercial legislation. This can never be properly done until a high and independent Department is created for this express object, with a sufficient corps of officers to open communication with every part of the world, gather information, and to digest and arrange it for the use of the Government and the Legislature.

The objections which will be made to such a plan are of little weight. To that of the expense, we shall pay no attention. We believe the saving to the Government in those branches of the service placed under the supervision of this new Department, as we said before, will be amply sufficient to meet all expenses. Besides, if it is not, it will be only the most narrow, suicidal policy which will raise this objection, if the expediency of forming such a Department be once proved. A similar objection, but perhaps a more plausible one, would be one made to the increase of patronage consequent upon the establishment of any new Department of Government. The reply is that whatever evils may result therefrom are the necessary result of the growth of the country, and the increase of the revenue.

A more formidable obstacle is likely to arise from a dislike of increasing the number of the Cabinet. But we do not see the necessity, however great may be the expediency, of the the head of the Department of Commerce being a member of the Cabinet. If we remember rightly, the Postmaster General was not until 1829. The Cabinet in this country is almost as much a growth outside the Constitution as it is in England; and the probability is that, as the heads of Departments increase — and they certainly must and will, however reluctant we may be to have them — only a portion of them, and not always the same ones, will be summoned to the Cabinet. But as the revenue is of so essential importance to the Government, and as the revenue depends principally upon the commercial and mercantile prosperity of the Union, it would seem to be particularly important that a man representing these interests, and intimately acquainted with their wants, their weakness, their capabilities, and their strength, should be present at the consultations of the highest Council in the Republic, to aid the President by his information and knowledge.

For the reasons thus imperfectly expressed, we feel that it is incumbent upon those representing the various branches of trade to agitate earnestly the subject of forming, at Washington, a Department presided over by a high officer of State, having the especial superintendence of the Trade and Commerce of the Union. Such a Department would be far more efficient than any voluntary organizations, and would, by communications with every part of the Country, and by correspondence with the various local Boards of Trade and Chambers of Commerce, prove a great bond of union among them, and do much towards harmonizing interests far more antagonistic and conflicting in appearance than in reality.

The other method for uniting the mercantile interests of the community is by a voluntary organization. The advantages of such a plan are, that it can be done at once without waiting for the action of Congress, and that it would be entirely out of the political arena. Indeed, even should a National Department of Trade be created, some union of the several Boards of Trade and Chambers of Commerce might be expedient, although not so essential as it will be if Congress refuses to take action.

But if it is thought absolutely necessary that some voluntary association should be formed, we think it might be done in connection with the other. The Massachusetts State Board of Agriculture consists in part of persons appointed by the Governor, and in part of members elected by the various Agricultural Societies. An advisatory Board, elected by the various local Trade Associations, and summoned occasionally to assist the Government on vital questions, might be organized with little trouble and at little expense.

The Committee beg leave to present the following resolutions:

Resolved, That in order to relieve some of the departments of the General Government, and especially that of the Treasury, from many of the details with which they are now crowded and in order to secure for the various industrial interests of the country the benefits of a systematized, experienced and permanent Board, it is the judgment of this Convention that a Government Board of Trade should be formed for the especial oversight and care of all questions relating to our agricultural, manufacturing and commercial interests, for the compilation of statistics for inquiry into casualties and for such other subjects as may properly be included in such a department.

Resolved, That the Secretary of the Board of Trade of Boston be requested to prepare and present, in behalf of this Committee, a memorial to the Congress of the United States, asking, in view of the immense industrial and mercantile interests involved, its early consideration of and action upon the subject.

Resolved, That the Board of Trade of Boston be, and is hereby requested to invite the Boards of Trade and Chambers of Commerce of the United States, to submit a plan for a National Chamber of Commerce, to the Board of Trade of Boston, whose duty it shall be to compare them or select from them the plan which, in their judgment, shall be best adapted to the purpose, or, in the event of no one of them fully commending itself to their judgment, to prepare one from the plans of the several Boards of Trade and Chambers of Commerce for their ratification, and two-thirds of the several Boards of Trade and Chambers of Commerce consenting thereto, the same shall be adopted, whereupon the Board of Trade of Boston shall cause to be taken the necessary steps for the organization of the said National Chamber of Commerce.

The report and the accompanying resolutions were unanimously adopted.

The Committee on Weights and Measures were authorized to submit their report after adjournment, and publish it in the proceedings.

Mr. Richeson, of St. Louis, offered the following resolutions:

Resolved, That the thanks of this Convention are due, and are hereby tendered to the Hon. Hiram Walbridge, for the courteous, impartial and dignified manner in which he has presided over its deliberations, and to the Secretaries, and other officers of the Convention.

Resolved, That the thanks of this Convention are due and are hereby tendered to the Detroit Board of Trade for its courtesy, liberality and public spirit in assembling here representatives of the respective Commercial Associations and Communites in the United

States and the British North American Provinces, with a view of securing a full, frank and unreserved interchange of opinions and information upon the important subjects suggested for consideration, affecting, as those subjects do, the prosperity of so many million people.

Resolved, That the thanks of this Convention are also tendered to the Citizens of Detroit, for their generous attention and hospitality.

Mr. Kennedy, of Philadelphia, moved to amend by including the lines of Railroad, to whose courtesy the members of the Convention are greatly indebted. Carried.

The resolutions, as amended, were then passed by acclamation.

Mr. Elliott, of St. Louis, presented the following resolution:

Resolved, That the American Delegates to this Convention have experienced much pleasure in mingling with the delegates from the British Provinces, and we trust, that the intelligent gentlemen who have lent us their presence, may bear to their homes as pleasant memories of us, as we shall retain of them.

This resolution was received with loud applause, and passed by acclamation. Hon. Mr. Coles, of Prince Edward's Island, briefly returned thanks.

The question of printing the official proceedings of the Convention was raised, when Mr. Joy stated, by authority, that the Detroit Board of Trade would take entire charge of that matter.

The following resolution, moved by Hon. Thos. Ryan, of Montreal, and seconded by Hon. W. McMaster, of Toronto, was presented as the sense of the delegation from the British Provinces:

Resolved, That the delegations from the British Provinces attending the Commercial Convention at Detroit, cannot separate without acknowledging with thanks, their sense of the uniform courtesy, kindness and respect which has been extended to them by the Chairman and the United States members of the Convention during its session.

Hon. J. V. L. Pruyn moved that the thanks of the Convention be returned to the reporters. Carried.

Hon. S. Treat, of St. Louis—I move that this Convention now adjourn *sine die.*

Gen. Walbridge then delivered the closing address:

Gentlemen of the Convention—If my unexpected designation as presiding officer of the largest and most important body of commercial and business men that ever assembled on this continent was gratifying, I can assure you, the unanimity which has marked the passage of the resolution, complimenting me for the manner in which I have presided over your deliberations, just passed, is accepted with unfeigned gratitude, and I beg to tender you my sincere and heartfelt thanks. No kindred Convention has ever been held within the limits of the United States, composed of the representatives of the constituencies of the great Cities of St. Louis, Chicago, Milwaukee, Detroit, Toledo, Cincinnati, Cleveland, Buffalo, Oswego, Troy, Albany, New York, Philadelphia, Boston, Portland, Bangor, Pittsburgh, and the other constituencies here represented. These are the constituencies who created, together with the people of the States in which they are located, that sound public sentiment which had sufficient power to call to the field two millions of men, to maintain the Constitution of the United States, and to extirpate from our body politic the only refractory element inconsistent with the Christianity and civilization of our age. These are the communities who have most cheerfully assumed, for the preservation of the life of the nation, 'our vast debt, for the payment of which we have pledged the entire and almost illimitable resources of thirty millions of people, and the liquidation of which the commercial men of this country mean to make as inevitable as the coming of the day of judgment. To preside over such an assemblage, thus represented, is enough to satisfy the ambition of any man. But how immeasurably is that honor increased, as I stand in the presence of the commercial wealth and mercantile character of the two great Empires on this Continent — the one representing thirty millions of men under a written Constitution and the representative principle; the other an Empire, recognizing constitutional monarchy in its most liberal form. This Convention marks an epoch in the commercial history of North America. Eras may be forgotten; epochs never. And whatever may be the immediate results flowing from the aggregation into one body of the commercial representatives of the great Cities of the Republic of the United States, and the great commercial communities of the Provinces of British America, I am confident that, sooner or later, the result of our deliberations will be felt in the formation of that correct public judgment which insists that peace hath its victories no less renowned than those of war. I am indeed proud to have been called to preside over a body representing the commercial enterprise, the commercial energy, and the commercial honor and integrity of the loyal Cities of the United States and the great Cities of British North America, which are here represented. I congratulate the Convention on the unanimity and cordiality with which its deliberations have been marked. And if at one period of our organization our harmony was disturbed, it was the legitimate conflict of interests where such great and important results were to be attained. And I congratulate the Convention that temporary disorder was not suffered to interrupt the deliberations of this august assembly. Whether our deliberations shall result in any governmental action, it has contributed to a more thorough knowledge of the wants and necessities of the great constituencies we represent, and must, sooner or later, eventuate in drawing into still closer and fraternal association these great communities whose honor has been confided to our keeping. Assembled, as we were, without previous acquaintance or association, it was almost impossible, in the adjustment of the details of the Convention, to have met the entire wishes of all. Yet the Chair hopes to carry from this Convention to his home, the conscientious opinion of all, that he endeavored to discharge his duties so as best to promote and facilitate the business of the Convention, and secure the respect of the community for its deliberations. If his rulings have seemed at times arbitrary or oppressive, they were dictated entirely by the desire to advance and expedite the business before the Convention. Nor did the Chair feel himself called on to insist upon that strict line of parliamentary law which is absolutely indispensable in political organizations, where men struggle for place and position, regardless of honor, dignity, character, or renown. Nor still did he desire to insist upon the rigid observance of these rules, always to be observed when you come within gunshot range of decayed and decaying politicians. On the contrary, the Chair remembered that he was presiding over an Association of business men, many of whom had, at a great sacrifice of time, and at considerable inconvenience, come thousands of miles from their distant homes to discharge a public duty, in the conscientious belief that their labors might tend to advance the honor, and contribute to the renown of their Country, and to draw into still closer relations the commercial representatives of the Western Hemisphere. In behalf of the City of New York, which I have in part here the honor to represent, I desire to say, we came to this Convention with no intention of presenting any name as its presiding officer. When, however, the Convention decreed otherwise, my associates — to their honor be it said — with a dignity and modesty befitting the great constituencies they represent, requested me not to call them to important positions in the organization of the Committees. And I have cheerfully responded to their wishes so far as I could in justice to the commercial and business interests they have here so worthily and ably represented.

Having learned that my name was presented by the delegation from that beautiful City whose shores are washed by the Father of Waters, I here tender to them my sincere thanks, not more for its presentation than for the flattering compliment they have extended in submitting the resolution you have so unanimously passed. If they have not obtruded themselves frequently upon the notice of the Assembly, it is from the calm consciousness that they are the representatives of that Great Valley of the Mississippi, within the limits of whose boundaries and its tributaries the seat of political empire is to be located during the next two decades. I congratulate them and this Convention that if the suggestions of the Convention shall secure requisite legislation hereafter, not only themselves, but the beautiful City of Chicago, at the head of the hydrographic basin of the North American Continent, are to have two great outlets for their trade—one down the Mississippi to the Gulf, the other through the basins of the Great Lakes to the Atlantic by the River St. Lawrence.

It is in accordance with the law of nature, and in accordance with the law of nations, that those whose habitations are on the head of navigable streams, are permitted to find access to the Ocean through their mouths. This Convention has declared by its action, that such are its convictions of public policy and public duty, and that it is the duty of the Canadian Government, temporarily in the occupancy of the River St. Lawrence, to give adequate water communication to the Ocean, so that this illimitable West may place its products in Eastern markets, and in foreign ports, at a price below that at which they can be produced in the old, exhausted countries of the Eastern Continent. The action of this Convention, in calling upon the Governor of the great State of New York to request its Legislature to meet the growing necessities and demands of this gigantic West, cannot but exercise a salutary and decisive influence in conducing to attain that result. No single community on this Continent will feel a greater pride and satisfaction at the recommendations of this Convention, than that of the commercial metropolis of this Country, for its commercial sentiments are of a broad and catholic character; national in the significance of the benefits which are to be conferred upon all. The City of New York recognizes exclusively no East, no West, no North, no South. She recognizes only one common Country, and she stretches her hands out to her sister Cities of Buffalo, Detroit, Milwaukee, Chicago, Cincinnati, St. Louis and St. Paul, and while extending greetings to them, urges them to press on that great enterprise, the completion of the Pacific Railroad, which is destined by its iron bands to draw into fraternal brotherhood the great communities that line the shores of the distant Pacific, as well as those that are on the Eastern slopes of the Alleghanies. A sentiment was expressed in the Convention, that it was indelicate to express its opinions, lest it thereby should be regarded as dictating to the Government. I am gratified that the more just, more wise, more dignified and liberal views prevailed, and embodied the expression of of the house in the passage of resolutions calling the attention of the Government to overcoming the natural obstructions which heretofore have interrupted the passage of the products of the West on their way to the Seaboard. And I am gratified that that expression was placed purely upon the grounds of commercial necessity. Nations are respected as they demonstrate their ability to enforce their decrees. The exhibition of the power and strength of the arms and armaments of the United States, so suddenly called into requisition for the suppression of the rebellion, cannot but command the respect of our neighbors on the North. And if the result of the deliberations of this Convention shall terminate in a formation of a just, proper, legitimate Treaty between them and us, while it is negotiated for our benefits, and is consistent with our interests, I trust it will not be inconsistent with the honor or inconsistent with the interests of those with whom the negotiation is made. For so broad and liberal, so magnanimous, just and generous are the sentiments of the United States, that in my judgment, they prefer flourishing opulent neighbors in the North, as they intend that there shall be no European adventurers to harrass us on the South. (Cheers.) Gentlemen, if in reviewing the brief intercourse that has existed between us, the Chair cannot recall a single instance in which his decisions have been overruled, he believes it is due more to the generosity and forbearance of the House than to any merit of his own. But he cannot accept this compliment without himself also personally tendering at the same time his thanks to the gentlemen who have been associated with him as Secretaries to this body, for the prompt assistance they have given him, and for the fidelity with which they have preserved the record of our proceedings, so accurate that not a single correction on the journal has been made, notwithstanding the multiplicity of our business, its conflicting character, and the confusion incident to so large a deliberative assembly. The Chair wishes the members God speed in their return to their families, and hopes they will find their business interests unimpaired and uninterrupted during their absence. I now declare this Convention adjourned *sine die.*

ADDENDA.

THE TRANSIT COMMITTEE.

DETROIT, July 13, 1865.

The Transit Committee met this morning at the Biddle House.

The resolutions of Mr. Littlejohn being under consideration,

Mr. McGiverin said:

In addressing the Committee on behalf of Canada, he desired to submit for their consideration the advantages of the various transit routes through Canada to the Seaboard. As the discussion of the Reciprocity Treaty is precluded from this Committee, as well as the Trade relations between the two Countries, the field for discussion becomes comparatively limited, feeling, as he did, that the navigation of our Rivers and Canals, the traffic over our Railways, and the Reciprocity Treaty are so intimately connected with each other, that it was difficult to separate them. But, as another Committee had been named to consider the commercial relations, he would endeavor to place before them the advantages Canada offers as a competitor for a portion of the vast and rapidly increasing commerce between the Western States and Europe. We had constructed Canals connecting the great grain-producing country bordering on the Western Lakes with Tide-water, at an outlay of nearly twenty-five millions of dollars. We had constructed a magnificent railway system, extending from the extreme Western section of Canada to Portland, in all involving an expenditure of one hundred and three millions of dollars. We had the Great Western Railway with its branches, connecting Michigan and New York; the Buffalo and Lake Huron, from Goderich to Buffalo; the Northern Railway, from Collingwood to Toronto; the Welland Railway, from Port Colborne to Port Dalhousie; and the Grand Trunk Line, from Sarnia to Maine—all these routes having been thrown open, without any restriction to the commerce of the West, and he should have stated, that the producer in the West has enjoyed privileges and advantages not conceded to the Canadian producer and the Canadian merchant, viz: that freight has been, and is now being transported at much lower rates for the people of the United States, than for our own people. In the same way discriminating tolls in favor of the United States have been imposed. Whilst the Western shippers can transport grain from any Western port to Montreal, at reduced rates, passing through both Canals, the people of Canada, bordering on the shore of Lake Ontario, have to pay full rates of toll through the St. Lawrence Canals. As this question had to be discussed in a purely commercial sense, it became his duty to point out to this Committee what seemed to him the superior advantages of the St. Lawrence waters for the shipment of produce to Europe. He called their attention to a few facts which will serve to convince every one that the natural water communication to the Ocean must afford superior advantages to artificial routes through the United States.

On the 10th September, 1861, sixteen thousand bushels of wheat were purchased at Chicago, of which ten thousand bushels were shipped *via* the St. Lawrence, and six thousand *via* New York.

ST. LAWRENCE ROUTE.

	DAYS.
Shipped at Chicago, 13th September, arrived at Port Colborne 18th,	5
Passed over Welland Railway same day; shipped at Port Dalhousie 19th September, arrived at Montreal 22d,	2
Detained one day at Port Dalhousie,	1
Shipped at Montreal, per steamer, 22d, and from Quebec 29th, arrived at Liverpool on 8th October,	10
	18
Detained between Quebec and Montreal,	8
In all,	26

CHARGES.

	CENTS.	CENTS.
Freight to Port Colborne,	16	
Welland Railway,	2	
Port Dalhousie to Montreal,	8	
Montreal to Liverpool,	26	
		52
Insurance from Chicago to Montreal,		2½
Insurance from Montreal to Liverpool,		1½
Charges at Liverpool and Commission,		11
Per bushel,		67

NEW YORK ROUTE.

	DAYS.
Shipped at Chicago, 13th September, arrived at Port Colborne 8th,	5
Passed over Welland Railway, same day; shipped at Port Dalhousie, 25th September, arrived at Oswego on the 26th September,	1
Detained at Port Dalhousie six days,	6
Shipped at Oswego, 26th September, arrived at New York 6th October,	10
Shipped at New York, 10th October, arrived at Liverpool 3d December,	54
	70
Detention,	10
In all,	80

CHARGES.

	CENTS.	CENTS.
Chicago to Port Colborne,	16	
Welland Railway,	2	
Port Dalhousie to Oswego,	4	
Oswego to New York,	11	
New York to Liverpool,	25½	
		58½
Insurance from Chicago to New York,	2¾	
Insurance from New York to Liverpool,	2¾	
		5½
Charges in New York,	3	
Charges and Commission in Liverpool,	11	
		14
Per bushel,		78

Were the proposal, which has long been favorably entertained, of enlarging the Welland, and enlarging and deepening the St. Lawrence Canals, carried out, it becomes apparent that the freight could be conveyed from Chicago to Liverpool in much shorter time, and at a reduction of at least twenty cents per bushel from the figures quoted. The people of Canada are alive to the great and important interests involved in the enlargement and improvement of our Canal system. The rapid growth of the West has brought into existence a class of propellers, with a carrying capacity of thirty to thirty-five thousand bushels of grain, which cannot, from the small single locks, and want of sufficient depth of water, pass through our Canals; this class of vessels are necessarily compelled to discharge their cargoes at Buffalo. The several Canadian Boards of Trade convened a meeting at Toronto, and unanimously agreed to urge upon the Canadian Legislature the importance of enlarging the Welland and St. Lawrence Canals to admit vessels of one thousand tons burthen, or possibly larger. He thought he was warranted in stating to this Committee that the Government policy is to consummate such a desirable object.

In reply to a member of the Committee as to the size of the proposed locks and depth of water, Mr. McGiverin stated that it had been generally understood that both Canals were to have locks two hundred and fifty feet by fifty feet, drawing thirteen feet of water. He regretted, as representing Canada, that the consideration of the Reciprocity and the Transit questions had not been submitted to the same Committee, but as that could not now be arranged, he would close his remarks for the present by expressing the hope that the consideration of the several questions in which Canada was interested would be viewed by the people of the United States free from prejudice; that whatever may have occurred to temporarily mar the good feeling which has hitherto existed, he felt convinced that the great mass of the Canadians were strong in their desire to renew and perpetuate. the Reciprocity Treaty, and cultivate the most friendly commercial relations. It should be borne in mind that in every free Country the right of liberty of speech was acknowledged, and before condemning all of Canada for the aspersions of a minority, they should bear in mind that there are two great parties in the United States whose views differ as widely as do those in Canada.

Reserving the privilege of again appearing before the Committee should it desire any further evidence, Mr. McGiverin closed his speech.

Mr. G. H. Perry said:

The River St. Lawrence is the natural outlet of the surplus waters of the great Lakes. It drains an area of 600,000 square miles, of which 355,000 belong to Canada. Ninety miles above the highest point at which it is affected by the tide-waters, its channel is interrupted by a fall of forty-five feet, known as the Lachine Rapids. The head of this fall is six miles above the City of Montreal, and from that point the river is obstructed by a series of similar rapids for the distance of one hundred and seven miles. To render the navigation of this noble river available, the Provincial Government have constructed a series of Canals, varying in length from three-fourths of a mile to eleven miles, of uniform size and dimensions, the lock chambers being two hundred feet in length by forty-five feet in width, with a depth of nine feet of water on the sills of the locks. They are capable of admitting vessels one hundred and eighty-six feet in length, forty-three feet beam, and drawing eight feet of water, of a capacity of three hundred tons burthen. The machinery and all appliances are of the most durable description of material, and all that art and science could effect for the purpose has been laid under contribution for the purpose of rendering the navigation perfect. In these climates the navigation is necessarily limited by the shortness of the season, but these Canals are available for two hundred and twenty days as a maximum, and two hundred and ten days as a minimum; last year they were opened about the 15th of April, and rarely close before the 1st of December. Taking, however, the present state of these Canals, and that they can be worked to the extent of a lockage in six minutes, or ten lockages per hour, a total movement of through freight would take place amounting to 15,840,000 tons for the season, and an upward movement of 7,920,000 tons, and a corresponding downward movement, as the maximum of usual effect. These Canals open the St. Lawrence and Lake Ontario to the head of the latter expanse of water; they overcome a fall of two hundred and thirty-four feet between the level of its surface and tidal waters, and complete the connection with the Seaboard for that portion of the outlet. The communication between Lakes Ontario and Erie is interrupted by the Niagara

Falls. A canal twenty-eight miles in length, known as the "Welland," renders the navigation perfect and completes the remaining link between the upper Lakes and the Seaboard. Its locks are one hundred and fifty feet in length, twenty-six and a half in width, with ten feet of water on the sills. This Canal is capable of admitting vessels of four hundred tons, and as it is open from ten to fifteen days earlier each season than the St. Lawrence, its period of navigation will be two hundred and forty days as a maximum. Applying the same data as to the lower series of Canals, it is capable of affording transit to 23,040,000 tons of freight annually, or an upward movement of 11,520,000 tons, and a downward of like amount as its maximum of greatest useful effect. This Canal overcomes a fall of three hundred and thirty-five feet, and has twenty-seven locks, while the St. Lawrence Canals have a length on the aggregate of forty-eight and a half miles, and also twenty-seven locks. The total fall between the level of Lake Erie and tide-water is five hundred and sixty-nine feet. It has been the intention of the Canadian Government to enlarge these series of Canals to the full size which the harbors and internal waters to which they give access will permit, so that it is not at all beyond the bounds of probability, if a fair and equitable reciprocity continues between the Imperial Government and the United States, to see these Canals admit vessels of *one thousand* tons laden with the produce of the Western States, to meet the Ocean steamships at Montreal. From the immense hydraulic power at command, their expansion would be illimitable, and can only be prescribed by the wants of commerce or the physical or natural obstructions in the waters to which they give access. Most of the rapids on the St. Lawrence *can be descended* by steamboats, and it has been at one time the intention of the Provincial Government to deepen the channel so as to permit *laden crafts* to descend. This would at once double the capacity of this channel for freight. In the event of that expansion of Western commerce so eloquently described by its advocates, Canada presents another route for consideration, forming a direct communication between Lakes Huron, Michigan and Superior with the Ocean by the Ottawa and French Rivers. The Ottawa River bifurcates about twenty-five miles above the City of Montreal, forming the island on which it stands. The North channel, known as "Riviere des Prairies," joins the St. Lawrence at Boute de L'Isle, sixteen miles below the City; the South mingles its dark waters with that stream at Lake St. Louis, above the head of Lachine Rapids. The proposed navigation would use its channel for a distance of three hundred and five miles above Montreal, then ascend its tributary, the Mattawan, passing a small height of land of four and a half miles in width, enter Lake Nipissing, and descend the French River to the shores of the Georgian Bay, opposite the Straits of Mackinaw, from which it is only distant by the width of Lake

Huron. The whole route has been surveyed, at the expense of some $90,000, by the Provincial Government, and its entire feasibility established. It will have sixty-eight locks, a lockage of sixty feet upwards from Lake Huron, and six hundred and twenty-two feet downwards to tidal waters. Its length will be as follows: Ottawa River, three hundred and five miles; Mattawan, forty and one-half miles; height of land, four and one-half miles; Lake Nipissing, thirty-one miles; French River, forty-nine miles. Total, four hundred and thirty miles. Its piesent condition has twenty-one miles of Canal, including the Lachine, and forty-four miles obstructed. The open navigation actually existing is three hundred and sixty-five miles, of from five to twenty feet in depth. The locks are designed to be of the largest possible size — two hundred and fifty feet long, fifty feet wide, with twelve feet of water on the sills, calculated to admit vessels of two hundred and thirty feet in length, forty-eight feet beam, drawing eleven feet of water, and of one thousand tons burthen. Taking the data heretofore used for the season of navigation, and admitting only six lockages per hour, the capacity of this channel for freight would be 31,680,000 tons each season — an upward movement of 15,840,000 tons, and a like downward movement, would be its greatest useful effect. Its course from Montreal is about in a straight line for the Straits of Mackinaw, and its actual canaling will be just thirty miles, including the Lachine Canal. If an independent outlet is necessary, the Riviere des Prairies furnishes it, with seven miles less Canal.

One hundred and forty miles to the southward of the mouth of French River, Nottawasaga Bay, at the foot of the Georgian Bay, affords facilities for the construction of another channel to Lake Ontario. It is known as the Georgian Bay and Lake Ontario Canal. It is designed to be of the same dimensions as the Ottawa and Lake Huron, and will have the same capacity of 31,680,000 tons per season; it has eight hundred and five feet of lockage to the Seaboard, or five hundred and seventy-one to the surface of Lake Ontario, and eighty miles of canal. The Chambly Canal, on the River Richelieu, opens the navigation between the St. Lawrence and Lake Champlain; its capacity enables 3,168,000 tons of freight to be placed annually on that Lake. A comparison of the distances by each of the routes submitted would be as follows: St. Lawrence, from Chicago to Montreal, and thence to Liverpool — Lake, one thousand, one hundred and forty-five miles; River, one hundred and thirty-two miles; Canals, seventy-one miles. Total, to Chicago, one thousand, three hundred and forty-eight miles. Time — Lake and River, at eight miles per hour, one hundred and fifty-nine hours; Canal, at two miles per hour, thirty-five hours; lockage, five hundred and thirty-five feet at one minute per foot, nine hours. Total, one hundred and ninety-three hours. Ottawa and

Lake Huron Navigation — Lake, five hundred and thirty miles; River, three hundred and seventy miles; Canal, thirty miles. Total, to Chicago, nine hundred and thirty miles. Time — Lake and River, one hundred and thirteen hours; Canal, fifteen hours; lockage, six hundred and eighty feet, twelve hours. Total, one hundred and forty hours. Georgian Bay — Lake, seven hundred and seventy-five miles; Canal, one hundred and forty-one miles; River, one hundred and thirty-two miles. Total, one thousand and forty-eight miles to Chicago. Time — Lake and River, one hundred and thirteen hours; Canal, seventy hours; lockage, thirteen hours. Total, one hundred and ninety-six hours. To Liverpool from Montreal — Quebec, one hundred and fifty miles; to Liverpool from Quebec, two thousand, five hundred and eighty-five miles. Total, by way of St. Lawrence from Chicago, four thousand and eighty-one miles; by way of Ottawa and Lake Huron, three thousand, six hundred and sixty-five miles; by way of Georgian Bay Canal, three thousand, seven hundred and eighty-five miles. It will thus be seen that Canada can offer, with her Canals and Railways, outlet to 16,000,000 tons annually, in their present condition, as follows:

	TONS.
St. Lawrence Canal,	7,920,000
Welland, a surplus of	3,600,000
Chambly Canal,	3,168,000
Railways,	1,000,000
Total,	15,688,000

Enlarged, the same channels would be equal to *Sixty Million* tons annually. For any quantity beyond that it would not be possible to find freight.

Mr. McLennan, of Montreal, made the following statement:

The receipts in Montreal by the Lachine Canal in 1862 were:

Wheat, bushels,	7,779,727
Flour, reduced to wheat, equal to bushels,	3,861,935
Indian corn, bushels,	2,661,261
	14,302,923

Shipments, same season, by sea-going vessels, exclusive of vessels, to Provincial ports:

Wheat, bushels,	6,500,795
Flour, equal to wheat, bushels,	2,987,385
Indian corn, bushels,	1,774,548
	11,262,728

As evidence of the quantity of stuff that can be passed through the Lachine Canal in its present state, though this is not all that could be done, the entire quantity of grain and flour passed in May and June, 1863, was equal to 5,361,685 bushels.

There is storage for grain in elevating warehouses on the Lachine Canal to the extent of 1,040,000 bushels.

The water power now used on the Lachine Canal is estimated at 5,124 horse power. The supply of water from the Lachine Rapids that may be made available when required, is practically unlimited, being estimated at the equivalent of some millions of horse power.

The clearances were fifty-three steamships and four hundred and thirty sailing vessels.

Illustrating the capacity of the harbor of Montreal, it appears there were in port on the 6th of June, 1861, one hundred and seventeen sea-going vessels. There are now on the route from Montreal to Great Britain, eight mail carrying steamships, (carrying also freight,) and ten freight steamships.

The average cost of grain freight from Chicago to Montreal, during the last three years, has been fourteen cents, and from Montreal to Liverpool eighteen cents; from Chicago to Liverpool, per bushel, thirty-two cents.

Comparative tonnage of American and Canadian vessels passing through the Welland Canal in 1863:

3,425 Canadian vessels, tons	521,808
3,474 American " "	808,289

As evidence of the value of the route in respect to climate and the conservation of grain, he would state that during five years that he has been actively engaged in the grain trade between Chicago and Milwaukee and Montreal, he has had but one cargo of wheat out of condition. The quantity handled during each season has ranged from two hundred thousand to five hundred thousand bushels.

The estimated full capacity of the Welland Canal is equal to the passage downwards of one hundred and fifteen millions of bushels of grain in the course of the usual season of navigation, about two hundred and twenty days.

After further discussion, the question was taken on Mr. Littlejohn's resolutions, and they were adopted.

Duncan Stewart, Esq., of Detroit, presented the following additional resolution, and asked that it be added to those already adopted:

Resolved, That in the event of the negotiation of any Treaty of Reciprocity between the United States and the British Provinces, our

Government should be careful to secure in such a Treaty a guarantee of a sufficient depth of water to enable screw steamers of not less than one thousand tons cargo carrying capacity to pass from Port Colborne, Canada West, to tide-water.

Mr. Littlejohn — I think the other resolutions cover the entire ground. So there can be no need of the one just offered.

Mr. Stewart — One of the other resolutions states that it gives us pleasure to learn that the Canadian Government intends to enlarge its Canals. The West is done with intentions, and demands unmistakable action. If the intention to enlarge yields us pleasure, a guarantee that will secure enlargement must largely increase that pleasure, therefore I will now take the liberty to present some few figures, to show the advantage of deep water down the St. Lawrence, and I will be as brief as possible in their presentation.

I take the ground that, as regards the commerce of the Lakes that seeks an Ocean outlet, Port Colborne, which is the entrance to the St. Lawrence outlet, and Buffalo, which is the entrance to the Erie Canal outlet, *via* New York, are the two starting points of competition. All points West, Northwest, and Southwest, that use the lake route to the Seaboard, stand in precisely the same relative condition to these two important points. The question now arises: By which of these two outlets can the West reach those markets of the Old World where its products are most in demand in the speediest and cheapest manner? This brings us at once to an examination of the advantages and disadvantages of each of these great channels of communication. At the present moment, all the advantages are on the side of the route through the State of New York. With a proper enlargement of the Canadian Canals, the case would be reversed, greatly to the advantage of the entire West. I will examine the question on the basis of an enlargement of the Canadian Canals, as compared with our present facilities *via* New York. I will take up the Erie Canal first, and examine it as to time, cost of transportation, incidental expenses, etc.

The Erie Canal, as you are all aware, joins the waters of the Western Lakes with those of the Hudson River. It enters Lake Erie at Buffalo, and the Hudson River at West Troy. Its length is three hundred and fifty miles. It has seventy-one locks; they are seven feet deep, one hundred and ten feet long, and eighteen feet wide. Boats of improved build can navigate it with two hundred and twenty net tons of cargo. The boats are towed by horses, and the average rate of speed is one and an eighth miles per hour. At this rate of travel, it requires twelve days and twenty-three hours — say, in round numbers, thirteen days to pass the Canal. This is the case if no break occurs or accident happens; but as all Canals, as well as other means of transport, are subject to breaks and delays, I will only use the actual time needed to reach tide-water in my calculations. One day more will place boat and cargo in the harbor of New York, which is one hundred and fifty miles from West Troy, making the entire distance five hundred miles. No gentleman interested in the Erie Canal will, I think, venture to say that I have not made a fair statement of the case. I will here remark that if, in my figures and calculations, any errors have crept in, I will be most glad to be corrected, as my intention is to make a dispassionate statement, and carefully avoid straining either facts or figures. The charges on a bushel of wheat intended for shipment abroad are, from Buffalo till it is put aboard ship at New York, as follows: Canal tolls paid to the State of New York, six and a half cents per bushel; shipping charges at Buffalo, one-quarter of a cent per bushel; elevating charges at Buffalo, one and three-quarter cents per bushel; measuring at New York, half a cent per bushel, and shipping charges there, one cent per bushel; in all, ten cents per bushel. This is entirely independent of the freight. For the past ten years the average rate of freight has not been less than nine cents per bushel additional. We are thus able to lay down as a rule that the lowest possible average figure at which a bushel of wheat can be delivered on board ship at New York, *via* Buffalo, and from that point, is nineteen cents. Here, again, I will call the gentlemen interested in the Erie Canal to bear witness to the correctness of my figures, and the moderation of my estimate as regards the average cost of freight. The figures are correct. The estimated average rate of freight is under, and not over, the mark; so that, in all things, I present the most favorable aspect that can by any possibility be presented of the Erie Canal outlet to the Ocean. The summing up is both short and simple: Time from Buffalo to New York, fourteen days; cost on a bushel of wheat, nineteen cents. This tells the whole story as regards the Erie Canal.

I now turn to the water route through Canada, and the great advantages a moderate enlargement of the Canals would secure to us. The Canals are as follows:

	LOCKS.	MILES.
Lachine Canal,	5	$8\frac{1}{2}$
Beauharnois Canal,	9	$11\frac{1}{4}$
Cornwall Canal,	6	$11\frac{1}{2}$
*Farren's Point Canal,	1	$0\frac{3}{4}$
*Rapid Platte Canal,	2	$3\frac{3}{4}$
*Iroquois Junction and Galops Canal,	3	$7\frac{5}{8}$
In all,	26	$43\frac{3}{8}$

The Welland Canal, connecting the Western Lakes with Lake Ontario, has twenty-seven locks, and the Canal is twenty-eight

* Known by the name of the Williamsburg Canals.

miles in length. It follows that the number of locks which must be passed to reach the Ocean by the St. Lawrence River is fifty-four, or seventeen less than there are on the Erie Canal. The number of miles on the Canal between the Seaboard and the Lakes in this direction are seventy-one and three-eighths miles, or, in round numbers, seventy-two miles, which is two hundred and seventy-three miles less than the Erie Canal. I would earnestly mpress two great facts on the minds of the members of this Committee, more particularly on the minds of the gentlemen from the West: that there is twenty-five per cent. fewer locks on the St. Lawrence route than on the Erie Canal, and that there are five miles of canal on the latter route for every one mile on the former. No further argument is required to prove which of these ways Nature designed as the great highway from the West to the outer world beyond the Ocean. Man, with all his wonderful powers, creative genius, and perseverance, will never fail to be right if he follows where Nature leads. In this particular case let us lay the lesson to our hearts.

I now come to a comparison of distances:

	MILES.
From Port Colborne to Kingston,	188
" Kingston to Montreal,	180
" Montreal to Quebec,	180

Making the total distance from Port Colborne to Quebec five hundred and forty-eight miles, or forty-eight miles more than from Buffalo to New York; but as the distance from any given point west of Port Colborne is twenty miles less than to Buffalo, the actual difference is reduced to twenty-eight miles between the great starting points of competition for the Ocean trade and tide-water. I trust the Government of Canada will give us fourteen feet depth of water all the way from Port Colborne to Montreal. If they do not give it to us now, they will have to commence another enlargement within twenty-five years. Suppose, however, that for the present we must rest contented with twelve feet six inches, this would admit of propellers of a carrying capacity of 30,000 bushels of wheat reaching tide-water without breaking bulk. While jaded horses, driven by semi-savages, whose blasphemous expressions shock every feeling of decency every time they apply the whip with merciless severity to the sides of the tired animals placed in their charge, drag the canal boat along at the rate of one and an eighth miles per hour towards tide-water on the Erie Canal, the magnificent screw steamers of these inland seas would be proudly plowing their way through the pure waters of the St. Lawrence at an average rate of eight miles per hour, including the time required to pass the Canals, reaching tide-water at Quebec in two days and twenty and a half hours, not consuming three days in the passage;

whereas fourteen days would be required *via* the Erie Canal, making a saving of eleven days in favor of the St. Lawrence; or, in other words, running the distance in less than one-quarter of the time necessary on the New York outlet.

I now come to the cost of transportation. A propeller, or vessel, carrying 30,000 bushels could net twenty-five to thirty per cent. of her cost every year, with an average freight of five cents to Montreal, and six cents per bushel to Quebec. Allow that the Canadian Government charged two cents per bushel for tolls on the entire length of the Canals, and that the Elevator charges at Quebec and Montreal were half a cent per bushel, including ten days' storage and re-shipment, the entire cost from Port Colborne to Quebec, and putting the wheat on board ship, would be eight and one-half cents for all charges, against ten cents of incidental charges *via* Buffalo; or one and one-half cents per bushel less than the charges other than freight on that route. Add the average freight of nine cents from Buffalo to New York, and we have a saving of ten and one-half cents per bushel to the Western farmer in the difference of the two routes to the Atlantic. This statement as to the saving of time and expense is a most astounding one, and one not readily to be believed by those not practically acquainted with the details of the business; but I stand here to-day, before the assembled mercantile wisdom and experience of one-half of the United States, and the combined talent, wisdom, and commercial experience of the British Provinces of North America, and solemnly declare that I am correct in every detail and particular of the statements I have made; and I further am convinced that no gentleman on this Committee can upset either my reasoning or my figures. I know that of which I speak.

I have examined with care and impartiality the highways to the sea from the West. I have placed your cargoes on shipboard at Quebec and New York; now let me examine further the balance of the way to Liverpool from either point, and carefully note the result. The distance from Quebec to Liverpool is two thousand, five hundred miles; from New York to Liverpool is three thousand miles — making in favor of Quebec a distance of five hundred miles, or fully two days' sail, assuming that freight steamers would make an average run of ten miles per hour from either point to Liverpool. Add this two days to the eleven days saved by steaming down the St. Lawrence, instead of towing by horses down the Erie Canal, and we have a total saving of thirteen days between the West and Europe — enabling us to reach the ports of the Old World in not much more time from Port Colborne than it now takes us to reach New York from Buffalo. The entire time required to make the passage from Port Colborne to Liverpool being thirteen days — allowing two days for transhipment at Quebec — our wheat and other products would reach Liverpool with more certainty in fifteen days than they now have of reaching New York in fourteen days.

The gentlemen of the Committee will have remarked that I do not speak of the screw steamers from the Lakes crossing the Ocean. I do so deliberately, because I consider that, with twelve feet six inches to fourteen feet water down the St. Lawrence, it will always be more profitable to transfer at Montreal or Quebec than attempt to cross the Ocean with lake-going steamers. The reason of this is that, in reaching Quebec, they need not put on board fuel for more than a run of two hundred miles at a time, thus saving a vast amount of freight room; whereas in crossing the Ocean they must put fuel on board for the run of twenty-five hundred miles, and a surplus to cover contingencies. It would be unwise to have that surplus less than two days' run — enough to run three thousand miles. Every gentleman who has any experience in this business will see at once that it would take fifteen times more tonnage room for fuel to cross the Ocean as it would take to run down the river. In going down the river there would be no need to have over twenty-five tons of coal on board at any one time, including the surplus, because twenty tons would be sufficient to run a screw steamer of one thousand tons cargo capacity, with a low pressure engine, two hundred miles, leaving nine hundred and seventy-five tons for cargo and twenty-five tons for coal — only two and one-half per cent. of the carrying capacity being reserved for fuel; whereas for the Ocean voyage it would be unsafe to leave port with less than two hundred and fifty tons of coal, or twenty-five per cent. of the carrying capacity — leaving only seven hundred and fifty tons for freight room. I think this clearly demonstrates the economy of a transfer of cargo at either Montreal or Quebec. On the other hand, I think that cargoes by sail, intended for a foreign market, should not be transferred, but that the sail vessel should be towed with promptness from Kingston to open sea navigation below Quebec, and then left to the use of her sails. A sail vessel of one thousand tons burden would make money rapidly for her owners by carrying wheat to Liverpool from Port Colborne for the rate it now costs to put it on board ship at New York from Buffalo.

I hope these dry, practical details are not wearying or tiring the patience of the Committee. I have been as brief as possible. I have not been, I know, eloquent, fanciful, or entertaining, but I do hope that I have been clear and intelligible enough to be understood.

The benefits, not only to the United States and the Canadas, but to the world at large, cannot be over-estimated. Deep water down the St. Lawrence will open a new phase in the World's History. It will be a fresh starting point on the road to increased prosperity and greatness of the two great members of the Anglo-Saxon Family. A feeling of sincere friendship and respect will take the place of unworthy passion; unfounded prejudice will disappear. The petty malice, engendered by mean jealousy, will no longer beget strife and breed distrust. We will stand before the World in our true character; foremost in deeds of Christian charity and benevolence, foremost in all good works, foremost in all that tends to elevate mankind, and foremost in the championship of civil freedom and equal rights. I believe the measures that will be adopted by this Convention will bring all these things to pass.

With deep water down the St. Lawrence, no interest will be more benefitted than the lumber interest. Instead of ruin, swift and sure, overtaking this branch of our industry, new life, animation and vigor will be imparted to it, if the treaty is renewed, with a deep water clause affixed. With boundless, and almost inexhaustible forests of valuable timber, pine is the only kind that is of any present value. Let ships of one thousand or fifteen hundred tons load at the wharves of our Lake Cities, and, as if by magic, oak, black walnut, white wood, maple of all kinds, white ash, tamarack and spruce, would at once become ten times more valuable than they are at present. The cabinet makers of Europe would furnish a market for your fancy woods; the West Indies would take every oak stave you could turn out, sending back, in return, her sugar, molasses, and other rich products, which, being purchased from first hands, and landed without any extra charges but the freight, at your own doors, would enable our merchants to sell these products at greatly reduced rates, thereby adding to the comfort and happiness of the great mass of the people. The railways of Great Britain would give you a limitless market for your spruce and tamarack of small growth for ties; and the wealthy cities of London, Liverpool, Manchester, Glasgow, Dublin, Bristol and Birmingham, would become competitors with Chicago, New York and Boston, for your best qualities of white pine. An open market with all the world will pay the owners of timber lands better than a limited home market; and with the class of vessels named, to carry the products of our forests to foreign lands, the rates of freight would be as low to any of the ports of Great Britain as they now are from any given point west of New York or Boston, while the prices to be obtained abroad would be much better than attainable in either of these markets.

I know it will not be considered patriotic to draw trade from our own Cities, and the cry will be raised that all this tends to enrich another country rather than our own. All I have to say is, that if the State of New York and Cities of New York and Buffalo, cannot do the business of the West as cheap as any one else can, they must expect to lose it, and deserve to do so.

The West means to do her business where she can do it to the most advantage; and if our Canadian friends afford us such facilities as will enable us to reach tide-water for a lower rate of freight and canal tolls, than the incidental expenses incurred passing through the State of New York, my humble opinion is that they will secure the business.

Which party is most deserving of our consideration? Men who profess feelings of friendship for us, and call themselves our fellow-citizens, yet retard our prosperity, and charge us double what is fair or reasonable, for every service they do for us, because we are in their power; or those who present themselves as strangers, but offer us advantages which our friends refuse to grant us.

A few more words and I am done. Some years ago, the farmers, in certain portions of the West, could not obtain over eight cents per bushel for their corn. Some professors of political economy say this was the result of a great crop, and nobody to eat it. This is a grave mistake; there were hungry men enough to eat up the whole of it! Nobody to eat! The want of transportation facilities ate it all up! That year, forwarders got in many instances twenty cents per bushel from Chicago to Buffalo; and the canal rates rose as high as twenty-five cents from Buffalo to New York. In plain English, the farmer of Illinois had to give the carrier the price of five and a half bushels of his corn to get him to carry one bushel from Chicago to New York, a distance of fifteen hundred miles by water. Twenty-five cents, including canal-tolls, would have laid the same corn down in Liverpool, had there been a chance to navigate the St. Lawrence with vessels of one thousand tons or upwards, and the owner of the craft would have been richly remunerated at that price; but on top of the forty-five cents to New York from Chicago, were the charges at that point, and another charge of twenty cents per bushel to cross the ocean, making the charge from Chicago to Liverpool not less than sixty-seven cents per bushel, when it would never have exceeded thirty cents had the right kind of vessels been able to pass down the St. Lawrence. This would have enabled the farmer to get forty-five cents for his corn, instead of eight cents, per bushel. With sixty bushels to the acre, the amount secured in the one case was four dollars and eighty cents; in the other it would have been twenty-seven dollars. This is no fancy sketch; it is a positive fact. After such a statement, I will leave it to the Committee to say, whether or not, the West has not just reason to complain of insufficient outlets to the Seaboard. With these facts placed before our Provincial friends, I trust they will go on and improve their lines of communication whether the treaty is renewed or not. They can offer such inducements for the trade of the West as will draw a large portion of it into their harbors, in spite of unfriendly legislation or unfounded prejudice. I have never known one single American merchant, and I have had some experience among them, who would give me twelve and a half cents per barrel, to carry flour to Buffalo, from Detroit, if the Grand Trunk or Great Western Railways would carry it for twelve and one-eighth cents; or who would give an American vessel eight and one-tenth cents per bushel to carry a cargo of grain to Kingston, if a Canadian craft stood ready to do it for eight cents. And this is the correct principle in trade. Trade knows no country or color; she will agree with those from whom she can obtain the best bargain. These are simple facts, which, I hope, will be duly considered by the gentlemen of this Committee.

The resolution was then put and carried, every member of the Committee voting for it, except Mr. Prosser, of Buffalo.

THE COMMITTEE ON RECIPROCITY.

DETROIT, July 13, 1865.

The proceedings of this Committee commenced last evening, when it was organized under the chairmanship of Mr. Joy, of Detroit, and speeches were made by the Hon. Mr. Howe and several other gentlemen. It was, however, agreed that the business part of the proceedings should commence this morning, and at 9 o'clock — the hour of meeting — the American Committee invited the Canadian and Lower Province delegates to express their views.

Hon. Thomas Ryan, of Montreal, the Chairman of the Provincial Delegations, handed in copies of the Report of Hon. Mr. Galt, on Reciprocity, of the Report of the Montreal Board of Trade, and of the Prize Essay of Mr. Harvey.

Mr. Ryan then desired to draw the attention of the Committee to the fact that Canadian imports from the States of certain important articles, which were increasing year by year, would certainly be stopped if the Treaty were not renewed. They (the Americans) had sent us in 1855 but 50,000 tons of coal, while in 1863 they had sent us 100,000 — a quantity which would increase from year to year.

Hon. Mr. Reppelier, of the Philadelphia Coal Exchange, called attention to the fact that Mr. Chase's return gave but 80,000 as exported in 1863.

Mr. Joy — The fiscal years do not correspond.

Mr. Fry, of Quebec — Our returns are from the Custom Houses, and are returns of imports, which must be more correct than those of exports supplied to Mr. Chase.

Hon. Mr. Ryan — The American tables make no allowance for "short exports," but if these were added to the American figures they would very closely correspond with the Canadian.

Mr. Joy — No doubt your figures are, upon that account, the most exact.

Hon. Mr. Ryan — I desire also to draw attention to the fact that the tonnage of vessels which have passed down our Canals is greater than that which passed up, which shows that, under the Treaty, the Americans of the Northwestern States have found a market for a new manufacture — viz., ships — and have, besides, been able to send craft down to the Atlantic, when they were needed, to assist in the blockade of Southern ports, or in transporting provisions for the armies, or munitions of war. Something has been said about our tariff having been raised. This has been rendered necessary, because we have built Railways and Canals, perhaps larger than we ourselves wanted, with a view to assisting the transportation of the products of the West.

Mr. Hatch, of Buffalo — Why were your duties made *ad valorem?*

Hon. Mr. Ryan — No doubt our duties were made *ad valorem*, instead of specific, with a view to give encouragement to trade by the St. Lawrence. At first sight they seemed to militate against New York, but the system has been changed within the last two or three years. I can now import Teas from China *via* New York, and leave a portion of the cargo there while the rest comes to Canada, and *vice versa*, so that the *ad valorem* system gives to the St. Lawrence a comparatively trifling advantage. If we have lately sold to New York large quantities of Teas imported into Montreal, it has been owing to the state of affairs produced by the war. In ordinary times it is, I believe, a shade cheaper to import *via* New York.

Mr. Henry Fry, of Quebec — Besides, when we changed from specific to *ad valorem* duties, we were only returning to our previous system.

Mr. Joy — What we of the West want, Sir, is to have your River and Canals made deep enough to admit vessels of fifteen hundred tons to pass between the Lakes and the Ocean.

Mr. Worts — Perhaps Mr. Ryan will read the resolution passed at the Toronto meeting relating thereto.

Hon. Mr. Ryan — Certainly, for it will show the Committee the feeling with which we meet you here. The third resolution passed at the Toronto meeting of the delegates from all Canada, was as follows :

"That this Convention will urge upon the Government of Canada the importance of immediately enlarging the Welland and deepening the St. Lawrence Canals, and it will favor the construction of such new routes through Canada for the transportation of Western produce to the Seaboard, as may be found requisite for the wants of that extensive traffic, and not inconsistent with the financial position of the country."

I was named one of a deputation to submit this resolution to the Minister of Finance, Mr. Galt, and he said the Government were anxious to enlarge the Canals of the West, and would do so as soon as they had the means. Mr. Galt said further that the Government would not have the least objection if the people of the West wished to join in the construction of new routes, or the enlargement of old ones, but would be quite willing to go into the matter. With respect to Reciprocity, Mr. Galt said — and I think I am at liberty to repeat his words — that if the Convention should take a view favorable to Reciprocity, the Canadian Government would receive every overture in a fair spirit; for they thought that, although Canada could do without it, it would be an inconvenience to both sides if Reciprocity were stopped. I asked when the negotiations would go on. He replied that they would wait to see what was done at Detroit; that if the commercial men of the States advised a policy hostile to us, we should have to shape a new policy for ourselves.

Mr. Hatch — Is it not understood that Sir Frederick Bruce has been authorized by the British Government to negotiate ?

Hon. Mr. Ryan — I inquired of Mr. Galt about this, and was told that Sir Frederick Bruce would do no more until he heard from Canada, after the Convention. Perhaps, Mr. President, I may here allude to a subject not of the pleasantest character. If you, Sir, drive us to do so, by adopting a policy hostile to our interests, we may have to change our tariff, and resort for revenue to direct taxation. If we had free trade, your citizens would find such facilities for purchasing in our market, and conveying goods into your country in an illicit manner, that you would find great difficulty in maintaining your present tariff of duties. Of course, however, it would be much more agreeable to us to meet the Government of the United States in another way. There are two or three minor points we talked over at Toronto. Your system bears very hard upon some things we deal in. For instance, I may mention flour. You exact duty on flour manufactured in Canada from United States wheat, which we do not in the contrary case. Your consular fees are very onerous and troublesome; but perhaps you feel that as much as we do.

Mr. Joy — Yes, Sir.

Hon. Mr. Ryan — Reverting to the flour question, the Treaty says that articles, the growth and produce of the United States and Canada, shall be admitted reciprocally free. Now, flour ground in Canada from American wheat is excluded by the strained interpretation of the word "and." Again, we thought it would be desirable to make the article crude petroleum reciprocally free. It appears that our petroleum is of a different quality from yours, and the two together make the best combination for distilling. In the article of metals, too, we think it would be of mutual advantage if metals smelted up to a certain point were not to be charged with duty. At the Bruce Mine we used to produce a great deal of low per centage ores, the transportation of which was too heavy to allow of our sending them to market in the crude state. Now, we could reduce it by the use of wood or charcoal to a degree which would enable it to be sent to market. Of course, ores can be sent to coal cheaper than coal can be brought to the ores, and the result of the change of which I speak would be that we should be able to sell our poorer ores, while your consumption of coal would be increased, and employment given to your smelting works. If you were to go into details, I should like to show you how, under Reciprocity, we consume a quantity of cut meats of yours, and send you live animals; while, if there were not free trade in these articles, we should use our coarse grain in raising more animals, and should not import cut meats from you, but, on the contrary, become a competitor with you in European and other markets.

Mr. Joy — We shall not have time to go very deeply into details, I fear.

Hon. Mr. Ryan — You will also please to look at the transit trade in grain. Now, you supplied the Lower Provinces in 1863 with 3,000,000 bushels of wheat and wheat flour. It appears, also, that you imported from Canada a precisely equivalent quantity.

Mr. Burnett — That shows that while the Lower Provinces can be most cheaply supplied in New York, certain parts of New England draw their supplies most cheaply from Canada. The trade is reciprocal.

Mr. Joy—We have many letters from Michigan people complaining that, before the Treaty went into effect, they supplied their white wheat to the New York and New England markets, whereas now the Canadian white wheat gets there first, and injures their market. The quality of wheat grown in Canada and Michigan is better for certain purposes than any other.

Mr. ——— —They make crackers from that flour in New England, and supply the American, as well as, perhaps, the Provincial fishermen with them.

Hon. Mr. Ryan—I must not forget to point out to you that, by one clause of the Treaty, the Government of the United States engages to urge on the State Governments to give us the use of the several State Canals. Now, whether they have or have not urged this very strongly, we have not the use of the New York Canals.

Mr. Fraley, of Pennsylvania—That is perhaps owing to the United States navigation laws. Every vessel, with or without masts, engaging in canal trade, must be registered and licensed as a coasting vessel.

Hon. Mr. Ryan—The Canals do not belong to the United States, but to the States.

Mr. Fraley—That makes no difference in the case. The navigation laws would prevent your going beyond the first reach of the Canal to deliver freight.

Mr. Joy—The New York people won't let others meddle with their Canals. That is always their policy, even towards other States.

Hon. Mr. Ryan—I must also speak something about the fisheries. I have to state that the fishing industry of your Atlantic States, exclusive of the whale fishery, amounted, in 1860, to $4,500,000, of which $3,000,000 was taken in British waters.

Hon. Mr. Howe here entered the Committee Room.

Hon. Mr. Ryan—I see that the Hon. Mr. Howe, of Nova Scotia, is now present, and I leave the subject of the fisheries to him.

Hon. Mr. Howe—One of the delegates from Prince Edward's Island has handed me a paper respecting the fisheries in the Gulf, which is signed by Messrs. Dean and Law, two American merchants settled at Charlottetown, which so clearly shows the advantages of the Treaty to the Americans that I must read it to you. It is as follows:

"For some years previous to the time the Reciprocity Treaty went into effect, the Americans fishing were embarrassed in consequence of the three mile limit, and the construction put upon it by

Colonial officers, that it meant three miles outside of a straight line from headland to headland, which, in many localities, where the buoys were deep, would make them many miles off, and the continual harassing and capturing of our vessels — so much so as to nearly ruin the business as a whole — a loss, and the tonnage engaged fast depreciating, and at the time the Treaty went into effect the fishing fleet in the Bay and Gulf of St. Lawrence was much smaller than it had been some years before. We think that, for one or two years previous to the Treaty, there could not have been more than two hundred and fifty sail of American vessels in these waters, averaging seventy-five tons each; value, three thousand dollars each, and manned by eleven men each, with an average catch of mackerel of two hundred and seventy-five barrels each; estimated value, twelve dollars per barrel gross, and ten dollars net. Gloucester having a majority of the fleet, being most daring in the pursuance of her business. In the two last years, we think, there have been employed six hundred vessels; average tonnage, ninety each; value, five thousand dollars each, and manned by fifteen men each, with an average catch of five hundred and twenty-five barrels of mackerel; estimated value at the time of landing, fourteen dollars and a half per barrel gross, and twelve dollars net. At first, many of our fishermen feared that the letting in of Colonial fish free of duty would lower our prices, but it had the contrary effect. With the large increase of catch, it gave a stimulus to the trade, and prices largely increased. Should there now be a very small catch for a few years, it would tend to reduce prices, for want of sufficient interest to keep merchants in the business.

FOR TWO YEARS BEFORE THE TREATY.

Tonnage,	18,150
Value of vessels,	$750,000
Men employed,	2,750
Barrels caught,	68,750
Gross proceeds,	$825,000
Net proceeds,	$687,500

FOR TWO YEARS UNDER THE TREATY.

Tonnage,	54,000
Value of vessels,	$3,000,000
Men employed,	9,000
Barrels caught,	315,000
Gross proceeds,	$4.567,500
Net proceeds,	$3,786,900

"In the above estimates the difference between the gross and net proceeds is the cost of salt, barrels, packing, and incidental expenses. The wear and tear of the vessels and men are to be paid from the net proceeds.

FOR TWO YEARS BEFORE THE TREATY.

"Vessels of ninety tons catch three hundred barrels of mackerel.

Value of catch, ...		$3,600 00
General charges deducted — For bait, ...	$ 75 00	
For barrels and packing, . .	300 00	
		375 00
		$3,225 00

FOR THE LAST TWO YEARS UNDER THE TREATY.

"Vessels of ninety tons catch six hundred barrels of mackerel.

Value of catch, ...		$8,700 00
General charges — For bait, ...	$200 00	
For barrels and packing, ...	780 00	
		980 00
		$7,720 00

"And at least double the quantity caught.

"WM. B. DEAN,
"MOSES LAW.

"CHARLOTTETOWN, P. E. I., July 3d, 1865."

There, said Mr. Howe, is the whole thing for you in a nut-shell.

Hon. Mr. Ryan — I have no doubt these figures are more valuable than mine, being compiled on the spot.

Mr. Joy — They are substantially the same as yours, Sir, I perceive, on comparing them.

Hon. Mr. Howe — Then, Sir, I must tell you that you supply our market with a great deal of the food that our fishermen require.

Mr. Joy — We have the figures, Sir, which were given, in your absence, by Mr. Ryan.

Hon. Mr. Howe — And you send us, in the ships which bring produce, a number of unmanufactured articles, too. A great deal of leather, and almost all the spirits we get in Nova Scotia, come from the States in vessels, which return laden with fish. Almost all the tobacco, manufactured and unmanufactured, comes from the States. Now as to Newfoundland. I regret that there is no gentleman here from that Colony; the time given was too short. I may say on its behalf, however, that the people there do not go into the mackerel fishery. Their fish is cod, which goes to Spain, Portugal, and the Mediterranean. It is cured specially for those markets. No pickled fish is sent to the United States, except what is taken by United States fishermen; while as for the dry fish, they often have not enough for their Spanish trade. But the bulk of their supplies for the fishermen and the population depending on the fisheries, comes from the United States. Their market is, therefore, one of great advantage to you.

Hon. Mr. Ryan then introduced Mr. Bolton, of New Brunswick, to the Committee.

Mr. Bolton, of St. John, would not take up the time of the Committee at that moment, further than by stating that the freights given by New Brunswick to American vessels amounted to $6,000,000. The navigation laws of the States gave Provincial vessels no such advantages.

Mr. Joy — Have you any official figures relating to that branch of the subject?

Mr. Bolton — Yes, and I can lay them before the Committee in a short time. Then as to the competition of our lumber with that of the United States. I am surprised that our friends of Bangor speak about that. The whole amount we send to the United States is only 13,000,000 superficial feet, while Bangor manufactures 150,000,000. Our lumber trade is principally with Europe; and it should be noticed that American lumber coming down the St. John is now shipped free of export duty, with which, before the Treaty, it used to be charged.

Mr. Fry, of Quebec, wished to remove an erroneous impression, which he had heard prevailed among some members of the Convention, that Canadians purchased no lumber from the Americans. Now the fact was that, although we had lumber of an inferior grade on the Ottawa and the Trent, which found a ready market at Troy and Albany, and exported thither more than we imported from the States, yet he could state that one of the Quebec merchants was at that moment engaged in getting lumber down from Michigan. One of his neighbors, besides, had a contract for getting $50,000 worth of Saginaw deals to Quebec this summer. The quality of lumber obtained from Saginaw was very superior. Quebec merchants could give a very high price for it, for it was wanted for machine making in Manchester and elsewhere. Size and quality were getting scarce on the Ottawa, and the lumber trade with Michigan would increase largely if the Treaty remained. In staves, too, there was a large trade, and an increasing trade. Oak was getting scarce in Canada, and the lumber merchants were glad to purchase Michigan oak. There was another article in which Quebeckers were interested — viz., ship building. Now, we had been in the habit of registering American-built ships in Quebec and Montreal, free of all duty whatever. During the past two years a large amount of tonnage had passed into the hands of Quebec and Montreal folks, and he had himself made two or three very good bargains in New York. Now, why should not Americans register Colonial-built ships in the same liberal way? It would be for the advantage of both parties; for the Colonial ship builder would find a good market, while the American ship owner would buy cheaper vessels than at present. A great deal of lumber for ship building was now being sent to Maine and Massachusetts from Canada by rail — hackmatack, knees, etc. — and, indeed, there were American ship builders who had bought yards and houses in Quebec, and two of them were now building ships for New Orleans, though how they were to be registered, or under what flag they were to sail, he did not know. The point he wished to make was, that it would not be unwise for the American Government to offer to its subjects every facility for acquiring cheaply the vessels on which their commercial position so much depended. It would be an act of justice to Canadians, and a privilege to Americans, if the registration of Canadian ships were allowed to take place on the same footing as that of American vessels in Canada.

The Committee then, at nearly 10 o'clock, adjourned.

MEMORIAL FROM THE BOARD OF TRADE OF ST. PAUL.

The Board of Trade of the city of St. Paul, Minnesota, respectfully presents to the Commercial Convention sitting at the City of Detroit, the following facts, relating to the Railroad connection now being made between the Mississippi River and Lake Superior, from this point:

The line of road located by the Lake Superior and Mississippi Railroad Company, and now being constructed from St. Paul to the head of Lake Superior, is intended to form the connecting link between the navigable waters of the Mississippi and Lake Superior—between "the largest River on the continent and the largest Lake in the world."

The actual distance from St. Paul to Fond du Lac (head of the Lake) is one hundred and thirty-three miles.

The purpose has been to make the line of this road a direct one, and this has been favored by the almost uniform level surface of the country over which the line passes, and as no divergence has been allowed for town, site or speculative purposes, this object, so desirable, has been successfully accomplished. The line is almost a direct one.

The distance from St. Paul to Fond du Lac, is, as above stated, one hundred and thirty-three miles. The St. Louis River, which passes through the Bays of St. Louis and Superior, being navigable to that point. From St. Paul to Lake Superior proper, the distance is nearly one hundred and fifty miles, the line passing along the northern side of the Bays of St. Louis and Superior. The line has been carefully surveyed and located, and the grading and work upon the road are being vigorously prosecuted, and thirty miles of the grading will be completed the present season, and those connected with the management of the road believe that its construction will continue to be pushed forward without interruption until it is fully completed and equipped.

The importance of this line of road to the merchants and producers of Minnesota, and as an auxiliary to the business of the Cities upon the Great Lakes and Seaboard, cannot well be overestimated, as the following facts and figures sufficiently indicate.

The distance from St. Paul, and from the central settled portions of the State, to the City of Chicago, is four hundred and fifty-one miles. Distance from Chicago and the head of Lake Superior to New York City is practically the same, to wit: nine hundred and seventy-one miles. The distance from St. Paul, via Chicago, to New York City is one thousand four hundred and twenty-two miles. From St. Paul to New York City, via Lake Superior, one thousand one hundred and twenty-one miles; but as lake navigation may be said to commence at the "head of the lake," the distance may be put at eleven hundred and four miles, making the difference in favor of the Lake Superior route over three hundred miles. The distance, by rail, from La Crosse to Chicago is two hundred and eighty miles; difference in favor of St. Paul over La Crosse, to reach lake navigation, is one hundred and forty-seven miles. Produce and freight upon the connecting lines of road that centre at St. Paul, one hundred and forty-seven miles distant from St. Paul, and that much further from the Lakes, can reach lake navigation without being transported more miles than freights at La Crosse must be carried to reach lake navigation. The distance from La Crosse to Milwaukee, however, is only two hundred miles, which places St. Paul sixty-seven miles nearer the Great Lakes than La Crosse, by this, her nearest route. The competition between the great Cities of Chicago and Milwaukee seems to have indicated that the correct basis upon which to make such comparison is to take the distance from La Crosse to Chicago as the proper one.

It will be seen, therefore, that the many millions of bushels of grain, with a relative proportion of other products, to be exported from Minnesota, and a portion of northwestern Wisconsin will naturally seek transit over the line of this road, as its cheapest and shortest route to market.

St. Paul is the center of the Railroad system of this State, hence the St. Paul and Pacific, the St. Paul and Winona, the Minnesota Valley and the Minnesota Central form a common center. The Eastern outlet to which, so far as lake navigation is concerned, is to be had over the line of the Lake Superior and Mississippi Railroad, and produce, upon the lines running South and East from this city, for at least a distance of one hundred and forty-seven miles, and all the produce on the lines coming from the West and North, would pass over this line to the Lakes, as its most direct and best route to market. The saving to the producers of our State, which will result from the opening of this important line of road, can scarcely be overestimated. Freight on grain from St. Paul and other River Towns north of Winona to Chicago, is now thirty cents per bushel, and has most of the time, for the last two years, greatly exceeded that figure. Such onerous and ruinous charges could not be made with a competing road from St. Paul to Lake Superior.

The same causes will insure to this line of road a large proportion of freights, on merchandise coming into the State. These considerations, and others of like weight, have induced the City of St. Paul to guarantee to the Company a bonus of $250,000, upon condition that this road is fully completed in five years from July 4th, 1864. The State has also donated seven sections per mile of her swamp lands, and Congress has made a grant of ten sections to the mile of the public lands to aid in its construction, which lands have been granted to the Company, making a magnificent grant of over 1,600,000 acres.

The line of this road passes through a heavily timbered country, affording an inexhaustible supply of pine and other lumber, not to be reached in the ordinary method of driving upon streams. This, with the opening up of a large area of arable country suitable for settlement, is expected to add to the general prosperity and property of the country. The Falls of the Snake, Kettle, and St. Louis Rivers are upon the line of this road, furnishing water power equal to any other, in the vicinity of the lumber, and other material so abundant in the Lake Superior region, and which only needs the opening of this road to be developed.

It is proper to add that the connecting roads, above spoken of, are being pressed to completion. The Minnesota Valley road, which, with the Superior road, will, when completed, furnish a continuous line of road from Lake Superior to Sioux City, Iowa, there connecting with the Union Pacific, is now graded and bridged a distance of fifty miles from St. Paul; the iron is being laid, and some thirty miles will be constructed and equipped during the present summer, and the people of St. Paul have great hopes of having the Sioux City connection made at an early day. The fact that the great South Pass, through which the Union Pacific road must of necessity go, is nearer the head of Lake Superior than it is to St. Louis, and about two hundred miles nearer Lake Superior than it is to Chicago, demonstrates to our people that our railroad connection with the Pacific coast will naturally come through the Sioux City line.

To all of which we would respectfully call the attention of your Board.

Dated St. Paul, Minn., July 7th, 1865.

VIEWS OF THE NORTHWEST.

A LETTER FROM HON. THOS. CLARK, OF SUPERIOR, WISCONSIN, TO THE PRESIDENT OF THE DETROIT CONVENTION.

Superior, Wisconsin, July 2, 1865.

To the President of the Detroit Commercial Convention:

The undersigned, a delegate appointed to attend your Convention, being unable to do so, respectfully offers the following for such consideration as your honorable body may be pleased to award it:

There are 200,000 of population in Minnesota and Wisconsin, whose districts of settlement in the aggregate average three hundred miles from the western shore of Lake Michigan. The annual surplus agricultural product of these districts may be estimated safely at 3,000,000 bushels of wheat, a like quantity of coarser grains, and half as much in weight of the products of animals, amounting to 225,000 tons of exports.

This estimate may be below or above the actual amount, but for the purposes of this inquiry it is adopted as a basis. Yet it is proper to add that it is the product of less than one of every twenty acres within the district capable of producing a like amount. The region had in view is the Northwest third of the State of Wisconsin and the South half of Minnesota, containing 60,000 square miles. The proportion of waste land in this region is considerably less than in the Middle States; and, if filled up to their average, we would have a population of 3,500,000, capable of producing from the region described an exportable product of 4,000,000 tons; or, to express the amounts in detail again, this upper garden of the Mississippi and St. Croix Rivers contains the soil and acres to produce and export 60,000,000 bushels of wheat, as much more of other grains, and like increase in other products.

This 60,000 square miles has been open to settlers fully ten years, and during the latter portion of the time the Mississippi and St. Croix Rivers have been connected with Lake Michigan by three lines of railway, giving the producer residing near the rivers facilities of export. Yet it is a fact patent to all that the increase of population and product has, during the last five years, been scarcely appreciable. True, the National struggle has had its retarding effect, and the Indians have greatly added to the check; yet it is not in the power of the sweat of the brow for the farmer to raise wheat, and contentedly give one bushel for moving two to tide-water. A district so subsidized cannot prosper and increase to the measure of population and product, that time and the soil would effect, with the commercial facilities enjoyed by the producer three hundred miles nearer tide-water.

At the coin-currency price of grain and freights in 1860 and '61, the lowest price for moving wheat from St. Paul to Lake Michigan was nineteen cents per bushel. During the currency rates of the subsequent years the freight ran up to thirty or thirty-five cents, but, relative to the price of wheat, the rise was but little more burthensome. The greater difficulty lay in the over-burthened facilities, and consequent detentions at the transhipping depots.

In view of this it was that the Illinois Canal was pressed as a commercial, as well as a military policy. The effect of this improvement upon the district in view would be that wheat might be moved from St. Paul to Chicago, on five hundred and fifty-six miles of River, at five mills, and three hundred and twenty miles of Canal at one cent four mills per ton per mile — the Erie Canal rates — amounting to seven dollars and twenty-six cents per ton, or *twenty-two* cents a bushel. Attempts have been made to make it appear that the cost of transportation upon River and Canal may be reduced to a lower figure, but this estimate is as low as the antecedents of Mississippi and Erie Canal boatmen warrant.

The Fox and Wisconsin River improvement is another project to relieve the district. This would give St Paul access to Lake Michigan through two hundred and thirty-one miles of River and two hundred and twenty-five of Canal, which, at the above prices, will be a fraction less than thirteen cents per bushel on wheat. It is this improvement, then, which will disenthral the 60,000 square miles.

The chain of Great Lakes — the common highway of the British Provinces and Northern tier of States — constitutes a commercial channel of seventeen hundred miles, from Quebec to the head of Lake Superior. However forcibly artificial improvements may for a time deflect the movement of trade from the great Mediterranean of North America, the developing energies of these two commercial, pioneer, and progressive peoples will follow Nature's engineering to and from the extremities. There intervenes but one hundred and seventy miles to connect Lake Superior, at Bayfield, with the upper limit of continuous navigation on the Mississippi; and one hundred and thirty-five miles to connect the latter with the head of the Lakes, and less than seventeen hundred miles to complete this international highway from Lake Superior to Puget Sound.

Impressed with the need of these connections, Congress, at various times, has made land grants; and finally, during the first session of the thirty-eighth, the former grants were extended, and the amount increased to ten sections per mile for the first roads, and twenty for the last, or Pacific and Lake Superior line of railway — while the upper Mississippi connection was among the formerly endowed projects. Our Government has placed at the disposal of the States of Wisconsin and Minnesota 3,500,000 of acres of lands, to connect the upper Mississippi with the head of the Great Lakes; in addition to which, the State of Minnesota has devoted seven sections per mile, or 600,000 acres, of her swamp lands, to aid the St. Paul and Lake Superior route of one hundred and forty miles. The grant for the Pacific route within the State of Minnesota amounts to 1,500,000 acres. Thus has Congressional and State legislation stamped *imperative necessity* upon these artificial improvements, to connect the Mississippi and Pacific Ocean with the western lobe of Lake Superior. These grants were made, relying upon the good faith of the applicants, whose representations assured Congress that the improvements would be immediately prosecuted, and that the applicants were endowed with ability and means to fulfill the behests of Government.

The commerce of a quarter of a century has tested the vital importance of these Lakes, and their utility in equalizing the tariffs of transportation, and keeping within bounds the railway rates. The West Coast of Lake Michigan is literally the Seaboard of the district — the 60,000 square miles under consideration. The average cost of Lake and Canal transportation per bushel of wheat, from Chicago to Liverpool, during the years 1860 to 1862 inclusive, was: Chicago *via* New York, forty-six cents; *via* Montreal, forty-one and a half.

This is compiled from Mr. Stewart's Report to President Lincoln of March 24, 1864, who adds: "During this period the cost of transportation ruled at very uniform rates between Chicago and New York, ranging from five dollars and fifty cents to six dollars per ton, giving about two dollars for Lake transport and three dollars and fifty cents to four dollars to the Erie Canal, and fifty cents per ton to the Hudson River, and *via* the Oswego route and through the Welland Canal from Chicago one dollar per ton additional on Lake transport, (with small vessels compared with those between Chicago and Buffalo,) and one dollar less on the Canal to the Hudson, making the cost substantially the same by either route." These rates, reduced to wheat, show the transportation from Chicago to New York twenty-five cents, and to Montreal seventeen and a half cents per bushel.

The navigability of Lake Superior, the Sault Canal and River, suffer in comparison with that of Lake Michigan to Lake Huron, by sixty miles in distance, the Sault locks, and fifty miles of River; while the head of Lake Superior penetrates two hundred and sixty miles further, to a point five hundred miles nearer Puget Sound, one hundred and eighty nearer the Central Pacific Trunk, and *one hundred and ninety miles nearer the center of the* 60,000 *square miles district in view.*

During the infancy of the Railways connecting the Mississippi with Lake Michigan, it was natural for the Lake Cities and Road Companies to dissuade the connection of *Lake Superior* with the River, when, especially, the productive capacity of the upper valley had not been tested. But now that those roads, and their River and Lake depots and markets, are overburthened, and the Northwestern producer is groaning under a tariff of *fifty-five* cents per bushel on his wheat, to the Seaboard, and from *twenty*—the least—to *fifty* dollars per ton on his imports of iron, salt, agricultural implements, groceries, and dry goods.

Now, National economy demands every pound of exportable produce to keep down the balance of trade, and every honest inducement to immigrants to fill up the rich acres of Wisconsin, Minnesota, and Dacotah. Now, the time has come when to dissuade, or not to encourage, the earliest possible opening of cheaper modes of transport, is unfriendly to our British neighbors, most oppressive to the agriculturist, and *disloyal* to the interests of our Government, which so pressingly demands the fullest remuneration for every blow struck by the artisan, sailor, and farmer.

Any one of the proposed Railways to connect the Mississippi with Lake Superior penetrates the district in view at the confluence of the St. Croix and Minnesota with the Mississippi, and near that of the Wisconsin with the latter River, and at the grand junction of the Northwestern Wisconsin and all of the Minnesota Railways, which are now being rapidly constructed and equipped. This *centre* is one hundred and thirty-five miles by proposed rail from Lake Superior, and over three hundred and fifty from Lake Michigan by Rail and River, and three hundred and twenty-five miles by the shortest projected Railway between this *center* and the latter Lake. Here are the market towns of the present population of 200,000, whose exports amount to 225,000 tons, costing them, at Lake Michigan, never less than *seven* dollars a ton, or nineteen cents a bushel on wheat; this population import over 60,000 tons, at from nine to fifty dollars, from Seaboard, the annual aggregate of their freights being $3,075,000. Give this people the Illinois Canal improvement, and their freights on the above tonnage will be $1,712,510, a relief of $1,360,000 — a relief which would stimulate an increase of more than ten per cent. annually in population and product; and without such relief every effort to induce immigration into the district must result in succeeding hardship or disappointment. The able and full discussion in Congress and Committee in favor of the Illinois and Michigan Canal deserved a better fate. But its estimated cost — $13,450,000 for three hundred and twenty miles of improvement — appeared too formidable an amount to meet with the favor of Congress, when the Government needed its energies and credit in the Nation's struggle.

Whatever arguments and premises went to establish the utility of that improvement, likewise were applicable to the Fox and Wisconsin project. This latter involves two hundred and twenty-five miles of similar, if not less expensive, work; and it is *the* work needed for the upper Mississippi Valley and its Western and Northwestern districts — the work demanded for the relief and prosperity of the district particularly in view. While this improvement gives a water route from St. Paul to Lake Michigan of four hundred and fifty-six miles, it shortens the Lake Michigan transportation two hundred miles. This, then, would involve a freight of four dollars and thirty and one-half cents River and Canal, and a deduction from the Chicago and Seaboard cost of the two hundred miles; so that, instead of seven dollars and twenty-six cents per ton and twenty-two cents per bushel on exports, and from nine to fifty dollars on imports, the tariffs would be reduced on the above tonnage to an aggregate of $1,586,500 — a saving of $1,488,500 annually for the district.

These two improvements, involving a cost of $23,000,000, would result in an annual saving to the present million of producers and consumers of the Mississippi Valley of three dollars per ton — not less than $4,000,000 — more than double the interest and sinking fund to liquidate the original expenditure. The policy which prevailed in deferring these improvements, however conservative and wise, would have defeated Clinton in constructing the Erie Canal, and left the grand West as undeveloped as it was a quarter of a century ago.

But the Nation's debt stands out in such emphatic numbers, that these undertakings, in the judgment of Congress, had to be postponed, and corporation enterprise left to take hold of the munificent grants to construct railways into the suffering districts.

The mineral resources of Lake Superior are no longer a speculative myth. The annual yield of copper — 10,000 tons — and of iron — 500,000 tons — may be swelled to ten times thos^ quantities, and will be, so soon as the miner can be fed at the producer's prices of provisions, and the metals moved at lower rates of transport to the markets demanding them. The Marquette iron range is only an evidence of what will be developed. Wisconsin has as rich and extensive an outcrop, and the Minnesota geologists have just come in with the richest specimens yet found on the Lake, from an outcrop of length, base, and height enough to supply the Mississippi demand for centuries, without an appreciable reduction of the deposit. This, with the copper, slates, and marble at the lake termini of the proposed roads, will always reload the cars from the agricultural districts, developing an exportable product from the lake regions of Wisconsin and Minnesota, which, without these roads, must remain, to the country, as valueless as the dunes of a desert.

The cost of transportation to and from the head of Lake Superior to the Seaboard cannot exceed one per cent. more than from the head of Lake Michigan, while from the Mississippi, at the center of the "district" of 60,000 square miles, the cost will be, on one hundred and thirty-five miles of rail, two dollars and seventy cents per ton, or eight cents per bushel on wheat.

It is claimed, in view of this subject, that with a railway from the center of the *district* to Lake Superior, the immediate demand and market at the Lake, which now, in its infancy, is 60,000 barrels of flour, and the usual proportion of other provisions, together with the reduction of transportation from five dollars to two dollars and seventy cents per ton, and from *twenty* to *eight* cents per bushel on wheat, will render the market price of produce at St. Paul, Hudson, and Prescott as good for all time as upon the west shore of Lake Michigan.

It was this, perhaps, more than anything else, that induced Congress to postpone the consideration of the improvements between the Mississippi and Lake Michigan; and the following demonstration can but satisfy the country that it was, so far as the *upper* Mississippi producer is concerned, a wise decision, provided the corporations now endowed of the land grants redeem their pledges to avail themselves of the munificence.

The cost of transportation of wheat from St. Paul, Hudson, and the central towns of that district, to Lake Michigan, has ranged from fifteen to thirty-five cents per bushel — twenty cents may be about the coin rate; other exports at two cents per ton per mile by Rail, and five mills by River, would amount to four dollars and ninety-four cents.

The comparisons of cost are:

St. Paul to Lake Michigan, by the present facilities, per bushel, .	$0 20
Or per ton, ...	4 94
St. Paul to Chicago, *via* River and Illinois Canal, per bushel, . .	0 22
Or per ton, ...	7 26

St. Paul to Lake Michigan, *via* Fox and Wisconsin Canal, per bushel,	$0 18
Or per ton, ...	4 30
St. Paul to Lake Superior, per bushel, ...	0 08
Or per ton, ...	2 70

Adding the Lake and Canal routes to the Seaboard, and the rates will be:

	CENTS.
St. Paul to New York, by present facilities, per bushel, ...	45
Or to Montreal, ...	37½
By the Illinois Canal, ...	47
By the Fox and Wisconsin Canal, ...	36
Or to Montreal, ...	29
By the Lake Superior route, ...	33
Or to Montreal, ...	24½

These facts have prevailed to stimulate the people of Lake Superior, and capital elsewhere, to embark in mining; but the price of provisions, augmented by a thousand miles of freights, has had its retarding effect. In the absence of a through traffic, lake freights are kept up, and the miner must pay from twenty to thirty per cent. more for his supplies than even the *distance* would indicate. The Bay de Noc' and Marquette Railway to a great extent alleviates the miner in that locality, but as yet it is of little relief to the west end of the Lake. Produce of the Mississippi Valley must pay five dollars per ton to Lake Michigan and five dollars more to Lake Superior, when it should be delivered for two dollars and seventy cents; this difference is the miner's loss — a tax upon the copper and iron of Lake Superior, which, when removed, will augment the exports of those metals to figures beyond sanguine estimate. Open the Mississippi Valley as a market for this iron, subject to a railway freight of two dollars and seventy cents per ton, and of River five mills per mile, and 1,000,000 of population will be supplied, who now pay from seven to ten dollars freight per ton.

The opening of this connection will extend a full line of commerce through the whole chain of Lakes, and hasten the extension towards the Pacific; the people of the Red River Valley be brought in connection with their sister Provinces; the trade and commerce of both Nations, flowing through a common channel, will institute a *union* which, under Heaven's blessing, shall never be broken. It will be the connecting link between the interior extremities of the two great lines of internal trade of North America, and second only to that between the two Oceans. Any measure to retard, any project which does not favor it, alike checks the internal trade of the country, and keeps the exportable products from their legitimate end — the restoration of *equal* commerce with other Nations.

Respectfully submitted by your humble servant,

THOS. CLARK.

At a meeting of commercial and business men at Superior, Wisconsin, Gen. H. Walbridge and Thomas Clark were appointed delegates to represent this locality in the Commercial Convention to be held in Detroit on the 11th of July, 1865, with authority to substitute others, should they, or either of them, be unable to attend.

JAMES EDWARDS,
Chairman.

E. W. Anderson, Jr.,
Secretary.

THE RIVER COMMUNICATIONS

OF THE

BRITISH AMERICAN PROVINCES.

Commerce demands a ready market, and an open, direct, and easy highway thereto. The natural streams of any country form its primary means of communication between the Interior and Seaboard. They are, where thoroughly available, the cheapest and readiest means of transit for agricultural and natural produce, and their connection by artificial channels is the direct step towards trade extension.

Placed in competition with Railways, or macadamized roads, as modes of conveyance for all descriptions of heavy freights, they are much more available for the wants of commerce; and no Country dependent upon the latter accessories alone for transit, if its interior is far removed from the Seacoast, can ever become an active commercial centre.

The limited capacity of Railways as conveyers of freight is due to the difference between motive power as applied to land and water. In the first case the haulage has to be effected over a comparatively rough surface of great length. The inertion of the whole load has to be overcome, and its actual weight, as it were, lifted from the surface. As there must be a limit to the width of bearing surface that is attained on Railways, by a gauge or width between the rails of five feet six inches as the medium, and consequently the capacity of conveyance is necessarily limited thereby, a railway car forty feet long, ten feet wide, on the outside, carries generally about ten tons, and *ten* of those cars is a good load for an ordinary locomotive.

On the other hand, a canal boat, with an engine of seventy horse power, one hundred and fifty feet long, thirty-five feet beam, and drawing nine feet of water, will take three hundred to three hundred and fifty tons, according to stowage, (or three to four railway trains), and will not require as many hands or as costly machinery as the Railway.

The question of speed is a more serious matter. It is in favor of the Railway, but at a cost of material by no means, nor in any case, commensurate with the sacrifice of material by which it is gained. It will be, on the part of the Railway, about thirty per cent. of gain; but while the Canal can accommodate four to five million tons annually, working in this climate only two hundred and twenty days, the Railway, with three hundred and twelve days' work, can hardly accommodate one million and a half tons.

The question before the Convention is, "The best means of communication with the Seaboard," and the problem it involves can be only solved by the natural and artificial water-bays passing through the British North American Provinces.

It is said the destinies of a Country are determined by its physical geography. If such be the case — and to a considerable extent it must be true — then a great future is before the Empires bordering the Great Lakes, penetrating from the Northeast to the Northwest, through seven degrees of latitude and twenty-three of longitude. Those magnificent reservoirs present a length of over two thousand miles, and a coast navigation of over double that distance.

Draining an area of 600,000 square miles, the disposition of those great reservoirs and their outfalls are as follows: Beginning from the Seaboard, the River St. Lawrence, from Point des Monts, at the head of the Gulf of St. Lawrence, in N. Lat. 49 deg., 18 min., W. Long. 67 deg., 13 min., to Kingston, at the foot of Lake Ontario, in Lat. 44 deg., 15 min., Long. 76 deg., 22 min., is six hundred and ten miles in length, varying from one mile to thirty in width, and diversified with islands and scenery of the most magnificent description.

Lake Ontario is one hundred and eighty miles in length, and fifty-eight miles in greatest width; it is two hundred and thirty-four feet above the level of the sea, and its greatest depth is six hundred feet; it covers eight thousand two hundred square miles of area. At its western extremity it is joined to (or, rather, receives the surplus waters from the upper Lakes through) Lake Erie by the Niagara River, on which the magnificent falls of the same name are situated, and which render it unnavigable. Its length is about thirty-two miles, and its width varies from *two miles* to eight hundred and fifty feet. The most westerly point of Lake Ontario is in 43 deg., 20 min., N. Lat., and 79 deg., 52 min., W. Long.

Lake Erie has its eastern extremity in 41 deg., 53 min., N. Lat., and 78 deg., 50 min., W. Long.; its western in 41 deg., 41 min.,

N. Lat., and 83 deg., 32 min., W. Long. It is two hundred and fifty miles in length, eighty-two miles in width, nine hundred feet greatest depth, and covers eleven thousand eight hundred square miles of area. It is five hundred and sixty-nine feet above the level of the sea, and is joined to Lake St. Clair by the Detroit River, twenty-four miles in length, from one and one-half miles in width to twenty-six hundred feet.

Lake Saint Clair has a north and south course. Its lower or southern end is in 42 deg., 25 min., N. Lat., 82 deg., 55 min., W. Long., and its northern end in 42 deg., 55 min., N. Lat., and 82 deg., 20 min., W. Long. It is the smallest of the Lakes, as well as the shallowest, being only twenty miles in length by twenty-five miles in width, with an extreme depth of eight to twenty feet. It covers three hundred and ninety-two square miles of area, and is connected with Lake Huron through the St. Clair River, which is twenty-eight miles in length, and about one mile average width.

Lake Huron has a general north and south course. It is divided into two parts by the Manitoulin Islands, the eastern division known as the Georgian Bay. Both cover an area of twenty-eight thousand five hundred square miles. The Lake is two hundred and sixty miles in length, one hundred and sixty-six miles in greatest width, and seven hundred and five feet greatest depth. Its southern end is in 43 deg. N. Lat., 82 deg., 25 min., W. Long.; and northern in 46 deg., 21 min., N. Lat., 84 deg. W. Long. It is joined to Lake Michigan on the west by the Straits of Mackinac, in 45 deg., 50 min., N. Lat., 84 deg., 48 min., W. Long.

Lake Michigan lies nearly parallel with Lake Huron. Its general course being northeast and southwest, it describes a long curve, not unlike a long cucumber in shape. Its southern extremity is in 41 deg., 37 min., N. Lat., and between 86 deg., 28 min., and 87 deg., 30 min., W. Long. It is two hundred and thirty miles long, eighty-two miles in width, nine hundred feet greatest depth. It is nearly on the same level as Lake Huron, the latter being five hundred and seventy-two feet above the sea, and the former five hundred and seventy-four feet. The area is twenty-one thousand two hundred square miles.

Lake Superior — the largest of all the Lakes — is joined to Lake Huron by the River St. Mary's. The length of this River, from the foot of St. Joseph's Island, is forty-five miles. It is broken by Rapids, known as Sault Ste. Marie, and the navigation is continued by a Canal of large dimensions, in the territory of the United States. The width of the River is over one mile. The size of canal locks, three hundred and fifty feet long; seventy feet between the quoins; twelve feet water on sides. Length of Canal, one mile. The Lake is four hundred and twenty miles in length, one hundred and sixty miles in width, and one thousand feet in greatest depth. Its southern extremity is in Lat. 46 deg., 28 min., and 84 deg., 32 min., W. Long., and its northwestern in Lat. 46 deg., 40 min., W. Long. 92 deg., 20 min. Its level is six hundred feet above the sea.

Having thus described that great series of Lakes and Rivers by which the surplus produce of an area of 800,000 square miles of the richest and most productive soil on this Continent must reach the Seaboard, it will now be necessary to detail more particularly the artificial means already in existence for overcoming the natural obstructions to their complete navigation, and what facilities exist for the construction of other artificial channels of equal or greater capacity, and more than commensurate value.

Between tidal water at Three Rivers and the foot of Lake Ontario a difference of level of two hundred and thirty-five feet has to be overcome. It is concentrated in the one hundred and six miles which intervene between the foot of the Lachine Rapids at Montreal and the summit of the Galops Rapids. In this distance there are seven distinct Canals, of an aggregate length of forty-three miles, as follows:

Lachine Canal, at the City of Montreal, eight and one-half miles in length, having *five* locks, each two hundred feet long, forty-five feet between the quoins in width, nine feet water on sills — (those are the dimensions of the locks throughout the whole of the St. Lawrence Canals.) The height of lift to be overcome is forty-four feet nine inches.

The Beauharnois Canal is eleven and one-quarter miles in length, has *nine* locks, with a lift of eighty-two feet six inches.

Cornwall Canal, eleven and one-half miles in length, has *seven* locks, with forty-eight feet height of lift.

Farren's Point Canal is *three-fourths* of a mile in length, has *one* lock, with four feet of lift.

Rapid Platte Canal is four miles in length, has *two* locks, with eleven feet six inches height of lift.

Point Iroquois Canal has *one* lock, is three miles in length, has six feet nine inches height of lift. This Canal is joined to the upper Canal by a recently constructed link two and five-eighths miles in length, without any locks.

Galops Canal is two miles in length, and has nine feet height of lift, with *two* locks.

The total length of Canals would be thus forty-three and five-eighths miles; number of locks, twenty-seven and total lift two hundred and six feet six inches. At foot of Lachine Canal the surface of the River is twelve feet nine inches above tidal water, which reaches Three Rivers, ninety miles below, while fifteen feet six inches is due to the natural inclination of the surface of the River in the thirty-five miles of still water which intervene between Kingston and Montreal, equal to 1.37 inches to the mile.

At Montreal a cargo downward bound meets the Ocean steamship, as the navigation of the St. Lawrence is uninterrupted to that point for vessels drawing over twenty feet of water, for which much praise is due to the energy and enterprise of the Montreal merchants.

The River, above the Galops Canal, is navigable for large craft to Kingston, sixty-five miles, and thence to the head of Lake Ontario, one hundred and eighty miles more; but at that point a check is interposed by the Rapids and Falls of the Niagara, and an ascent of three hundred and thirty-four feet three inches has to be overcome before the surface of Lake Erie is reached.

This is accomplished by the Welland Canal of twenty-eight miles in length, having twenty-seven locks, each one hundred and eighty feet long, by twenty-six feet six inches between the quoins, with a depth of water on sides of ten feet. It opens the navigation to the heads of Lakes Huron and Michigan.

The St. Lawrence Canals admit vessels one hundred and eighty-six feet in length, forty-three feet breadth of beam, drawing *eight* feet of water; maximum burthen, three hundred tons.

The Welland Canal admits vessels one hundred and sixty-two feet long, twenty-five feet beam, drawing *nine* feet of water; maximum burthen, four hundred tons.

As the series are limited by the St. Lawrence at present, their value as channels for freight can be easily determined. Assuming the maximum of work for the season of navigation, which may be taken at two hundred and twenty days, at six lockages per hour, or a lift of one foot each minute, we would have 6 x 24 x 220 x 300 = 9,504,000 tons, representing a downward movement of 4,752,000 tons, and an upward of equal amount.

But the limit of the capacity of these Canals has not been yet reached. It is, unfortunately, governed by Lake St. Clair, which will not allow its being navigated by any vessel drawing over *nine* feet of water; therefore, the capacity of the St. Lawrence Canals will be attained when the first section is deepened to *ten* feet of water on the sides of its locks, and the chambers enlarged to a length of two hundred and fifty feet by fifty feet, admitting vessels of seven hundred and fifty tons. The lengthening and widening of the Welland Canal to a similar capacity is a work of time and great expense.

The yearly capacity of the Canals so enlarged would be equal to 23,760,000 tons annually, or a downward movement of 11,880,000 tons, with an upward of similar amount.

It would appear that, unless a large sum of money is laid out on Lake Saint Clair, those noble Canals will then have attained their utmost useful dimensions.

The distance from Chicago to Montreal by this route is as follows: Eleven hundred and forty-five miles Lake navigation, one hundred and thirty-two miles River navigation, and seventy-one miles of Canal—making a total of thirteen hundred and forty-eight miles.

Time occupied: Lake, at eight miles per hour, one hundred and forty-three hours; River, eight miles per hour, seventeen hours; Canals, *two* miles per hour, thirty-five hours; lockage, five hundred and forty feet, at *one* minute per foot, nine hours. Total, one hundred and ninety-five hours, or eight days and three hours.

From Montreal to Quebec is one hundred and fifty miles, thence to Liverpool two thousand, five hundred and eighty-three miles; the whole distance between Chicago and this latter port is, therefore, four thousand and eighty-one miles.

The cost of transmission of a ton of agricultural or other produce would be as follows: Chicago to Kingston, twelve cents per bushel, four dollars and forty-four cents per ton; Kingston to Montreal, including transhipment, etc., six cents per bushel, two dollars and twenty-two cents; Montreal to Liverpool, twenty-five cents per bushel, nine dollars and twenty-five cents. Total cost, forty-three cents, equal to fifteen dollars and ninety-one cents, to which must be added insurance, four cents; commission, six cents; Town and dock dues, three cents; light-house and Imperial dues, three cents; making a total of sixteen cents per bushel additional, and, at thirty-seven bushels to the ton, an additional charge of five dollars and ninety-two cents. Total cost per ton to Liverpool, twenty-one dollars and eighty-three cents, or fifty-nine cents per bushel.

If the Western trade contains any of the great elements its advocates claim for it—and there is no reason to doubt the gigantic proportions it might assume if all restrictions were removed by the action of the people of the United States, or their Government—this route could be filled to its greatest present capacity, and a much greater reduction effected in the transmission downwards, by having return cargoes, which the route does not at present furnish.

The quantity of water passing over the Niagara Falls is equal to 14,359,844 cubic feet per minute. It is fully one-third greater at the head of the St. Lawrence Canals, as the Lake and Rivers receive several large tributaries, and drain a vastly increased area.

Now, the Canals require at their greatest enlargement 12,500 cubic feet of water per minute for actual work, and, therefore, their extension for navigable purposes can only be limited by their profitable employment.

The St. Lawrence is the only direct line of *existing* Canals, belonging to the British North American Provinces, which can afford facilities for the accommodation and development of Western commerce; and if the restrictive policy pursued by the Government of the United States was removed, a large proportion of the grain trade would seek it as an outlet, and an impetus would be given to the settlement and productiveness of the Western States, which they now seek in vain.

But the capabilities of the British Provinces are not confined to the St. Lawrence alone. There are facilities for the construction of other routes, possessing many substantial advantages over that great outlet, of equal if not superior capacity, and which the increase of Western traffic will call into existence.

It must be borne steadily in mind that the great advantages those routes offer to the producer are, the *shortest*, *most capacious*, *cheapest*, and *safest route to the Ocean*, and that a cargo descending the Great Lakes to Montreal has accomplished all those conditions, inasmuch as it has reached the head of Ocean navigation by the most direct and available route in existence.

At Montreal the St. Lawrence is joined by one of its principal tributaries from the Northwest, known in the days of French dominion as the *Grand River* or *Ottawa*, since, by the latter name exclusively.

Twenty-five miles above Montreal it bifurcates, forming the island on which that City is built, one stream, (the southern arm,) flowing in front of the City, and mingling its dark brown waters with the deep blue of the St. Lawrence; the other and northern arm joins the same River sixteen miles below that City.

It is a stream of seven hundred and eighty miles in length, draining an area of 87,700 square miles, or one-fourth of the whole of the Province of Canada. Its course, for three hundred and five miles above the City of Montreal, is nearly due west, and a straight line drawn from thence to the center of the Straits of Mackinac would clearly define its course for that distance

At this point the same River turns sharply to the northward, but the direct course is continued by a tributary which joins it from the westward — the Matawan. This stream is forty and one-half miles in length; it drains an area of nine hundred and fifty square miles, and at its western extremity the ridge which divides the Catchuart Basin of the St. Lawrence and Ottawa Rivers interposes.

Its greatest elevation is just ten feet above the surface water of the Upper Tortu Lake, the same of the Matawan; and an excavation of fifteen hundred feet in length, by an average depth of less than five feet, would cause the waters now flowing eastward to the Ottawa to descend the western slope to the St. Lawrence.

This summit is four and one-half miles in length, at which point the eastern end of Lake Nipissing is reached. It is sixty miles in its greatest length, twenty in its greatest width, and stands six hundred and thirty-two feet above the level of tide-waters. It is the second of two large Lakes, which receive the drainage waters of an area of nine thousand square miles. The first, known as

Lake Temiscaming, has an area of three hundred and fifty square miles. It is connected with Nipissing by the Sturgeon River, and with the Ottawa by a chain of Lakes, and a swift stream, at the confluence of the Montreal River, one hundred and fifty miles above the junction of the Matawan.

The greatest length of Lake Nipissing is, from east to west, midway on its southern shores, thirty-one miles from the foot of the Portage to Tortu Lake, its affluent. The French River carries the waters of its Catchuen Basin to Lake Huron, from which it is forty-nine miles distant, and which it joins at a point two hundred and seventy miles from the Straits of Mackinac, and five hundred from Chicago. Thus the whole distance between these points is nine hundred and thirty miles — viz., Four hundred and thirty from Montreal to mouth of French River, and five hundred thence to Chicago — making the distance shorter by four hundred and eighteen miles than by way of the St. Lawrence and the Lakes.

As time is an essential element in any system of transit limited to a certain season in each year, one of its most important advantages is found in this, the shorter route. As it is, however, the only actual advantage at present, it will be necessary to investigate all the conditions of this line of communication, for the purpose of establishing its claim to be, when constructed, the shortest, and cheapest, and safest yet designed.

At the point where the Matawan joins the Ottawa, the latter River is over thirteen hundred feet in width, and it discharges 2,511,936 cubic feet per minute on the average, its depth in the open reaches being from *five* to *twenty* fathoms; and from the peculiar formation through which its course is prolonged, it consists of a string of moderate sized Lakes, united by short reaches of rapids, generally in the form known as cascades, or short falls, which bear a very small proportion to the navigable portions, not averaging twelve per cent. of the length required for the purposes of communication, nor, indeed, of that of the whole River.

The Matawan discharges 65,122 cubic feet per minute, but, owing to the fact that its head waters are confined to an area of a few square miles, it will be necessary to draw the navigable supply from Lake Nipissing.

This latter Lake is the reservoir of a drainage of nine thousand square miles, the upper portion of which is occupied by Lake Tamangaminque. Its discharge by the French River is equal to 477,369 cubic feet per minute. The requirements of navigation at its utmost development, allowing six lockages per hour, would not be more than 12,500 cubic feet per minute; so that, as far as water supply is concerned, no doubt of the capacity of this route can be entertained.

The design for the proposed navigation is such as to adapt any vessel using it to the capacity of the principal lake harbors. It is stated that eleven feet of water is the greatest depth that of Chicago will allow vessels to draw. Consequently it is proposed to have twelve feet water on the sills of the Ottawa and Lake Huron Canal locks, and they are to be of corresponding dimensions — two hundred and fifty feet in length, by a clear width of fifty feet, admitting vessels of two hundred and thirty-four feet in length and forty-eight feet beam, drawing eleven feet of water, and of a capacity of one thousand tons.

On the whole length of four hundred and thirty miles between Montreal and Lake Huron, on this route, thirty miles in length of artificial Canal will be required, and that includes eight and one-half miles of the St. Lawrence Canals at Montreal, which will be common, but not necessarily so, to both channels.

In fact, there is no limitation to the Ottawa route for freight capacity, because it reaches, by the north channel — better known as the Riviere des Prairies — what may be called the head of Ocean navigation, at the Boute de L'Isle, sixteen miles below Montreal, without interfering with the artificial channels of the St. Lawrence in any way; and the improvement of this North Channel would lessen the actual canalling on the main route by at least *seven* miles.

The character of the North Channel prescribes the nature of the works necessary for rendering it navigable, which would be four dams of very moderate dimensions, not exceeding in each case six hundred feet in length by ten feet in width, and as the City of Montreal is rapidly extending, the Boute de L'Isle, will become her principal Port where the sea-going steam or sailing ships will meet the Lake craft laden with the produce of the Western prairies.

Throughout the whole of this proposed navigation, the greatest length of artificial Canal will not exceed ten miles. The works necessary in nearly every case will consist of weirs, restoring the River course to its original regime, and the only excavation requisite will not exceed 6,000,000 cubic yards beyond what is necessary for the lock sites. At the summit level the greatest length of artificial channel occurs, and it is within the limits stated.

It is manifestly evident, that doubling the capacity of the channel by the erection of a second series of locks, would be an achievement of no extraordinary difficulty, and would cost less than one-half the original outlay on the first series, because the weirs, the most expensive portion of those works, render the construction of the second series a matter of convenience, (if the trade require it) easy of accomplishment, at the same time furnishing motive power to a very large amount, and from which a considerable revenue could be derived.

The capacity for freight at *six* lockages per hour, and for a season of two hundred and twenty days, during which the navigation would remain open, would be 31,680,000 tons annually, or 15,840,000 tons of a downward movement, and the same upward.

It is a navigation peculiarly adapted to large screw propellers, because the large and frequent expanses of open water and the small extent of Canal along the route enables a high speed to be maintained throughout, which is unattainable in every other case.

The distance for navigable purposes between Chicago and Montreal would be as follows: Lake, five hundred and thirty miles; River, three hundred and seventy; Canal, thirty. Miles total, nine hundred and thirty.

Its relation to time will be as follows: River and Lake, nine hundred miles, at *eight* miles per hour, say one hundred and thirteen hours; Canal, *two miles* per hour, fifteen hours; the lockage will be six hundred and eighty-two feet, of which sixty feet will be upwards and six hundred and twenty-two downwards, at *one* minute per foot, twelve hours. Total, one hundred and forty hours, or five days and twenty hours.

From Montreal to Quebec the distance is one hundred and fifty miles; thence to Liverpool, two thousand five hundred and eighty-three. Total distance between Chicago and the latter port, three thousand six hundred and sixty-three miles.

The act of transmitting a ton of freight between these Ports would be, by this route, as follows: Chicago to Montreal, thirteen cents per bushel — $4.81 per ton of thirty seven bushels; Montreal to Liverpool, twenty-five cents per bushel — $9.25 per ton; dock dues, commission, light-house and Imperial duties, sixteen cents, per bushel — $5.92, being a total of $19.98 per ton, or at the rate of forty-five cents per bushel.

Penetrating a mineral region, rich in all the useful metals, and furnishing from its inexhaustible forests a choice of return freight, the Ottawa possesses many claims to general attention; for it is by the agency of that stream alone the Western States can ever hope for full and profitable development, or the resources of the Northwest territory of British North America for settlement and commerce with the outer world. It would place Fort William, on Lake Superior, within one thousand and fifty miles of Montreal, by water, from whence a Railway of one hundred and ninety-two miles in length would touch Rainy Lake, which may be taken as the head of navigable water to Lake Winnipeg.

The effect of opening this region to commerce and settlement is obvious. It covers over 500,000 square miles of territory, and contains, within that area, large deposits of valuable coal and other minerals, as well as a fruitful agricultural country; but its chief recommendation is that it forms the intermediate plain over which the Pacific Railway must be carried, from the Northwestern slopes of the Alleghany range in Canada to the Northeasterly slopes of the Rocky Mountains, overlooking the valleys of the Sankatchewan.

But large as this Canal project may be, it has not exhausted the resources of Canada in surface formation, favorable to the construction of artificial Water Ways.

Lake Huron is divided, longitudinally, with two unequal portions by the Manitoulin Island, and the Peninsula known as Cape Hurd; that to the Eastward is known as the Georgian Bay, and covers an area of six thousand square miles. It is about one hundred and forty miles in length and fifty-five miles in its greatest breadth.

The French River enters this bay, within thirty miles of its Northern extremity, opposite the channel between Cape Hurd and the Great Manitoulin. At the Southwestern extremity the capacious expanse of Nattawassaga Bay is to be found, and at the Southeastern the Severn carries the surplus waters of twelve hundred square miles, of which Lake Simcoe acts as collecting reservoir.

This latter lake is five hundred and sixty-four square miles in area, and thirty-five miles in greatest length, and eighteen in greatest width. It is seven hundred and four feet above the line of the sea, four hundred and seventy feet above Lake Ontario, and one hundred and thirty-two feet above Lake Huron.

It is proposed to excavate a Canal from head of Nattawassaga Bay for seventeen miles, to the Western extension of Lake Simcoe, known as Kimpenfelt Bay; thence along that Lake for some thirty-two miles of open navigation to Cook's Bay, at its Southern extremity; thence by the Holland River and across the summit of the Blue Ridge to the source of the Humber River, down the channel of which it is continued to the mouth in Lake Ontario, a distance from Cook's Bay of forty-eight miles. The total length of excavation or Canal being sixty-five miles, and lockage one hundred and thirty-two feet up and four hundred and seventy feet downward, six hundred and two feet to reach the level of Lake Ontario, which is three hundred and thirty-eight feet below Lake Huron.

The dimensions of this Canal are proposed to equal that of the Ottawa navigation with locks 250 x 50 x 12, and consequently its capacity for freight will be equal, viz: 31,680,000 tons per annum, (all the elements of the calculation being the same,) 15,840,000 tons down and the same quantity up.

At the mouth of the Humber, the cargo will have the option of crossing the Lake to Oswego, and thence, by Erie Canal, to New York, or descending the St. Lawrence Canals to Montreal.

The distances by this route are as follows: Chicago to Montreal, by the proposed route — Lake, seven hundred and seventy-five miles; Canal, one hundred and forty-one; River, one hundred and thirty-four miles — total, one thousand and fifty miles. Time, Lake and River nine hundred and nine miles, at eight miles per hour, one hundred and thirteen hours; Canal, one hundred and forty-one miles, at two miles per hour, seventy hours; lockage on Georgian Bay Canal, six hundred and two feet. To this must be added two hundred and five feet lockage downwards in the St. Lawrence, making a total of eight hundred and seven feet, which, at one minute per foot, would be thirteen hours; total time, one hundred and ninety-six hours.

As time is the mainly essential element in the transmission of freight along these routes, the cost by the Canal would be probably one cent per bushel more than by the St. Lawrence, or between Chicago and Liverpool, sixty cents, which will be $22.20 per ton of thirty-seven bushels.

Should the time come when the Western freight shall fill all the channels previously enumerated, and an outlet of large capacity be constructed from the Southern end of Lake Champlain to the Hudson, at Albany, this proposed route would become a valuable auxiliary for the distribution of cargo over a portion of the Eastern States. As an outlet to the Ocean, its theoretic value is at present negative.

Between Ottawa, the capital of Canada, on the River of the same, name, and Kingston, at the foot of Lake Ontario, a navigable channel known as the Rideau Canal was constructed by the late Colonel By, of the Royal Engineers.

It is the best example of hydraulic engineering, as applied to the improvement and control of natural water courses on the continent, or probably in the world.

The channel of the Rideau River is rendered navigable by a series of dams, for a distance of *ninety miles*, to the natural summit level between its water shed, and that of a small stream known as the Cataraqui, where, by cutting through an isthmus less than one mile in length, the navigation is perfected by another series of dams and weirs, and the whole extent of actual canalling, in a length of one hundred and twenty-six miles, is sixteen miles. It has forty-seven locks, and a lockage of four hundred and thirty feet and four inches, of which two hundred and seventy-three feet and ten inches is ascent from the Ottawa, and one hundred and fifty-six feet and six inches descent to Lake Ontario. Its locks are one hundred and thirty-three feet in length, thirty-three feet in width, with five feet and six inches water on the sills. It passes vessels of two hundred tons, one hundred and twelve feet in length, thirty-two feet broad, drawing four feet and six inches water.

Using the data hitherto employed, its capacity for freight would be 6,336,000 tons, or 3,168,000 up and the same down, per annum. Its principal traffic consists in the transportation of flour, grain, partially manufactured lumber and iron ore, of which large quantities of the best black muriatic oxyd is to be found at the summit and at Ottawa. It also furnishes access to a country rich in galena, plumbago and copper.

The upper part of the Rideau and Cataraqui Rivers is composed of large Lakes, with small elevators above the summit level, and it is upon and within easy reach of those Lakes the principal ore deposits are formed.

As an element in the great canal system, which is eventually to control the traffic of the Western States, the Rideau must only play a subsiding part, principally for local purposes, and the distribution of such portions of the general downward movement which may be required for local purposes.

It will always play an important part in the distribution of the export lumber trade to the State of New York, and in the development of its own mineral resources.

The next important channel is that afforded by the Richelieu River which discharges the surplus water of Lake Champlain into the St. Lawrence at Sorel, fifty-six miles below Montreal.

This River is rendered navigable by a Canal at Chambly, twelve miles in length. It has ten locks, each one hundred and twenty-two feet long and twenty-four feet wide, with six feet water on the sills, admitting schooners or barges one hundred and ten feet long, by twenty-two feet broad, and drawing five feet water. To pass through the height of lockage is seventy-four feet.

Applying the data previously used, and allowing this Canal to pass vessels of one hundred tons, a total yearly movement of 3,168,000 tons, on 1,584,000 up and a like quantity down, would be the measure of its capacity; but it is controlled for useful effect by the Champlain Canal, in the State of New York, which leads from Whitehall, at the southern extremity of the Lake, to the Erie Canal at West Troy, a distance of sixty-six and three-fourths miles. It has an upward lockage of fifty-four and one-fourth feet, and a downward one of one hundred and fifty feet, making a total of two hundred and four and one-fourth feet of lockage.

The locks are twenty in number, ninety feet in length, by fifteen feet in width, with four feet water on sills, and it admits vessels of fifty tons. Its yearly value would be equal to 1,584,000 tons, or 789,000 tons upwards and the same downwards.

It has been proposed to construct a Canal from Caughanawaga, at the head of the Lachine Rapids to St. Johns, on Lake Champlain, a distance of thirty-six miles. It was to have two locks, each two hundred and thirty feet long, thirty-six feet wide, and ten feet water on sills. It was designed to admit vessels of eight hundred and fifty tons burthen, which would give, per annum, 26,928,000 tons as its greatest freight capacity; but its value entirely consists in the probability of the enlargement of the Champlain Canal, and the possibility of using the Lake as a summit level.

If this could be effected, the enlargement would be useful, because it would relieve the St. Lawrence and the Ottawa Canals from such portion of the freight as would be compelled to pass in front of Montreal, and would be a very useful auxiliary to the Erie Canal.

There can be very little doubt that the only improvement possible in the New York Canals is to be found in this direction; and the small elevation of Lake Champlain over the St. Lawrence and Hudson will render the operation of enlarging the Southern Canal easy of accomplishment.

Between Montreal and the City of Ottawa the navigation is maintained by eleven locks of various dimensions, but all governed by one of ninety-six feet in length, nineteen feet wide, with four and a half feet water on the sills.

It admits barges of ninety tons burthen, and a large proportion of sawed lumber is shipped annually in craft belonging to the United States, which passes down these Canals and the Lachine, and ascends the Richelieu to Lake Champlain.

Using the elements of capacity hitherto employed, these Canals have a yearly capacity of 2,851,000 tons, or a downward movement of 1,425,600, and the same upwards.

A large proportion of the heavy local freight passes up there, and they were within the last twenty-five years the highway between tidal-water and the Lakes, by way of the Rideau Canal.

The facilities afforded by the British North American Provinces for water communication between the Western States and the Ocean, have been described, and their values freely detailed. The results must be pleasing to those who have faith in the development of the Great West, because they can rest assured that no matter how large the extension may be, natural and artificial channels of corresponding navigation will be ready to afford it easy, cheap and safe transit to the Ocean.

Existing lines of communication within the United States have failed to accommodate the grain trade in a corresponding degree with its development, because of the absence of the natural agents necessary; in other words, the water-ways of the country were insufficient and inapplicable for the purpose.

Those improved by artificial means consist of three great lines, the most westerly being the Illinois Canal, reaching from Chicago to the Mississippi, which it enters at Grafton, thirty-two miles above St. Louis. It is about three hundred and fifty miles in length, and its cargo is delivered one thousand two hundred and fifty miles from New Orleans, while it would have to perform a voyage of over six thousand miles from Chicago to Liverpool.

This Canal is of small dimensions, and if it were possible to enlarge it, there are obvious reasons against its affording an outlet to the grain trade in the great length to market, and the danger to cargo from the intertropical climates through which it must pass. It will become a valuable auxiliary whenever the cotton of the South comes to be manufactured on the Ottawa.

The next line of value are those Canals which communicate with the Ohio. This River, which is one thousand miles in length, enters the Mississippi at Cairo. It drains an area of 200,000 square miles, and has a difference between its highest and lowest waters of sixty-three feet, and on the upper reaches its waters are often reduced to two feet in depth in the channel.

Its downward navigation is carried on principally by *flat boats* built at the wharf, and sold where the cargo is delivered. The upward traffic is by steamboats of peculiar construction, but in any case its traffic is very limited. It has navigable communication with Lake Erie at Toledo, Sandusky, Cleveland and Erie, and may be said to be navigable from Pittsburgh, in Pennsylvania, to its mouth, a distance of nine hundred and sixty-five miles, and this point, known as Cairo, is one thousand and thirty-eight miles above New Orleans, which is one hundred and forty miles from the mouth of the Mississippi, and this latter point is five thousand one hundred and sixty miles from Liverpool.

A cargo shipped at Erie would travel one hundred and twenty-nine miles to Pittsburgh, two thousand and three miles to New Orleans, and five thousand three hundred miles from there to Liverpool, making a total of seven thousand four hundred and thirty-two miles by the Ohio.

There are several lines of canal or navigable waters connected with this River, the principal of which are through the Wabash and Sciota Rivers, and the connecting line between Pittsburgh and Erie.

Highlv valuable as an agent for local trade and development, it is quite evident that this line can never become the great highway of Western staples, nor even an efficient feeder of the commercial centers on Lake Erie.

The next, and most successful of all existing routes, is the Erie Canal, connecting the waters of the Lake of that name with the Hudson River.

If the man who made two blades of grass grow where one only grew before was a public benefactor, and deserved well of his country, of how much greater honor was he worthy by whose genius, patriotism, and perseverance the Western wilderness was converted into a granary for this Continent, and, at no distant day, for Europe also.

Honors may be heaped on the successful soldier, statues may be erected to the enlightened and patriotic statesman, dignities may be achieved by the talented lawyer, and wealth may be realized by the successful and persevering merchant; but none of those things can enhance the fame of De Witt Clinton. The proudest monument which could be erected to him is the creature of his own genius — the Erie Canal — and "*Clinton's folly*" stands far above the loftiest pillar a Nation's gratitude could construct.

Whether viewed in a political or commercial light, this great work is the noblest inspiration of far-seeing and comprehensive genius the world has ever witnessed; and, although the commerce it has created has outgrown its capacity, or even profitable or possible development, it will exist as a memorial of the greatest benefactor of his race which the present age has produced, and one who deserved well of his country.

It is not necessary to enter into a history of this remarkable channel. Commenced in 1817, it was completed in 1825, and has since been enlarged to many times its original dimensions, and its greatest attainable capacity.

The length of the present Canal, from Buffalo to Albany, is three hundred and fifty and one-half miles. It has seventy-one locks, one hundred and ten feet in length by eighteen feet in width, with seven feet water on the sills. It allows boats seventeen feet beam, ninety-eight feet in length, and drawing six feet water, to pass through; capacity, two hundred tons.

At Syracuse a branch joins the main line from Oswego. Its length is thirty-eight miles, and it descends one hundred and fifty-five feet to the level of the Erie Canal at that point.

The lockage on the main line is six hundred and fifty-four feet. It has two summits — that at Lake Erie, and that at Syracuse. The latter is fifty-three miles in length, and is supplied by a series of small Lakes, whose area cannot be extended artificially, and therefore the capacity of the Canal is limited.

Its freight capacity, taking two hundred and twenty days as a maximum season's work, and *ten* lockages per hour, and capacity of vessel as equal to two hundred tons, would be 10,560,000 tons, or a downward movement of 5,280,000 tons, with a similar upward movement.

For ordinary purposes of comparison the theoretical values given are sufficiently correct, but in practice it is found that a little over 3,500,000 tons of a downward movement will fill the Erie Canal to its utmost capacity, and that is due to its great artificial length, and the accidents consequent on the amount of mechanical appliances employed in its working and construction.

It follows, therefore, that, amongst the other requisites, *a line of communication by water* must embrace the minimum of artificial channel, or the shortest possible length of Canal.

A comparison of the routes described will be necessary, but previously we must consider the *time* and *expense* involved in transit by the Erie Canal, as fôllows: Chicago to Buffalo, one thousand miles; Erie Canal proper, three hundred and sixty miles; Hudson River, one hundred and sixty miles. Total, Chicago to New York, fifteen hundred and twenty miles. New York to Liverpool, twenty-nine hundred and eighty miles. Total, forty-five hundred miles from

Chicago to Liverpool by this route. Time: Lake and River, eleven hundred and sixty miles at eight miles per hour, one hundred and forty-five hours; Canal, thirty-six miles at two miles per hour, one hundred and eighty hours; lockage, six hundred and fifty-four feet at one minute per foot, eleven hours. Total time, three hundred and thirty-five hours, or nearly fourteen days.

It is well known that a cargo generally occupies that time in passing the artificial channel alone, but, as an element of comparison, this data is sufficiently near for all purposes.

The cost of a ton of produce between Chicago and this route is: To Buffalo, eleven cents per bushel; Buffalo to New York, sixteen cents; *lighterage*, weighing, screening, brokerage, stamp duty, and incidentals, one cent; insurance, New York to Chicago, two and one-half cents; commission, one cent; average Ocean freight, twenty-four and one-half cents; primage, five per cent. on freight, one cent; Imperial duties at Liverpool, three cents; town and dock dues, weighing, etc., three cents; commission, three cents. Total, seventy-one cents per bushel, and, at thirty-seven bushels to the ton, the total cost of a ton between Chicago and Liverpool will be twenty-six dollars and twenty-seven cents.

A further comparison would show that the St. Lawrence route places Chicago within four thousand and eighty-one miles of Liverpool; Ottawa and Lake Huron Canal, three thousand, six hundred and sixty-three miles; Georgian Bay and Toronto Canal, three thousand, seven hundred and eighty-eight; Erie Canal, four thousand, five hundred.

The St. Lawrence is shorter than the Erie by four hundred and nineteen miles; the Ottawa and Lake Huron by eight hundred and thirty-seven miles; and the Georgian Bay and Toronto by seven hundred and seventeen miles.

In freight charges, the St. Lawrence will transport at twenty-one dollars and eighty-three cents per ton; the Ottawa and Lake Huron at nineteen dollars and ninety-eight cents; the Georgian Bay and Toronto, twenty-two dollars and twenty cents; the Erie Canal, twenty-six dollars and twenty-seven cents.

Therefore the St. Lawrence is cheaper by four dollars and forty-four cents than the Erie; the Ottawa and Lake Huron, six dollars and twenty-nine cents; and the Georgian Bay and Toronto, four dollars and seven cents.

As time is an important element in a climate which limits internal navigation to two hundred and twenty days each season, its value can be only reckoned to the Seaboard in each case. Therefore, between Chicago and New York, a cargo occupies fourteen days to traverse the Erie Canal.

Between Chicago and Montreal, by the St. Lawrence, *eight days and three hours;* between the same ports, by the Ottawa and Lake

Huron, *five days and twenty hours;* by the Georgian Bay and Toronto, *eight days and four hours.* The difference in favor of the St. Lawrence over the Erie would be *five days and twenty-one hours;* for the Ottawa and Lake Huron, *eight days and four hours;* for the Georgian Bay and Toronto, *five days and twenty hours.*

Taking the maximum time on all those channels, a vessel could make the trip from Chicago to New York and back in twenty-eight days, or say *eight trips* per season. From Chicago to Montreal by the St. Lawrence, in sixteen days and six hours, or *thirteen trips* each season; Ottawa and Lake Huron, eleven days and sixteen hours, or nearly *nineteen trips* per season; the Georgian Bay and Toronto, *sixteen days and eight hours*, or *thirteen trips* for the season.

The elements of the foregoing comparison show clearly the reasons of the high price of freight on the Erie Canal, and it is for this Convention to devise means whereby the accessible channels to the Seaboard will be rendered available for the development of the full proportions of the traffic centering at the Lake Cities, and thereby give an impetus to the commerce of the Country, and supply a stimulus much needed for its agricultural interests.

Whatever may be the impediment, it is certainly strange that a larger proportion of the wheat and coarser cereals of the Western Provinces does not reach Great Britain. As a general rule, they are cheaper here than in Europe, and yet, with her large outlays, it seems she is obliged to search Europe, Asia, and Africa for supplies, which are rotting in Wisconsin and Iowa for want of a purchaser, or, if report speaks truly, *burned*, as being cheaper than firewood at a dollar and a half a cord.

By opening up this country to settlement and commerce, DeWitt Clinton did more for the United States, and humanity, and civilization, than any man of his age, and second only to him will be those individuals who shall, by wise measures, open its agricultural treasures to the starving populations of the Old World.

Great Britain imports yearly £26,000,000 sterling worth of breadstuffs for her surplus population, and in years of scarcity it ranges as high as £40,000,000. The supply purchased with this enormous sum is gathered from the following Countries, and the proportions are such as to show they have little to spare beyond the wants of their own population, except the United States alone, whose miserable proportion is due to the fostering of pet interests to the prejudice of the agriculturist:

	Per cent. of all imported into Great Britain.
Russia,	19½
Prussia,	31¼
Mecklenburg,	8
Hanse Towns,	4
France,	6½

	Per cent. of all Imported into Great Britain.
Turkey and Principalities,	5¼
Egypt,	2½
United States,	7¼
Denmark,	11¼
Other Countries,	2½

It is true that, during the past season, a much larger proportion of United States agricultural produce has reached Great Britain, but as the exceptional cause which led to that event has passed away, we may look to the decline in quantity as a certainty, so long as hostile tariffs exclude British manufactured goods from the markets of the Western States.

This question of water communication with *the Seaboard* has been placed before you in its entirety. It is one of the utmost importance to your interests, as well as those of the British American Provinces, and the advantages to be derived from the various channels described depend in no small measure on the action of this Convention.

Connected with it is the very interesting problem of manufacturing the agricultural produce on its downward passage, because, as a general rule, the losses on grain transported for long distances in bulk greatly enhance its value in the market. Now, cheap food as distinctly means *cheap money* as any one value can represent another; and, in those days of financial enlightenment, cheap money means sufficient capital.

It is not, therefore, the interest of either the seller or buyer that the representative values should be enhanced, without profit to either, by intermediate accidents. Therefore, it is an essential requisite of the trade that manufacture takes place as near the point of production as possible.

From the same reasons which limit the possible extension of the Erie Canal, the manufacture of grain on its downward passage could be only partially effected; but on the Canadian routes no such want of motive power prevails.

On the downward passage from Chicago, *via* the Ottawa and Lake Huron navigation, the French River, after deducting largely for navigable purposes, on a fall of sixty feet, would supply a motor equal to 40,707 horse power.

The Matawan, with a fall of one hundred and forty-eight feet, would give 12,745 horse power, while the Ottawa, with an assumed available discharge of 1,000,000 cubic feet per minute, (about one-fourth of the actual quantity,) and a total available fall between the junction of the Matawan and Montreal, would give 497,159 horse power — making a total of 550,611 horse power.

To render the value of this more apparent, it is known that a French burr mill stone of *five feet* in diameter, making ninety-seven revolutions per minute, and grinding *five bushels per hour* — the speed and quantity proper for an export trade — will, with its corresponding machinery, about ten horse power, give 55,061, such machines grinding 36,000 bushels each annually, or a manufacture of 1,980,196,000 bushels — *five times* as much as the greatest enthusiast in Western progress can hope that fruitful country will ever produce for exportation.

And this is not more than one-fourth of the real motive power furnished by the River.

It has been stated that Great Britain *imported* from the United States, during the years 1861, '62, '63, breadstuffs to the value of £12,643,918 sterling, and that the transit expenses were £8,826,351 sterling, the original cost realized at Chicago being only £3,817,069. If such is really the case, how stand the facts in relation to your progress?

Why, simply, by multiplying your transit dues beyond all reasonable proportions, you have restricted the power of your best customer to purchase at remunerative rates, and you have wasted so much capital, which might have been in circulation for your own benefit, without a corresponding profit.

If any operation is so badly conducted as to require the labor of two men to perform the work of one, there is a waste of both capital and labor; the work is unremunerative, and progress is impossible. Yet in this transit matter that foolish game has been repeated many times over.

It is about as wise to prescribe by law what tools an artisan shall use to effect a given object, as to prescribe the dimensions of an expanding commerce by tariffs and trade restrictions. The law of convenience, supply and demand should alone control, as natural agents, its course; and when the principle is admitted that taxation shall be levied on the surplus of man's industry, and not on the necessities of his existence, commerce will then be treated as subject to known laws, arising naturally from its prosecution, and not from arbitrary enactments, too often the result of prejudice or self-interested convenience.

The wants of the Western trade demand the mighty outlets, of which a faint description has been placed before you. Taken in connection with the existing Railways through British North America, they would be equal to a downward movement of *sixty millions of tons* — a quantity that even the Western States could not hope to attain.

The blessings which unrestricted commercial intercourse would bestow upon both Nations is incalculable. As friends and neighbors, it would improve the good understanding which should exist between people having so many interests in common; and it would prove a blessing to the vast mass of the overpeopled Countries of Europe.

Hostile tariffs will not produce any of those effects which the advocates of Protection desire. They will not develop any of the resources of the Western States, nor will they add to the wealth or happiness of the vast mass of the people, or the prosperity of the general commerce of the Country.

It will not bring about the consummation so earnestly desired by your extreme politicians, of annexation. Perfectly satisfied with being subjects of the greatest Empire the world ever saw — first in civilization, in order, in justice — we have no prouder aspirations than our nationality, no higher glory than the name of Briton confers.

Content with our lower political life and greater personal freedom, we leave to the aspirants after new nationalities the higher political life they covet, nor do we regret the accompanying concomitants in our content with our own condition.

We revere our time-honored institutions, and we bow to the majesty of our law. We are devotedly loyal to our gracious Queen, whom God preserve, and we are not amongst those given to change.

Our political and commercial interests are bound up in those of the glorious Empire to which we belong. We participate in its glories, we feel its reverses, and we are thoroughly prepared to take our share in its dangers. Judge you, therefore, whether we are likely to risk our allegiance for a theoretic advantage of no present or prospective practical value, or whether we shall imperil our future prosperity because it suits your Government to impose a tariff hostile to our interests in appearance.

We wish to live as friends and neighbors, but we know our own advantages, and are convinced our true interests are best served by remaining loyal British subjects.

The abrogation of the Reciprocity Treaty will check the development of our Canals, and probably of the lumber trade, but the depression must be partial, and we have the remedy in our hands, which is to abolish import duties on British manufactured goods.

At present our whole revenue is raised in this way, while it operates as a premium in favor of the United States manufacture; but reverse the process, and what will be the consequence? Why your people will smuggle the cheaper goods at all hazards, and we will reap the profits by increased trade and investment of British *manufacturing* capital.

A comprehensive Reciprocity Treaty will be a blessing to all parties, but unrestricted *free trade* would best subserve the interests of both peoples, while a restrictive policy will be followed by great commercial distress.

GEORGE H. PERRY, C. E.,

Ottawa, Canada West.

THE LUMBER TRADE OF CANADA.

BY HON. JAS. SKEAD, OF OTTAWA, C. E.

Foremost amongst the natural productions of British North America, the inexhaustible supplies of pine drawn from the Canadian forests furnish an article of commerce which has been, is, and will be, for many years to come, a great staple of trade.

The pine forests which furnish so remarkable a feature in the physical geography of the Provinces, occupy a large extent of country, through *five* degrees of latitude and *eleven* of longitude, extending in Canada from the St. Lawrence in the South to the Arctic Ocean in the North. Not that this immense tract is one unbroken forest, but that it is the favored location of the peculiar and useful description of timber, which enters so extensively into domestic use, and contributes so largely to commerce.

Other countries produce greater varieties, but none such *fine* and *large timber*, in merchantable quantities, as Canada. The species peculiarly adapted to commercial purposes being the *white pine*, or, in botanical language, the *pinus strobus*, and the *red pine* or *pinus rubra*, both attaining their greatest magnitude of growth and most useful development within the geographical limits described.

Its value as an article of commerce may be ascertained from the fact that the yearly production of material equals *seventy* to *eighty* millions of cubic feet of partially manufactured timber exported, and the operations consequent thereon involve serious outlays, the effect of which it would be well to consider before proceeding to describe the *modus operandi* of production, and the bearing the whole trade has on the great questions of "*commercial intercourse*" and "*reciprocal free trade*," now before this Convention."

The trade employs in the forest alone fifteen thousand men, and the *partial manufacture* ten thousand men. The term *partial manufacture* is used because it only really embraces the operations necessary to prepare the timber for shipment, and is not, strictly speaking, manufactured at all. It is simply analagous to the case of *pig iron*, *pig lead*, or *crude copper*, none of which can be said to be manufactured, because the only operations they undergo is to separate them from the *stony matrix* in which they were confined, and render them available for the uses of the skilled workman, at the lowest possible cost of transportation.

Thus timber, *squared*, *sawed*, *planed*, *tongued* and *grooved*, cannot be said to be manufactured, because it is not actually made into the particular shape in which it could enter domestic service, except in very rough and ordinary cases, but only sufficient of the useless material has been removed as to render it available for the hands of the skilled workman, and prevent useless expenditure for freight.

Having defined what is meant by *partially manufactured lumber*, I may now state that in the operation alone twenty-six thousand tons of agricultural produce are actually consumed every year, and that in the transportation of the portion of this trade, which leaves the Port of Quebec for Europe, *seventeen thousand seamen* are employed, and if to that number are added those engaged in the navigation of our internal waters, and the transit of partially manufactured material to the United States, the total would be twenty-five thousand men engaged in transportation, or a total of fifty thousand employed altogether.

As an article of commerce, therefore, this trade is of great importance. Its freight for shipment amounts to over *one million and a half tons*, and its accessories half as much more. The extension of free trade principles will enable those prosecuting it to enlarge its dimensions almost indefinitely, because so great is the quantity on the area covered by pine in Canada, that the question of supply can only be regulated by demand, and that will be increasing for many years to come, both in the Eastern and Western States, where cheap lumber for the ordinary purposes of domestic life is an absolute necessity.

The abrogation of the Reciprocity Treaty, therefore, will inflict far greater evil on the people of the United States than on the people of British North America, for the simple reason that it will increase the price of what is one of the necessaries and comforts of life to them, while its only effect on the latter will be a decline not in prices but in *quantity*, from the inability of certain classes to purchase. As regards actual price, it will range higher in the producer's hands than previous to the consummation of that event.

Those remarks apply with peculiar force to the Eastern States, as they are almost completely denuded of timber — very few having even one year's supply within their own boundaries.

A very large proportion of the agricultural produce consumed in the manufacture and transport of lumber was drawn from the Western States. The abrogation of the Treaty will destroy that trade altogether, and compel the producers to look to the resources of their own country for supplies.

Hitherto it was more profitable to employ our surplus labor in the woods; but if any portion of it be set free by absurd tariffs, then the agricultural resources of the country will be developed, and there is no doubt if the whole of our surplus labor could be directed to that end, we would create, in a very little space of time, an *export trade* in cereals as large as the lumber trade, and fully as important.

The following statistical table will show the truth of this position :

STATEMENT,

Showing the Value of the Exports of Canada, the Products of the Forest, as compared with those of Agriculture for the last Seven Years, as appears by the Trade and Navigation Returns made to Parliament during that time, namely:

	1857	1858	1859	1860	1861	1862	1863
Products of the Forest	11,730,387	9,447,727	9,663,962	11,012,253	9,372,645	9,482,897	13,543,926
Products of Agriculture	8,882,628	7,904,400	7,339,798	14,259,225	18,244,631	15,041,002	13,472,134
Balance in favor of Forest in '57, '58, '59 and 1863,	2,847,825	1,543,327	2,324,164	....	....	....	71,792
Balance in favor of Agriculture in '60, '61 and '62,	....	....	....	3,246,972	8,671,986	5,558,105	....

From this statement it will be seen that the value of lumber exported in seven years, from 1857 to 1863 both inclusive, amounted to $74,223,837, and of agricultural produce the sum of $85,144,015, leaving a balance in favor of agricultural produce of $10,890,218. An inspection of the table will show that *four* of the *seven years* show a balance in favor of lumber and against agriculture, amounting to $6,786,845, but the last *three years* the balance was against *lumber*, to the amount of $17,677,063.

Those figures demonstrate clearly what can be done with agricultural produce, if Canada is compelled to look to it as a staple. In the case before us, a stimulus was given to production by exceptional causes which have happily passed away. And from the superior excellence of Canadian grown wheat, and in the event of abrogation of Reciprocity being consummated, our geographical position and the superior excellence of our chief agricultural products will easily secure for us, through local tariff arrangements, control of the English market, and secure a large proportion of the enormous sums she yearly expends for breadstuffs.

A description of the localities from which the lumber trade of British North America is drawn, will illustrate the favorable conditions under which its commercial value is realized.

First in order is the Saguenay Territory, *one hundred and forty miles* above the Point de Montes, at the head of the Gulf of St. Lawrence. The Saguenay River discharges, from the Northward, the drainage of

34

27,000 square miles. This River is navigable for ships of the largest burthen, for a length of seventy-five miles.

The Valley of the Saguenay is rich in *white* and *red pine*, *spruce*, *birch* and *tamarac*. Its surface is diversified by Lake, River and Stream, but the character of its soil forbids profitable settlement to any considerable extent. It must always continue forest land, and judiciously managed, can furnish an inexhaustible supply of lumber, as well as a large proportion of minerals.

Between the Valley of the Saguenay and the next great lumber region, the St. Maurice, a territory of eight thousand square miles interposes. The City of Quebec stands about midway between the Saguenay and St. Maurice, on the shores of this territory. Its surplus waters are discharged with the St. Lawrence by isolated but sufficiently copious streams. It is moderately well wooded, producing *white* and *red pine*, *birch*, *white cedar*, *spruce* and *tamarac*.

The St. Maurice River discharges the drainage of an area of *twenty-one thousand square miles* into the St. Lawrence, at a point ninety miles above Quebec. Its Valley may literally be called a "*land of many waters.*" A map of its territory resembles a section of a "*plum pudding*," where the fruit is uncommonly large and plentiful, more than any any other object, so thickly is it studded with Lakes and Lakelets.

It contains large quantities of *white*, *red* and *yellow pine*, *spruce*, *birch*, *maple*, *elm*, *ash* and *tamarac*. It interlocks with the Valley of the Ottawa and Saguenay.

Between it and the Boute de Isle, at the Island of Montreal, where the North branch of the Ottawa joins, the St. Lawrence, a small valley of nine thousand and six hundred square miles intervenes. It is drained into the St. Lawrence by its own streams, some of which are seventy to eighty miles in length, and good floatable Rivers. It possesses a great deal of *white* and *red pine*, *spruce*, *tamarac*, and some *ash*.

The Valley of the Ottawa covers an area of 87,761 square miles. It is traversed throughout its greatest length by the River from which its name is derived, and which may be said to encompass its whole area on the *South-West* and *North*. Its sources overlap the St. Maurice, and itself is overlapped by the sources of the Saguenay, the head waters of all these Rivers being within two days' journey, or forty miles, of each other.

Its tributaries are of great magnitude, many of them being from *three* to *four hundred* miles in length, while the main stream has a course of seven hundred and eighty miles, and is navigable for canoes to its source.

The Valley of this River is the principal site of the Lumber Trade, and has been so since June 11, 1806, when the first raft left the mouth of its great tributary, the Gatineau. Yet in the fifty-nine years which have since elapsed, little over 20,000 square miles have been denuded of merchantable lumber.

Its principal productions are *white* and *red pine*, both of the largest and best quality on this continent. It also yields *tamarac*, *spruce*, *ash*, *white oak*, of a very superior quality, *elm*, *birch* and all varieties of *maple*.

Between the Cataraqui River, or more properly speaking, the junction of the Rideau Canal and the St. Lawrence and the River Trent, a small area of 2,350 miles furnishes a quantity of *white pine*, and is rich in minerals.

The Trent drains a Valley of 6,200 square miles in extent. It furnishes limited quantities of *white* and *red pine*, *ash*, *oak*, *birch* and *tamarac*. The River is navigable for some eighty or one hundred miles.

This completes the series of Lumber Lands, whose Rivers run into the St. Lawrence and Lake Ontario, the total area of which is 161,-911 square miles; but to this must be added the territory extending from the Saguenay eastward to Blanc Sablon, on the Gulf of St. Lawrence, known as the Tadnescu Territory, having a coast line of one hundred and sixty miles, and an area of 65,000 square miles, which has not yet been worked to any extent.

It furnishes a large quantity of timber, available for ship building, and a quantity of the best description of *birch*, *maple*, *ash*, *oak* and *elm*. This would make the whole *pine* producing area 226,911 miles, leading to the St. Lawrence. It is penetrated in every direction by large navigable Rivers, with nothing to restrict the commercial value of material produced but the demand.

Between the Western affluents of the Ottawa and the shores of Lake Huron, limited on the South by the Severn and a series of streams connected therewith, and on the North by the French River, an area of 12,800 square miles supplies a choice quality of *white* and *red pine*, some *oak*, *elm*, *maple* and *birch*. It is well watered — several large streams discharging into the Georgian Bay — and is easily accessible. Its forests furnish splendid *spars*.

West of French River, to Pigeon River, on Lake Superior, an area of 48,000 square miles, with a coast line of four hundred and twenty miles, furnishes a quantity of *white pine*, of small but good quality. It produces a large quantity of other timber, as *birch*, *maple*, *oak*, *elm*, *spruce*, *tamarac*, *ash* and *white cedar*.

The whole area available for producing *pine* north of the St. Lawrence would be 287,711 square miles.

Of the 24,000 square miles, wholly or in part producing the *finer hard woods*, as *oak*, *elm*, *black walnut*, all the varieties of *maple*, *chestnut*, *hickory*, *sycamore*, *basswood* and *ash*, it is not necessary to enter into details. A large trade has been driven in this material for years, especially in *pipe staves*, and this will doubless increase as demand multiplies. But if a market could be obtained for the ornamental woods, the Western Peninsula of Canada would have a regular mine of wealth in her yet uncleared forests.

Having described the country from which the Lumber Trade is drawn, it may be necessary to detail the means whereby it is brought from the forest and placed in the hands of the shipper.

The principal part of the forest lands of British North America belongs to the Crown; in other words, they are public property, and are administered for the benefit of the people. The lumber manufacturer obtains the area on which he works, which is called a "*timber berth or limit*," by bidding the highest price for it at auction. It is generally supposed to be *theoretically* ten miles square, containing one hundred square miles, or sixty-four thousand acres; but owing to the topographical features of the country, the "*limits*" are of all sizes and shapes, from twenty-four square miles upwards.

The "*limit*" holder becomes a yearly tenant to the Crown at a fixed ground rent, and pays a duty of *one half penny* per cubic foot of *squared timber* got out, and of five pence per piece on each standard log of twelve feet in length and twenty-one inches in diameter, which is equal to twenty-eight cubic feet for sawed lumber.

All the operations connected with this trade are costly. Streams have to be improved—converted into *floatable* channels—roads, bridges and *chateaus* to be constructed, and very often extensive farms cleared from the forest for the pasturage of cattle necessary to transport the *manufactured* timber or the *saw-log* to the nearest water course.

Winter is the period during which the greatest part of these operations are completed. The *squared* timber must be selected with great care, nearly perfectly straight, and entirely free from *knots*, *shakes*, or other *blemishes*. It must be hewed perfectly square, and must carry the same thickness throughout, a very slight taper indeed being allowable. About *one twenty-fifth* of the standing price is available for squared timber.

It must be totally free from blemishes of any kind, over thirty feet in length, and should square at least fifteen inches. Fully forty per cent. of the remainder is available for saw-logs, the balance of thirty-five per cent. being undergrowth or useless, or damaged.

The loss in the manufacture of *squared* timber is enormous, especially when it is of large growth and will square over eighteen inches, it may be taken at twenty per cent., and that of the best cleared stuff. Very often splendid pieces of timber are left on the ground, because they will not square evenly throughout. Bringing the market nearer the point of production, will remedy this to a great extent.

When the whole quantity has been hauled out, which is generally accomplished by the middle of the month of March, and when the ice breaks up it is floated down to the main river and formed into cribs, each twenty-four feet in width, by *string-pieces*, *traverses* and *withes*—care being taken to avoid injuring the timber by any attachment. Seventy, eighty or one hundred of these cribs form a raft, which usually contains 100,000 cubic feet. Each crib consists of twenty-six to thirty-six pieces, and contains from eight hundred to one thousand cubic feet.

The raft descends the various falls on the river by inclined plains called slides, erected expressly for this purpose. A single crib is passed at a time, so that when all are over, the raft must be *banded* up again, or re-made. This occurs as often as slides are to be passed. Towing by steam is resorted to in the navigable reaches of the Rivers.

It is thus squared timber reaches Quebec, while the saw-logs either descend the falls singly without a slide, or are passed down after the descent of the cribs on the large open reaches, are moulinetted or enclosed by booms, and towed *en masse* to the head of the next falls. Those operations are repeated till the point of manufacture is reached.

The works connected with those streams are very extensive, artistic, and complete in their character, and wholly unique; and, it may be added, the best investments in public works the Country affords.

Full details of the statistics of this trade would cover a large amount of time, but the average quantity arriving at Quebec, and manufactured for other markets, during a period of five years, will show the value of the Canadian lumber trade.

	Cubic Feet.
Oak, average yearly quantity,	1,585,856
Elm, " "	1,438,706
Ash, " "	149,930
Birch, " "	92,714
Tamarac, " "	987,062
White Pine, " "	17,665,675
Red Pine, " "	2,566,360
	24,486,303
Sawed planks, 250,000,000 feet, B. M.,	20,833,333
" home consumption, 250 000,000 feet, B. M.,	20,833,333
" American market, 250,000,000 feet, B. M.,	20,833,333
Total,	86,986,352

Or over *one million and three-quarters* tons.

The manufacture of this material into *sawed* lumber employs over two thousand mills of all sizes, many of them costing $30,000 to $40,000, and some as high as $300,000.

The census returns for 1861 show that in that year alone 982,060,145 feet, board measure, were manufactured in Canada of a value of $8,243,735, exclusive of squared timber. The capital invested amounted to $8,621,149—the cost of raw material being $3,516,695.

The tonnage this trade employs at Quebec comprises about twelve hundred vessels of an aggregate freight capacity of 673,507 tons. The

Lakes and Canals employ over 500,000 tons, so that the trade, in way or other, furnishes a traffic of over *two million tons.*

As before stated, the supply can only be circumscribed by the demand, and new markets would open a trade unrivalled in magnitude. If all trade restrictions were withdrawn, and a portion of the traffic in breadstuffs passed down the Ottawa, a profitable return freight was a certainty on which the forwarder could reckon, which he can do on no other route.

This important commercial element will be very little affected in mercantile value by the abrogation of the Reciprocity Treaty, or any hostile legislation whatever. As a trade it was in existence before the Treaty was thought of as a possibility, and that to a very considerable extent too, although a heavy duty was levied on it by the United States Government.

Twenty years ago, in 1845, New York imported more than one-third the whole quantity now sent to the United States; and for thirteen years afterwards, from 1851 to 1863, the following table will show the relative value of this material to be not so greatly affected by Reciprocity as by the wants of the different markets, which cannot be supplied elsewhere:

EXPORTS OF LUMBER FROM CANADA.

	To all Countries.	To Great Britain.	To the United States.
1851	$5,085,628	$3,373,080	$1,147,268
1852	5,548,132	3,918,088	1,590,316
1853	8 666,160	6,162,568	2,383,184
1854	9,275,780	7,246,968	1,975,030
1855	7,127,104	4,370,668	2,694,236
1856	8,894,948	5,935,892	2,897,548
1857	10,427,656	7,212,132	3,121,556
1858	8,354,755	5,106,696	3,207,964
1859	8,656,691	5,204,248	3,301,819
1860	10,061,147	6,130,776	4,846,611
1861	8,693,638	6,408,789	2,065,870
1862	10,051,147	4,896,533	3,253,589
1863	12,264,178	7,713,316	4,165,290

EXPORTS OF PLANKS AND BOARDS TO THE UNITED STATES.

	Value.	Price per M.
1851	$ 774,116	$7 00
1852	1,144,092	7 75
1853	1,866,712	9 00
1854	1,579 821	9 75
1855	2,313,359	10 50
1856	2,483,687	10 75
1857	2.557,206	11 50
1858	2,890,319	7 75
1859	2,676.447	8 00
1860	3,027,730	9 75
1861	1 507.546	9 50
1862	2,279,567	9 75
1863	2,963,426	10 00

The liberality of the Imperial Government was manifested by allowing the Provincial Executive to suspend the operation of the *Navigation Laws* in 1847, so that vessels belonging to the United States actually shipped lumber at Ottawa, and actually traversed two hundred and fifty miles of our Canals and internal waters, on the same footing as British vessels, *seven* years before the Reciprocity Treaty was negotiated.

And since that event no circumstance has arisen which can be charged to either the Provincial or Imperial Governments as manifesting an intention, on their parts, to construe the terms of the Treaty in an unfair or illiberal spirit.

On the contrary, while well aware that one of its most important stipulations are yet unfulfilled, (that contained in the third paragraph of the fourth article, relative to the navigation of State Canals,) and that no attempt has been made to meet the conditions of the case by the United States Government; and that a very restricted and illiberal construction has been put on the *first*, *fourteenth* and *seventeenth* articles, to be admitted in the Free Schedule, yet the United States craft have been allowed to navigate our Canals, free of tolls, for more than one season, and on the same footing as British vessels. During the year 1864, the number of American vessels navigating these Canals were 1,433, of an aggregate freight capacity of 278,463 tons, while not one British craft was found on their waters.

We have admitted American manufactured flour, whether from home grown or Canadian wheat—we have admitted pig iron, pig lead and crude copper, free of duty; and it certainly must be a considerable amount of casuistry to make *tongued*, *grooved* and *planed* more of a manufactured article than the same material fresh from the saw.

The course followed by the United States Government is directly the reverse of this. They will not admit Canadian manufactured flour without an affidavit that it is not the produce of wheat grown on their own territory. They keep Consuls at our principal ports, from whom we must obtain permits before we can take a cargo of free goods to any of their ports, and pay for the privilege too. They levy duties on pig lead, pig iron, and crude copper, and planed, tongued and grooved lumber, as well as other articles of agricultural produce. The deny our ships register on equitable terms, and they engross our fisheries, which are valued to the Eastern States alone at $3,000,000 per annum, and for which we receive no equivalent whatever, so that, as far as we are concerned, Reciprocity is a misnomer, and its abrogation would not be that fearful evil to British North America which some people in the United States imagine.

The idea appears to be entertained by a portion of the people of the United States, that the abrogation of this Treaty would compel *annexation.* No greater political fallacy was ever broached. As a people, our interests, directly and indirectly, are bound up with those of the Great Empire of which we form a component part. Even our trade relations are more important with her than with the United States, because she manufactures more cheaply, and the abrogation of the Reciprocity Treaty will be far more likely to give these interests a preponderating influence than otherwise.

We thoroughly understand the effect of our abolition of import duties on British manufactured goods, and how it would be felt on the United States revenue. And you can picture to yourselves the effect a discriminating duty, in our own favor, will have on the Western farmer and merchant.

The issues are in your own hands. We have paid pretty dearly for the privilege of trading with you, but we knew our material progress and development required some sacrifice, and we were content to pay you $7,934,243 per annum to secure that. But your politicians, by presuming that, like Esau, we would sell our birthright for a mess of pottage, will find themselves wofully mistaken; and after having inflicted on their own people a lasting injury, will perhaps begin to understand what is meant by the term "*allegiance.*"

We are here to receive your overtures; to adjust with you our trade relations as reasonable and sensible business men. We responded freely to your call. We made no movement for the abrogation of this Treaty, nor did the prospect of that consummation affect us very much. We made no effort to stay the proceedings your Government wisely or unwisely had inaugurated; but when, like sensible business men, you proposed to talk this matter over in Convention, we acceded to your request, and are here to receive your propositions.

Sincerely desirous of preserving amicable trade relations with our neighbors, we are fully aware of the advantages we enjoy, physically, geographically and commercially, and are not disposed to throw them away for theoretical or speculative benefits, of more than doubtful character.

I have endeavored to place fairly before you the advantages the British North American Provinces possess in assisting the development of your own and their resources, and which, by a judiciously planned system of commercial intercourse, can be fully realized.

In concluding this address, I would remark that, as this is the first great Commercial Convention on record, it is to be hoped its proceedings will mark an era in the history of mankind, characterized by *peace*, *good will*, and the removal of national and sectional prejudice or jealousy, as well as the establishment of an enlightened commercial policy, more in accordance with the progress of civilization than that hitherto followed.

We frankly and freely extend to you the right hand of fellowship, content to live with you as friends and neighbors, though still devoted adherents of the British Empire, and loyal subjects of our Gracious Queen.

EXCURSION ON THE RIVER.

DETROIT, July 18th, 1865.

The Excursion given by the citizens and the Board of Trade of Detroit, to the delegates and the members of the press attending the Convention, was a splendid success. There were three steamers lashed together, gaily decorated with evergreens and flags, and loaded with people to the number probably of 2000. A large portion of the party were ladies. The boats left the Detroit and Milwaukee Railroad wharf between five and six o'clock, and sailed up and down the river for over five hours, passing the city repeatedly, and passing Fort Wayne once. On board, every preparation had been made for the comfort of the excursionists. The collation provided was excellent and ample, and with appetites sharpened by the river breeze, the people did full justice to the eatables. Music was provided and facilities afforded for dancing — of which numbers availed themselves. Early in the evening speech-making began.

Mr. Elliot, of St. Louis, made a humorous speech, and was followed by Hon. Jacob M. Howard, United States Senator from Michigan, who, in the course of his remarks, took occasion to refer to Mr. Potter's speech at the Board of Trade Rooms. He said he had been informed that to-day a gentleman, occupying a high position in Canada as functionary of the United States, had intimated that it was the policy of the United States Government to withhold Reciprocity, in order to bring about a closer Reciprocity called Annexation. That gentleman might have information which he (Howard) had not. Yet knowing, as he did, the temper and disposition of the members of the Cabinet, he (Howard) had no hesitation in assuring his Canadian friends that, if such a statement was made by that gentleman, or any other, it was totally unfounded. (Cheers.) The people of the United States wished to live as good friends with their neighbors on the other side of the border. They desired to see them prosper. They rejoiced to see a great and powerful community growing up beside them. They had no wish to go to war with them. They had had war enough in the United States to satisty the present generation at least. The events of the last four years would show posterity, he thought, that the American people were not fond of war, at the same time that they taught the world that that people were not afraid of war, when their liberties and their nationality were in danger. (Cheers.) He knew the people of Canada were loyal to their crown. He honored them for this, and it should be their pride, as it was their duty, to be true to their Government. He concluded amidst loud cheers, by expressing the kindest feelings toward the gentlemen who composed the delegations from the British Provinces.

Numerous other speeches were made.

WEIGHTS AND MEASURES.

The gentlemen composing the Committee on Weights and Measures are located at such remote distances from each other, that it has been found impracticable to embody a report for publication with the proceedings of the Convention. The Committee are, however, unanimously in favor of recommending the adoption, by Congress, of the decimal system of Weights and Measures.

THE PRESS.

The following is a list of the gentlemen of the Press, who have been in attendance on the Convention, with the names of the several journals which they represent:

NEW YORK CITY.

Herald — J. E. P. Doyle, D. A. Levien.
World — S. Hadfield, S. C. Howell.

CHICAGO.

Tribune — J. F. Ballantyne, George Buckley.
Times — F. B. Wilkie, Henry Binmore, David M. Philip.
Republican — Charles H. Wright.
Journal — C. H. Wingall.

TORONTO, C. W.

Globe — J. K. Edwards, W. H. Orr, H. P. Johnson, A. Harvey.
Leader — Charles Belford, George R. Gregg.

CINCINNATI.

Commercial — John A. Gano.
Gazette — L. A. Hine.

CLEVELAND.

Herald — J. C. Sage.
Leader — E. C. Hardy.

BOSTON.

Journal — Thomas Maguire.
Herald — E. B. Haskell.
Post — Walter Bartlett.
Advertiser — George B. Woods.

MILWAUKEE.

Wisconsin — L. Proctor.

PHILADELPHIA.

Inquirer — Joseph McFarland.

HAMILTON, C. W.

Times — John Maclean.

LONDON, C. W.

Prototype — John Siddons.

QUEBEC, C. E.

Le Canadien — Y. A. M. Provancher.
La Journal de Quebec — E. Gerin.

MONTREAL, C. E.

La Revue Canadien — Y. A. M. Provancher
La Minerve — J. Royal.

DETROIT.

Advertiser and Tribune — R. Haddock, C. K. Backus, George Buckley.
Free Press — H. M. Utley, R. M. Longan, W. Buckingham.

OFFICIAL REPORTER,

For the President of the Convention — J. O'Loghlen.

CPSIA information can be obtained
at www.ICGtesting.com
Printed in the USA
LVHW111959050422
715401LV00006B/296